Jeremy Hobbs

About the Author

Writer and journalist Nina Siegal was born in New York City, and grew up in Manhattan and on Long Island. She received her BA from Cornell University and her MFA in fiction from the Iowa Writers' Workshop. She has written for such publications as *The Progressive*, the *Wall Street Journal*, *Art + Auction*, and the *New York Times*. She was a finalist for the James Jones First Novel Fellowship in 2005, and received the Jack Leggett Fellowship and a Fulbright Fellowship to work on her next novel, which is set in Amsterdam.

a little trouble with the FACTS

a little trouble with the FACTS

a novel

Nina Siegal

HARPER

NEW YORK • LONDON • TORONTO • SYDNEY

HARPER

This novel is a work of fiction. Any references to real people, events, establishments, organizations, or locales are intended only to give the fiction a sense of reality and authenticity, and are used fictitiously. All other names, characters and places, and all dialogue and incidents portrayed in this book are the product of the author's imagination.

FIRST EDITION

Designed by Jan Pisciotta

Library of Congress Cataloging-in-Publication Data

Siegal, Nina.
A little trouble with the facts : a novel / Nina Siegal.—1st Harper paperbacks ed.
p. cm.
ISBN: 978-0-06-124290-8
1. Women journalists—Fiction. 2. Artists—Fiction. 3. Graffiti—Fiction. I. Title
PS3619.I37L58 2008
813'.6—dc22 2007032387

08 09 10 11 12 ID/RRD 10 9 8 7 6 5 4 3 2 1

For George Rood,
"as in discourteous"
(1934–2000),

and for
Joseph Edward Siegal
(2006–)

It is not funny that a man should be killed, but it is sometimes funny that he should be killed for so little, and that his death should be the coin of what we call civilization.

—Raymond Chandler, *The Simple Art of Murder*

a little trouble with the FACTS

1

The Death Beat

It was the high mercury end of July and no one was doing any dying. I wasn't getting much work done, just moving faxes from one side of my desk to the other and finding homes for stray paper clips.

A few reporters had been sent out to cover the heat—chat with the fan salesmen, check on the polar bears at the zoo. Metro columnist Clint Westwood was under his desk pawing through old columns for new ideas. White-haired Rusty Markowitz was on the horn with a stringer he'd sent to stalk a Broadway ingenue. He was red-faced and barking, "Listen, give her the cell phone. Well, if she won't take it just *shove* it right up to her mouth!"

The other Pulitzer Prize winners were out in the Hamptons putting the final touches on their next historical opus or cultivating a new patch of skin cancer. It was slow. Slow as a drunkard's grin.

I was about to go upstairs for a cup of coffee when the phone rang. I took my gum out of my mouth and stuck it onto the filing cabinet with the other pieces.

"Obits," I said. "Vane."

There was no voice on the line, but I heard a siren, the rattling of steel. Maybe the Brooklyn Bridge was calling.

"Valerie Vane, Obituary Desk," I tried again. "May I help you?"

Now there was a voice, low and soft. "Yes," it said. "I want to inquire about a story that ran in your pages today." The voice was male, deep and smoky, but tentative—a controlled burn.

"Which story would that be?"

"The piece on Wallace," he said. "Malcolm Wallace."

I reached across my desk for the morning edition and another stick of gum. Chelsea and Hillary were on the cover riding camels, next to our three-column overnighter on the heat wave—brownouts in Inwood, track fires in Chinatown, historic concessions lines at Jones Beach. I flipped past the genocide and nuclear arsenals, past the labor unrest and roaming bison, and found the story in the measly posterior of the Metro pages, one of the shorties below the fold.

"Famous for Writing His Name," read the headline with the subhead, "Artist Brought Street Life into Galleries." Malcolm Wallace, forty-two, painter—a graffiti writer self-dubbed Stain 149. The piece didn't have a byline, but I already knew who'd written it, because I happened to be chewing her gum.

"Is there a problem?" I asked the caller.

"Yes, I believe so," he said. "I'm concerned about the facts related in the story. You see, the article here says he took his own life."

I checked the first paragraph of the story, where indeed it said that Wallace had jumped from the Queensboro Bridge. "Correct," I said.

"Suicide," he said slowly.

"That's right, suicide." I said it the way he'd said it, using his rhythms, his elisions of the vowels so that it sounded like "Soocide." Killing of Sue.

"But that's not right," he said, and then he used the word again: "Suicide."

I did a quick mental check of the facts I'd gleaned the day before from DCPI, police press. It was my typical morning call to

Detective Pinsky for updates and confirms: Wallace, Malcolm A. Deceased black male found on the rocks near base of the Fifty-ninth Street Bridge, Queens side. Discovered Saturday, 5:47 a.m. Time of death: approximately 2:15. Body waterlogged, bloated, no visible marks. Jump from bridge. ID in breast pocket.

"Let me see." I pushed some faxes around my desk to make it sound like I was checking. "Yep, Sue Side is what we got." Each syllable on tiptoe. "Sue Side from DCPI."

We got calls like this from time to time from people who weren't happy when they saw the cold, hard facts in dark, gray ink. My first few months on the desk, I'd get nervous and run them by Jaime Cordoba, the chief Obit editor.

Jaime was an Orthodox Jew born in Cuba, raised in Georgia, and he'd gotten enough guff for just his name ("hymie at the hymie-town paper?") that very little rattled him. He had skin the color of ginger and a mane of curly black hair he kept under his yarmulke with a few dabs of Brylcreem. When I needed his advice, he shook that mane like a just-roused lion, and spoke with a Latin southern twang no louder than a whisper.

"People don't like to accept death," he'd told me. "It's like a railway that runs on a senseless schedule and we obituary writers are station workers cleaning up after the train's already left. We're wearing an official uniform so people think we can give them answers. But here's my advice: stick to pushing the broom. Just tip your hat and say, 'I'm sorry, mister, I don't have any control over departures.' "

Since then, I'd developed a system for phoners. Step one was to comfort: "It may take a little bit of time to get adjusted to your loss," I started, but the caller wasn't listening.

"Who said suicide?" he wanted to know.

"The police reported 'jump from bridge.' "

"Malcolm just put the down payment on a permanent space for a painting school," the caller said. "A man who's going to kill himself doesn't secure a mortgage. He doesn't say he's going out for ice cream and jump into the East River."

"No," I said. "Not usually. I know these senseless acts are sometimes hard to understand. We need to try and look at the big picture . . ." This was step two: Help the caller contemplate death in the abstract.

I was laying it on thick as cement, but I wasn't much interested in the caller. I was thinking about my cup of coffee getting cold upstairs. This Wallace fellow had already gotten plenty of ink. He'd been famous in the eighties—hell, he'd even been the subject of a 1985 Sunday Magazine feature—but only for as long as it took to shake up a can of spray paint. He'd since been scrubbed from history. I figured the main reason he'd made the page was the weather: 104 by day, a sauna in the shade. Jaime had been complaining about our section "looking geriatric" and when he found the Wallace notice, he said, "Finally, some young blood," slapping the fax on my desk. "This'll be fun for you, Vane. Has to do with art."

"Listen," the caller was saying now. "I know a lot of people don't mean much to some people. A lot of people are just some other guy. I don't know how the police concluded suicide, but I'm sure whatever they told you is wrong, because Malcolm Wallace would never kill himself. He wasn't that type of man."

Then something crept up my spine. It was Detective Pinsky from the previous day's morning call: "They're saying suicide but it's too soon to tell. You know the drill, Val," I now remembered he'd said. "DA's got it."

I'd made a follow-up call to Betty Schlacter, the flak for the Manhattan district attorney. We'd chitchatted about the supermodel slaying and then she'd cut it short, claiming a lunch date. She couldn't give me anything on Wallace, not even basics, she'd said. Investigations were off limits and off the record until they were closed. I'd jotted in my notes: O/B DNP (On

Background. Do Not Print.). And then Jaime had come by with a frosted cupcake.

You see, for two years, I'd been an up-and-comer, a star cub recruited from a glossy to write flashy features for The Paper's Style section. I'd covered society galas, celebrity soirees, and red carpet premieres. I'd been an all-access insider, behind the velvet ropes. But things had gone wrong somewhere along the line, and then they'd gotten worse, and then they'd gone all the way south. Ultimately, I'd been demoted to the Obit desk to putter out my remaining days with the washed-up hacks, the union stewards, and other miscellaneous nobodies.

The day before had been my six-month anniversary on Obits. Jaime meant the cupcake as a form of celebration, but to me it was more like a frosted nail in the coffin. I swallowed it down, and then excused myself for my half-hour lunch break and went in search of something to gnaw. Down the block, at the usual office haunt, there was no collegial patter at the cashier's counter. No office chums clapped my back. I bought myself a day-old bagel and walked to the kiddy park to watch babies waddle in the spray. I wrenched bite after bite from the stale dough and pitied my sad fate.

When I'd gotten back to the office, Jaime was waiting on the Wallace squib to move the page. I'd been late and now I was harried, thinking I'd messed up again for good. I'd whipped up the Obit to specs, including "jump from bridge." In my muddled state—I now realized—I'd forgotten all about Pinsky and Schlacter. I'd forgotten all about O/B DNP and "too soon to tell."

This, I understood more acutely with each smoky breath on the other end of the line, may indeed have been a mistake. Another mistake. I didn't say anything to the caller. I didn't even let myself think it too loud. If I had to tell my editor that we had to run a correction, it wouldn't look good for me.

I cleared my throat. "Sir," I said. "This is The Paper of Record. We write *the* with a capital *T*, as in 'The Truth.' Maybe you want to speak to the news desk, if there's news on this case. Maybe you'd like the cop shop, if there needs to be an investigation. At Obits, we don't do updates. We just stack 'em and pack 'em."

Once it came out of my mouth, even I was surprised by the harshness of the phrase. I could hear the anonymous mister breathing in short, smoky bursts, saying nothing. His pause sprawled about a yard and then stopped abruptly.

"Are you a reporter?" he asked.

The word jumped up between us. I didn't flick at it, didn't try to grab it out of the air. He said the same thing again, only louder. "Are you a reporter?" His words poked me in the chest like a frat boy looking for a brawl.

A year earlier if someone had asked me that question I would've guffawed. Who didn't know that Valerie Vane was a reporter? I wasn't just a reporter; I was the supreme scribe of the urban zeitgeist. Who *else* could have gotten upstairs at Moomba for the first celebrity karaoke night? Who *else* would have convinced transsexual heiress Zita Marlowe to do her first, and only, face-to-face after the surgery? *I* had identified gray as the new black, *and* Thursday as the new Friday. And later, when the trends shifted again, *I* was the one who'd let everyone know that Monday was the new Thursday. That's why Buzz Phipps, the Style editor, had always rushed over to my desk, breathless with the latest hot tip. He wanted every worthy story to get the Valerie Treatment.

Now, with the word *reporter* balancing on the line between us, I wasn't so sure.

"The name's Vane," was all I could offer the caller. "Valerie Vane."

It meant nothing to him. "Well, if you are a reporter or if you ever want to be one, don't just take down what you hear from the cops. Try doing a little research."

I opened another stick of gum and folded it under my tongue. "Who is this?" I said, chewing audibly. "I'll take your name. I'll get back to you."

The man laughed a slow, even laugh. "No, Valerie Vane," he said, his teeth clamped on the sharp *V* edges of my name, his throat coughing up the As. "I'll take down your name and I'll be calling you back. We'll see this mistake is corrected one way or another."

The word *mistake* buzzed in my ear like a fly about to land in my soup. "You haven't told me *your* name," I said.

He gave it a little thought and said, "Cabeza. Just call me Cabeza."

"Cabeza, as in—" There was a dial tone, hard and flat.

Head? I thought. Wasn't *cabeza* Spanish for head? Or was it beer?

The Paper's newsroom was on the third floor of the copper-topped fortress in Midtown. It was arranged in concentric circles of clout. In the center were the top brass, orchestrating the movements of the planets and scorching any Icarus who tried to fly too high. In orbit were the lesser gods: backfield editors, assignment editors, and design chiefs. Reporters were spun out on the periphery like comets beyond the orbit of Pluto. Obits was in deep, interstellar space, far from the action. Close to the exits.

The furnishing was Late-Century Nondescript. Gray Formica desks connected low-slung gray canvas cubicles, boxy computers, gray swivel chairs. All of it was gray upholstered, with beige carpeting wall to wall. On most days, the place was about as lively as an insurance office. No one yelled, "Stop the presses!" or ran through the newsroom snapping out patter like Rosalind Russell and Cary Grant. Reporters talked in hushed tones, and typed with their heads crooked solemnly over ergonomic keyboards. Clerks imported panini from the gourmet grocer and ate at their desks, swallowing three-dollar pink bottles of water called "Calm."

But if I listened intently, with the right amount of reverence, I could sometimes hear the two-finger *clickety clack* of old Underwood typewriters. I could imagine blue suits waltzing in like Clark Gable from a wet lunch with the beat cops at Jimmy's Corner. Or the boys in short pants running between desks yelling "Copy!" I could, just barely, if I listened with imagination, make out the subterranean rumble of the defunct printing presses, the throaty laughter of the newspapermen smelling of machine oil, cigars, and cheap scotch.

Most of them were gone, but a few still trolled the newsroom, like my cubicle mate, Mickey Rood. Rood had been at The Paper fifty-eight years and then some. He'd started as a copy boy at fifteen and had climbed the ranks until he hit a glass ceiling made of bottles of Wild Turkey. Some time ago, I didn't know quite when, Rood had "retired" to Obits.

During his early years at The Paper he'd moonlighted as a jazz pianist, subsisting on a quart of single malt and three packs a night. The veins of his translucent cheeks mapped long-closed Greenwich Village jazz, blues, and juke joints. His face had three neat slits: two for his twinkling, cantankerous eyes and another for his thin-lipped grin. He wore a navy suit jacket with a stain around the neckline and loose threads at the wrists. His button-down was jaundiced, and his slacks, two sizes too large, were cinched against his waist with a stretch of white rope. When he wasn't using his battered wooden cane, he hooked the handle to that rope. He trailed a smell of tree mold and shoe polish.

"Name's Rood," he'd said, clearing some phlegm and standing to offer me his hand, the first day I'd arrived at Obits. "As in discourteous."

I plopped down the sad cardboard box I'd hefted from Style and shook. His hand covered mine like a wet baseball mitt.

"Valerie Vane," I said.

"Vane," said Rood, still clutching my hand. "As in vainglorious. Boastful, proud." He was neither approving nor disapproving.

"Or idle, fruitless, futile," I said, meeting his eyes and swallowing down a lump.

Rood relaxed his grip and frowned. "You think you'll hate the graveyard," he said. "But you won't. You can learn a lot here about life and death and you'll get a first-row seat on the dispensation of immortality."

I felt sorry for the slope of his hulking shoulders under that polyester jacket, the checkered tie covered in little white crumbs. "The obituary can be the last word in journalism," he added. "An interesting life is an eternal fascination. To write an obit well, you have to know your subject inside and out, and you have to know how to probe to get to the dirt."

"Sounds like dentistry," I said.

"Or," he said, tilting on his cane and turning away from me, "you'll play your cards right and be out of here soon."

Rood had been right about one thing. In six months sponge-bathing the Grim Reaper, I'd at least gotten a line on him: poor people died in fires, rich kids by overdose. Teenagers in car wrecks and school shootings. Prostitutes were strangled, transsexuals thrown from windows or off cliffs. Businessmen drank exhaust overnight in parked cars. Politicos and ex-cops liked to eat their guns.

I didn't feel sorry for the dead most of the time. I figured there were a lot worse things than being dead. In fact, lately I'd developed a kind of envy for the freshly deceased. After all, the corpses we packed in our rose-scented boxes weren't any ordinary stiffs. They were corporate titans and political heavyweights, millionaire philanthropists and Tony Award winners, icons of the silver screen, pop princesses and peacemakers. Every name on our pages was synonymous with success. Even our mobsters and murderers were head of the class.

I would've been proud to lie down in that bone yard. But instead, I was in purgatory, pushing papers. And there was plenty of paperwork: paper files, clippings, background searches, Internet trolling, legal papers on assets, holdings, scandals, illness, distinguishing marks, cause of death, time and date, names of survivors, names of enemies and friends. Call the coroner's office to verify, call the cops to verify, and, finally, convince the editor to memorialize the sap.

When all the facts were lined up, the editors assessed the assets and did the numbers. The biggest celebs got the front page, that's A-1 and the jump—1,800 to 2,500 words with the full spread, as many as fourteen pictures. From there on down, your inches got shorter, your pix shrunk. Members of Congress pulled up to 1,800 words with just one or two headshots. Authors and actors, 1,000. On their heels, pioneering scientists and do-gooders—500 to 1,000. Notable criminals, especially the big splashy ones with high-priced crimes on their heads, got a good 400 to 800, and some of them trumped Nobel laureates. And when it was all done, if we still had space on the page, there were sometimes a handful of shorties, 100 to 300 words. The mention of a life, not quite worthy, but good enough for a filler squib.

This Wallace character had fallen among the last group. He ranked a cool three hundred. But if the Reaper's harvest had been richer that day, I didn't think he'd have rated ten.

I usually tapped Rood when I got angry callers. But he was at the center of the newsroom now listening to Jane Battinger crow. Battinger was the Metro News chief, a bottle blonde who'd mislaid the bottle. She didn't talk so much as squall, loud and shrill enough to rouse, well, the dead. And she was working on one just now: LaShanniah.

LaShanniah, the hip-hop soul queen at the top of the charts, had died over the weekend in an unexplained yachting accident. It wasn't that we'd missed the story. Rood had given her a generous write-up, turning her short-lived career of voice-enhanced canned drumbeats into a Cinderella story par excellence. Problem was the math. Instead of A-1, they'd put her on B-17, with just eight hundred words and one headshot. The tabs, by contrast, had splashed her across their covers for two days with second-day follows of her last harrowing moments and enough file photos to crush a librarian.

For two days Metro had been fending off angry phone calls and letters to the editor calling The Paper out of touch and—worse—racist. Now Battinger had it in her teeth, and she wanted to spit it out onto someone else's plate. Rood was an obvious, if civilian, target. He'd written the inches, but he hadn't worked up the numbers. It was the brass who assigned length and location. He'd just filed to their specs.

But Rood had been around long enough to know that if an editor wanted to yell, better to let her vent. So he squinted and took it until Battinger's voice faded to a hoarse, bitter squeak, and then he lurched across the newsroom on his cane.

He went straight for Jaime. He was flushed and his breathing was rough. He didn't like to be barked at, especially by a broad. Jaime nodded for him to sit, but Rood was too worked up, so he just stood and wobbled. Jaime didn't need to ask what had happened and Rood didn't need to tell him. The two of them just needed to look at each other for a while until they figured out a plan, and Jaime would execute it.

A few minutes later I saw Jaime climb the central staircase to the Culture desk. Next thing, he was headed back with the pop writer, Curtis Wright, on his tail. Then I got the picture: This was going to be a collaborative gig. Curtis was going to write the lead and get the credit, and some Obit hack would be dragged in to grunt it out.

I ducked my head behind my computer, trying to look swamped. I glanced up as they passed to get a look at Curtis, who was shaking his thick dreadlocks. He had on a told-you-so expression clear as the day is long. "Tomorrow is already three days late," he muttered as he passed.

Jaime affected the look of a beaten dog, ready to take his licks. Sure, he'd let Curtis ride him a bit if it meant getting the top Culture writer on board. Then, when he needed to, he'd tell him where to get off. Politely, of course.

"If you had anyone down here who kept tabs on youth," Curtis continued. And Jaime shot me a glance as they walked beyond hearing range. I'd volunteered a few days earlier to handle LaShanniah, but he'd told me I wasn't "ready" for anything that big.

I moved to the fax machine and pretended I had something incoming. "Try to advance it somehow," Jaime was saying. "I don't know a thing about this girl, so tell it to me like I was born yesterday. Or maybe like I was born a half century ago, because that's closer to the truth. That means I grew up listening to Dave Brubeck. And a lot of our subscribers still don't know what the word *hep* means." Curtis cracked a toothy smile. "I'm giving you Valerie Vane for research." Jaime nodded in my general direction. "Got that, Valerie? You two just get it out fast."

I headed back to my cube. Before I could wipe out the screensaver, Curtis was hovering. "Want a shot at an A-1 byline?" he said.

I couldn't complain. Curtis Wright was tall, and I could use a touch of Culture.

That evening, after the backfield edit and the slot edit and the copy desk rounds and the page one editors meeting and a final look from Battinger, Curtis and I had our feet up on the desk and were eating takeout lo mein. He chopsticked some hanging noodles between his lips and eyeballed me.

"I bet you're glad to be out of Style." He coughed a little laugh.

"I'm a real fashion *don't.*"

"Buzz misses you," he said.

"Sure." I crunched a piece of lemongrass between my teeth. "Like a house cat misses his mouse. Anyway, he's got Tracy."

Since I had left Style, a new girl, Tracy Newton, had taken my place. It was *All About Eve,* all over again. When I was on the desk, she was a freelancer, snatching side dishes after I nabbed the big roast, the Iowa chorus girl waiting in the wings for the leading lady to break her leg.

Tracy and I couldn't have been more different. She was dark and angular with jet-black hair, a nose to ski off, cheekbones doubling as scenic peaks. She gave new meaning to the term *legwork*; her endless trotters could cross the newsroom in four strides. Me, I'm a winding country road with cherry-blond hair. Everything on me goes round: big eyes, big lips, big everything. I wear my hair in short curls behind my ears, and apply an extra coat of mascara. Where Tracy Newton titters, I purr.

Curtis held his chopsticks before his lips. "Tracy," he said, "can't hold a candle to you."

It'd been a long time since anyone had flirted with me, and it was like easing into a hot bath. "You flatter me," I said. "Tracy has her good points."

"Yours are a few points higher," he said.

I was putting on my best coy smile, slow as a pair of long silk gloves, when one of the copy editors shouted from across the room, "Val, can you handle a call on Obits?"

I put down my carton. "Ring it through!"

The phone rang. "Vane."

I knew who it was by the metallic ache behind the silence. "Cabeza?" I said.

"I've got some new facts," he said, skipping the niceties. "I want you to investigate this murder."

A few minutes ago I'd been contemplating LaShanniah's string bikini and now the word *murder* was on the line. I turned to Curtis, batted my eyes a little, and pointed at the mouthpiece with a shrug. He nodded, lifted himself out of his seat, waved bye-bye, and went to talk to the slot. I hunched over in the swivel chair with the phone close to my chest. "Listen, Cabeza, Mr. Beer, whatever it is you call yourself," I said. "I think maybe you have the wrong idea about me. Gumshoe isn't my bailiwick. I'm more of a cocktails and furs kind of girl." It wasn't true anymore, and I knew it, but he didn't.

"I don't think I have the wrong idea," he said.

"When a body's gone, I like to leave it be," I said. "I don't dance with corpses."

He laughed. It was a tight little laugh, both feet on a dime. "You think I don't know anything about you, but I do. I know you wrote that article and I know that you also suspect you might've made a mistake. But where you are, people don't like to admit to mistakes."

"I'm sorry," I said. "I disagree." I reached out to put down the receiver, but before I could he spoke again.

"You can be a reporter again," Cabeza said.

I put the phone back up to my ear. He did know something about me, then. "All I'm looking for is the truth," he continued. "And if you're a reporter, that's what you want, too."

I thought about it for longer than I care to admit. I knew he heard me thinking, though there was no sound except for the two of us breathing at each other.

"Thanks," I said. "Not interested."

Then I hung up the phone.

2

Cinderella Redux

The truth was, I wasn't hard-boiled. I wasn't a lot of things I pretended to be, least of all a first-class news hawk. If I'd been a cocktails and furs kind of girl, it'd been too short a stint to stick.

In truth, I was born on the hardwood floor of a Mission District squat in San Francisco, circa 1972. And my given name was Sunburst Rhapsody Miller.

My mother was a Boston society escapee and my father a Harvard dropout. The two of them had watched Cambridge disappear in the rearview of my dad's VW camper in 1967. He was a chemist heading into his junior year, but classes conflicted with the Summer of Love. She was a high school songstress, good with a tambourine.

When I came along, five years later, they were holed up with a troupe of yippies and Merry Pranksters in a squat on Treat Avenue. Their pals organized Happenings and wrote agitprop plays with titles like *What Would Woody Do?* and *Tempeh for the Masses!* Rent was twenty-five smackers a month and no one's wooden bowl ever wanted for brown rice.

Those early years were the happiest I can recall. The pastel houses on our street lined up like candy jars at the corner drug. Our bay windows poured in buckets of sunlight. Our storerooms were full of costumes, wigs, masks, and face paint to daub a circus, so a little girl's life never wanted for playtime. By day, my folks got run out of public parks for their antiwar skits. By night, the house filled with friends and fans whose banjos, rain sticks, and didgeridoos sweetened the night air along with the thick smoke of Mendocino kind.

We weren't a family that stuck to schedules, but there was one thing we kept regular. Every Friday afternoon at four o'clock, my father would walk me over to Eureka Valley and he'd plunk down two dollars at the Castro Theatre box office, and then guide me inside the movie house. The Wurlitzer organ played and the Deco chandelier dimmed and my dad took my hand as we watched the screen flicker.

His great love, after agitprop, my mom, and me, was movies, the old black-and-whites. His own dad had taken him to the flicks once a week when he was a boy. It was the one aspect of his childhood in "the old country" (i.e., the East Coast) that he wanted to pass along to the next generation. And secretly, I thought he also liked to get a glimpse of the glamour he'd left behind, as directed by George Cukor, Billy Wilder, and Howard Hawkes: *His Girl Friday, Breakfast at Tiffany's, Sabrina, Bringing Up Baby, The Thin Man, Week-end at the Waldorf*. On the way home to our squat, we'd play the characters in the movies. He'd be Walter Burns and I'd be Hildy Johnson. I'd be Sabrina and he'd be Linus Larrabbee. He was Nick to my Nora.

Sure, he had a handlebar soup strainer and a Nehru-collared paisley shirt. But I always figured my dad for a classic screen idol. With his aristocratic roots, his broad-cut chin, and his Roman nose, he could easily land a big-bucks blockbuster. I'd be right there beside him, a curly-haired Shirley Temple costar. We'd leave this ragtag troupe behind and take our act to Tinsel Town. From Castro Street to Mission, we planned plots set on city streetscapes, drawn from his high-contrast past: debutantes' lily-white hands ringed thick with diamonds, street urchins turned men of industry, old ladies coughing blood into their hankies and signing their mansions off to their cats.

Back at the squat, though, we went silent. My mother, who was otherwise too slack, was strict about one thing: the East was the past, and we didn't mention it. Maybe she didn't want to miss everything so much, because she'd left so much behind. But my father wasn't so stony. He saw that my eyes glittered with the lure of New York celluloid and he fed my fervor. At night, when I was tucked under my homemade quilt, he dragged in his old steamer trunk and plucked out pictures. His top-hatted pop at the "21" Club; his mother in a Garbo-style gown at the Russian Tea Room; even a picture of Mom chasing pigeons near Central Park's Belvedere Fountain. One night, he brought me an old volume of *Vanity Fair,* and I read it cover to cover. Then I read it again, and again, and again, like a girl on a fantasy merry-go-round, all bells and lights and whistles and no brass ring.

San Fran was swell but we couldn't stay. My mother gave me the news at age ten: "Back to the land" meant swapping our flush toilet for a creaky outhouse, city sanitation for a compost heap. My mother's cheery tone didn't hide the truth from me: we were the worst pack of downwardly mobile, good-for-nothing hippies that ever passed the hat.

So one morning, we packed our props into the camper van and pointed our compass north. My dad strapped on an old duffel and climbed onto his Harley Road King. He was going to take the scenic route along Pacific Coast Highway and meet us there by midnight. Mom and I got into the van and watched the cityscape morph into evergreens and we arrived at our damp new cabin on the Eugene farm just in time for sundown.

The wind whistled balefully through the plywood wallboards and midnight came and went. It was the longest night that I ever knew, waiting wide-awake for the rumble of his motor up the dirt road. I counted the slats in the ceiling, reread my *Vanity Fair*, and counted the slats again, so I wasn't awakened when I heard my mother's endless wail. Somewhere along the Lost Coast, Dad had stopped for gas. When he turned back onto the road, an oncoming trucker didn't make out his bike's night beam and he was killed in a white-hot flash.

What words can I assign to that loss? I never had them. I don't know if I ever will. But I knew how I felt about Eugene. It had been a trip in the wrong direction. We didn't belong back on the land. We didn't need to be deeper into the dirt. I decided that first day that the farm, the West, the hippie life, wasn't ever going to be the way for me. I never got good at potlucks and sing-alongs. I couldn't sit cross-legged and bless my soy stir-fry. I was always too antsy, too ready for my screen test. As I saw it, life was high above this earthly gloom, somewhere in the skyscrapers that touched the clouds over Manhattan.

I arrived at the Port Authority by Greyhound bus on my twenty-third birthday, with everything I owned stuffed into my Guatemalan backpack. I had a few names scribbled on a piece of notebook paper in my pocket, those I could remember from my father's stories over his steamer trunk. But I hadn't counted on inquisitive doormen. And I hadn't realized how many Millers there were in the Manhattan White Pages.

So I gave up on the family reunification dream—for the moment—and started circling ads for cheap shares in *The Village Voice*. After my futon was ensconced in an East Fifth Street walk-up, I called Zachariah Winkle, the publisher of *Gotham's Gate*, a weekly glossy with a flair for the indiscreet. My English professor at Reed had given me his name.

"Call me Zip," he said. "Everyone does. I'm not hiring now. But I'm always willing to look at a fresh face." I offered to flash mine over coffee in SoHo, and landed an internship three days a week.

As it happened, I arrived during penguin suit season, that stretch of springtime when the city's nonprofits host the $3,000-a-plate suppers that keep them afloat for the year. Guests get poached salmon, duck confit, a few speeches, and a chance to demonstrate charitable zeal. Corporate bigwigs buy tables for $10K to $50K a pop, and promise to show their expensive mugs. But when the time comes for them to lift a fork, they beg off and fill their seats with hired hacks.

Penguin-suit soirees are a snore to anyone in the know. But I was out of the know. My first month in New York, I was a blank book wanting script. In the first weeks, I'd tasted my inaugural almond cookie at Veniero's on East Eleventh, played impromptu chess in Washington Square Park, skipped down the East Side promenade. One evening I'd even found myself on a fishing boat on the Hudson, drinking German Riesling while listening to a Czech opera with a Belgian chef. When Zip Winkle mentioned the PEN American Center Gala to this Oregonian wildflower, she very nearly swooned. "Oh, just do me one favor," Zip added. "If you happen to notice anything intriguing about any of the guests, call it in to Bernie."

Bernie Wabash was the *Gate*'s chief gossip columnist who penned "Inside Line," six inches on page three with a handful of bold-faced lies. He always needed items, and all the mag's lackeys were expected to supply them. I'd always wanted to get a tidbit on Bernie's page. This was my first inside shot.

At a secondhand shop on West Tenth, I found a pink gown with a three-foot train and matching satin gloves. My redheaded roommate pinned it up with safeties, and I dabbed my lips red until she said stop. I counted my quarters and took my first yellow cab, gabbing at the hack all sixty blocks north. When my pink-tinted pumps tapped the grand plaza at Lincoln Center, I figured myself for Sabrina, just returned from Paris.

Inside, I snatched a flute of champagne from a silver tray,

almost toppling the waiter, found my place card with my name at Table 13, and placed my satin gloves on my plate. I had nothing to do but read and reread the gala program, memorizing the names and titles of the listed sponsors, assuming they'd all be my pals by the end of the night.

The evening's honoree was Jeremiah Sinclair Golden Jr., son of the Vermont senator and founder of TriBeCa's Odyssey Pictures, the indie film giant known for cinematic milestones such as *Under the Milk Sink* and *Dancing in Moscow*. Not yet thirty, *People* magazine described Golden as "the glamour puss of the cutting-edge art set," praising his "indefatigable faith in unproven quantities." Tonight, he was being honored for promoting poetry slams in the former Soviet bloc.

I figured he would arrive trailed by baby bluebloods. But as the guests filtered in, I saw most were probably pulling Social Security. Not that any of them needed a government assist. A single mink stole offered to the coat check could've supported poetry slams worldwide for as long as slams stayed hip. I popped mini crab cakes and washed them down with champagne. I walked out onto the patio with my flute and waited for a debonair millionaire to sidle up behind me and wrap me in a mink.

But instead, I shivered until a young man in a tux politely rang a dinner bell and called us all inside. The speeches were to begin immediately. I was tipsy by the time Jeremiah Golden walked up to the mike, and maybe lightheaded too, because I almost fell off my seat. He was the very portrait of polite East Coast society, straight from the dog-eared pages of my ancient *Vanity Fair*. His Savile Row tuxedo wouldn't have looked any smarter on John-John. His black curls flounced. Yes, flounced. In place of a bow tie, he wore a yellow silk cravat, tucked into his black vest, with a matching display hankie. I guessed he wore Alfred Dunhill cufflinks and carried a compendium case. Forget the silver spoon; he was born with a whole table setting in his mouth.

I tried to listen. Really, I did. But I caught only a few phrases: "I couldn't string together two words of prose, let alone improvise a revolutionary sonnet like these young people I met . . ." "The real honorees here tonight are the Ukrainian freestyler . . ." "I've always believed in underground movements, and never had the chance to . . ." My head was too busy with snippets of imagined repartee between us that would, preferably, take place in his Connecticut horse stables before he helped me mount. I heard the laughter of the crowd, punctuating the cadences of his thank-you speech, and I heard the thunderous clapping when he was through.

"Think globally, slam locally," he said, returning to take another bow before the mike, a fist in the air, making a power-to-the-people gesture, though it read more like, "Go get 'em champ." He returned to his seat at Table 1, and I immediately began scheming for ways to position myself in the empty chair beside him.

But then I remembered Bernie. I was supposed to be collecting string. I hadn't gotten a single inch yet, not even the color of the room. We were between courses, so I took my notepad out of my purse and clutched my pen. I was standing on a gold mountain of gossip. All I had to do was mine. But how would I recognize any of the people I was supposed to be skewering? I didn't know a single face, and even if I asked for names, they wouldn't ring bells. These were all New York City insiders, after all, bigwigs with private bank accounts, not the kind of celebs appearing on *Entertainment Tonight*. Well, I thought, how hard can it be? I'm an attractive young woman in a spiffy dress. I hoisted my train and edged into a circle of gents. Their conversation stopped short and they all looked from my pen to my face and back again.

"Pardon me," I said. "My name is Sunburst and I don't know a thing about poetry slams. Can someone clue me in?"

"Starburst, you say?" said one of the gents. "As in fruit chew?"

The circle erupted in laughter.

"No, actually . . ."

"Do you come in assorted flavors?" More laughter.

"Why, I believe I'm your distributor!" said another gent, touching his watch chain. "We hold M&M/Mars." Guffaws from the group as I backed away.

After a while, the dinner bell rang. I took my seat at Table 13, still clutching my blank notepad. About halfway through supper, the gold-dipped septuagenarian at my elbow asked me to pass her a roll. I picked through the assortment and said, "Ooh, they have cinnamon raisin. Those are my favorite. My mother showed me how to make cinnamon raisin rolls and . . ." The septuagenarian smiled at me with her penciled-in lips, said, "That's very nice dear," and turned back to the Rolex at her right.

After a couple of hours listening to silverware tap fine china, I heard crunching crinoline as the gents led their ladies away. I stood at the edge of the gilded railing on the second tier and gazed at the mezzanine. I'd failed to get any items or any contacts. I hadn't managed a single round of witty quippery.

My celluloid fantasy was revived, though, because just then, Jeremiah burst back through the front doors and ran up the stairs. I wondered if I was imagining things, but he said, "I need to use the loo. Would you mind very much watching the door?" On his way out a few minutes later, he stopped. "This is no place for a beautiful woman in a scandalous gown," he announced. "Unless you're staying for the *Carmen* matinee, I could give you a ride anywhere you need to go."

Anywhere. It was a big offer for a girl fresh off the farm. I had nowhere to go except home to my redheaded roommate in her Peanuts Gang socks. I was all dressed up with nothing to show for it. Anywhere sounded like the place to be. I lowered my chin and said in my best Audrey Hepburn, "Yes, please."

If I'd been wise, I'd have made to the nearest pay phone and called an item in to Bernie: "Jeremiah Sinclair Golden Jr. seen making a trip to the WC and coming back glassy-eyed." If I'd been smart, I'd have said, "What would a man like you want with a wildflower like me?" But after his "anywhere," the room filled again with glitter, and all I could see was starlight.

"Where to?" he said, holding open the door of his stretch Lincoln Town Car at the edge of the grand plaza, as the fountain's waters glowed in triumphant arcs behind him. I looked around for Billy Wilder, to see if his ghost was directing the scene. I searched for Samuel Taylor, his scriptwriter, because I didn't know my lines. What would Audrey say? I told him the address of my tenement on East Fifth Street and he repeated it to his driver, adding, "Take the long way through the park," just like William Holden. He didn't need any prompting. Then he closed the glass partition with his remote.

It was one of those flawless New York City nights in the early blush of spring. The scent of lilacs drifted in through the cracked window. I leaned back on the soft leather bench and imagined the landscape montage that George Cukor would insert into this scene. We'd see the whole Central Park, from glorious glimmering Broadway down to the Plaza Hotel. The camera would pan out past the tinted glass of the limo, as I rolled down the window to smell the early blossoms. We'd see deer and elk frolic with foxes; see night shadows form on the Loeb Boathouse, near where—later in the movie—Jeremiah and I would have our first kiss in a rowboat. Swans would float in a moonlight-reflecting lake.

"You must be new to the city. I've never seen you before," said Jeremiah.

I opened my eyes. "There are eight million people in this city. You couldn't possibly have met everyone."

"But if I'd met you, I would've remembered."

My cheeks grew hot. "It's true. I just moved here."

"You see? I was right. You're new. The new new thing."

It felt like a kind of anointment. Then the old movies turned Blake Edwards–Technicolor. Jeremiah's limo pulled to a stop in front of Tiffany, where Holly Golightly took her breakfast. The light changed and the car continued down Fifth Avenue, and the whole glinting panorama came to life. The gold-plated shops were like so many old friends from my magazines: Bergdorf and Trump Tower, Gucci and Brooks Brothers, Cartier and Saks. We drove through the Disney glow of Times Square—I saw Carolines and the Walter Kerr, TKTS and MTV—and past the Fashion District all the way down to the East Village."

Jeremiah's leg was leaning against mine as we sat in the limo in front of my East Fifth tenement, and this was all the encouragement I needed to sit still and wait. The car idled and the driver's stereo played something jazzy and low. "Are you a fan of stuffed cabbage?" he asked. "I didn't even touch my poached salmon."

The car dropped us at Veselka on Second Avenue, a well-lit diner that specialized in kielbasa and cold borscht. The train of my gown draped into the aisle, tripping the Polish waitress. I was leaning on one fist, gazing into the black puddles of Jeremiah's eyes as he regaled me with stories of the film world, the art world, the poetry slammers, and the "sad, terrible struggles that artists face to get any recognition for their crafts." He talked a one-man symphony, conducting with his fork. I poked my blintz and memorized each note.

At 1:30, when our plates were lifted away, he mentioned martinis. I confessed I'd never tasted one. Minutes later, we were standing in front of a nondescript door in a darkened alley getting appraised by an electronic eyeball. The door swung open to admit us into a tiny room with a glittering wall of spirits. It was a drinking establishment all right. But the bartender, a Teddy boy in an Edwardian zoot suit, had vetted all the guests.

Teddy cleared a spot for us at the bar and Jeremiah helped me up onto a stool. He ordered us a round of dirty martinis. I asked him what made them dirty, and he said, "The person you're with," placing a hand on my knee.

I said, "Maybe you've got the wrong idea about me." But I didn't move my knee.

He said, "I've got a few ideas about you."

I said, "We'll have to start from the first idea and work our way down the list."

His first guess: "I bet in a few weeks you won't even remember the girl you are today, the girl in front of me in this cotton-candy dress, these pink pumps, the big eyes, hungry for a taste of everything. You'll be amazed to find that you're a creature of the city, through and through."

My naïveté was like so many buttons on a flimsy silk blouse. He'd undone them and I felt exposed. "I certainly hope that's true," I said.

He drained his martini glass. "Careful what you wish for."

The bar was a music box. It wound up each time a new group of sanctioned visitors waltzed through the velvet curtain. A guy in a smoking jacket told Jeremiah he'd loved the latest Odyssey release, *Chance Meeting at Midnight.* Jeremiah answered that he wished he could take the credit, but the real geniuses were the grips.

"Everyone said I was a born candidate, like my dad," he confided once his admirers dispersed. "But I'm really a very private person. Still, I needed to prove I was good for something."

"I'm sure you're good for plenty of things," I said, leaning closer.

He moved closer too. "To me, you see, the arts are a more powerful tool. An intimate tool." He moved his hand farther up my thigh. "A work of art can change everything, so I support groundbreaking artists. I buy their work; I encourage them. I give them the impetus to keep working. I can be very hands-on."

He certainly was hands-on. His hands were all over the place.

I'd known my share of commune boys out west. I'd dated at Reed, young men with carefully disheveled hair who were eager to quote Kristeva. But I'd never been this close to a man who was so willing to play the part. Jeremiah didn't apologize for having money; he flashed it. He didn't play down his connections; he dropped names like a barman drops ice into a glass. And he wasn't afraid to be forward. His hand sneaked unrepentantly from my knee to my thigh and I didn't move to swat it.

Just before dawn, when his Town Car was back on East Fifth Street, my battered tenement already seemed like a relic of the salad days that would be over soon enough. In three or four days, it would be all sorted out. I'd have that *Vanity Fair* job, thanks to a few calls from Jeremiah to the right people, and I'd phone my mother from under the plush duvet in his penthouse flat to tell her I was permanently engaged back east.

Jeremiah leaned in to kiss me, right on cue. And then he backed me up against the limo. "Wow," I said. "What a wonderful night. I can't wait to see you again."

"Mmmmm," he said, and pushed at the side of my gown.

"I'd better get inside."

"Sounds great," he said.

I moved to the side, to press him away. Even if things happened fast in the movies, the first kiss always ended with a polite hat tipping at the door, a happy skip in his step as the leading man backed away. But Jeremiah wasn't budging.

"Can I make you dinner next week? I'm a very good cook, and I . . ."

Now he stumbled back. He wiped his mouth with the back of his wrist. "No, no, not possible."

"Not possible?"

"I'm not going to meet your mom, okay?"

"Of course not, silly; she's in Oregon," I said. "I mean, if she visited—"

He leaned against his limo and shook his head slowly. "You seem like a very nice girl, and we've had a good time tonight. But, uh, this"—his arm swept the air, to indicate, well, everything—"this doesn't mean we're dating, okay?"

"But what about . . . ?" I was about to say it, to articulate my celluloid dream, as if he'd been in on it with me all along.

Jeremiah touched my face, placing two fingers under my chin. "Don't you read the papers, princess? I'm engaged to an Astor."

"You're engaged to an . . ." It took a minute to sink in. "I didn't know. . . . I thought . . ."

"Yeah. I know you thought. Funny. Girls and their ideas. Oh well." He hopped back into the limo and gave me a halfhearted wave. Then the car door shut with a decisive thud. I stood there for a long time, until I saw the sun coming up over Avenue C, like an egg over hard.

I have to hand it to Jeremiah. He taught me one essential lesson: never skip the tabloids.

After that, the city became my teacher, and she was a strict schoolmarm. She didn't like innocents and was suspicious of charmers. The city wasn't teeming with Larrabees, only colorful cads who'd twirl a girl at midnight and disappear by dawn. She was quick with a ruler when she saw me falling into George Cukor daydreams, and she taught me that success didn't fall out of the sky like pollen in springtime; it was won by hardscrabble sweat.

My schoolmarm's daily pop quiz asked one question, and one question only: Who's on top?

Who's on top? I didn't have the answer. I didn't even know where to begin. To find it, I tried loitering near the jockeys at the "21" Club and lingering near the Picasso stage curtain at the Four Seasons Grill Room. I idled in the velvet chairs at the Algonquin, sipping Earl Gray, watching for signs of a new Dorothy Parker salon. But my hours in these haunts were long and futile, as they were only living shrines to ghosts of cachet.

At the New York Public Library, behind the great lions, I began my research. I found clippings about the city's oldest families and the rise of the nouveau riche. I jotted notes from *Forbes* and *Fortune, Us* and *W, Interview* and *Details*. Between admin duties at *Gotham's Gate,* I searched the Internet for Mormon-style genealogies of Manhattan family trees. I tacked a map to my wall and marked off notable natives and recent arrivistes. I connected dots, and I followed my own routes, until I could've led a Hollywood-style Starline tour.

And then I did the tour. I pressed my nose to the glass at Pravda and Pastis, observing how the clientele swirled their $100 reds. Skulking around Gramercy Park, I took notes on where and how to walk a well-groomed pet. With my snoop's pad and pen, I lurked behind mailboxes and streetlamps, scuttled under canopies, and raised the suspicions of a thousand doormen, just to figure out who could be who.

Whenever I had a free minute from my admin duties at the magazine, I badgered Bernie Wabash for legwork on his column. Despite my coming up zilch at the gala, he gave me another shot and made me a sometime stringer. When I did well, he printed my tidbits. "Inside Line" under Bernie wasn't true gossip, but rather a stargazer travelogue of celebrity spa treatments, club sightings, and sunbathing shots on million-dollar cruises. So while I worked with Bernie, I took notes on how the column could be improved. I had a plan brewing: once I had enough ideas about remaking "Inside Line," I'd find a way to sell the idea to an even glossier mag.

It wasn't just career ambition that kept my fire fed. I also had a secret plan—to find my family, my father's family, and to secure my spot in my own blue-blooded lineage. If I could find them, I wouldn't be on the outside looking in anymore. I'd be more like *My Man Godfrey*, the society escapee who returned in the form of a butler and taught his society peers to see how the other half lived. Well, more like him, anyway.

But even with my private study, I still got it wrong. My school-marm asked me, Who's on top? And I didn't know. Because all I had were charts and maps and facts and lists. I was nowhere near the door.

Until one day—the day Bernie Wabash keeled over at his desk while he was eating a fistful of fries. Zip Winkle called me into his office and told me the news, saying he didn't have anyone else to replace Bernie, so until he could find someone permanent, I would need to keep the column afloat. Before he handed over the keys to Bernie's office, he said, "Trouble is, we can't have any Sunburst Rhapsody *anything* as a byline for a gossip column. You need to change that. Think of a name that will look swell in print."

I stayed up all night, pacing, trying to come up with something that would make Zip make me Bernie for good, and not search for another replacement. My plan: to scrap "Inside Line" and rename the column "Inside and Out." Instead of paparazzi shots on the *Law and Order* set or pillow talk from the masseurs at Bliss, I would dish out "power gossip." Who was an insider and who was still pressing against the glass? Who was getting a raise and who was getting the boot? I wanted to make and break Manhattan. I spent the wee hours jotting ideas for my new name. I wanted it to have the ring of an old-time starlet, to honor my father; it had to feel quick on the tongue. But mostly, it needed to be the kind of name that would make anyone famous in a day.

The next morning, I dropped some Visine in my eyes,

dressed in my best knit suit, donned a black felt cloche, and I went straight to Zip's office, looking like a cherry-blond Rosalind Russell. I introduced myself all over again. That was the last day of the Oregonian wildflower, and the first day of Valerie Vane. Zip leaned back in his massage chair and nodded. "Sounds about right," he said. "Sounds about right. You've picked the right time to do it. The city is on fire out there. I want you to show me every flame!"

Back in Bernie's musty office, I wiped down the coffee stains and flipped opened the Rolodex, containing the names of every has-been and never-was in Manhattan. I started punching numbers into the phone, knowing that I had to refresh that Rolodex fast, and if I could, I wouldn't be subbing for long. I needed sources in the worst way, and all I had for leverage was an expense account.

"Hello, this is Valerie Vane, the new columnist for *Gotham's Gate*'s 'Inside and Out,' " I said to the booker at Picholine. "I'd like to reserve a table for two for lunch each day this week." There was nothing like free urchin panna cotta and wild mushroom rabbit risotto, gratis, to make a source spill.

Next, I dialed Penny Highgrass, the city's top flack, and invited her to lunch. I told her about my new position at *Gotham's Gate*, and I said I was willing to place a few of her clients on the high board if she could get me victims for the ramp. She agreed. I called other flacks and made the same bid.

My first column was close enough to what I wanted to make more than a few people squirm:

> INSIDE: The cofounders of Spank, the new racy online literary sex magazine, Randall Fox and Charlene Dempsey, can make any restaurant buzz like a vibrator. Just ask Bar SOS, which hosted their recent "Cock Tales" story-telling soiree. It has been booked solid ever since.

OUT: In an as-yet-unnamed independent film, Rick Pantingelo plays a kosher butcher married to Paige Darling, but our sources say it won't ever hit the silver screen. The chemistry between the pair is so bad our spies overheard Darling calling it "a remake of *Beauty and the Beast*."

INSIDE: Is there anyone around town who hasn't seen Jolene Marburry-Rhode's big wad of bills? The new bride of high-tech industry analyst Charles Rhode has waved it around SoHo all week, while looking for a storefront for her jewelry design shop. "Money is no object," she told several potential sellers. "With the bonus Charles got this year, we could buy Thailand."

OUT: Have we forgotten about Michael Swanson yet? Unfortunately, no. That former Clinton administration insider reminds us of his good works every time some barely legal blonde shows up with herpes sores. Can someone tame that lion?

"The way to become famous fast," Walter Winchell once claimed, "is to throw a brick at someone who is famous." Instead of daisies, I now had bricks in my basket.

Soon enough I'd scared enough publicists that I was on every VIP list in town. I had tickets to any show and invites to every opening, just so I couldn't smear people for making me wait. And flacks did all they could to get me to anoint their clients or their clubs. I had too many items to handle on my own, so Zip gave me reinforcements. Soon, I had a team of stringers out partying across the city on my behalf. The tattlers at the other papers got boots in their ears for losing what I got weekly. They had to call my sources after they'd seen my item and say, "*Gotham's Gate* is reporting X, Y, and Z. What can we get for scraps?"

Now, whenever I got my quiz—Who's on Top?—I always had the answer. Because I wrote the answer.

"I never knew how smart I was," said Zip, puffing a cigar, a few months later. "You're the kid we've been looking for all these years. You're the kid with the golden key."

I rarely ate anything but canapés. I drank only promo specials. And soon enough, I found my crowd: a klatch of flacks named Tammi, Jenni, and Nikki. They were all twenty-five, all blond, and they were all pretti and perki. As children, they ate vine-ripened tomatoes from their mothers' rooftop gardens and smeared their morning baguettes with goose liver pâté.

One rainy night when cabs were scarce, the girls invited me back to Tammi's. As we downed RémyRed and ginger ale, they shared with me their master plan. "It's called, 'Don't Forget the *I*,' " said Tammi, hiccupping and covering her mouth. "You know, since all our names end in *i*?"

I got it.

"I mean, we want to have fun at parties, but how can we have fun if the right people aren't in the room?" she said. "What we'll do is ensure the right people get into the right parties, so even if the parties aren't that good, they'll be good."

I signed on. I told them they'd get a column inch for each bouncer I didn't need to kiss. Within a few months, they controlled the ropes. And I had the password to every PR tax shelter in town.

"Dog bone," I said one night, pushing past the bald man who'd eyed me through his peephole. I was at Motel, the Chelsea club the Three *I*'s were repping, where guests got anything delivered to their "room," paid for in half-hour increments. Down the nondescript hallway and an all-white stairwell, I found myself at the check-in desk, where one of Tammi's new recruits, Sari, glanced up and waved me through.

"Bill Maher is here," Tammi whispered as she ushered me to a corner. "First night out, everything primo. We just had Brazilian mangos delivered to each suite. We have peacocks in pens downstairs—they're so bii-iiig you wouldn't believe!—and the bellhop brings them up at exactly two a.m. One already died on the way here. Really bad karma. But who cares! Which room do you want? I can give you San Francisco mayor Willie Brown in six, Elle the Gender Bender in four, or Matt Dillon in two."

The parties, the clubs, the nightlife—it was fun for a while. But my dreams didn't revolve around a measly gossip column in a second-rate glossy. I wanted my own roll of bills, my own limo, my own classy clique, my own designer coif and duds, vetted by my own stylist, my own, my own, my own.

So, at the end of my twenty-fifth year, I decided to cash in. I asked Zip for time off the column so I could work on a feature. I wanted a yard, not just inches. It took me three weeks, but in the end I had a six-thousand-word exposé, a detailed tell-all about the habits and habitats of the celebs on the gold-plated clipboards.

"The *I*'s Have It: The Klatch of Blondes Who Stole Manhattan" was my first cover story for *Gotham's Gate*. It was somewhere between Candace Bushnell and Walter Winchell. The tone was lofty, strident with just the right touch of class-conscious alarm. It was full of substantiating detail, anecdotes no one could cull unless they'd *been there,* and delicious little morsels only an insider could snatch. I threw enough bricks, in short, to build a chimney.

It was a sensation; I was finally launched as a "journalist." I was invited to parties with *New Yorker* writers and auteurs from *Vanity Fair*. And after that, something truly miraculous occurred: Hollywood optioned the story. They planned to make it a screenplay and Gwyneth Paltrow would play Tammi. I asked how much and they told me we didn't even need to talk money. They would give me five hundred large up front and another two big bills once the picture was flickering.

It was the easiest half mill anyone ever made. People say that kind of thing never happens, but it did. First time out on a cover story for a glossy, and I made a killing. The facts of the transaction ran in all the insider rags. I got featured in a story in the Sunday Mag about big bucks for small fries—it was short and it was mean . . . but still.

After the splash, Zip gave me a Christmas bonus that could've bought me a bridge. Then he gave me a journalistic blank check: I could write anything I liked for my next story. I no longer needed to log daily hours. All I had to do was show my face in his office once a week and report my progress.

I got myself a loft in TriBeCa, and Chuck Uptite, the installation artist, did my interior design. It was all industrial chic, stainless-steel medical cabinetry everywhere. Rolling emergency-room gurneys as sideboards, medical instrument stands for tables. I mixed flavored vodkas at the glimmering glass bar. My recycling bin was full of gourmet takeout containers. I kept a stack of invitations by the toilet, so guests could cherry-pick premieres. I had two cell phones and a pager and never answered any of them.

The bartender at my new corner haunt concocted a cocktail in my honor: the Vanitini. Vanilla vodka, sweet vermouth, and a splash of grenadine. Vanitinis were sweet, but I didn't pucker. I was getting used to sweet: sweet as a perfect assignment, sweet as a five-figure bonus, sweet as a half-mill movie deal. The next time I got quizzed—Who's on Top?—the answer was simple.

The answer was Vane.

3

Night Rewrite

At The Paper, night arrives with the copy editors. Midnight rolls with the presses. Somewhere in between, the hands on the clock tend to bend.

When I hung up with Cabeza, I sat still for a few minutes, trying not to breathe. I put a new stick of gum in my mouth and chewed slowly. The right thing to do to was to confess a mistake, file a correction, and move on. But it wasn't so simple anymore. Jaime wouldn't smile at another slipup, and Battinger would make a paperweight of my head.

No, I'll wait it out, I thought, chewing a little faster. Cabeza wouldn't try again. A correction wouldn't fix what ailed him. He didn't want the truth; he wanted justice. And The Paper couldn't give him that. Maybe nobody could.

I looked around for Curtis, but he'd already gone back to Culture. LaShanniah had moved to graphics and out of our hands. The only people in the newsroom now were copy editors and the Night Rewrite boys huddled in their corner on the other side of Metro.

Night Rewrite was the 6:00 p.m. to 2:00 a.m. slot, aka the lobster shift, the dogwatch, the province of probationary reporters still proving their grit. The boys (and one or two girls) in that corner handled late-night shorties—boat crashes on the Hudson, shootings at the Latin Quarter—and reworked headline stories after the lead reporters killed their phones. When I was on Style, I had nothing but pity for the poor Rewrite boys, chained to the desk while the city skyline sang me serenades. That beat seemed like hours with your feet up waiting for someone to drown.

One night, I'd glided past Rewrite corner, on mule stilettos, wearing a white lacy two-piece number, on my way to the White Party at Lotus. Maybe I was tipsy from cocktails at Joe Allen, or dizzy from champagne at a Fashion Week presser, but as I passed, I'd tapped one of the boys on the shoulder and promised, with a laugh, to "bring back a doggy bag."

I shuddered now, thinking of it. Who had I tapped with all that disdain? Could it have been Matthew Talbot, who'd since been sent to Afghanistan to look for men in caves? Or Franklin Cook, who got the coveted biz-day posting in Silicon Alley?

Rewrite was where I ached to be. Maybe it wasn't the Milan runways or even white tents in Bryant Park, but it was better than a plywood box. After six months or a year on Rewrite I would've been able to move to a legit Metro assignment, like the Brooklyn Courts or Albany capital watch. From there, maybe they'd consider putting me back on Style.

But when the masthead had convened to decide my fate after the, um, Incident, Battinger said, "Style girls don't belong on Rewrite." Style pens, she said, trafficked in functional froufrou, pugs as the new pocket pet, fearless facials, while the rest of The Paper nabbed the apple out of the roast and stuck their forks in the meat. Maybe Battinger was right. But that wasn't the reason she didn't want me on Rewrite. Obits was penance, plain and simple. And I didn't miss the gist.

Maybe it was my longing glance at Rewrite that caught Randy Antillo's attention. "Hey Val," he said, and waved me over. I got up and walked across the newsroom. Randy was hovering over Travis Parsons's desk saying "Oh, yeah baby." I didn't ask, figuring Internet porn. "Dude, can you *do* that?" Randy added.

I took a step closer and looked at Travis's screen. It was Mullets Galore, a Web site honoring Midwestern eighties hair. Randy was rapt. "So, Val, you write that quick hit on Stain 149?" he said, without looking at me.

"The obit today?" I asked. "Oh, right, yeah, I . . ."

"Pretty cool, Val," he said, standing up straight so I could get the whole length of him. Randy was a six-foot-three-inch matchstick with a cap of red hair. His byline, R. Horacio Antillo, had the sound of a hard-bitten scribe, but he was just a Williamsburg trust-fund hipster who wore his sideburns two inches too thick. Battinger had brought him in from Jersey briefs and put him on the night shift so he'd start his Metro climb. He wasn't much to look at, but even I could see he was destined for glory.

"I loved Stain," Randy was saying. "When I was thirteen, he was, like, my idol."

"Every rebel has-been is your idol," said Travis, a twenty-five-year-old Harvard Crimson alum with familial links to The Paper's masthead. He'd been donated to Battinger as a lackey. But, as a Yale grad, she didn't like handouts from Harvard, so she put Travis on Rewrite and let him stew for thirteen months. "You never told me you were a graffiti artist," Travis said.

"Yeah, I did. I was a *writer*," said Randy, correcting Travis. "That's what they say—not 'graffiti artist.' Writer. I was one of the original Queens Bombers."

"Queens Bombers?" Travis said. "I've heard of the Bronx Bombers, but not *Queens*. Hey, anyway, didn't you grow up in Jersey?"

"So?" said Randy. "I took the train in." He swiped at Travis's head, putting a few hairs out of place. Travis smoothed his dirty-blond swoop, drew his chair to his desk, and sulked on his fist.

"I can't believe they let you get Stain in the paper," Randy said to me. "He was such a genius. That piece he did with Haring right off the FDR? I can't believe how *awesome* that is. And it's never ever been touched. Not a single buff. So, what's your theory?"

"Theory?"

Randy pantomimed yanking a noose around his neck. His tongue flopped to the corner of his lips. Then his eyes brightened. "Come on, you must have some idea," he said. "Why'd he do it?"

"Maybe it's tough being a graffiti artist when you're forty-two."

"He seemed like a pretty happy guy when I saw him last."

"You saw him?"

"Sure, at that anti-Giuliani rally downtown a few weeks ago. He was throwing dung at a painting of the mayor. I wrote it up. Didn't make it into the paper, though. They said it was 'too incidental,' but what they meant was 'too radical,' you know? Man, I wish I'd gotten that in. It would've been good timing, the underground hero taking his last licks."

I couldn't really hold up my end of the conversation on Stain. I'd gotten the fax and made two calls. I'd pulled a couple of articles off the Internet, and checked The Paper's digital archives. I'd read the Sunday Magazine feature and then I did what I usually did when I had a three-hundred-word squib: I cribbed from the press release.

Now, I figured it wouldn't hurt to recheck. I left Randy venting to Travis. When I got back to my desk, I found my stack of paper clips strewn everywhere. For no particular reason, I was unnerved. I typed in "Malcolm Wallace." After blinking at me for a minute, green letters flashed on the screen: "Please contact the morgue."

The morgue was The Paper's newsprint archive. Jaime had told me a thousand times that I should use the morgue to do the bulk of my research on anything pre-1985, the year The Paper had begun digitizing. But so far I'd done all of my research from my desk. *Are you a reporter?* I asked myself. *Are you a reporter?* said that smoky voice.

I went into the text documents on my computer to find my page of notes from my morning chat with Pinsky. There it was:

"Wallace, Malcolm A. Deceased black male found at water's edge near base of the Fifty-ninth Street Bridge, Queens side." Et cetera. I scrolled down to the part where I'd written "Jump from bridge possible. O/B DNP," and I put my cursor on the end of the line and backspaced.

My heart sank a little—for myself—but at least now my notes substantiated my story, in case anyone asked. I could go home and climb into bed, and in the morning there would be a fresh paper on the newsstand, full of all kinds of new problems for people to worry about. That was the nice thing about news. By tomorrow, today's paper would be fish wrap. It would be shredded for kitty litter. It would be taped inside shop windows to indicate the place was closed.

The humidity fell on me like a raccoon coat when I pushed through The Paper's brass revolving doors. A thin spread of gray clouds hovered low over the skyscrapers. Underneath it, the sky was illuminated almost to daylight by the glow from Times Square. It wasn't the usual incandescence of the Great White Way, more like a postnuclear haze. It was coming from my left, where, at the corner of Seventh Avenue, NASDAQ was putting the final touches on its colossal video screen. To test the green LEDs, they had turned the wall of lights all green.

Blinded, I took a few steps back and bumped into something. I thought it was a fire hydrant until I saw Battinger. She was standing in front of the building having a smoke, and I'd stepped on her toes. "Valerie," she said, wincing and pulling her foot away.

"Oh!" I said. "I'm so sorry."

She looked down to assess the damage.

"Nothing a little polish won't fix," she said. But she didn't mean it.

Battinger had never liked me, not since the first day I stepped into The Paper's marble foyer. She'd been opposed to hiring a twenty-six-year-old straight from a glossy. She didn't like my five-thousand-word piece on personal party planners. She told me she "couldn't follow the thread" of my story on fit models for thongs. When I had trouble with my features, she was the first to tally up my corrections. By the time of the Incident, I'd already depleted whatever sense of humor she had left.

It made no sense that Battinger was outside having a smoke. Her shift had ended hours earlier, a few squawks after she'd finished with Rood. I wondered if she couldn't find a bar like any other self-respecting alkie. "So are we finished with this LaShanniah business now?" she said.

"Yeah. I think Curtis got us out of the woods."

"I hope so." She took a long drag off her butt. "It's why we put young people like you on the Obit desk, you know. To keep abreast of this new generation."

She looked about to spit. We both knew the real reason they put people like me on Obits. Battinger stubbed out the last of her cigarette on the hydrant. "I got a call today from some character who wouldn't leave his name. Said he was interested in an obit that ran today. Unbylined. I told him that probably meant you wrote it. You hear from him?"

I swallowed. "Yes, I think so."

"Think so?"

"Yes, I talked to him."

"Any problem there?" she said. She stared me dead in the eyes.

"No. He just had some questions."

"He sounded like he might be upset about something." She flicked her butt into the gutter. "But when I pressed him he said he'd take it up with you. Asked me a lot of questions, though. How long were you on Obits; did you write for other sections; were you working with Metro? Guy was damn curious."

That raccoon coat started to weigh tons.

"I guess you spoke to him," she continued when I didn't answer. "So, if it's a problem, I'm sure we'll hear about it tomorrow. Meantime, you're looking a little haggard. You should get some zzzz's."

"You too," I said, and then tracked back. "I'm beat."

But the truth was, I was as alert as a hummingbird. I wanted to know what Cabeza had told Battinger. Had he already sold me out? She walked past me and, maybe sensing this question, looked back before she hit the revolving door. "Anything else?"

"No. No, Jane. Mrs. Battinger. Have a good night," I said.

"Good," she said. "Hopefully that's the last of it."

"Hope so." I turned quickly on my heel and headed west.

On another night like this, nearing midnight with the sky so phosphorescent, I probably would've called a private car to dash me off to Asia de Cuba for grilled baby octopus and balsamic portabellos. In my Style days. Or if I was feeling chatty, I might've headed down to Chelsea to meet the post-art-opening crowd at Lot 61 to sit on a high stool and flirt with the gay barman.

Tonight, I had nowhere to go, nothing to do. I heard the patter of feet, the crunch of rubber through wet potholes, the burst of horns forcing their way out of Times Square. I moved into the crowd toward Eighth Avenue.

A group of teenagers in matching pink tank tops and low riders pushed past the door of the local welfare hotel, linking arms and screaming a show tune. An old woman stepped out, wearing a housecoat stained in wide circles under the arms. A wiry Indian man sat on a lawn chair next to a tree stump and sucked on a brown bidi. At the corner, a family in long shorts, big tees, white Reeboks, and socks piling up their ankles stood outside Ben & Jerry's. As I passed, the little girl in a pink overall dress said, "Look at all those little lights up there, Mommy. Do people really live up that high in the sky?"

The whole family—Homer, Marge, Bart, and Lisa—gaped up, their plastic spoons pressing their tongues into their mouths. I looked up to see what they were seeing. They weren't looking at anything, just skyscrapers filled with little lights, all the little boxes where we New Yorkers make our tiny lives. It didn't look like much, did it? A whole lot of people in their little rooms, each of them trying so hard to light up the sky. Ultimately, each one would shut out their light, but the New York sky would still be filled with eight million more. So what was the point?

After playing tourist, my neck hurt. I turned off Forty-third Street and onto Eighth Avenue, where walkers and diners and laughers and smokers cluttered the sidewalk. I pushed on, watching my feet chew up the wet pavement, watching the marquee lights swirl in onyx puddles. Up ahead of me, there was a darkened stoop. A man in a trench coat leaned forward, his face hidden under the shadowed brim of an old fedora. I saw the red tip of his cigarette, smoke obscuring the lineaments of his face.

Cabeza, I thought. He's followed me. I saw the green lantern of the subway stop and, just as I realized I was being paranoid, took the stairs quickly down.

I pushed my key into the door on Broadway near Eightieth Street, and smelled fresh-baked bagels from the H&H bakery below. The foyer was dark and empty, the brown and tan tiles polished to a patent sheen. I collected my mail—nothing but circulars and bills—and began to climb the narrow stairway.

The first landing smelled of untended cats and I could hear the grunts of our resident Deadhead investment banker either catching the game or getting lucky. A bag of garbage had pushed a door ajar on four, and I could see a couple chopping vegetables on the floating butcher block in their duplex. I counted the eight stairs between each landing until the sixth floor, where I caught my breath. I found my keys and opened the door to my studio. It had to be about 110 degrees inside, as I'd forgotten to open the windows and turn on the fans. I locked all four Yale locks and kicked my way through balled-up socks and piles of laundry to get to the windows and flick on the A/C.

For six months, I'd submitted to the cruelty of an ordinary life: the hollow echo of the dripping faucet in a barren apartment, the alarming, persistent hum of a midsize refrigerator, the mismatched dishes piling up in the sink. I'd tasted sobriety and I didn't like it. It had the rubber texture of sushi from the corner deli, looking for takers since noon.

My new apartment had all the charm of the inside of a tennis shoe. Five hundred square feet of wall and floor divided by white Sheetrock; a mini-bake oven; a refrigerator large enough for condiments; a place to blow your nose. It was all one room: half bedroom, half dining room, and half kitchenette, which left minus one half for living.

I'd moved uptown to get away from all the people who had known me when things were swell. But I hadn't really committed to the place yet. The walls were bare and the bookcases empty. Most of what I owned was still in boxes piled on the floor. There were four pieces of furniture: a sofa, a coffee table, a chair, and a mattress on the floor. The phone rang, and I kicked away some boxes to answer it. No one was on the line. I listened for a while, wondering whether I'd hear that smoky voice, but finally it was a dial tone, and I put down the phone.

The apartment's best asset was a large picture window that overlooked the Broadway Mall, a strip of grass and cobblestone where, at the moment, some neighborhood drunks were passing a bottle in a brown paper bag and I felt jealous. I had no pals; I was officially off the booze. My new nightlife was all on the small screen. I'd started watching old movies again, famous black-and-whites. But this time, I passed over the screwball comedies that made the city swirl in gleeful symmetry. Instead, I traveled to the dark side of the screen. My new companions were fedora-clad detectives, dames pursing cigarette holders between (presumably) bloodred lips, cackling mobsters, faceless trench coats silhouetted in the hall. They weren't pretty and they didn't end happily. I'd adopted them all from the gap-toothed VHS peddler down the block. The titles dropped me deeper and deeper into the darkness.

Tonight I had *Sweet Smell of Success*. I needed only a Vanitini. I gazed out the window at my drunken neighbors on the median. Oh, hell. Just one wouldn't kill me. I went to the cupboard and pulled down a tumbler. I lifted the ice tray out of the freezer, cracking it hard. The Russian landlord had left me a bottle of Vladimir, as some kind of welcome gift. I'd saved it for a moment like this, when I wanted to leap headlong off the wagon. So what if it wasn't top shelf? I poured some vodka into the martini shaker. Then I remembered the grenadine, but I didn't have any. So I poured out some of the juice from the maraschino cherry jar. No vermouth, either, but I had a tad of cooking sherry, so I waved it over the top of the shaker, and rattled it up fast.

I downed my Vanitini—the first one I'd had in months. It was definitely a sad pour. The cherry juice made it sweet, but its aftertaste bit back. Still, it reminded me of a feeling I hadn't had in months: weightlessness. I mixed myself another, rattled it up, and slugged it back. I pressed *Sweet Smell* into the VCR.

The opening credits rolled and the jazz blared. Burt Lancaster, Tony Curtis, screenplay by Clifford Odets and Ernest Lehman. I went back to the kitchen and poured myself a third Vanitini as the soundtrack swelled. I drank that one standing up. Pouring myself another, I moved to the couch and kicked off my shoes. A city skyline full of bright lights. The camera comes up on the back end of a printing press as workers throw stacks of newspapers into delivery trucks. Blaring horns grow louder as the truck bumps through Times Square, past the blinking CANADIAN CLUB sign, past the hot lights showing off showgirls, past the dime stores and all-night hot dog stands.

Sidney Falco walks onto the screen. He's a pretty boy with slicked-back hair and a starched shirt, but his pretty is the menacing sort, the kind you know means trouble. He yanks one of the papers out of the stack on the sidewalk and scans a gossip column by J. J. Hunsecker. Whatever he's looking for isn't there, and Falco scowls and dumps the rag into the trash. He is a flash of nerves as he climbs the stairs to his second-floor office, where his name, SIDNEY FALCO, PRESS AGENT, is taped on the door. He moves into the back room, where he coincidentally also sleeps, and changes into his clothes for an evening on the town. His girl Friday follows him into the bedroom, sits primly on the edge his bed, and stares up at him, doe-eyed. "Where do you want to go, Sidney?"

On my couch, in my Vanitini haze, I recite the words along with Curtis:

"Way up high, Sam, where it's always balmy. Where no one snaps his fingers and says, 'Hey Schmitt, rack the balls,' or 'Hey mouse, mouse, go out and buy me a pack of butts.' I don't want tips from the kitty. I'm in the big game with the big players. My experience I can give you in a nutshell and I didn't dream it in a dream, either: Dog eat dog. In brief: From now on, only the best of everything is good enough for me."

I tipped my head back to get one last sip out of my tumbler, but nothing was coming. My head fell into the cushions and the glass tumbled to the floor. The blue shadows of the TV light danced on my plaster ceiling. It was beautiful and wild, a fantastic waltz of light against the darkness. *The best of everything.*

Then everything went black.

4

Shoot the Works

The scene: a housewarming party at my very own three-thousand-square-foot loft. Glitterati on the davenport, fashionistas on the fire escape. Uptite shows a humming brood of design aficionados through the room. Caviar on the medical sideboards, crudités on the gurneys. I'm playing hostess in a fitted silk gown that plunges back and front. But tasteful. Understated. Hot. My hair is coiffed by Jules Freelove, Broadway stylist. My barman is handing me a bottle of Veuve Clicquot.

Not a VHS-induced dream. It happened. That was me, back then, when I was shiny spanking new, and it was all my own, my own, my own.

And Jeremiah Sinclair Golden Jr. walked through my door. He was bracketed between two sets of silicone implants he'd filched from a *Penthouse* party uptown. He was grinning, and who could blame him, given what he had on each arm?

It'd been a year since he'd left me on the East Fifth Street curb, and since then, my tabloid study had informed me that his Astor heiress left him at the altar. She'd complained to Liz Smith that his $20,000 budget on her gown "simply wasn't sufficient," but the scuttlebutt had it she'd become aware of his extra-premarital affairs. Jeremiah rebounded fast, and the string of socialites he'd dated since would've made a mighty pricey necklace.

Now he walked right up to me, and said, "May I?" He took the champagne from my hand and popped the cork. The fizz spilled down the neck of the bottle and onto his hand. He licked it off, saying, "That's tasty." When he caught my grimace, he added, "I'm enchanted to finally meet this Valerie Vane I've been hearing so much about."

He was looking right at my face. He could've read the birthmarks on my neck like tea leaves. He was close enough to smell my Obsession. And he didn't recognize a thing. "It's amazing we've never met," he said.

Amazing, indeed. In a sense, though, he was right. That girl he'd left on Fifth Street, the one who'd wept into her pillow while her roommate stuck needles in a voodoo-doll Golden, was playing banjo elsewhere with Holly Golightly's pre–alter ego, Lulamae Barnes. I'd shed Sunburst Miller's skin when I'd put that cotton-candy gown down my incinerator shaft. And now, I didn't even blame Jeremiah for the way he'd spun me and let me fall. I blamed that bumpkin I'd been, so ripe for a grifter's scam.

I poured Jeremiah a glass of Veuve Clicquot and he and his silicone twins worked the room. I watched them admire Uptite's design, the chrome surfaces, the glass beakers, the framed forceps and scalpels. The Three *I*'s assembled—*"Isn't he . . . Ohmygod, that's totally Jeremiah Golden . . . Yikes, lose the bimbos!"*—and prattled. They were still my posse in spite of the exposé, since all press was good press, as publicists all agreed.

Eventually, Jeremiah circled back. "I'd like to get a delivery here, if you don't mind," he said.

I knew what kind of delivery he meant, but I told him it was okay. Plenty of people had already suggested doing lines off my medical cabinetry—the irony, it seemed, was far too inviting. By the time his dealer arrived, his silicone sweethearts had already huffed out the door. At five a.m., my glass coffee table was powdered white and Mr. Golden was a fixture on my Eames settee. I was too bemused to complain.

"You ever try one of these?" he said, taking a cigar out of his jacket and pointing its obscene length at me. "My D.P. brought this Cohiba back from Cuba, but I haven't had a good reason to smoke it yet. I thought I'd save it to celebrate something, and now seems like the right moment."

I took the cigar from him and twirled it between my thumb and forefinger, sizing it up. "What are we celebrating?"

"It seems to me," he said, looking from one end of my loft to the other, "you've got plenty to celebrate."

"And what about you?"

He took the cigar back, cut the tip with a silver cigar razor, and considered. "My good luck in meeting you. I've been reading your column," he said. "You've managed to skewer all my favorite people. And boy, did they deserve it." He laughed at his own joke for a minute, but I didn't join him. "You don't just feed the beast," he added, "you really draw a picture of the city, you give a sense of the whole scene. I bet you're a native. Am I right?"

My cynicism was so thick I could've cut it like a cake. This was the same exchange we'd had so long ago, only in reverse.

"Native?"

"Native New Yorker. Am I right?"

"What makes you think so?"

"Ha," he laughed one note. "Only a native New Yorker would take offense. And, of course, the column. You know everyone in town."

"I'm not on the column anymore," I said. "They've got me on features now."

"They had to!" he declared, his voice cracking oddly. "With what you know, you could be filling that entire magazine. Am I right? The gossip stuff is good, but you've got real insight."

I put the cigar to my lips and wondered if I'd really been quite so blind to flattery in the past.

"Light it," he said. "Go on. I think you'll like it. It's actually sweet." He moved next to me and pressed a hand to my thigh. It was as familiar as an old song you played over and over for a month until you got sick of it and tossed the whole CD. He flipped open a Zippo and I inched toward its blue flame.

"You know how to do that? You've got to puff it a few times and don't inhale. Just go slow, sweetheart. There you go."

A plume of smoke enveloped me. The taste was tart and strong and it nipped my tongue. Not exactly sweet. I knew I'd be coughing something awful in the morning. I politely passed it back to Jeremiah, and then I moved a little away. He was a charmer; that was a fact. But he no longer looked like a Larrabee. He didn't hold that sway over me, because now I could hold my own. He no longer had his Astor. And I wasn't about to let him get close enough to let me down again.

"It's been a long evening," I said, yawning.

"Of course, of course," he said, standing fast. "I've overstayed my welcome."

"Not at all," I said. "But it is getting late."

"Of course," he said again, pulling on his jacket and nervously patting the pockets. "I'd love to take you out to dinner some evening. Could I? Might I take you somewhere nice?"

Well, wasn't that touching? Suddenly he had time for dinner dates. "I don't really do dinner very often these days," I said. "I'm so busy."

"I guess that's a no, then?" he said, turning it over like a foreign currency he'd never used. "You don't hear that very often."

"You don't?" I led him to the door. "It was lovely to meet you," I added, suppressing, the "again." I let him kiss my hand.

After I heard his footsteps make the ground floor, I went back to the settee. I surveyed my new loft. Everything was in its place. I picked up Jeremiah's Cohiba where he'd left it burning and put it between my teeth. Maybe it did taste a little sweet.

• • •

The next morning, The Paper came calling. I was padding around my loft in socks picking up empties when the phone rang. Burton Phipps introduced himself and said he'd been following my work in *Gotham's Gate*. He wanted to know if I had any interest in newspaper work "of the slightly more urbane sort.

He said, "Why don't you come over and have lunch? There aren't any jobs here at the moment, but we should get to know each other in case something opens up. They call Zachariah Zip, over there, don't they?" he said. "I love that. If it makes you feel more at home, you can call me Buzz. Some of the reporters here do already. It's kind of a tease."

I was pretty sure this Phipps just wanted to eyeball me so he'd know how to spot me in a room. But I realized at my interview that he'd be my future boss, if I'd have him. He flipped through my stack of clips and clucked, "Quite a nose for news."

Buzz Phipps had a face like a new BMW sports car: sleek aerodynamic curves and a buffed, hot-waxed patina, tested for maximum performance on scenic mountain roads, seen idling in French hamlets before quaint patisseries. Around town, I knew, Buzz kept a harem of hair-care specialists, massage therapists, manicure-pedicurists, personal trainers, wardrobe consultants, eyebrow experts, ear-and-nose-hair pluckers. And there were fashion designers and boutique managers throughout Manhattan who'd rescheduled a Rothschild to offer Buzz a fitting.

I told him I wasn't seeking a job at The Paper.

"Nonsense" was his answer. "You're no slouch, but working for that glossy doesn't say so," he added confidentially. "Even a year here would make you legit. But you should already be thinking about your career, big picture. Not just your next little scoop."

Nothing on him moved. A Kansas-style twister couldn't put a single hair on Buzz Phipps's pate out of place. His blond hair cambered off his brow with a gravity-defying curl. His slacks were pressed along the fold, his fine leather belt polished black and his buckle shined. A form-fitting shirt revealed a neat thicket of brown hair just beneath his bronzed throat. His lips were ample and pink, his teeth porcelain. And his eyes were, with the aid of contacts, pale blue verging on gray.

"I'll think it over," I said.

On the way home, I considered my mother back in Oregon, who paid five dollars weekly for the Sunday edition. She'd moved off the farm some years back, but she still had her ideals. Even if I didn't work for the investigative team, writing for The Paper would prove I'd made something of my life.

The next day, I told Zip I wouldn't be able to cash his blank check after all. He leaned back in his massage recliner and turned the volume to throb. "They were smart to steal you; you're just what they need to shake up that sleepy section. But if you ever get tired of the scholarly life, come join us again in the gutter."

I learned quickly that my life at The Paper wasn't going to be cush. First off, the hours were a working stiff's. At *Gotham's Gate* writers arrived at noon and milled at the water cooler till six. At The Paper, reporters started at ten, worked till ten, and called home nightly to say they were running late. Second, there were new rules I had to obey: I couldn't accept freebies over twenty-five bills—none of the gentle exfoliating cleansers, acid-free jojobas, or aloe vera extracts that arrived on my desk by the ribboned bagful. I had to bundle those off to Goodwill. No junkets, and free tickets were allowed only if I was really writing about the event. The bigger glitch for me, though, was the almost-outright ban on unnamed sources. I couldn't quote half my friends. It was like running a pub during prohibition: traffic only in teetotalers.

The Paper was rigorous with the facts. Everything that appeared in print had to be both true and verified. This was new territory for me. So, in my first few months on Style, I inadvertently became a star feature in the "Corrections" column, on page two. The copy desk checked stories before they ran, but if they missed the smallest fault, there were always a million amateur fact-checkers among our readership ready to point out a mistake. When the Letters desk got a call, Buzz got a call, and then I got a call, and I had to oblige with a correction.

After some months had passed like this, Buzz called me into his office and sat me down in his Aeron chair (a gift from his partner, not the manufacturer or its flack). He leaned close and produced a silver tube of L'Occitane shea butter and offered me a dab. I shook my head. I didn't need any lubrication. If he was going to chide me, I'd take it dry.

"I want to go over something with you," he said, taking out a marked-up copy of my most recent story on Nora Sumner, the editor in chief of the glossiest fashion glossy in town. "First off, I want to talk about a few words you've used here: *editrix*."

"Editor, you know, but with a touch of dominatrix."

"Oh, I *get* it," Buzz said flatly. "I'm *familiar* with the term. That's just not what we call one of our media colleagues. How about we go with plain old editor?"

"Sure," I said, and swallowed.

"Okay, now. We're talking here about a rumored affair with an unnamed millionaire fund-raiser for the Democratic Party. And this just pops up in the sidebar, unattributed."

"It's attributed—"

"It's attributed to 'the Sumner camp.' Where, may I ask, is that? Rhinebeck?"

"It's on good authority from two executive secretaries. They don't even know each other. They work in different departments."

"Hmmm. That doesn't give us the right to call it a 'none-too-secret dalliance.' And meanwhile, her lawyer says she's not seeking a divorce. We have him on the record. His statement is going to stand up against two unidentified secretaries. I suggest we scrap this sidebar altogether. There's nothing on this loin once you remove the gristle."

"Okay, Buzz, but I know we'll look silly if we don't even mention it. Everyone else in town is running it already."

Buzz leaned back in his chair and sighed. He took the tube of L'Occitane off his desk and squeezed some yellow cream into his palm. "That's just it. We're not everyone else, Valerie. This paper writes the first draft of history. We can't afford mistakes, and we can't be putting out unverified items about any old *editrix*. If you get something wrong here and, by some fault of our system, it gets in print, it stays wrong. It gets reported in other papers wrong, it goes out on the Internet wrong, and then it turns up wrong in the history books. Then it's always wrong, and it's our fault. That's a big burden we shoulder, but it's one we all share."

The way Buzz was rubbing the lotion into his hand made it seem like he was working up to something. He wielded the word *wrong* like a battering ram.

"So, you're saying we need to cut that section about the affair? What if I got some more publishing world insiders?"

"I know what's happening here," Buzz continued. "You never worked anywhere but *Gotham's Gate,* and that's the kind of reporting you know—the kind where facts don't ever get in the way of a good story. Maybe you had fact-checkers who were supposed to comb for flaws, but they were using their combs for their bangs. *Gotham's Gate* is as full of mistakes as a colander is full of holes. I knew all this when I hired you, and I blame myself for not taking the time out to help you. I've been remiss."

I started looking around for my purse. I wondered if they'd let me finish my lunch before they showed me the door.

"Don't look so glum," Buzz said. "We'll fix it. We'll make it right. From now on, you sit down and circle every fact in your story. Check it against your notes. Check it with your sources. Check against your gut. Is something not right here? Is this not exactly the truth?"

He stopped making circles on the back of his hand and handed me the tube of lotion. This time I took it and smoothed some into my palm, then rubbed it against my neck, massaging slowly. He wasn't firing me. He was giving me a second chance.

"I understand," I said. "I promise to do better."

Buzz smiled. "Of course you do."

After that talking-to, I followed Buzz's advice and kept my stories lean as a triathelete. I avoided the promo specials, made sure my sources were sober and on the level, vetted my info with people The Paper had already quoted ten times, and made no mention of any camp, save the one to which Charles Rhode's daughter went for tennis (which happened to be in Rhinebeck). As a result, my stories were dull as dust, but, at least, I was off the Corrections page. Not a single complaining call, not a single private conference. I even got buddy-buddy with the staff fact-checkers, who didn't brush their hair.

As a reward for my vigilance I was appointed to a new Style beat: Society. It was what I'd always wanted, and I'd never imagined I could do it at The Paper. The opportunities before me seemed vast; maybe I'd finally find some of my father's childhood chums or my great-grandmother's other great-granddaughters. But I was still a newbie.

On my first assignment, a patron's dinner for the Met, Grand Dame Mitzy Carlisle grabbed my hand as I was scribbling her quips on my notepad under the table. She tapped me on the thigh and whispered that I should join her in the Ladies', where she was going to powder her nose.

"It's fine if you quote me," she told me as she leaned in to, in fact, powder, "and I'm sure it's fine if you quote most everyone here. But leave that notebook in your purse. You are among people who don't appreciate a paper trail."

"But I've got to take notes," I said. "How else will I get their quotes right?"

"You'll just have to develop a colorful memory, darling. And take lots of bathroom breaks."

As I soon gathered, Mitzy had missed her calling to be a gal reporter for the *International Herald Tribune* in the 1920s when she gave up her slot in the London bureau to marry an Oxford purebred. She told me she'd followed Brenda Starr's fortunes in the Sunday funnies through the years with the tragicomic sense of remorse.

After dinner, she took me to a diner on Madison Avenue and tutored me on everything from the appropriate amount of frisée to leave on my plate at dinner to the proper pronunciation of sommelier. She wanted to ensure that I'd never get lost in a sea of bejeweled blue-hairs again. Working with me, she said, was her last chance to dance with the fourth estate. Mitzy didn't care if what I printed was flattering to anyone; she was happy for a little scandal in her circle—"jazzed things up a bit," she said. She just wanted it to be correct.

And after a year had elapsed covering my elders without a single mismatched pantsuit, Buzz pulled me into his office for another conference.

"Are you familiar with the term *zeitgeist,* Valerie?" he said.

At first, I thought I'd spelled it wrong in a story. "Sure, zeitgeist," I said. "It's the general *gestalt.*" Just replacing one German word with another. "The cultural climate, the, I don't know, spirit of the times. The way things shake."

"Zeitgeist," he said again, without looking up. "You own it. Your new beat."

• • •

The zeitgeist, as I saw it, was the dominant paradigm, at its most Hegelian extreme. New York, Big Picture. It was math geeks building technology empires on venture capital magic dust and art moguls turning the city's oldest museums into international franchises offering Picassos like Big Macs.

For four months in a row, my splashy cover stories on Style came every other week. I introduced the term *fashionista* into the paper's lexicon; I busted the dog-run wars open wide; I single-handedly popularized the pashmina. Love me or hate me, everyone read me. Valerie Vane was the name they flipped to after ordering their eggs Florentine.

Suddenly, I was always in Jeremiah Golden territory. I ran into him at Thomas Kren's businessman collector's preview at the Guggenheim's motorcycle show, John McEnroe's pre–U.S. Open Bloody Mary brunch, Tanya Steele's "second sweet sixteen." At Madam O'Hara's pet-hospital fund-raiser, I noticed him notice me, and at the pre-opening imported sake tasting at Nobu Next Door, he insisted I try one milky and unfiltered. When Zita Marlowe held her Botox Buffet, he lay down on the gurney next to mine, too late for me to bolt out of my IV.

I paid attention to my schoolmarm's ruler and when she saw him coming and tapped in a frenzy, I paid heed. She'd been good to me, after all. The more I kept focused on "Who's on Top?" the better I could supply the answer.

My rebuff from that night at my loft still seemed to sting him, though, so he kept asking me if I'd let him take me to dinner. I kept saying no, without exactly saying it. And the more I said it, the more persistent he became, until I took pity and switched to "Not anytime soon," and then "Not this week," and eventually, "Not today." When I finally offered up a "Maybe," he grinned like a Cheshire cat.

"Maybe," he said. "Now, that's what a man likes to hear."

Then one night, I happened into Ilin Fischy's bathroom. Ilin was a Chinese-Slovakian artist who had just won a MacArthur "genius award" for her "ethnographic videography," after spending a year filming herself "passing" as a man in various settings—men's clubs and cigar bars, locker rooms and bathhouses. The party, as stated on the invitation, was her Official Coming Out. "As what?" was the question on everyone's lips. Her hostess-wear didn't provide answers. She appeared in a latex minidress, revealing both her ample breasts and the contours of an impressively masculine crotch.

In the bathroom, Jeremiah, one of her early collectors, was with Lance Glutton, Arty Guzzler, and Paul Bakanal, his Dalton cohorts, cutting an eighth on the mirrored sink. Arty marveled, "I guess she models her dildos here?" Seeing that access to the facilities was barred, I headed back to the party. But just as I was clearing the door, Jeremiah took my hand.

"Would you like a line?" he said. "There's plenty to go around."

In my travels for zeitgeist reporting, I'd happened into many a stage door and green room, even a corporate boardroom or two—after hours—to find bold-faced names in the midst of this kind of illicit business. I wasn't judgmental and it didn't get into print. I knew that for the ambitious among us, leisure often came in a pipe or a pill or a powder and only the meanest of gossip writers had the audacity to do that kind of damage.

I'd been offered my fair share, and I hadn't dabbled. Growing up among hippies had been plenty mind-bending and the space-cakes by us didn't fly anyone anywhere great, so I'd never been a fan of the scene. These days, I had to keep alert. At any moment there could be a subtle power play, a slip of status, and my schoolmarm taught me that the best way to catch it was to befriend sobriety and to be the only one in a room steady on both feet.

I was about to demur again, but now Jeremiah had my hand. "Maybe, maybe, maybe. You're too full of maybes," he said.

Maybe I was too full of maybes. Maybe I was too uptight. I'd been pressing my nose against the glass for a long, long while. Maybe it was time I joined the party. Maybe I could stand to fraternize a little with the boys. Just once, anyway, couldn't hurt.

I heard my schoolmarm's ruler tapping, but I took the straw from him anyway. I leaned over the sink. I'd seen Jeremiah do it so many times; I figured it was simple. But the first snort was way too fast and ached in my face, so I put a hand up to my temple to try to stem the pain. "Somebody better help her out," declared Paul, while the others laughed. "Can't have a Valerie Vane OD on our hands."

Jeremiah eased over, silencing the laughter. He took up a razor and cut another line. This one was shorter and narrower. "That was made special for you," he said. He rolled up a bill and held it to my nose. "Nice and easy. Nice and slow."

I did it his way and won some praise. "Fast learner," said someone, as my schoolmarm's tapping got louder. Jeremiah seemed to be proud of his new student. After I tried a second line, my schoolmarm had resorted to SOS in Morse code. There wasn't too much left on the mirror now, but Jeremiah said, "Shoot the works, baby. The rest of it's yours." I decided I could ignore the code, just this once.

And so, after Ilin Fischy's genius party, I let Jeremiah put me in the back of his Lincoln Town Car. It went north this time, toward the cherry-wood doors of his Sixty-third Street town house. The first three floors were musty, decorated in various shades of brown and maroon: velvet club chairs draped with chenille throws, a lot of empty crystal vases. Scattered about the walls, in the appropriate nooks, were landscape paintings and still lifes of plums and pears. "My grandmother's," he said, as if it needed saying.

"I don't spend any time down here," he said, leading me upstairs. "There's only one floor that's really mine; it's really where I live."

The fourth floor was practically a Hammacher Schlemmer showroom. A life-sized replica of R2-D2, complete with remote. An antique pinball game and a foosball table—original, circa 1976. A tower of high-end electronics and two subwoofers shaped like trucks. And then there was lots of Pop Art. Behind the taxi-yellow leather couch was a series of photographs of teenage boys captured in 1980s bar mitzvah glory, each in a multicolored rococo frame. "I got those at the Armory show early this year," said Jeremiah. "A really cool artist named something-Marti. He's going to be a superstar."

He walked me over to a giant abstraction that looked like a blue Rorschach blot. "Elephant art," he said. "These two New York artists give elephants paint brushes and let them go at the canvas. Amazing, huh?" Above the fireplace mantle was an enormous orange silkscreen that was unmistakably Warhol: a mangled car wrapped around a tree. The driver still in the wreckage, the body curled over the steering wheel.

"My newest acquisition," Jeremiah said, striding to the fireplace. "It's from his death and disaster series. I picked it up at Sotheby's in May. It depicts the American dream turned nightmare. The car is our emblem of progress, the industrial revolution, America's most generic status symbol, and it's all wreckage." Jeremiah poured the contents of his plastic bag onto the coffee table and started shaping it into smaller mountains of dust. "At least that's what the auction catalog said."

I walked toward the Warhol, drawn by the repeating image of the driver crushed behind the steering wheel. The car was completely mangled, ruptured, and yet there was something peaceful about the way the body was just slumped there.

"It's hard to look away, right?" said Jeremiah. "Sort of like pornography."

"Pricey pornography," I said.

"But at least with this one I can be sure I'm not going to

lose money. Not that I'd ever sell this baby. But the others"—he shrugged—"you don't know. Elephant art could be dead in a year. Or it could be worth millions. Here, let me show you something."

He took my hand again and led me upstairs, into the attic, where he kept what looked like about a thousand canvases, all pressed against one another. He started flipping through them, one after another. "A collector has to be willing to make mistakes," he said, showing me one work after the next, the way Jay Gatsby tossed his silk shirts on the bed for Daisy Buchanan. "These are mine."

In the dim light, all the colors were shades of gray but I knew these were colorful paintings, post-Warholian, 1980s retro-kitsch, though I suspected he bought them when they still seemed cutting edge. Pop Art turned on a spin wheel; splatters of color and symbols and references to cartoons.

"I've guessed wrong on hundreds of artists people went crazy for when the market was hot in the eighties," he continued. "Japanese collectors would've paid hundreds of thousands for some of these. I was just a kid, but I had a pretty nice allowance and people offered me things cheap. I had the idea I was going to get really rich speculating on art, make my dad proud. Each one felt like a sure thing. Today, these wouldn't fetch a nickel at a farm auction. These days I try to invest in tangible assets," he said, taking a step closer. "I like something that's a little out of my reach. This work of art, right here"—meaning me—"would be worth the risk. I think. But my bids keep falling flat. Tell me, what does it take to have a shot at this masterpiece?"

I took a step back. This move was a bit corny, I knew. But I listened for the sound of my schoolmarm's tapping ruler and didn't hear it. "I don't know," I said. "Sounds like you might lose your shirt."

I bumped into an old rocking chair and the ghost of his grandmother revived. Jeremiah took another step forward and steadied the rocker. "And a few other garments."

My defenses were down. The attic was small, and he was so close. Plus, I'd lost my bearings somewhere back in Ilin Fischy's bathroom, and now I couldn't tell the difference between badinage and a corny come-on.

Jeremiah backed me into the chair and I sat as gracefully as possible. He leaned over me. "Tell me what it takes," he said, "to win you."

The rocker rocked again. His breath was warm on my lips. Why was I so resistant, anyway? After all, I wasn't like the naïf back on East Fifth Street. I reached up and put my hand through his black curls. They were welcoming. He knelt down in front of me and put his hands around my waist.

Just this once, I thought, for the second fatal time that night. He moved in to kiss me, and before my lips assented, I heard my schoolmarm's ruler one last time. One final, distant tap.

Now I had two new bad habits: Jeremiah and his ever-present companion, devil's dust. At first, we were a happy threesome. Things looked simple through a haze of white. Life was happier without the constant tapping of that vigilant ruler. And I'd convinced myself that I was so good, I didn't even need to be that alert.

Jeremiah, too, made it all seem simple. Devil's dust for him was de rigueur. How else could we keep up with our busy social schedule? Who cared if we spent half the day in bed? No one asked questions, and no one else mattered. If I started to make a few mistakes at The Paper, who was the wiser? People had learned to value Valerie Vane. A few corrections here or there wouldn't fell me. And best of all: I no longer felt sad or angry, or anything, really, about that girl I'd left on East Fifth Street. Who cared where I'd come from? To live in Manhattan was to be born again and again and again.

So, three months later, when we were sprawled on the floor of Ilin Fischy's bathroom, snorting off the toilet seat, I found the opportunity to share my secret with Jeremiah. We'd been at it for three days. Hopping from party to party, bathroom to bathroom, dumping vial after vial on mirror after mirror. I'd blown off work for a few days as the stories I was working on were, I kept telling Buzz, "taking up all of my time."

Jeremiah gave me my cue. "You know what's funny?" he said, sniffing and knuckling his nose. "Ever since I met you I've had this funny feeling."

"What's that?" I slid across the floor and took the straw. We were running low again.

"Like I'd known you before. Like we went to the same elementary school or something. You know? A weird sensation, like I knew you somehow before."

"You just don't remember," I said, getting on my knees over the toilet. "We met."

"We did?"

I took the razor from him. "We went to Veselka. We drank dirty martinis. We kissed, and I suggested we eat dinner sometime. Then you gave me a little lecture on New York City manners and sent me home."

Jeremiah thought it over for a moment and I saw his eyes brighten with the distant memory. "The pink dress? The matching gloves?"

I nodded.

"The country cook?"

"The country cook."

He sat stunned for a moment. Then he crawled across the bathroom floor and took my face in his hands. "Valerie Vane was once that girl? Oh, honey. What a marvelous transformation!" He laughed for a while, holding me. He pushed stray hair behind my ears. He brushed some dust onto my lips, then put a finger in my mouth and rubbed it into my gums.

"That was me."

He climbed on top of me. "Isn't it romantic, Valerie? Maybe someday we'll be married and we'll tell our kids about our first date, how you were a bumpkin from the sticks and I was a fancy-pants socialite and how I converted you." He cradled my head as he kicked off his loafers. "My very own Eliza Doolittle. My Cinderella. My jewel in the rough. A pea in the mattress."

"Yes, kids, your grandmother was once a string of clichés."

Jeremiah started unbuttoning his pants. "Maybe I should," he said. "Maybe I'll take you down to city hall and make an honest Oregonian out of you."

"Jeremiah, stop . . ."

"Why? You think I wouldn't? You think I only want some aristocratic princess? I could. I would marry a girl just like you. A real girl next door."

"Come on, Jeremiah. Don't tease like that. It's not fair."

"I'm serious," he said. "I've always wanted to believe a girl would change for me." Suddenly, he was full of sentiment. His eyes got moist. He took my hands and pressed them to his chest. "You did, didn't you? You changed for—for me?"

What was the right answer? *You flatter yourself, Jeremiah, that's absurd?* But the truth, if I was going to admit it, was that I had, sort of. I'd molded myself into someone who could handle a Jeremiah Golden. Then I'd been what he wanted me to be.

He rolled off me and started to take off his pants. "That is so hot. You're so lovely," he said, tugging them off. "You did that for me! Oh, sweetheart. Would you? Would you marry me?" He pushed up my skirt and yanked down my panties.

"Marry?"

"Betroth. Wed," he said, tossing my panties into the tub. "Would you be my wife? Mrs. Jeremiah Sinclair Golden Jr.?"

Context, as they say, is everything. I ignored the fact that we were on the bathroom floor, two days into a three-day binge. That girl from East Fifth Street, the one who still believed in fairy tales and Linus Larabees, was there with us, still.

She took it for a genuine proposal, even though Jeremiah wasn't exactly on bended knee.

"Would you?" he asked. "Would you," with every thrust.

"Yes," I cried at last. "Oh, God, Jeremiah. Oh. God. Yes!"

5

An Invitation

There's nothing like the acrid scent of half-brewed coffee and a fresh stack of death faxes to make everything seem normal again.

When I arrived at my desk in Obits the next morning, I looked for a memo asking me to attend a correction meeting. I didn't find one. I looked for a note from Jaime saying, "Talk to me." But it wasn't there either. The only thing I found was the morning edition, with LaShanniah smiling up at me from under the fold.

Nine a.m. staccato: fingers clicking keyboard, headset pressed to lips, tone commanding.

"That was 12:34 a.m.," said Detective Pinsky.

"One two three four," I said. "Confirm. We got *D* as in daylight, *A* as in aspirin, *B* as in blinding, *R* as in radio, *O* as in off, *W* as in water," I said. "*Ski* as in bunny."

"Dabrowski. That's right."

"We got middle initial *P* as in prick."

"*P* as in pick your poison," he repeated.

"Two middle initials?"

"*O* as in operator."

One of the clerks dropped a white envelope on my desk. I picked it up. "V. Vane" was printed in careful calligraphy on the outside. I turned it over in my hands, feeling the weighty cardstock.

"*O* as in . . . ," Pinsky said, searching for me. "Oh, Valerie?"

"Oh, wait a sec." The envelope was sealed at the back with a faux wax stamp. I touched the raised label, the edges of the wax. It was an invitation. A genuine invitation!

"As in, *other* people calling. Can't spend the whole day on the phone with one reporter."

"Right," I said, as if from a slumber. "I'll have to call you back." I felt blindly for the cradle and hung up on Pinsky.

I held the envelope up to the light. Could it be? A real invitation? Could it be that my exile was finally coming to an end? That I was to be admitted back into society? I took a stab at the possibilities: Madame O'Hara's unveiling of her new penthouse? A backstage pass to the Dalai Lama's Central Park appearance? I began to tear the edge of the envelope, then I stopped. Could it be? Dare I imagine? An invite to Janis London's annual picnic on Liberty Island? Wherever it was, I'd walk in like a traveler just returned from the wilderness, a little dazed, a little emaciated. "What was it like out there?" Janis would say. Or Madame O'Hara. Or the Dalai Lama.

I dropped the envelope and felt around in my drawer for the silver letter opener that my mother had given me when I'd started on Style. It was the only gift I'd received from her in years, antique Deco with a firefly just above the handle and a long thin blade. I didn't use it for just any old letter. I used it for important invitations, the kind with mulled-over guest lists. I found it enclosed in its velvet case at the very back of the drawer.

I slid the letter opener's narrowest edge under the envelope's fold and carefully slid it back and forth. I reached inside and took out the card, relishing the soft crinkle of the paper. I saw the words, stenciled elegantly into the front of the plain white card, understated and stark: "In Memoriam." I put down the paper knife and pushed open the card. "Please help us celebrate the too-brief life of Malcolm Wallace, who touched us all."

Without thinking, I clenched the letter opener in my palm and it nicked me, a shallow slice. It clattered onto the desk. I grabbed one hand with the other and jumped to my feet, glaring over the top of my cubicle wall accusingly. But I'd forgotten about the cord of my headset, which tugged at my head and choked me. I sat down and tore the headset off my head with my good hand and stood up again. It would've been comic if it wasn't so sad. Who was to blame? Was it the clerk with the red ringlets? No, she was chattering on the phone, looking innocent. Maybe Will, the mailroom clerk? I started to call out, but his name stuck in my throat.

Cabeza. There was no question. He wasn't going to get gone easily. No matter how many days and how many death faxes passed between us, I knew now that he'd be there, waiting for a correct.

I was sucking the slice at the base of my palm when Jaime leaned over the top of my cubicle. "Nice work," he said, holding up the late edition. "We're finally in the clear."

He opened the paper to show me LaShanniah's spread: LaShanniah in a gold bikini, LaShanniah in a glittering black gown, LaShanniah driving her gold-plated Humvee through Compton, and a candid at the beach with her last boyfriend, Bo-Charles of the boy band Flex. Then there was a large panoramic of fans during a candlelight vigil at her beached and busted yacht. My name wasn't on it. The byline only read Curtis Wright.

"You guys really gave us the whole deli counter," he said.

"Everything but the pickles." I was about to tell Jaime that I could've delivered a whole platter of dills, if he'd given me a shot the first time. I had contacts for her stylist from her Edible Panties tour, and two phone calls would've gotten me the butler at her Santa Monica ranch and the driver of the second yacht involved in the collision.

"As a reward for your hard work," Jaime said, "I'm assigning you an advancer." Advancers were standing obituaries on people we expected to pass posthaste. Obits had a three-drawer padlocked metal filing cabinet filled with them. They included not just the elderly, but also some A-listers who didn't take well to terra firma: actors revolving through rehab, action heroes hell-bent on lethal stunts. Your Robert Downey Jr.'s, your Jackie Chans, your David Blaines. They were written by a kind of carrion club, who were rumored to keep a "ghoul pool," wagering on the dates their items would run. "I want you to look at Sally Firehouse. I think she should be fascinating for you. The morgue will have most of what you need. Take your time with this one, give it that classic Valerie Vane flair."

I already knew a thing or two about Sally Firehouse. But then, who didn't? The celebrated 1970s Lower East Side performance artist set off alarms all over town with her "feminist bonfires." For thirty years, she'd crowded punk clubs for her acts of self-immolation. But she'd come through miraculously unscathed and survived to an anarchist's cozy old age on Avenue C.

When Jaime left I turned to Rood, who was hunched over his desk, having his lunch. It wasn't so much a meal as a sacrament, performed each day at exactly 11:45. Mickey opened his filing cabinet and pulled out a crumpled brown bag. From it, he removed a tin of sardines packed in oil, a pint of apple juice, and a package of vanilla sugar wafers. First, he ate the wafers, pulling each layer apart from the next. Then, he opened the sardine coffin and plucked them out with a white plastic fork. After the service, the fork would be washed in the men's room behind the International desk, and returned to his pencil holder. Then, and only then, he drank his apple juice.

I held my breath to abate the stench, and I told him about my prize for helping with LaShanniah. There were cookie crumbs on his chin and white chunks in his teeth. "Lunatic dame," he said. "But good news for you, Val. Means Jaime is warming to you. Work your heart out on that one. No one's done the prebit interview yet. If you do it well, Old Man Cordoba might throw you a bone."

I folded a congratulatory piece of gum under my tongue. I punched Firehouse's name into the digital archives. The first thing I looked for was her age: fifty-five. Not a good gamble for the ghoul pool. Still, how well could she be faring with a lifetime's worth of sucking smoke? And she was still performing. At any moment, a match could stick in the wrong place or a fire could get out of hand. Encouraged that I might soon get my own byline, I picked up the phone and dialed the morgue.

This time, I wouldn't cut corners. I'd do all my research. I would circle my words and triple-check my facts. I was turning over a new leaf—hell, I'd upturn an oak if needed. While dialing the morgue, I had another smart idea: I'd get the file on Malcolm Wallace and set that straight as well. A woman answered the phone at the morgue and I asked her for both files.

"Fifteen minutes" was all she answered. "Ninth floor."

Rood tapped me on the shoulder. "By the way," he said, "put me down for April. Those lungs can't last forever. Five bills."

I had fifteen minutes to kill. I called Pinsky back and started again with *O*.

Curtis Wright was walking across the newsroom. I sat back to take in the view. He was wearing a clean white button-down, brown tapered slacks, and a pair of square-toed shoes. He was better groomed than the majority of men at The Paper. But it was the mug that really set him apart. His pecan skin was flawless. As a Style reporter, I've logged hours with million-dollar faces—supermodels, actors, princes, and people bred to look that way. Most of them needed a little airbrush here and there so the cameras weren't too damning. Curtis could take any kind of light.

"I came looking for you this morning," he said, at the edge of my cube. "I wanted to apologize that you didn't get the byline. I tried to convince Battinger but she refused to double it up."

"Having my name next to yours would've only caused you trouble."

"I wouldn't mind that kind of trouble," Curtis said.

"Don't speak so fast," I said. "Your tongue might not like it."

"My tongue goes where I go," he said, and winked.

I heard the sound of my schoolmarm's ruler for the first time in months, and I took heed. "I seem to have lost my tongue."

Curtis smoothed his hand across his pate and back over his dreads. "Listen, Val, there's something else. I've been getting a lot of calls the last few days about a graffiti artist who died, someone I knew back in the day."

"Yeah?"

"A guy named Wallace. Quite a character. I saw we ran an un-bylined Obit. Was that you?"

"Oh, right," I said. This was it. It was already starting. Curtis knew about my mistake. Cabeza had called Battinger and now he'd called Wright. "Yeah, yeah. The Stain guy."

"Good. I'm glad we got something into the paper, even if it was short. Some folks called over the weekend saying we should do a feature. They say he was an unsung graffiti great. I'm thinking about it. There's a lot of resurgence of that history now. You know, people who want us to finally do the definitive treatment on Curtis Blow or Fab Five Freddy. I can see what they're getting at, since these folks didn't really get their due in their day. But I don't know. Is it worth a spread? What do you think?"

I didn't know if Curtis was playing cat and mouse. Why would he be asking my feedback on a story idea? I didn't rate as a peer, even. "Who's making the argument?" For the moment, I didn't want to give anything away. I would go for neutral. But I kept my hand on the clutch so I could shift into reverse if we hit a snag.

"A few people, at least one heavy hitter who might have influence with the masthead. But I'm not convinced. You're the closest to the story. It's sad he killed himself. Did you think he was worth more words than what he got?"

Neutral was working out fine so far. "Everyone down here thought three hundred words was plenty. To be honest, I just filed a quickie, and I guess I thought it was plenty, for what I knew. But you probably knew him better. Was there a lot I missed?"

Curtis let that marble roll on his roulette wheel for a while and finally it found a slot. "Wallace was quite a character. We go way back, actually. He used to call me with so-called scoops. A real golden gadfly. He was always talking about someone who'd been wronged, how the community was being ignored, he was often threatening to sue people, but I don't think he ever really did. I liked him well enough. Actually, I love these conspiracy theorist dudes. Just . . . well, I had to take it all with a salt lick."

He scratched his head. He had long fingers, and they danced like a daddy longlegs through his dreads. He looked pensive for a moment, and then almost sad. "When someone dies you start to wonder if maybe you should've done things differently, you know? I guess, mainly, I didn't really listen to his pitches because what he was talking about was all too small for us: some Bronx artist ripped off some style or some club fight erupted over long-time beefs. The real style wars, the petty crap. *Village Voice* material, maybe. That's what I told him. Call Michael Musto."

"Sounds like you were probably right. No need to feel bad."

"I do feel bad, but you're right, Val. We gave him plenty. Most artists don't even get an obit."

Exactly.

"Okay, it's time I confess," said Curtis. "The real reason I came down was to ask you if you'd like to join me for a Bollywood film festival at the Film Forum tonight. I've got to do a feature for Weekend. What do you say? A good nine hours of singing and dancing in Hindi, and hundreds of soaking saris?"

Two invitations in one day. And I hadn't received a single one since the Incident.

6

The Incident

It was ruthlessly cold that January night, but my ego left my coat at home. I wanted to show off some strapless shimmer, a retro chic number I'd adopted at Saks.

In walks me to Club Zero after the bubbly's already poured. But I get no entrance. My stiletto gets stuck in the velvet curtain a few steps past the door. I kick at it but it's got me good. I dance with the curtain until the hostess pulls me through.

She doesn't consult her clipboard. She doesn't ask my name. She knows exactly who I am. I am the VIP section, whole and entire. My backup is waiting on me, a few steps above the floor.

I feel good about that, but the curtain dance has set me back. I'm no good at clumsy. I'm good at slink. I'm good at glide. My breastbone can make an entrance. My hips can open a door. Not my feet. My feet get in the way. And devil dust won't have it. Won't have mistakes. It likes things tidy. It likes things neat, controlled, sure.

Up in the VIP, the glasses are full but the seats are empty. I turn to my hostess and yell in her ear. She shrugs and says they were here a minute ago. *Maybe they're dancing. Maybe they're out on the floor.* When I try to look, I get strobe lights in my eyes.

Walking among the dancers, I scan the bobbing heads, the flickering sequins, the loosening straps. I seek familiar shapes and finally I find them. Jeremiah's cohort is dead center, the heart of the throb. Paul Bakanal is a sack on the shoulder of a short brunette. Lance Glutton is deep in the ear of an unraveling blonde. Arty Guzzler is on his knees, awestruck by a set of red toenails. Jeremiah is nowhere to be seen.

It's funny. I haven't heard from him all day. He left the loft early after I said Uptite had designs on our wedding buffet. Our engagement had been hush-hush until now, but there are ten thousand ticks on the to-do list: crosscheck caterers, find florists, and on and on. So I badgered, just a little, for the right to announce it to a person or two. *Uptite?* he said. The last thing he said, on his way down the stairs, was "Can't we just wait?"

Wait? Sniff, sniff. Wait for what?

There's a high squeal behind me and it's Tammi, linking arms with a new member of her flack team she introduces as Cyndi. Tammi has a touch of white powder on her upper lip. I wipe my own and she mimics and says thanks. The puddle black of Cyndi's pupils leaves no question she's an initiate, in more ways than one.

"You girls come from the bathroom?"

"Mmmmhmmmmm," says Tammi.

"Any left for me?" Sniff, sniff. Not like I need more. I finished up my stash at home.

"Sorry," says Tammi. "But we're expecting a delivery."

"How soon?" Not like it matters. I can wait. Like I said, I covered the bases at home. Sniff. That was a little while ago, though, and I wouldn't mind a bump. Just a small one. Just to get the to-do lists out of my mind. To get into the mood.

"Have you seen Jeremiah? I want to make sure everything's okay."

Tammi swings her head from side to side. Maybe she's looking, or maybe she's saying no.

"Have you seen him?"

I'm a jumping LP. I sound like I need to know where Jeremiah is every second. Which I don't. I don't need to walk into a room and know. I just got here. I'm here for the party. I'm here to have a good time with all my good, good friends. We've got champagne on the dash. We're expecting a delivery. Nothing big is happening anytime soon.

"He's around here," Tammi says and I'm relieved. "They came from some art opening at Deitch about an hour ago. They were up in the couches before Cyndi and I went to the bathroom."

"They?"

Tammi doesn't answer; Jenni and Nikki have just arrived. She and Cyndi are waving their hands like baby dolphin flippers high above the bobbing heads. There's squealing. There's air kissing all around. There're little bleats and beeps.

"It's so crowded down here," says Nikki. "Where's our section?"

The girls lure the boys and their cronies back to the VIP and soon we're a saturnalia a few steps above the throng. We sit on silk pillows or toss them on the floor. We pop a new cork and spill as we pour. Arty assembles a bouquet of red toes between his paws. Lance finds the ear of the blonde and creeps back inside. Paul's brunette gets at home between his thighs. Tammi, Nikki, Jenni, and Cyndi form a honeycomb and buzz.

In walks Demi, a genuine celeb. She's Tammi, Nikki, and Jenni's new friend. She's trailing a posse and half a dozen shutterbugs who've weaseled their way in the door. We carve out a central spot for her in the VIP and the paparazzi start to swarm.

But she doesn't sit with us; she drops her faux-fur fox on our sofa and stands there in a tube top and terry short shorts. The shooters get some snaps. Then Demi bounds out into the thick of it, her hands above her head, her tube top sinking. Murmurs in the crowd so loud we can hear them in the VIP. I dig in my purse for my pen, and all I get are nails full of tobacco.

I should follow her for comment, call in a scoop to Rewrite

and make the early edition. It should be easy. She's hankering for ink. Anyone in the room can read it. She's sweating out her pores for print. All I have to do is walk over and oblige.

Tammi runs back. "Someone saw her nip," she says. "Did you see that, Valerie?"

"Her nip?" says Nikki.

"Yep, nip," says Jenni.

"Left or right?" says Cyndi.

"Goooood question," says Tammi, pointing at Cyndi and jotting something down on a notepad. "You're going to be so goooood at this. You're going to be really, really goooood!"

I ogle Tammi's notepad. I could borrow her pen, but I can't bring myself to do it. It's okay. I've got a colorful memory. I don't need a pen. I ask Tammi, "When's your deliveryman coming?"

"Should be here by now," she says.

"You called Ken?" says Nikki in a conspiratorial whisper.

"Yeah, I called Ken."

"Oh, you called Ken?" says Jenni. "Great. When's he getting here?"

"He should be here by now."

They all look toward the door, then look back at one another and shrug.

Demi and her flock fly back and perch, downing our bubbly. I should stand up and talk to Demi, get a comment. But I'm deep in my silk cushions with two men on my mind: Jeremiah and Ken. Standing up could take an hour. Sitting back down could be another month. I could get sidetracked; I might miss Ken. I should see Ken before Jeremiah. Not that I need Ken, but Ken would cheer me up. And before I see Jeremiah, I should be cheery. Maybe this morning I was cranky. That's it. Though I'm not sure why. Sniff, sniff. Everything's swell. Sniff. I'm a bona fide big deal. I'm on top of the top. I'm going to be a Golden. Though no one knows but me. *Can't we just wait?*

Demi leans over to grab her faux fox. She smiles at me faintly, maybe because Tammi told her she could milk me for ink. I know I'll wake up to see her smack in the *New York Post*, even though Richard's not in the room. Buzz will say, "Weren't you *there*?" And I'll say, "Of course I was there. But she didn't show me her tits." Or maybe I'll write it; maybe I'll call it in quoteless. Once Ken comes. I'll get up my gusto and work the room. Someone sighted a nip. Then I'll have done my share.

But already Demi and her entourage have departed. I am relieved. The room wants less of me. Tammi's cell rings. She puts it daintily to her ear. "You're outside? Great. I'll be right there." Tammi snaps her phone and grins. "Anyone want to come meet Ken?"

Obviously, me. Sniff, sniff. Outside, I climb up into the high backseat of his shiny black Escalade as Tammi climbs into the passenger seat. Ken sits in the front but I don't get a look at his mug; all I see is his cowboy hat in the glow of the hot blue dash.

"Hey, *Kenneth,*" says Tammi, pouring on the sugar as if she's meeting a boy for root beer. "We've been missing you too long."

"Let me tell you about this traffic," he says. "I've been up to Harlem and down to Alphabet City. Lot of orders tonight."

"Alphabet City?" says Tammi. "Get retro! We call it the East Village now, doll."

"Grew up on East Fifth," says Ken. "It'll always be Alphabet City to me."

I remember something about East Fifth. I remember a girl there, a girl in a pink dress. If she'd been engaged to my Golden she'd be singing it from a hilltop like Maria von Trapp.

"Hey, I grew up on East Fifth Street, too," I say. "A tenement share with handmade curtains."

Tammi flashes me a worried grin. "That's just silly, Val. Park Avenue doesn't even go *down* to Fifth Street."

But it's true. All of a sudden, truth feels so good. So welcome, so new. I want to tell Ken all about East Fifth Street, I want to tell Ken about everything. "No, really. I had a roommate and she was nice. We had no money. I remember one day I found a ten-dollar bill. I went to the bodega and bought tofu, broccoli, a head of garlic, a lemon, soy sauce, and Ben & Jerry's New York Super Fudge Chunk. It seemed like a feast!"

"What are you *on* about, Val?" says Tammi. "This is *so* not true."

That girl had a name. A name, a name . . . Sunflowers or Barley or something organic. Sniff, sniff. In the last few weeks, things have been getting away from me. Things that shouldn't get away from me. That girl's name. It disappears like a marble down a manhole.

"Val has been working on a crazy deadline. She's deliriously tired," Tammi apologizes to Ken. "She's been working on it, like, for*ever.* It'll be out in Style on Sunday. Right, Val?"

"Actually, I missed my deadline," I say, still wondering where that name dropped.

"Oh," says Tammi, "Well, next Sunday, then. Valerie has big stories all the time." She adds some more sugar and stirs. I clench my fist around something, but I don't have my vial. I'd like my vial. I wonder why it's not in my hand.

"Val wants one, too," says Tammi to Ken. And she says to me, "You want one, don't you, Val?"

"Totally." I push a sweaty wad of twenties into an outstretched hand. I don't bother to count; I counted long ago. I've had the bills ready in my hands since Tammi mentioned Ken. It's the first time I know it. That's what's been jabbing at my palm.

Ken takes the money and slips his hand back behind Tammi's leather seat and hands me the tiny glass vial. I crunch it in my paw and it feels cold with soft curves, not unlike a marble. Holding my marble, the image of the girl climbing the stairs on East

Fifth Street dissolves, but on goes the search for the name: Rainbow, Starshine . . .

Before I get out of the Escalade, I twist open the black lid of my vial and take out my keys. I hold the vial between my knees and lean to get a quick sniff.

"Hey," barks Ken. "People can see."

I just need a quick one. Sniff, sniff. Just one. A bump.

"Come on, Val," says Tammi, knocking on my door. "It's freezing out here. Let's go back in."

My skin smarts as soon as it hits the air. I put my arms around my shoulders, and head back in through the doors, past the bouncers, through the velvet curtain, up the stairs, past the bar, over the dance floor, through the hallway, alongside the dance floor, and back into the VIP. Even though Demi's gone there's a posse of paparazzi leaning on the back of our banquette. Maybe a half dozen shutterbugs. Maybe a handful of Sidney Falcos in the bunch.

Tammi is teasing them with promises of fresh meat. "Nas said he'd be coming by," she says to Nikki.

"Oh, Nas is always here. This is his second skin."

"Second skin; funny Nikki," says Jenni. "I'll wait for Nas if you wait for Nas."

"I'll wait," says Cyndi, not quite in on the inside joke.

"Anyone seen Jeremiah?" I say.

Paul gazes at me dull-eyed. Lance points to his left and to his right, and then up toward the ceiling, before he makes himself dizzy and retreats under his blonde. Arty is already lying on the floor.

"They were here when I came in," says Tammi, plugging numbers into her cell phone.

Again. "They?"

"Angelica and him."

"Angelica?"

"Angelica?" says Nikki.

"Angelica's here?" says Jenni.

"Who's Angelica?" I ask.

"You don't know Angelica?" says Nikki. "Oh, that's weird. You should know Angelica."

"I don't know Angelica." Sniff, sniff.

"That's baaaaad, Val," says Tammi. "Where have you beeeen? Angelica Pomeroy is the new *it* girl. She's the new new thing. You, of all people, should know Angelica Pomeroy. You should do a piece. Totally—actually."

I grind my teeth. "*Who* is Angelica Pomeroy?"

Tammi says, "VH1 VJ?"

Nikki says, "Crazy skinny?"

Jenni says, "Balloon boobs?"

Cyndi gets in the act. "She's, like, nineteen or something. She was an underwear supermodel. Now she works the whole backward baseball cap thing."

"She is *not* nineteen," says Nikki. "She's like twenty-*two*."

"She's from Long Island."

"Long Island? *Nobody's* from Long Island."

"Yep. I'm not kidding."

"Are you teasing?"

"Not teasing! Somewhere like Great Neck or Ronkonkoma or Patchogue. I don't know. Out there somewhere." She flicks her wrist.

"Don't write that, Val."

"Oh, so, now she's our client?"

"Everyone," says Tammi, as if it is a dictum, "is our client."

Sniff, sniff. But Jeremiah shouldn't be with any new new thing. He's my Golden. We're making it official any day now. Aren't we? *Can't we just wait?*

I claw my skirt. He's got to be here. He's got to be here somewhere. I'll go find him and find out about this whole Angelica thing. So down again I go back across the floor, dizzy in the spinning lights. I push through the mass of dancers. I get a paw on my ass and a hand on my hip and a tug at my bra. I get a blinding eyeful of bodies, but no sight of him. I back off to climb the stairs. Maybe I'll get a better view one landing up. Now I'm at the ladies'. I reach into my pocket and finger my marble. Sniff, sniff. Maybe just a quick bump and then I'll search.

I push through the door before I hear the groans, moans. I don't think much of it. It's a club bathroom, anyway. This kind of thing is routine. And it's normal to use the other stall. At first, they don't strike me as familiar, so I take another step forward. But then there it is, the image to end my life. His black curls thrown back, his dimpled ass, and someone else's bare thighs, someone else's breasts. His button-down is open, her hands around his neck. Her alligator shoes are tipped over on the floor. All the pieces fall into place quickly. Jeremiah has VH1 VJ Angelica Pomeroy, *the new new thing*, pinned to the bathroom sink.

I scream so loud I don't even hear myself. A girl looking for a stall assesses the scene and scuttles out the bathroom door. Jeremiah hears me and pulls back from Angelica, and she comes tumbling off the sink, headfirst into his chest.

Anyone with any sense would back out of the bathroom and run. But devil's dust is in me and it doesn't like good sense. I lurch forward, claws bared. I kick Jeremiah, and then ram my heel hard into his foot, to hold him steady while I dig for Angelica's eyes. She has no idea what's come at her, what kind of rabid bird, but I claw and scrape at her face and her hair until I've got some sort of hold. I don't know what I've got, exactly, but I've got some sort of hold.

The stall girl must've gotten her friends, because a crowd of onlookers is now in the bathroom door. Angelica's panties are still below her knees and her skirt is hiked up near her bra. But I don't give her time to assemble; I grab a clump of hair.

"You low-rent Ronkonkoma reject," I cry. "How dare you fuck my fiancé?"

She gasps, "What? You didn't tell me—"

"I swear, Angelica, this woman is not my fiancée."

"This woman!" I scream, to drown him out. "Now I'm *this woman?!* This morning I was your future wife—"

He is holding me back and talking fast. "She's talking crazy, Angelica. We are not engaged. Do you see a ring on her finger? If we're engaged, where's the rock? Where is it, Valerie?"

"But you . . . don't you . . ." I scream, now crying, then clawing. "How could . . . !"

Next, the VIPs are at the door with Tammi at the front, shouting, "Val, back off! You've got to let it go!"

And Nikki and Jenni chiming in, "Back off, Val."

But I don't back off. Devil dust won't let me. No, I don't hear Tammi, Nikki, and Jenni. And now Jeremiah's chums are also on hand. Lance is pushing people away. Paul is yelling he'll call the police. Even Arty Guzzler is fully alert.

"How dare you do this to me!" I yell at Jeremiah and Angelica, and then again at the assembled mass. "Don't you know who I am? I'm Valerie Vane! I buy ink by the barrel. I could ruin you. One article under my byline and I could destroy all of you!"

Jeremiah is trying to hold me out of scratching distance of Angelica, but his pants are still on the floor and all he does is waddle. He manages to get me in an elbow lock around the waist, so I need to bend over to reach her where she is, still pressed against the sink. I kick with my back hoofs like an angry nag, and I claw at her eyes like a wildcat. And it is this hybrid beast that the paparazzi manage to capture and splatter the next day on the front page of every tab in town.

"Don't you know who I am?" I'm screaming, my mouth as wide as Oregon. "Don't you know who I am?"

7

The Morgue

There are two ways to get to the morgue: out the window or up the stairs. I weighed my options. The window was a quick fix. But then again, I'd already logged six months in a state of disgrace. The gesture would be belated. The other morgue, the one upstairs, held Firehouse. And Firehouse could get me back on top.

I stood in The Paper's elevator bank—Italianate marble, Art Deco brass doors reflecting my distorted face—and debated whether I dared take the lift. The Paper's elevators carried editors in chief and ad men, rabbis and imams, activists and apologists, columnists and clerks. During election season, they lifted presidents and hopefuls to the publisher's penthouse. Come springtime, their yellow doors emitted a stream of admin assistants in strappy dresses that let their shoulders lap up the sun.

When I'd arrived at The Paper, I was happy to get into those boxes, standing shoulder to shoulder with the redwoods and heading upward. But these days, I was a mere cut sapling in an old growth forest, easily trampled underfoot. I moved into the hallway and waited to see if I could catch a ride with a bike messenger or janitor. Today I promised myself that if anyone mighty were standing in the cab when the doors went wide, I'd pass the ride and hoof it up.

The brass doors opened in front of photo chief Bob Torrens.

A hard call. He was powerful, but cheerful. A slip of a man in a pale yellow suit and red bow tie. Not on the news side, so he couldn't quite sneer. He'd always been a chum when I'd worked on Style, assigning me top-notch shooters and schmoozey free-lancers who could stargaze without missing the shot. "Nice work on the singer, Val," he said in a clipped English accent, a bit of an affect to go with his Savile Row suit.

"Thanks," I said, feeling safe enough to step into the cab.

"Eight pix," he said. "More than Elvis—but then again we weren't quite as generous in those days. Still had trouble choosing. Prom dress, mermaid costume. We almost went with a shot of her in a cobra bikini, but we knew the editorial board would choke on it." This was fine. The numbers were ticking up. We'd chitchat our way to nine, no sweat. "If you were still on Style you could've done a fashion postmortem." He turned to face me. "Hey, maybe even Week in Review."

The elevator stopped at four.

"Well, that's me," he said. "Anyway, next time I hope you get a byline," he said on his way out. "It's a shame, Valerie, considering your name used to be all over this rag."

I looked down at my feet and took in the blocky toes of my beat-up heels until I got to the ninth floor. From now on, I'd take the stairs.

At nine, I got out. The corridor was dark and silent as a mausoleum. As I walked toward a flashing light at the end of the hall, Cabeza's voice smoldered in my ear, joining with my Sidney Falco hangover: *Are you a reporter? All I'm looking for is the truth. And if you're a reporter, that's what you'll want too—the truth. Way up high, Sam, where it's always balmy. Where no one snaps his fingers and says,Hey, Mouse, Mouse. Are you a reporter?*

Maybe Cabeza had known a hundred girls like me, fresh in town from nowhere in particular. Maybe he was the type who asked where you were from and didn't accept a coy smile as an answer. Maybe he was one of those people who didn't let things go so easily.

I could hear Burt Lancaster as J. J. Hunsecker in *Sweet Smell* saying to Falco: "You're dead, son. Now go get yourself buried."

That night in the ladies' of Club Zero turned out to be a stellar photo-op for the paparazzi that hadn't followed Demi out the door.

There was the shot of Jeremiah in boxer shorts. The shot of panty-less Angelica edging out from behind the sink and fleeing past me. The shot of me biting Jeremiah's finger when he wagged it in my face. Blood on the ladies' room floor. The shot of Jeremiah raising his finger and screaming. The shot of the cops parting the crowd. The cops wrestling me to the floor. The cops frisking me. The cops discovering my marble. One cop holding up the drugs—this one copied widely, with the vial in focus in the foreground and my pathetic profile in soft-focus in the background. And of course, the shot of me being cuffed as I insisted, screaming, that they couldn't take me anywhere because I'd pour barrels of ink on all their heads. The most oft-used caption was "Don't you know who I am?"

The story splattered the tabloid front pages for four days. Gossip columnists milked it for at least a month, and incidental items still popped up now and again. The shocking parts—Jeremiah's and Angelica's unclad privates—were digitally blurred in the interest of good taste. So the image showed me strung conveniently between Jeremiah and Angelica, like the crossbar of an *H*. Angelica, by some horrifying photographic distortion, came off looking quite proper, her mouth agape as if she'd been attacked out of nowhere while sipping pekoe tea with the queen. Jeremiah, also quite improbably, came out looking heroic, his chest bared as he yanks me away from his new new thing.

The "Club Zero Incident," as it came to be known—or just

"Club Zero"—turned out to be my big publicity campaign for that fine Midtown establishment. If anyone hadn't been there before, they went there now to glimpse the tabloid landmark. The club obliged tourists by hanging a framed copy of the *Post*'s "VANE-GLORY" cover in the ladies' room at the scene of the crime.

The Incident only lionized Golden and Pomeroy. It turns out they announced their engagement while I was being processed through Central Booking. No wonder he wanted to wait. A week later, they appeared together on *Entertainment Tonight*—Angelica still with Band-Aids on her cheeks—to announce that they would co-executive produce a new Odyssey Pictures release, *Terror in the City*. It would be a neo-noir cinema verité—that is, a thriller based on a couple's encounter with a madwoman modeled on yours truly, except that my character would be a *Basic Instinct*–style serial murderess named Victoria Vile. The role would've been perfect for Joan Crawford. They could even have used clips from *Sudden Fear*. Angelica, however, had decided on a career in pictures, and so she would star as herself.

For all my promises of blotting Jeremiah and Angelica out with my pen, it turned out I didn't have the power of even a Bic. The barrels of ink came spilling on me—me, the cuckolded ex. Sure, now I was a bold-faced name but not in the way I'd ever wanted to be. Maybe there aren't a lot of wet eyes on that account. And I don't guess there should be, considering how easily I'd always thrown bricks. Live by the swordfish, die by the seared tuna, as they say.

Tammi bailed me out, but when she dropped me in front of my TriBeCa loft, she said, "I'm sorry, Val, but this has got to be it. I've got to cut you off," just like Paulie Cicero to Henry Hill when Henry crosses the mob boss in *Goodfellas*. "You're no good for business."

I knew she was right. It wasn't just the marble; it wasn't just the fact that I'd clawed the face of a television personality. We both knew. I'd never be let back into another VIP section. I'd never get past a bouncer, even if my name was the only name on his clipboard. My face was all over town, like a Western wanted ad. I'd become a media piñata, and everyone in town was taking a whack.

"You'll need to hide out for a while," said Tammi, in the most comforting voice she could muster. "Do you know anyone in Spain?"

Then the lawyers came in and grazed. Angelica and Jeremiah didn't press charges, but, after some consideration, they decided they would sue me for my TriBeCa loft. Club Zero even got a cut—they said the crime scene investigation had cost them four days' bar. There wasn't anything left to go around after that, because I'd already blown the rest on, well, blow, for myself and all my so-called friends.

The Paper was even less forgiving. When I arrived at my desk Monday morning, Buzz didn't have nice things to say, like "We'll fix this." Or "Would you like some shea butter?" This time, he said, "There's a special editors' meeting called for today and the subject is Valerie Vane."

The masthead convened. A memo was distributed to every bureau from Roanoke to Rangoon: If you're appearing in print elsewhere, don't expect to stay on here. To look like they cared, they offered me a month in rehab. After that, they got out their carving knives. They couldn't fire me outright because of certain obscure union rules a discomfited news steward explained to me over coffee. I had at least a year left on my contract and if they broke it they'd have teamsters on their backs. I got a few calls from tabs that thought my "party girl" persona could come in handy for a nightlife columnist, but I wasn't that cheap. Well, maybe I was, but I didn't care to exploit my own shame with vegetable pulp all over my face.

It was Jaime Cordoba who caught my fall. He was short on obituary assistants, he said, and he could use me. He promised Battinger he'd keep me under wraps, out of the limelight. I'd be doing administrative work, mostly, and if I wrote much of anything, I wouldn't get a byline. All in one lift of Jaime's hand, I was saved and I was damned: at twenty-eight, I'd be a lifer without any hope of a life.

The morgue was at the end of the hall and light flashed like a lighthouse beam. I continued down the corridor, my eyes fixed on the flashing light, but the closer I moved the farther away it seemed, like some camera trick from Hitchcock's *Vertigo*.

Are you a reporter? No, I wasn't a reporter. I didn't know the first thing about Truth with a capital *T*. I was about as easily led astray as a donkey.

I found the door to the morgue and turned inside. Clerks in gray were methodically moving files from one shelf to another. A photocopy machine flashed and hissed, sliding back and forth, back and forth, with a metronymic hum. A female clerk in a shapeless gray dress noticed me. She stepped behind a long wooden desk and sat down. She adjusted the tortoise-shell glasses on her nose. "You must be here for the Firehouse file," she said, handing me one of two files in the tray.

"Yes," I said. "Also the file on Malcolm Wallace."

"That's here for you too." She put them in my hands. I placed the Stain file inside the Firehouse file, hiding it, and put both under my arm.

"Just a minute," she said. "You've got to sign both of those out."

I took the pen from her and leaned over to write out my name. "That ever get to you?" I said, nodding toward the copier.

"Nah," she said. "It's like living with a bad smell. You don't even notice it after a while."

She watched me write my name. Then she picked up the paper and read it. "I'm sorry, but doesn't that say Valerie Vane? I thought she was . . ."

I smiled. "Nope," I said. "The rumors were greatly exaggerated."

"Must be hard living with that," she said.

There's a reason people pay twenty-five cents to flip to page ten for Page Six every day. It's because they sit in windowless rooms where copy machines make their lullabies. I grabbed the pen out of gray girl's hand and took the files. I proudly scrawled my signature, big and bold, under my name. "Why don't you take that and sell it for a hundred bucks?"

I cleared my desk and put the files down. The Firehouse folder was stuffed with about a hundred clips. They were all brittle and folded, taped together with small strips of yellowed Scotch tape with running dates scribbled in ink across the newsprint. But I wasn't interested in that file. My fingers twitched nervously over the Wallace file, which was, I was horrified to learn, just as bulky.

I'd never been much for research. Files, paper, history. Yellowing papers and ancient ideas didn't help me capture the zeitgeist. But I figured this research on Wallace wouldn't take long. I knew what I was looking for—something to exonerate me—and I was sure it wouldn't be hard to find. Something that showed this Stain had plenty of reasons to let go of that rope to which he'd been clinging. An open and shut suicide.

I tried to organize the clips by date so that I'd create a basic Wallace timeline. The first was June 24, 1971, and the headline read, "'Tonka 184' Makes His Mark." There was no byline, but there were two photos showing scribbles on a wall, and scribbles on a street lamp. The pull quote read: *"It's just a name. It's like what can you make out of it?"*

> Someone has been making a name for himself all over the city, without ever showing his face. He writes Tonka 184, everywhere he goes. Small scribbles on subways, tiny signatures on walls from Broadway to Canal Street and beyond.

His scrawls have now become omnipresent, as familiar as the subway stations themselves. And now he has hundreds of imitators, including Joe 136, Stitch 131, Eye 156, Yank 135, and Stain 149.

Stitch 131 is a tailor's son who lives on 131st Street in Harlem. Eye 156, from 156th Street, says his name is just "about seeing."

"It's just a name, it's like what can you make out of it?" said Stain 149, a lanky 14-year-old from the South Bronx with Afro-style hair. He says everyone calls him Stain, because "I mess it all up." He says writing his name is a form of "self-advertisement."

He focuses on subway walls and doesn't go outside the five boroughs. Unlike the others, he chose 149 for his number because that's the subway stop where he watches his scrawls go by on trains. His adopted name and number are now omnipresent, as familiar as the subway signs themselves.

So, Wallace was a graffiti pioneer, one of the first noted taggers. That made him interesting; even I had to be impressed. The next clip, dated October 17, 1974, was a short art book review about Norman Mailer's *The Faith of Graffiti,* and it started with a description of Mailer's book party, which was attended by a handful of taggers, including Stain. "None of this matters," Stain told the reporter, waving his hand toward Mailer's buffet table, the caviar and pâté. "It's all about the trains. It's about getting your name up, not about having your name in a book." The art critic suggested that the impulse to tag was more akin to the need to stand on a soapbox and shout. "Among the kids I met at the opening, I got one feeling: ambition. Nobody wants to be nobody. All of them want to be famous," the critic concluded. "If you take them at their word, every teenager in this room is Goya, Michelangelo, or da Vinci."

I felt a tinge of zeitgeist envy. It was hard to imagine a time when graffiti was everywhere on trains. Wouldn't happen that way anymore. Subways were now paint-resistant silver bullets. Parks were green as an Irish holiday. No squeegee men menaced windshields and Penn Station wasn't a homeless haven. Not even heroin was chic anymore. All that had been replaced by quaint trends without any edge: swing dancing, Prozac parties, Tae-bo. In retrospect, even jogging and leg warmers seemed cool.

From the file I pulled an article from a 1985 Sunday Magazine, "American Graffiti in Paris," with a photo of Wallace taking up half the page. The picture was grainy and slightly faded, a shot taken on a subway, with Wallace standing, his arms crossed in front of his chest. Eighties hip-hop cool: red knit polo shirt with collar stitching, white cords, white Pumas. On his head was a maroon corduroy applejack titled to one side. His eyes were wide-set and heavy-lidded. His nose had a flat bridge and a broad tip. Though he was striking an aloof pose, he had a sweet prankish smile that made his face as round and luminous as a harvest moon.

I stared at the photo for a long time. It was hard not to like Stain; he obviously had pluck. I could tell he was going somewhere and picking up speed. I could tell he liked the feel of the wind on his face. His eyes flashed innocence, rebellion. *Take me on,* they said. *Try me.*

I read for a long while more. Maybe a couple of hours. It felt good to be doing research; to have my nose in papers that didn't contain any reference to the era in which I lived. *You can be a reporter again.* Doing research felt healthy, noble. Maybe Cabeza was right.

Firehouse sat alone in her folder while I went on the ride with Stain—the kid who leaves home at sundown and sneaks into rail yards. Climbs fences with a spray can in the pockets of his Adidas sweats. Rough-and-tumble kid gets his name up.

Gets known. Makes the downtown scene. Gets a gallery, gets fame. Goes anywhere. Rides all the way to Europe on a cloud. Bronx kid in Paris. Bronx kid in Milan. It was like *Sabrina,* only when he returns from Europe he's the literal *Talk of the Town*. Maybe someone made a cocktail in his honor. The Stainerini? Stain and Tonic? Stain on the Rocks?

Right, that wasn't funny.

I put the materials back in the folder and closed it. Underneath was the envelope marked, V. Vane—my invitation to his wake.

8

The Last Borough

The Bronx, a sultry summer night: a dance with a two-three rhythm and I didn't know the steps. It wasn't my kind of dancing anyway. Too close and all hands. Its breath was hot on my neck, its palm wet on my spine. Hot pavement, cold calm. Men leaning on cars. Girls in tight skirts, toppling breasts. Boys in cut-offs airing their shorts. Hungry eyes graze exposed thighs, sweaty belly flesh. The air clashes with the sound of ice cream bells and storefront speakers blaring, "hot hot hot." Kids' sticky fingers on push-up pops. Broken hydrants, squealing cries, a cruising van's deep bass, hearty laughs. Car alarms sound, sirens wail.

Up the pitted sidewalk. Past unknown words, unknown streets. Intervale Avenue, *cuchifritos*, *botanica, potencias*. No up- and downtown. No familiar grid. Every block a cha-cha-cha deeper into chaos.

"Excuse me, ma'am," I asked a woman with a carriage. "I'm looking for this address on Spofford." I showed her my invite.

"You're almost there," she said, looking up from her infant, a bundle of white ruffles. "You just have to cross Bruckner Boulevard." Bruckner Boulevard: eight lanes of speeding traffic under a ramshackle highway, deserted and littered and dark. As I waited for the light to change, I nervously hugged my dress. It was fear plain and simple; this was the kind of place where a girl could easily fall into a shadow and drown.

I could turn around right now. Sure, I could. And maybe I should. I'd wobble on these heels all the way back down Southern Boulevard and hoof back up the rickety subway stairs and take the 2/5 elevated back to Manhattan. I could find myself in the safety of the humdrum Upper West Side and climb to my empty little apartment, watch my standing fan whir. I could pretend it was all pretty, just an endless ride on the colorful carousel.

But what would I do then? Bite my nails awaiting Cabeza's next call? Sink a VHS and imagine myself Audrey Hepburn all over again? Rattle up a weak martini until Battinger rang up to say, "You're through." No. If I went back I'd have to go farther than that. Much farther, past the Upper West Side, past The Paper, past my TriBeCa loft and my fancy friends, past Buzz and Zip and "Inside and Out." I'd have to go all the way back to where I went wrong. But where was that?

The invite said apartment eleven, so I climbed four flights of stairs and came to a pair of snake eyes. I paused and listened to the swell of voices behind the steel door. For a moment I imagined stepping right back into that same old cocktail party I'd left six months earlier, the one with all the people I knew, their flushed faces ripe with fine wine, their repartee senseless. That cocktail party was still taking place somewhere in Manhattan. It always was. It only changed locations so the guests could badmouth someone else's decor.

I pushed through the door without knocking. This was a different kind of party all together. There was no music, no clinking of glasses, no blustery cheer, no giddy boasting with fifteen-dollar words. There was a hush, a downbeat, a murmur. People moved slowly, as if they were weightless. They dawdled in pools of respectful silence. Death was a visitor in this room and he'd turned the treble down low.

But where the soundtrack was muted, the visuals were deafening. The whole space, about two thousand square feet, was covered floor to ceiling with graffiti. There were murals on the walls and tags on the ceiling, drips and splatters on the hardwood floor, on the pillars, on exposed snaking pipes. I couldn't make out what they said, mostly, but the bright colors were as garrulous as publicists.

It was obviously a painting studio of some sort, but not furnished. No tables or sinks or workbenches, just about two dozen folding chairs, a couple of beat-up sofas probably dragged in for the occasion, and a wooden podium standing empty up front. *He just put a down payment on the painting school,* I remembered Cabeza saying on the phone. *A man doesn't secure a mortgage. . .*

So, this was Wallace's big last investment. This place was going to be a school for aspiring painters. It didn't look like much, but a painting studio didn't need much. The question was, how would I find the owner of that voice in my head? There were about a hundred guests and any of the men could've been Cabeza. I didn't want to dawdle; I wanted to get in and get out, find Cabeza and make whatever deal he wanted to get him off my back.

Then something large stepped in front of me. It was about six feet tall and three feet wide and blocked out the light. I stepped back, but the shadow overtook me again. I was going to plead for mercy, but the voice stopped me. It was high-pitched and cracking. "May I help you?" he asked. I looked up into the face of a mere child, a boy of maybe sixteen, with curly eyelashes circling big brown eyes. His skin was the color of molasses. His face was soft and supple as a ripe plum.

"Hello." I offered him my envelope. "I was invited."

"That's all right." He waved it away. "Everyone's welcome here. I just thought maybe you were lost."

"I came for the Malcolm Wallace memorial."

"You're in the right place. I'm Kamal Prince Tatum." He offered me his hand. "Stain's nephew." His eyes shone the same way Malcolm's had in the Sunday Magazine. It was a straight line from the kid in the eighties to this one here, give or take about a hundred pounds. "Some people call me Prince. Some people call me Kamal. You choose what you like."

"I'll take Kamal," I said. "You look a lot like your uncle. I'm very sorry for your loss."

"Thank you," he said. "I'm sorry if I don't remember meeting you."

I looked down at my feet. "I didn't know him personally. I actually came here to, to, support a friend." I felt my throat constrict. "Listen, I think I'd better . . ." I was about to make an excuse about something I'd left in my car.

"You look a little pale, Miss. You'd better come over near the fan. We've already had a couple of faintings. Must be the heat and the paint fumes."

"It is very hot in here." I wiped my brow and found it surprisingly wet. "But I think I . . ."

"I'll get you something to drink," he said. "It's much cooler over by the window. It's too hot to be standing in this doorway."

I couldn't protest. The teenager was already ushering me in. He was right. The closer I got to the windows, the better I felt. They were only cracked open, but they emitted a languid breeze. The space would've cost a cool million or two in Manhattan with its pressed-tin ceiling and high iron windows with a clear view of the dusky sky.

I didn't know what I was looking for as I scanned the crowd for Cabeza, probably someone ugly, too short or too wide, with a humpback or a missing limb. There were about a hundred people not sure what to do with their hands. Everyone looked either overdressed or underdressed. One man wore a bandanna around his head, tied at the back, and a T-shirt with holes in the shoulders. Someone else with a pencil-thin mustache and long narrow sideburns sweated in a three-piece suit. There were jeans and hoodies. Do-rags and spiffy fedoras. Scarf tops and Sunday church hats and a few tie-dyes. Children shifted from foot to foot, tugging uncomfortably at their bow ties and hair ribbons.

"Here you go," said Kamal, handing me a plastic cup and asking me what I wanted to drink. The table had a variety of options, including a bottle of scotch, which looked tempting, and a pitcher of a clear drink full of mint leaves and lime slices that Kamal said was caipirinha. I opted for the Pathmark Orangeade and swallowed a cup in one slug. He refilled it. "Who'd you say your friend was?"

I looked up from my drink back into his brown eyes. His eyelashes curled like angel's wings. I didn't want to have to start lying again. "Cabeza," I said, hoping that would cover it. I didn't have a last name. Or maybe I didn't have a first. I didn't know if Cabeza was a real name or some sort of hip-hop alias.

"Oh, yeah. He's somewhere around here," Kamal said. "I saw him earlier. He was talking to some of my friends."

I was about to ask Kamal to describe Cabeza. Did he have pockmarks or acne scars? A forehead dead-ended in a thicket of greased gray hair? "You think you could help me find him?" As if the kid didn't have anything better to do than waltz me around the room. He looked at my face as if he were trying to piece together a puzzle.

"What did you say you do?"

"I'm a writer," I said, and realized that this could be taken two ways. "A journalist." Of course, Kamal wouldn't have taken me for a graffiti artist anyway.

"Oh, that makes sense. Cabeza knows a lot of writers. You know Henry Chalfant? He's here, somewhere, too. He made a movie about graff. Wrote a book. There's some reporter up here from *New York Press* and some writer from *Spin*." Then a sour expression crossed his face. "You pretty tight with that guy?"

Nobody likes lying to kids. I adjusted my skirt and pulled at my neckline. "We know each other through work." I swallowed it down with another gulp of Orangeade.

An elderly man in a pinstriped suit stepped to the podium and started adjusting the mike. "Everyone, everyone," he said. "Okay, now. Everyone come up to the front of the room, because Amenia Wallace Tatum, Stain's sister, would like to say a few words. Please everyone, give her your attention for a few moments."

The crowd assembled and Amenia Wallace Tatum walked slowly to the front of the room. She was a tall, lithe woman in a fitted sundress made of hand-dyed African cloth with a headdress to match. The yellow wrap and her calm, elegant gait gave the impression of a giraffe. Her arms were bare and sinewy. As she moved through the crowd, people shook her hands.

As soon as she'd gotten comfortable with the mike, she started speaking. At first, her voice was soft and tentative, but as she got further into her speech, I could tell that she was a trained speaker, someone who felt natural in front of crowds. "Thank you, everyone. Thank you for your attention, and thank you, Clarence, for that introduction. Most of you heard my eulogy at the burial, and I hope many of you could attend. But I had a few other words I wanted to offer in this context, because I've been thinking so much about my brother in the last few days, and there's so much more I feel I need to say, to express, before I don't have the chance to be with you all in this way."

Her voice was gaining clarity. "First of all, I want to thank everyone for coming up tonight from all over the neighborhood, the city, the country," she said. "We have a few people who came in from California to be here, and at least three writers from Germany, who came to pay their respects. And I particularly want to thank all of the artists who took time in the last few days to cover these walls of the studio with such beautiful testaments of love." She opened her palm and gestured in a wide arc to all the paintings in the room. "Bigs Cru, Mosco, Spkye, N/R, Crash, Revs, and RIF." Some people murmured approval, other people clapped softly.

Amenia cleared her throat and looked down at the floor; she slowly unfolded a piece of paper and cleared her throat again. "A lot of you who've known me through the years will remember that, for a long time, I didn't understand my brother. I didn't understand why, ever since we were kids, he seemed to have this need to go around marking up the world. I was always in the books, studying the word of Elijah Muhammad, and here was my kid brother running around with a spray can, making a mess of things."

She smiled and paused for a moment. "That's all right," said someone up front.

"By the time I got to high school, I thought, Well, at least he isn't selling dope or stripping cars, like some of his classmates. But I still didn't understand it. To tell you the truth, I'm still not sure I understand it. When I'm riding around on trains and looking at all those scratched-up windows and doors, all those ugly tags, all that destruction, sometimes I still think, what's all that for? How does that help our cause? I thought maybe with Stain it was just a way of getting back at the world because we didn't have a father, because he was frustrated that my mom had to struggle through everything with us alone. You know, I didn't even understand it when he got his first gallery show. I just thought, Those stupid rich folks, they'll buy anything."

People laughed softly.

"That's because they don't know any better, I thought. Because they don't understand it's all just his rage." She stressed that last word, sighed, and shook her head. She paused for a long time. "I didn't go to his first solo exhibition in SoHo, the one that got him on the covers of all those magazines. I didn't attend the fancy openings or the award ceremonies. When Momma showed me his name in print, I wouldn't look at the stories. Can you imagine? I didn't want to know about my own brother. I was that arrogant. I have to live with that. But Malcolm didn't need my approval; he didn't bother himself with my disdain. He just kept inviting me. He offered to fly me to Austria and Brussels, to Paris. But I didn't go."

Her face struggled with tears. The room held its breath. But Amenia lifted her chin and raised her chest, and it passed.

"I'm telling you this now because I know I was wrong. I was wrong about my brother. I didn't give him credit for who he was at that time. But luckily, I saw the error of my ways before it was too late. I only wish it'd been earlier. As all of you know too well, the art establishment, those society folks downtown, got tired of the graffiti trend after a while. They used Malcolm and abandoned him once they'd had their fill. It was then that I finally went to see him. To my everlasting shame, only then, when he was broken down and alone. That's when I realized how important he was to me."

She clenched her jaw and took a moment to look around the room. Her eyes brightened as she saw the paintings on the walls. "I knew he'd gotten messed up by everything, and I was angry at myself that I hadn't been there to protect him. I went to see him when he was living on Thompson Street. He could barely lift his eyes to meet mine."

There were people nodding their heads in agreement. This, I guessed, had been Wallace's breaking point. Something had happened and he'd left the art world. I tried to remember what it had been.

"But I looked around me and I saw that it hadn't just been all about that. His room was full of canvases, beautiful canvases, art like nothing I'd ever seen in my life. It was music in paint, our music. I sat down with him on the floor, and I put my arms around my brother and I held him. It was then I saw it: my brother is a real artist. An artist. He isn't doing this just to express his anger or to get someone else's approval. His art said, 'I'm here. I exist.' "

That stopped her short. She dropped her chin and cried for a while, dabbing her eyes with a crumpled Kleenex. The audience waited with heads bent.

Amenia started again. "Malcolm said, 'I exist,' and I said it right back to him. 'You exist, my brother, and you exist for much more than this.' He cleaned up and he left that other life behind and made a new life. A lot of people forgot about Malcolm when he left the art world. But that was, in many ways, when he really became the man you all knew and loved. He went on to teach other young people that they could also say 'I exist.' That's why today we're standing in one of three art studios that my brother, Malcolm Wallace, brought to life here in the Bronx. And why there are aspiring painters here from all over the city who knew him as an artist, as a teacher, as a poet on our city trains and walls. And that's why no one in this room believes you killed yourself, no matter what the papers print, and no matter how they try to destroy your reputation, even in the afterlife. We're all here, Malcolm, saying we loved you. We still love you, and you have our respect. You have our love."

The room filled with murmurs of assent.

"And that's why we honor you today and why I pledge to continue on with your work here," Amenia continued, looking up beyond the ceiling. "Everyone in this room is going to honor your legacy and see to it that these three art studios get the support and the students they deserve. We are going to see that your goals are achieved and that there are generations upon generations of young Malcolm Wallaces springing from the Bronx each year."

Amens all around. "That's right," said someone. "That's our pledge," said someone else.

"Thank you everyone," said Amenia. "Thank you, Malcolm."

Amenia turned from the podium and everyone who wasn't already standing got up. The elderly man in the pinstriped suit went back up to the mike and thanked everyone and mopped his brow with a handkerchief. "Please feel free to stay and have something to drink. There's soda, juice, and snacks on the table. A few more people will talk in a bit."

Kamal was still by my side, watching the crowd form around his mother. He asked me if I was feeling better and I nodded and he left me to join her. I poured myself more orangeade and tried to play the fly on the wall, thinking I'd spot Cabeza if I just stayed put. *A man doesn't secure a mortgage* . . . I felt something climbing up my spine again, and this time it had pincers. I was beginning to think maybe Cabeza was right. Maybe I had made a bad mistake, and maybe I'd better pay for it. I moved my hand through the bowl of chips and packed a few into my mouth, out of nervousness.

Kamal returned to the table to grab a bottle of water for someone else. "You find Cabeza yet?" He was a polite kid. "I saw him over there with Bigs Cru. You know them?"

I shook my head.

"Aw, they're pretty famous," Kamal said. "They do murals for Tommy Hilfiger and Coca-Cola. They did that piece over there," he said, tipping the bottle toward the far wall. I could see that the wall had lettering on it, big bulky letters in green and blue, painted three dimensionally, thrusting into space. I couldn't make it out. I cocked my head to one side, thinking that might help.

"What does it say?" I asked Kamal.

"Can't you read it?" he asked. "It says Stain 149."

I couldn't read it. I stared blankly, feeling like a guest at a pool party who doesn't swim.

Kamal laughed.

"Look," he said, raising his finger and tracing the shapes of the letters in the air. "There's the *S,* which is sort of coming at us. See, the top is bigger than the bottom, and the bottom sort of has the feet, in the distance."

Now, I could see what he meant. Yes, there was an *S.* I nodded.

"And see the *T* is wrapped around the leg of the *S,* and its squiggle is kicking up dust into the *A.* Right?"

Put that way, I could see it. Sure I could. Then the other letters coalesced. Sure, I could read it—Stain, all twisted and tilted, dancing out into space. The letters had life then. They had motion. "Cool," I said. "You do this stuff?"

"Sometimes," he said. "But I'm trying to be a journalist. Like you."

"Oh, well, maybe I can . . . I could help."

"I'll introduce you to Bigs Cru." Kamal led me through the crowd and as he went he pointed out other paintings. "That one was done by Mosco—he's a Mexican graff king. Over there you got Crash and Daze. They came down on Monday night. That's Zephyr."

I was happily getting a dose of subculture, nodding and sipping my orangeade, when we passed a group of women and I overheard one of them saying, "Amenia is heartbroken about that story."

"You really expect that paper to get things right about our community?" another woman answered. "When was the last time you saw a reporter up here unless it was a fire or a murder? Did they write about anything that's positive? Why should we expect anything they print . . ."

Kamal pushed farther into the crowd, weaving fast, and I didn't want to lose him.

"S'up, Smudgy?" someone said to Kamal. I turned to see a good-looking man in his early forties with a high forehead, a gold canine, and a pair of wide gold-framed glasses. He reached for

Kamal and pulled him into a tight hug. "We got a wall," he said. "Diaz Pizzeria on Two Hundred Seventh, the whole side of the building. You think Amenia and your auntie would be okay with that?"

"Sure," Kamal said. "Anywhere."

Kamal made introductions. There were three members of the Cru: the tall one, named Wicked Rick; a shorter, rounder, soft-spoken one named Clu, who took my hand with a formal, "Pleased to make your acquaintance"; and a third named Rx. He was seated in a folding chair next to the window, and he tipped his cap.

"Rx? Like prescription?" I asked.

"Raw Excellence," he said.

Kamal explained to them that I was looking for Cabeza. They looked at one another, as if each of them thought the other had seen him, but none of them had seen him himself. No one seemed to want to offer anything. "I'm a journalist," I said, hoping this would make a difference. "I thought I'd write about Stain," I added, trying it on for size.

"Oh, I see," said Rx from the folding chair, his sunglasses slung across the bridge of his nose. He was sucking on a toothpick. "Man's got to die so they put him in print. What about all the times he tried to get press for his art studios for kids? How come you didn't come up here then?"

Wicked Rick waved the air, clearing Rx's words. "Don't mind him. Cabeza's around here somewhere."

Rx started moving the zipper on his velour running suit, playing peek-a-boo with a patch of chest hair. "What you going to write about Stain?" he asked. "You going to talk about anything other than 1983, '84, '85?" He counted the dates off on his fingers.

Wicked Rick scowled at Rx, but Clu moved closer and gazed at me earnestly to see how I'd answer. He seemed shy and low on words, but he must've said something someone didn't like once, because he had a pink scar that started at his jaw and ran all the way to his ear. I moved my orangeade from one hand to the other. "I thought I'd look at his influence on the community here." It sounded like what they might want to hear. "He was a great inspiration to the young people."

Rx slid lower in his chair, the toothpick tipping so it arched his upper lip. "Yeah," he said. "I thought so. A nice light feature, huh? So his murderer gets off scot-free, and his art goes missing. You reporters are whack."

"Yo, Rx, step off," said Wicked Rick. "She's a guest."

Rx looked at Rick, then at me, and bent down to polish his sneakers. Then he sat back up again. "You're not from that paper, are you? The one that wrote that lie about Stain killing himself? Did they send you up here to make nice?"

I stammered out something like "Nobody sent me. I came up because I care about . . ." I kept talking after that but I don't think my words resembled a sentence. I tried to get a final slug of my orangeade but there was only a drop. Then everything slowed down. The shapes in the room began to sway back and forth, leaving a kind of rippling wake.

"I'm sorry," I said to Wicked Rick and Kamal. "I shouldn't be here, I . . ." I wobbled on my feet and took a step back. But I knocked into a big woman wearing a flower-topped hat, knocking it right off her head. "Oh, my, let me get that," I said, stooping to pick up the hat. I bent down but I didn't feel like coming back up. I felt myself losing my footing and there was nothing I could do about it. Everything in my body went limp, as if I'd been resisting collapse and now it was imminent. Next thing I knew, I was sprawled out on the floor clutching a huge Sunday church hat.

When I came to, I lay there for a while, watching the shapes move above me, eyes looking down at me. I didn't try to get up.

It was weirdly comforting to be on the floor. Maybe I'd stay a while. People could just walk right over me if I was in the way.

An arm reached down to take my hand. It was a muscular arm at the top of which was a white shirtsleeve. I looked up to see the rest of the shirt, a Cuban guayabera with embroidered stitching running up a broad chest under a gray jacket. On my way up from the floor I noticed the gray pleated slacks. Then I saw a narrow-rimmed white Havana hat with a brown ribbon encircling the crown.

"*Aqui linda,*" he said, his voice smoky and dark. "*¿Tienes dolor?*"

I knew in an instant. It was the voice from the phone, the voice in my head.

Then I was on my feet. Before me stood a man of sharp good looks, angular features, and a square chin, with a brush of stubble and a rush of black hair speckled at the temples with gray. His shoulders were broad enough to carry a trunk, but he wasn't the sort of man who hauled much of anything. His hands were elegant, but not too small to grab hold of a woman and steady her.

My thought: Robert Mitchum in *Out of the Past,* one of my favorite noirs. Mitchum plays a former private dick who's tried to leave his sleuthing days—and a gorgeous, lethal Jane Greer—behind. But he can't escape his past. I opened my lips to talk, but all that came out was a croak. He put a hand on my lower back. It felt warm there. "Do you need to sit down?"

The members of Bigs Cru were around me, Clu and Wicked Rick each with a hand on my shoulder. Rx stood a little bit back, squinting at me. If I hadn't just fallen, he'd have been saying something about what he thought of me, and not softly. I tried to catch my breath, but I was wheezing. Kamal ran and came back with a cup of water. I drank it down, wishing I could drown myself in it.

"I'm fine," I said. "Really, I'm fine. I just need a little fresh air."

I pulled away from the group of men and backed slowly toward the door. Wicked Rick took a few steps forward, and I said, "I'm okay, really. I'll be right back."

I weaved through the crowd back to the stairs. Still dizzy and uneasy on my feet, I descended, my calves buckling. I slipped twice and crashed my kneecaps on the sharp edges of the steps. *You've done this before,* I told myself, *you've done this since age one. Just put one foot in front of the other and walk.*

I was afraid that Rx would follow. I was afraid Kamal would follow. They'd want answers. I wouldn't have answers. *Please forgive me,* I'd say. But they wouldn't. *Please don't tell on me.* But I didn't deserve their mercy.

At the bottom of the stairwell, I pushed through another heavy door, out into the night. The more I thought about it, the more I realized it wouldn't be Rx or Kamal or any of the others. It would be Cabeza.

Outside, the air was dense and punishing. Behind a black cloud, the moon glowered. Someone stepped out of a dimmed doughnut shop, backing into me. I started. He produced a bracelet of keys, jangling them benevolently. I jogged across the street, clutching my dress. My heart was pulsing in my throat; my nape was wet with sweat. Behind me, something crashed and I jumped. It was the doughnut shop's gate.

I told myself to take it easy, but my feet kept moving. I was walking in the street, avoiding the darkened stoops. A battered gypsy cab zipped behind me, flashing its lights. I didn't know what it wanted from me.

The light was red at Bruckner Boulevard. I'd have to wait to cross back over those thousands of lanes. The traffic was warfare; cars flew by like bullets, trucks were mortar shells. A step off the curb could mean a sedan in my spine. I looked back again, expecting to see Cabeza, his shadow looming long across the macadam. He wasn't there yet. Not yet. But he'd be coming.

9

Dicey Intersection

I didn't flinch when I felt his hand on the back of my arm or heard his voice just behind my ear, "*Cuidate.* This is a dicey intersection." I didn't turn around, because I already knew what was there. White guayabera, pressed gray slacks, brown-ribboned Havana hat. He was close enough that I could smell the breath on his caipirinha.

"Don't worry about me," I said. "I can manage."

"Of course you can," he answered, hot against my ear. "But it's unfortunate you left the memorial. Some people would very much like to talk to you."

"I know who you are," I said. "I know what you want. I've paid my respects to Mr. Wallace. I think it's time I get home."

I saw him out of the corner of my eye. The shadows of the expressway slashed his face in slices of dark and light. The brim of his Havana hat obscured his brow. I saw the whites of his eyes and the pearl of his teeth. It was a Richard Widmark close-up straight out of *Kiss of Death*.

"I don't blame you for that story. The police thought it was a suicide, open and shut. You have no reason to think the cops would lie to you. These people up here think different. All you need to do is explain how you came to your conclusion."

His grip was firm but not vigorous. Suggesting, not insisting. At that moment, I could've done as he said. I could've tried to explain myself to the grieving folks back in that room. But I wouldn't be able to, because I had no excuse. I didn't have the facts. I didn't have the word of the cops to substantiate my story. I couldn't fall back on a sterling reputation. Not even the name of The Paper seemed like a worthy defense.

There was nowhere to turn except deeper into fiction. I thought of Barbara Stanwyck and Gloria Grahame. Their characters always played ruthlessly and they played smart, and they made it out alive—well, mostly. I figured I could try a few of their best lines. I'd placed my silver letter opener in my purse earlier in the day, just in case. Maybe I could use it now, just as Barb might use her compact pistol, to crack some space between us.

I twisted fast and turned to face Cabeza. I pressed myself against him, to let him know my curves. I threw my head back and kissed my knuckles, then bit my nails. I'd seen these gestures used to great effect.

"You've got to help me, you've got to," I said, trying on Mary Astor in the *Maltese Falcon*. "I'm in a terrible bind. I can't explain everything. And even if I did, you'd never believe me. I'm so mixed up; don't you see? If I could fix this, I would. I'd do anything, anything. But you must believe me. It will only make matters worse. I know it doesn't make any sense. I know. But I've got no one else to turn to. And you're my only hope. You must believe me. You must. If you don't believe me—"

Cabeza's eyes gleamed. "What's this all about?"

I pressed myself closer and put a hand on his chest. At the same time, I slipped my free hand into my purse and felt around for the letter opener. I didn't want to hurt Cabeza, just hold him off once he'd gotten wise to my damsel in distress act.

"There, there," he said. "There's no need to be upset, really. There could be another way around this."

My fingers twitched against the lining of my purse, and I

turned to give him a bit of my thigh. I was having trouble getting the handle of the letter opener in a businesslike grip. "I never meant to hurt anyone, I . . . I . . . The cops told me one thing, the editors wanted something else. I didn't know how I would make the story work, but I couldn't do anything, I . . ."

He was putting his hand through my hair now, shushing me. "It's okay, don't worry. Don't worry, really." His face was getting closer to mine, his lips parting. My hand was on the handle. Now was the time to act. I intended to jerk the silver blade out of the purse. Then I realized I couldn't go through with it. It was absurd. It was high melodrama, camp. I moved my arm to release the blade, and that's when he felt my hand jerk.

"Whoa," he said. "What's going . . ." He grabbed my wrist and held it tight, pulling it out of the purse, and there in my hand was the letter opener. "What have you got there?" he said, taking a step back.

I looked at the letter opener as if I'd never seen it before and I dropped it. It pinged against the pavement. Cabeza looked down and laughed. "What is that?" he said. "A butter knife?" He steadied me against his hip and reached down to pick it up. He held it up to the streetlight and it glinted. "What were you going to do with that," he said, chuckling, "butter me to death?"

I tried to say something. All that came out was "I . . . no . . . I'm just so . . ."

"I'm really amazed at you," he said. "Even a little impressed. That was a cute act, and I almost bought it. But I didn't expect this."

I buried my face in his chest. "I'm sorry, I'm sorry, I'm sorry," I said. "I don't know how to do anything, I'm such a failure. I can't get a single thing right. Those people back there in that room must hate me. And they have every right to hate me. I'm horrible. Ridiculous. I've never been any use to anybody."

"Listen, what is all this silliness?" he said. "I don't really understand the game we're playing out here, or what kind of scenario you've concocted in your head for me next, but I'm perfectly willing to be reasonable, and I certainly didn't mean to harm you or intimidate you or make you afraid. You didn't need to go to all that trouble. We really should just talk. I think that would be best."

His voice was level, compassionate. He wasn't threatening me. He was reassuring. Soothing. But I was ashamed of myself, and I couldn't find the words to tell him how sorry I felt. It was true that I wanted to fix what I'd broken, but I didn't know how to fix anything. I wanted to fold up and disappear.

"*Linda,* are you hearing me? I really think that if you were willing to talk a little, we could work something out," Cabeza continued.

It was so pathetic, all so pathetic, and all I could do was just cry. I wanted him to let go of me and let me fall down right there in the gutter, where I belonged. I didn't have the will even to stand anymore.

He held me still in the crook of his arm. "Hey, there," he said. "You okay?"

"I . . . I'm sorry," I muttered. "Can't you just let me? Leave me?"

Cabeza just held on, and his arms were strong. His chest was warm. "What is this all about, *linda*?" he asked, softly. "You can't tell me?"

There was a white flash in the sky and a simultaneous blast of thunder, then a downpour. Within moments, we were both drenched. Cabeza urged me to move, but I didn't want to go anywhere. Nothing better than crying in the rain. Cabeza encouraged me to walk and I said, "I can't, I can't." My face, I realized, was smeared with tears, and I was soaked.

Cabeza drew me under his Havana hat, into his chest. I smelled his caipirinha breath again and the tart scent of his sweat, peppery, vinegary musk. His voice was tender. "Come on, now. We can't stay here." He put his jacket over my shoulders and guided me across Bruckner Boulevard.

In the dusty glow of a streetlight on the other side, he hailed us a gypsy cab, and when it sloshed to a stop in the puddle next to us, he bundled me through the door.

The M&G Diner is a twenty-four-hour greasy spoon on the corner of 125th Street and Morningside in Harlem. The hot pink neon out front reads OLD FASHION' BUT GOOD. Inside, it's a well-lit room behind high, greased-up windows, with a linoleum floor and orange Formica tabletops. There's an L-shaped counter where you have to sit if you're solo, no matter what time of night, no matter how empty. We'd been offered the counter at the door and Cabeza had answered, "No thanks. We're together."

There isn't anything to smell at the M&G except sizzling batter in the deep fryer and fresh-made black coffee and sweet potatoes baking and short ribs smoking on the grill. There isn't much to hear except the sway and groan of R & B from the jukebox by the window. Cabeza had plugged coins in the slot and now the juke was playing Al Green's "Look What You Done for Me."

Before me sat a red-rimmed white plate covered with orange candied yams, a hunk of golden fried chicken, and two half-eaten yellow muffins. I was still wearing Cabeza's jacket and I had dried my hair a little using the hand dryer in the cramped bathroom. He was still damp, but he didn't seem upset. Between his thumb and forefinger was a fried chicken thigh, suspended over a plate of Belgian waffles.

On the way downtown, the storm had hammered the roof and I'd watched Cabeza in the light of the passing streetlights. The shadows of the rain-streaked window played against his cheeks like Robert Blake's Perry in *In Cold Blood*, just before he's hanged. Cabeza hadn't looked at me in the car. He'd just kept a hand on my forearm and let me cry it out, not asking anything, not talking, just giving me a tissue to pat my face.

Now that we were in the full fluorescence of the M&G, I saw what I hadn't in the shadows: eyes so pale green they could make a forest feel gaudy. They were underscored with sleepless purple half moons and topped with a furrowed brow and crow's feet. They were creased at the sides like bed sheets tucked in in a hurry.

"You're not supposed to eat chicken and waffles until after you've danced eight hours to the sixteen-piece swing band," he said.

"You'd better get them to wrap that up." I nodded toward his airborne thigh. "Got a place in mind?"

"You're not bad," he said. "You can just turn around on a dime."

My face still felt raw from crying, but Cabeza had filled me with a few cups of black coffee and fed me hot corn muffins. "Where are you from?" I asked.

He brought the paper napkin to his lips, smoothing away the shine left by the chicken. "Puerto Rico. A seaside town called Aguas Buenas. *La ciudad de las aguas claras,*" he added with some fanfare. "City of clear waters. I left the island when I was eighteen for Hollywood, imagining I'd soon be a big American director, but no one seemed to agree I fit the bill. They didn't have room for Mexican directors, they said."

"Mexicans? But you are—"

"Precisely. Hollywood wasn't interested in geography. When I got there, even Latino bit parts were played by gringos bronzed with shoe polish."

Now that he mentioned it, Cabeza reminded me a little of Ramon Miguel Vargas, the narc border cop played by Charlton

Heston in *Touch of Evil*. Heston was supposed to be a Mexican, but he was about as Mexican as Judy Garland.

"So I switched coasts and went into documentaries," he continued. "I had family in El Barrio. I got a cheap camera and started shooting stoops in my neighborhood. Then, an Austrian director who was trying to document the burning of the Bronx heard about me and asked me to help him out. It was a big break, in a way. I've been at it ever since."

He set down his chicken and used the napkin to tap the corners of his mouth. I could tell that despite his man-of-the-people jive, he was an aristocrat by breeding. It didn't matter that he sat on a stool at a Formica table. Every table at which he sat was cut from aged oak. Every paper cup that met his lips was crystal. His napkin, on his lips, turned to linen.

"And what kinds of films are you making now?"

"My work still focuses on the urban landscape, working-class families and their struggles," he said, in the language of a grant application. Then he looked up at me and laughed. '*Con los pobres estoy,*'" he sang. "'*Noble soy.*'"

I knew just enough Spanish to get this: *I'm with the poor. I'm noble*. But he said it in jest. Self-mocking. I must've been smiling at him, because he smiled back. It was a nice smile. As big as a house with a few extra rooms.

"So," he said. "You want to talk to me about what happened out there? I may not be so terrific on the telephone, but I've been told I'm not a bad listener one-on-one."

I looked down again at my corn muffins. No one had asked me to articulate my feelings for a long time. I chewed some yams for a while and he waited. I lifted my eyes. He was still waiting.

"I . . . It's just . . ." I stopped.

"You don't have to talk to me."

I didn't know why I wanted to tell him things, but I did. Maybe it was because his jacket was still warming me, and he hadn't asked for it back yet. Maybe because it seemed like we were at a diner at the edge of the world. "It's not going to make a lot of sense," I said. "My father died when I was ten. It was a long time ago, I know, but since then, it's like I've never known who I was supposed to be. It's like I'm always trying on costumes that never quite fit."

Cabeza laughed. "I think that's probably true for most people."

"You think so?"

"I don't know. Sometimes it's true for me." I took a sip of my coffee. He kept talking. "Nobody in New York is who they pretend to be. You think the people back in that room are all genuine? Nah. Everyone has something they're hiding about themselves. You're right at home with the phonies if you live here in New York."

He was cutting his waffle into wedges, slicing along each radius. It didn't faze him. Everything he said made me feel better. Just the sound of his smoky voice this close made me feel there might be ground under my feet.

"I'm not trying to dismiss what you're saying, *linda*. It's a terrible thing to lose a father. I have something like that too. I lost a brother very young. I sometimes feel that I'm always trying to make up for that. Sometimes I think it's how I got so close to Malcolm. I thought he'd be my new brother. In some ways, he was."

I put my hand out across the table and touched Cabeza's arm. "I'm so sorry about Malcolm," I said. "I should've said it earlier. I'm so sorry for your loss."

"Look, it's not your fault. But you can help us. If you want to redeem yourself here and help us at the same time, we can work something out."

"How?"

"We don't need a correction," he said. "We just want the truth to come out. I think you want that too. Maybe you didn't want it before, but now that you've seen how devastating his loss was to so many people . . ." He went back to cutting his waffle. "If we can get a story out about what happened to Wallace, we'd be happy. If you can get the story, I think it would be beneficial to you too."

"I think you're assuming I have power. I'm not even allowed to write under my own byline. No one would give me any story—let alone a story that big."

He put some waffle into his mouth and chewed. When he was done chewing he started talking. "You may temporarily be in somewhat of a bad position, I'll grant you that. But because of where you are—still working at that paper—you're a very powerful girl. Maybe you don't realize how powerful you could be. We come from a place that isn't covered much in the media. The fact that you came up to the Bronx today was a sign that you're tougher than you think. You came this far; maybe you're willing to go a little bit further. You could help us find out who killed Malcolm. You write about it. We all win." Cabeza dipped his waffle in syrup. "Malcolm was a real art star, perhaps the most important black artist in contemporary art, after Basquiat. I hate those distinctions—black artist, Latino artist, woman artist—but that's how people thought of him. And if you check your art history, you'll see there aren't too many black artists allowed through the gates. If you found out who murdered him, you'd have a very big story on your hands. It would be the kind of story your editors couldn't ignore, no matter who brought it to them."

I was starting to get his point. I was starting to understand why he'd gone to all the trouble to invite me to the memorial and then to bring me in from the rain. He could've just called Battinger back to file a complaint. Anyone in that room could've done that. But he'd seen an opportunity I hadn't seen—as long as I was still on staff, I could still make it right. But first I needed to know why everyone had ruled out suicide. "Why are you so sure that Wallace was murdered?"

He stopped chewing. "Because I know he didn't kill himself. He wasn't that type of man. It just wasn't in him."

I'd already heard this logic. I moved my silverware around on my plate. Cabeza could sense my dissatisfaction, and he didn't let it slide.

"And because there was too much intrigue going on around him at the time of his death. You see, Malcolm spent the last several months looking for some paintings that had gone missing. He'd been down to see his old dealer, a woman named Darla Deitrick, who has a space on West Twenty-fourth Street by the West Side Highway, because he thought she still had some of his works."

I knew about the Darla Deitrick gallery. Darla was a famous dealer who'd recently gotten attention for an exhibition called "Good Cop," a series of portraits of New York's men in blue just weeks after the Amadou Diallo shooting in the Bronx. It had caused a great commotion, and The Paper had covered the show at least three times. If Darla Deitrick indeed had something to do with Wallace's death—even tangentially, even if I could merely mention her name in the same breath—it would indeed be the kind of story I could pitch to Battinger.

"I've tried to reach Darla about those paintings, but she doesn't return my calls," he said. "I imagine working for that paper qualifies you to go to art galleries and ask questions, no matter what subjects you're supposed to cover."

"You can't possibly think a gallery owner would kill one of her artists."

"I'm not saying any such thing." He chewed politely for a while, and then swallowed. "I'm just trying to figure out if there's any connection between these missing paintings and the fact that he ended up dead."

"For instance?"

Cabeza's movements were all fastidious, deliberate. He held his fork suspended before eating another bite. "For example,

Malcolm told me he thought Deitrick had sold his work but she hadn't reported the sales, not to him and not to the IRS. If he was right, she committed a federal crime. That would be a good story for your paper, I think."

Darla Deitrick committing tax fraud? Yeah, that would be a story for us. I could probably even go past Battinger, maybe even to the Culture desk. I swallowed a big sip of coffee, but my cup was getting cold and empty. The waitress came over and hovered above us with a pot of coffee that smelled like fresh peat. "She'll have a refill," Cabeza said. "None for me."

"Let's say I find something. How does that serve you?"

"I find out whether Malcolm was onto something. If he was, I can follow up. I can help the Wallace family secure his works, if she still has them. They would want them back. But I don't know how it will all play out right now. All I know is I need someone who can get in there and snoop around."

I finished my chicken and put the bones down on my plate. "I won't be able to do any of this if I get canned for my mistake on the Obit."

"Don't worry about that," he said. "I'll see to it that no one makes a fuss. I'll let them know we're working together to make it right."

"How will you do that?"

"I'm going to, that's all. Ms. Deitrick has got a show going up just now, some minimalist *mierda*. So she's got to be nice to reporters this week. That gives you an in."

The waitress came by and lifted Cabeza's plate. "Weren't hungry, I see," she said.

"It's the chicken I can't stand," he said, passing her his bone-littered plate and winking. He routed through his back pocket and came out with two Handi Wipes, offering me one.

"Never touch them myself," I said. "How did you meet Wallace?"

He was wiping his hands with the Handi Wipe one finger at a time. I got a whiff of its sweet alcohol scent. "In 1973, I made a documentary about a group of graffiti writers, the early ones tagging. I did most of the filming at the Bench, the subway stop on 149th Street where everyone would watch the trains go by. That's where Wallace got his name, you know."

I nodded. Stain 149. A name and a street.

Our waitress dropped our check on the table. Without looking at it, Cabeza removed a crisp twenty from his pocket, folded it the long way, and tapped her arm. *"Gracias,"* he said. *"Lo retenez."*

"I was very young myself," he continued. "We were all kids. I shot the movie on sixteen millimeter and it wasn't in great condition, but it got a pretty good play underground, so to speak. Malcolm was always with me, no matter what I did. I helped him get stretchers when he was short on cash. You could say I was a patron, of sorts. I also dated Amenia for a little while, years ago, before she converted to Islam. Shall we?"

He stood up and wiped the front of his shirt. He took his Havana hat off the table and put it back on his head. I stood up with him. I was mostly dry by now. The comfort food had made me feel brand-new. "Where did the rest of them end up?"

"Who?"

"The other graffiti kids you filmed. Other than Wallace?"

Cabeza walked me to the door, reached around me, and opened it for me. He was gentlemanly that way. "The truth is a lot of them are already dead," he said. "Shot or overdosed, bad drugs, bad beefs, bad doctors. Some are in jail. Some still write. There's a place in Brooklyn where some writers work on legal walls. Stain was one of the few who made it out whole."

The air was lighter outside, since it had stopped raining. Cabeza asked me where I was headed and he hailed me another gypsy, handing me a ten-dollar bill. "You going to be all right getting home?" he asked.

I handed back his cash and took off his jacket. "Reporters aren't allowed to accept gifts over twenty-five dollars from sources," I said, handing it to him. "And you already paid for the meal."

"That was just a meal between friends," he said. "But should I take that to mean you're willing to work with me to find out what really happened to Malcolm?"

I knew it was risky, but I also didn't see any other road to redemption.

"Yes," I said, stepping into the cab. "I'm in."

10

White on White

I sat on a white leather ottoman before a white marble desk in a white room in the back of a white gallery, looking at a white man in a white linen suit.

I was fidgety.

The man had a white phone to his ear and showed me the whites of his eyes to let me know he was on hold. "This will just be a minute."

"Nice suit," I said. "Dolce?"

He nodded and pursed his lips. Then he pulled the receiver away from his ear. He whispered, "All the assistants wear Dolce. She gives us a clothing allowance, but only for her designers."

"Only Dolce and Gabbana?"

"Dolce, Paul Smith, Prada. The usual suspects."

"Ah," I whispered back. "A strict constructionist."

He cupped his hand over the mouthpiece. "You don't know the half." Then there was a buzz on the other end of the line and he turned his chair to show me the white shell of his ear. When I'd walked into the gallery, I'd thought he was bald, but now I noticed a soft blond down on top of his head, cropped so close it shimmered.

"Listen, I've got someone in my office who wants to do an interview with Darla," he said into the phone. "A drop-in. I should . . . Of course we're opening tonight. Aren't you coming?"

I'd been sitting on the ottoman looking at Blondie for twenty minutes, waiting for him to finish up on the phone. "Of course you don't go at two o'clock," Blondie said, twisting the phone cord around his white finger. "It doesn't get fun until five! I usually get there at about three thirty so I don't have to deal with the hetero crowd clogging up the coat check. So? Take a disco nap."

The gallery was everything a gallery should be, long and wide and pristine with cold polished granite floors, its cool minimalism showing high-class restraint. It was sealed airtight with soundless central A/C, so I forgot the 100-degree swelter beyond the glass doors. Before taking my lunch break to Chelsea, I'd conducted a little more research on Darla Deitrick. It was much more fruitful than the hour I spent searching "Cabeza" on the Internet. His name generated 39.4 million Web hits, none of them very helpful: the sixteenth-century Spanish conquistador Alvar Nuñez Cabeza de Vaca; Spanish medical sites about *dolor de cabeza*—a headache. The closest I got was info about a documentary called *Wild Style*, and a site that called itself a "cyber-bench."

By contrast, there were buckets about Darla. Cabeza had been spot-on about her publicity lust. As a twenty-year-old junior at the Rhode Island School of Design, she'd strolled into MoMA one afternoon, pulled a can of spray paint out of her patent-leather purse, and hissed the words *Paint Makes Art* onto the surface of Jackson Pollock's, *One: Number 31, 1950*. She'd turned toward Matisse's *Dance (I)* when three security guards tackled her.

Once the Pollock was restored—she'd used water-soluble paint—and Darla had done her jail time and finished up her degree, she opened a gallery on Greene Street and positioned herself as a champion of illegal art underdogs—namely, Bronx and East Village street vandals she showcased like prize poodles. She moved to Chelsea from SoHo in 1995. Her first show there became famous because the artist distributed workable stun guns. People downed wine and cheese and zapped one another until Darla was carted away in cuffs. She'd gotten the address of her new gallery in every rag in town.

I'd been to her Chelsea space once with Jeremiah, back when things were swell, to attend an opening for Tan Rififi. The artist had been naked, save a loincloth, and he crouched like a sumo wrestler over a pail of cow's blood. He leaned in and soaked his hair, then took sumo strides to a canvas on the wall and shook his locks like a dog shaking off a bath. Jeremiah and I had gone straight to the dry cleaners from there.

Now I was considering Darla's current exhibition: "PURE: A Retrospective of White-on-White." All the paintings were white, or shades of white, white lines on white backgrounds, white boxes on white squares. One had a small red square in the corner of a white box. That was pretty exciting.

I didn't know many of the artists in the show, but according to the catalog on the desk, they were something special: Cy Twombly, Robert Ryman, Ad Reinhardt, Agnes Martin, Kasimir Malevich, Josef Albers, Piero Manzoni. There was one I recognized: Jasper Johns's white-starred and -striped *White Flag*. It was on loan from the Metropolitan Museum of Art—which had agreed to hang it with Darla under the strictest of conditions, the catalog made clear—and it was hanging in its own alcove, with its very own guard. I figured I was standing in the most expensive whitewash ever produced—perhaps $50 million's worth.

Could Cabeza be right? Why would a woman who obviously had high-level connects care one way or another about a small-time graffiti dude who ran a paint school in the Bronx? She didn't need to be bothering with minnows, when she was frying up great whites. And why was Cabeza so concerned about these paintings of Wallace's anyway? I knew from my days on Style that everybody has an angle. What was his?

I strolled through the space and tried to name the paintings:

Snow falling on igloos. Bald man quick-sanded in a dune. Cloud descending over a first communion. Ghosts in smocks. I spent about ten minutes at that, got bored, and went back to Blondie. I watched his white skin play against the white wall for a while.

"I know, it's tedious," he was telling his friend on the phone. "The bouncers think they're the maître d' and the maître d's think they're the cooks, and the cooks, of course, are celebrities! Please. Stop flirting with Courtney Love and get back in the kitchen!"

Drawn by a dab of color, I got up again and stood before a wall of framed snapshots. There were two dozen pictures, dating back to when Darla was paying fines for her Pollock. I saw from the photos that she was a redheaded pixie with tresses that fell in two cords in front of her chest. I recognized some of the people in the photos: Warhol, Bowie, Mailer, Madonna, and Leonard Lauder—and finally, in one picture in front of what seemed to be her SoHo gallery, Wallace. He was in the back row, all the way to the left, wearing the same smile I'd seen in the 1985 Sunday Magazine shot. I wished I had a pen-sized camera, so I could take a little spy-shot of that and bring it back to Cabeza.

"Bye, kiss, gotta go, bye!" said Blondie, finally. I turned as he placed the phone in its cradle, and breathed deeply, a yoga Kapalabhati breath. Then he stood up and attempted to smooth the folds in his linen pants. They resisted. He frowned and tried to smooth them again. They didn't budge. "Hate the summer!" he said to the pants.

Then he turned his back to me and thrust open the sliding door. He went inside, saying, "This will just take one second." A moment later, he came out again. "I'm sorry, Miss, what did you say your name was again?"

He hadn't asked me before. I cleared my throat. "Valerie Vane," I said.

Blondie straightened up as if he'd touched an electrical wire. He thrust the sliding glass door into its casing with a thud. "You?"

he said, and then he took another yoga breath. He started again. "You. Are. Valerie. Vane?" He swallowed. "Oh my *God*." He scampered toward me, scanning my face. "You are!" he declared. "You. Are. Valerie Vane! Oh my God. I *LOVE* you! I mean, Lit-er-al-ly. I *LOVE* you!" He folded his arms and looked me up and down as if I were *David*, on loan from Florence.

"But your hair is darker. You're a little, well, you put on a touch of . . . nothing, really! You're gorgeous! And I didn't realize how tall you were! An Amazon! Oh, heaven have mercy." He plunked down in his seat again. "I cut out your 'Blondes' cover story from *Gotham's Gate* two years ago. It's *still* on my refrigerator. A work of genius. *Genius.* Oh you got it dead on. Really, *dead* on. It made me dye my hair. And it's still blond!" He put his hand through the moss on his head, surprising himself, and shook his scalp at me.

"It is still blond," I said.

Blondie was just like the gray girl I'd met at the morgue, or maybe the flip side of the same coin. They were both entranced by infamy, but where she found schadenfreude, he found envy. He walked back behind the desk, picking up the phone. He started to laugh, "Oh, my *God,* I kept you waiting for so long while I was on the . . ." He laughed a little bit more and started to punch numbers. "Charles will die. He will simply die when I tell him I have the real Valerie Vane right here in the gallery staring at me. You'll talk to Charles? Will you talk to him?"

I didn't say anything, but it's possible I frowned. Blondie reconsidered the receiver. "Of course, you didn't come here for that. I'll go get Ms. Deitrick."

He looked like he would go get Darla this time, but he stopped, pivoted, and leaned his knuckles on the desk. "You know, I am so sorry about what happened to you," he whispered. "That Angelica Pomeroy is, frankly, a whore. Lord knows we all have tacky friends, but please! Can you believe that she—"

Darla Deitrick stepped into the frame of the sliding glass door. She posed for a moment with one hand against the frame and the other teapotted against her hip. She was no more than five foot one, hoisted up on a pair of scaly red stilettos. Her hair might've been called red, but pumpkin was more accurate. Her black Dolce pencil skirt was all business, transacted through Swiss bank accounts. Her face was powdered white and her eyes were encircled with black kohl. Her temples had the stretched-thin look of trampolines. I guessed a Botox buffet, though she was not yet pushing fifty. She wore glasses with heavy frames, black with leopard spots. Against all the white, she looked like a popup cutout.

"Gideon," she said, sternly, stepping through the glass.

Blondie turned around. "Oh, Ms. Deitrick. I was just coming to get you. You've got an appointment with Valerie Vane. She's a reporter from the Style section," his voice was outright shrill, "and she wants to talk to you about the exhibition. Isn't that wonderful?"

Darla glanced at Blondie vaguely and her lip turned up a little. "Of course, I recognize your name," she said, though obviously she didn't. "It's nice to finally meet you in person. I am very close with Tyler Prattle," she said, referring to The Paper's top art critic. "I hope we'll see him tonight at the opening. You'd be coming then, I assume?"

"Ms. Vane is of course invited this evening," Blondie put in. "Silly me, I completely forgot to give you your invitation." He turned to Darla. "I'm afraid I've made Valerie wait, but she's been eager to speak with you." Then back to me. "Is it okay if I call you Valerie? I feel as if we're old friends."

"Sure," I said.

Blondie clearly hadn't heard about my demotion, and that was because The Paper kept a lid on internal reassignments; as far as the public was concerned, I could've been in Baja or Siberia. Being fawned over had its perks. I felt around in my purse for a business card.

Darla stepped through the doorway and clip-clopped on her heels a few inches closer. She offered me her hand and shook weakly. Her left eyebrow, plucked almost to invisibility, twitched.

"I'd love to discuss the show," she said. "Unfortunately, I've scheduled clients for the entire afternoon. If all goes well we'll be sold out before the case of Stags' Leap even arrives. Is Tyler coming?"

I said, "I have only a few questions. It will take just a minute." I tried to make it sound like a barter: a minute for Tyler. I couldn't produce Tyler, but I figured I was good for a minute after waiting twenty. Darla shifted on her feet, cocking her head to look at a small old-fashioned alarm clock on the marble desk. She was going to give me a minute. But not sixty-one seconds.

Darla looked at Blondie now, and ticked her neck to the side, so he'd skedaddle. "So nice to meet you," I said, and reached out to shake his hand. I pressed my card into it, keeping an eye on Darla. She didn't notice. Then Blondie scuttled out through the glass door with a slavering smile.

"It's about Malcolm Wallace," I said, once we were alone. "Stain 149."

Darla's face didn't register any particular expression, but her eyebrow twitched again. "Well, I haven't heard that name in years. Is he showing again? What *is* he doing these days?"

"Not too much," I said.

"Ah. And how does that warrant a story for the Style section?"

If she'd already heard about Wallace's death, she'd have found a way to say it then. And if she knew but wasn't saying, her expression didn't betray her.

"I have some bad news, I'm afraid," I said. "Wallace passed away on Sunday morning."

"Malcolm?" Her face collapsed, and then her body did too, into the ottoman. Her knees were bracketed together, her fingertips to her nose. She gave the impression of a cocktail umbrella folding. "How?"

"It's unclear. He was found below the Queensboro Bridge."

She gasped. "How horrible!"

"I know this is a difficult subject, and I'm sure it will take some time to get adjusted to your loss, but I hoped you might be able to answer just a few questions about Wallace. We're trying to put together a story about his artistic career. The family said I'd find one of his best works here."

"This is terrible news," she said. "Malcolm was a dear, dear friend. And in his day he was a wonderful artist."

What registered on her face wasn't the loss of a friend, though. She seemed just a tad irked that the joy had been stripped from her opening day, and that now she had to discuss a subject that wasn't on the agenda.

"He was such a lovely man," she continued. "When I knew him he was just a boy. A sweet boy. Well, I was a baby then too! But I'm afraid you are misinformed. I haven't represented Malcolm Wallace in twenty years." She was talking to me absently now, as if working on an equation in her head.

"You were the last dealer to represent him," I said.

Darla nodded slowly, and her hands fell to her lap. "Yes, I was. He didn't want a dealer after he left me. He didn't want anything to do with SoHo."

"Why not?"

"The eighties," she said, as if that explained all of it.

I shook my head.

"You say you're putting together a story about Malcolm? Will it be a big piece? When will it appear? I can tell you everything.

I can put you in touch with all the right people. But not just this moment; this is a bad time." She caught herself. "It's never a good time, is it?" She stood up again, stroking the tresses of her hair. "I'll tell you what I can now, and then we'll talk more later. Okay? Will that be okay?"

I thought this would be the best I could get. I nodded, and then waited, while she assembled her thoughts. Then, without much ramping up, she launched in: "I remember when he first came into my gallery, he was like a Molotov cocktail. I've seen a lot of kids who think of themselves as artists, but there aren't that many like Wallace. I was of course the first dealer in New York to recognize the power of that genre. People dismissed graffiti, but to me it was the next natural step from neo-Expressionism, the last gasp of modernism. There's a direct line from Rothko to Rauschenberg to Basquiat. Stain's work had an additional charm—it was evasive, somehow, withholding."

Darla was all over the place. Pseudo-nostalgia, self-aggrandizement, a touch of critical theory. I wondered if this was how she processed grief.

"He did well for you?"

"Oh, he did fabulously! Probably the best of his group. Some of them had talent, but not like Malcolm. He was genuinely brilliant. And believe me, I use that word advisedly."

"You represented a lot of graffiti artists."

"Of course. I was the first. People have held it against me for years. Some people said it was 'fad art,' but no one would convince me of that. Some people called it scrawls; I said, then what's Dubuffet? Every artist working today references outsider art and primitives. I got the feeling some collectors just didn't want people from the *outer boroughs* in *our* galleries. They appreciate that much more in Europe. I say: You just don't know where good art will come from. If it comes from the gutter, it comes from the gutter."

She reconsidered what she'd said. "That sounds wrong, maybe too dismissive. Divisive? What's the word I'm looking for? You're a writer. You can fill it in. The thing was, Wallace wasn't really graffiti. He was much more than that, a true painter. Also, he had irrepressible charisma. Let me say that. He was also a gorgeous kid. Beautiful! You could see it emblazoned on his face: 'I will be famous or I will die.' Putting his name on things was just a small part of it; Malcolm *needed* to be recognized the way fish need gills to breathe and elephants need those huge ears to, well . . . you know."

Darla was exactly the kind of creature I'd come to know so well on Style, and maybe that's why Cabeza knew I'd be able to get her talking. Just feed her ego a little birdseed and she'd go on singing like this for hours. But I didn't need the entire eighties flashback. I just needed to know one thing. "Do you still have some of his pieces?"

"No, no, no, no, of course not. I sold everything. All the pieces he gave to me, personally, I sold while the market was high. I would've sold more to collectors, too, if he'd given me more. I had a waiting list of buyers."

"Why'd he stop giving you things to sell? He stop working?"

"No! He was very prolific. *Constantly* working. His studio was wall-to-wall paintings, scraps of metal, shoes, pants. He painted on his pants! Stop working? Never!"

Darla started clicking back and forth in front of me.

"Why did you let him go?"

"I didn't, exactly. He got back from his European tour and he had this whole new modus operandi. He didn't want to talk to the collectors. He didn't want to 'make nice,' as he put it. The more I tried to sell, the more he told me that he didn't belong on gallery walls. His only credentials were street credentials, he said. And so forth. I'm sure you know the argument."

"I've heard something about it."

"The trouble was, he was having a lot of fights with other graffiti writers. Beefs, they call it, sort of like little gang wars. He'd write his name somewhere and someone else would buff it—you know, write over it. Who knows why he still wanted to be doing that. He was famous. Genuinely. He didn't need to be scrawling on walls anymore, tempting arrest. It was like he still wanted to be the tough kid on the block. And well, there were all these street urchins here all the time and it was getting out of hand and I didn't really want them wreaking havoc. I was paying for his very high lifestyle. Limos and hotel rooms, painting supplies, trips to Europe, with lots of hangers-on. I didn't like that. Not too many dealers would, frankly."

"Sure," I said. "I can understand that." I jotted some notes on my pad.

"You don't need all this," Darla said. "In fact, strike that last part. I don't want to be quoted on that."

I didn't bother to pretend to cross out my notes. She wasn't watching anyway.

"Do you really want to hear all this? It's a sad story. It's not going to be important for your piece. But I'll tell you, if it can stay off the record. It got worse. He got deeper into drugs, and then he became very radicalized. Paranoid, if you ask me. He said he didn't want his art to be sold, so he started painting on his own skin. He showed up at an opening at Sidney Janis one night with the word *slave* on his forehead. He tapped people and offered to let them examine his teeth. It was all very hard to take."

"How deep was he into drugs?"

"Did I say he was? Actually, strike that too. I don't know. I try not to get too involved with the personal lives of my artists. Once you get into that territory, there's no coming back."

"What about his friends?"

"Well, he had that group of sycophants, you know, always

around him. I'm sure some of them were dopers. You know kids from that neighborhood, there's always that element. But dear, I'm telling you. I handled the works of art. I didn't spend my free time with the boy. He had a pretty rough crowd."

The word *boy* rang in my ears. I didn't know much about how artists related to their dealers, but a woman like Darla would've noticed a lot of things even if she wasn't using her free time to get to know Wallace.

"As you can see, I'm a businesswoman. I run a small business where I sell pictures for a fee," she gestured toward the million-dollar paintings, as if this were a poster shop where a van Gogh sold for twenty bucks. "If you don't want to sell art, you don't need me. I think we parted in 1987, but I could be mistaken." She fastened her lips politely and turned the clasp. Apparently my time was up. "I'd love to tell you more but my clients will be here any minute. We'll reschedule, yes?"

I thanked her. But I knew she didn't have clients arriving anytime soon, at least to buy these works. Nobody was going to be buying works on loan from major museums. She walked me to the foyer of the gallery, stopping in the middle of the space before the Robert Ryman. "Now, this," she said, "is where conceptual art meets abstraction: emotion essentialized. Have you ever seen anything more beautiful in your whole life?"

I looked at the all-white painting. I felt like Scott of the Antarctic.

"Critics like to say that the white canvas is the endgame of fine art. They are wrong. It is the pinnacle. You don't get to white immediately. You have to arrive at white. You have to be a perfect classicist—life drawing, color, perspective, mastering figurative painting, exploring abstraction—before you get to white. You strip everything down and you go closer and closer to the essence of expression. White is the last possible painting. It's a kind of religious moment, a paradigm shift that makes anything possible."

We'd finally gotten to the heart of Darla too. Strip down all the exterior varnish and what you've got was a saleswoman. The entire time I'd detained her with Wallace, she'd been preparing her pitch. And here it was, as polished as a press release. I had to marvel. "Fascinating," I said.

Darla breathed in the Ryman and exhaled. Every time she looked at the work, this was meant to suggest, she experienced a new conversion. "Well," she said. "At least your visit down here was profitable in the end, I hope. Please call me in a couple of days and I'll put you in touch with anyone you'll need for your Wallace story. He deserves a big feature. And in the meantime, we'll see you later at the opening, yes? Perhaps you'll travel down with Mr. Prattle. If need be, I can have Gideon arrange a car."

We'd come full circle. My payment was due. I looked down. "Lovely shoes," I said. "What are they, may I ask?"

"Aren't they cute?" she said. "Irrawaddy cobra. I just brought them back from Bangkok."

"Adorable," I said. "I'll send a note to Prattle when I'm back at my desk. Just one more thing. Why do you think Wallace thought you had his paintings?"

Her eyebrow twitched again, but her face was stolid. "Did he?"

Darla reached behind me and grabbed the stainless-steel door handle, pulling it open to let in the swelter. "You're some sort of celebrity journalist, I take it? Is that what Gideon was saying? I'm always pleased to speak with anyone from your paper. However, I hope next time you come you'll give us a ring and let us know you're coming down. Just so that we can make sure we give you the proper attention. I hope you understand."

"Certainly," I said.

"We'll see you at the opening tonight," she said again. She didn't wait for my answer. The glass door swooshed softly closed behind me. I was back out on West Twenty-fourth Street, a gray block of cement buildings with an abandoned stretch of railroad overhead, garbage strewn into the rutted pavement. I smelled the vague scent of rancid meat and motor oil.

Okay by me. I was tired of all that purity.

11

Gone Fishing

When I got back to the office, I found a note on my desk, scribbled in the looping script of Rood's hand:

> *Gideon, gallery assistant. Don't phone.*
> *Meet at Twilo, Saturday Night, 3:00 a.m.*
> *(I gather he means Sunday.) The Power Bar.*

Blondie. And I'd forgotten to say good-bye.

I shredded the note and looked around for Rood, but he was unaccountably absent. Despite the previous night's downpour, the newsroom was still on heat-wave tempo. Clerks glided somnolently back and forth like ducks in a shooting gallery. Randy Antillo was sling-shooting rubber bands into the Manhattan map on the office wall. Clint Westwood was replacing his penny loafer insoles. Rusty Markowitz was cursing at his monitor, "*Active* quotes, damn stringers! How can I use this crap?" Battinger was wearing her headset tipped back like a tiara and typing, a burger in her kisser.

Jaime called out, "Firehouse pre-bit coming along?"

Firehouse. Right, Firehouse. "Yes, just fine," I said. The Wallace file was covering up the Firehouse file, so I switched them. I put an article in front of me and dragged my eyes over the words, but nothing sank in. I picked up the phone and dialed Betty Schlacter, the DA's flack. When I asked her about the Wallace case, she said his name back to me, as if he were already filed on microfiche.

"Graffiti guy. Queensboro Bridge. Saturday."

"Doing follows now on obits?"

"You know how slow it gets in summer."

"What was the name again?"

I told her and there was a click. She left me with Bernadette Peters singing *Oklahoma* from the soundtrack. Just when the wind was sweeping down the plain, she returned. "That case is still active. You know we can't discuss anything under investigation."

"Sure," I said. "I know that."

"How about this: I'll let you know when we've solved it and give you everything. I still have your number around here somewhere." These government flacks had a way of making you feel small. Fishing wasn't allowed at city hall. But before she'd let me beg off, she asked, "Do you still have any juice with Buzz Phipps, Valerie?"

"It depends on how hard I squeeze him."

Silent pause. "I have something new on the supermodel slaying," she said. "But never mind, I'll call Tracy." Then she hung up. It was a low blow, and I had to sit there and take it. Tracy was getting "Drop Dead Gorgeous" and I was getting the dial tone.

I tapped the eraser of my pencil on the desk for a while. I needed to get something on Wallace—anything—enough, anyway, to get Cabeza off my back. Enough to satisfy my newfound curiosity about him too. But how would I do it? News hawks didn't get their information from flacks, did they? Gumshoes didn't go around asking press agents for scraps. Jake Gittes knew he had to go to the orange groves. Marlowe had to go to Mexico to find Terry Lennox. But how did he know? And when did he know?

I scanned the collection of reference books on my cubicle shelf: a Zagat restaurant guide; a hot pink guide to Manhattan sex haunts; a thick *Gotham's Gate* special edition, "Who's Who in the Hamptons"; and a thin volume of celebrity yoga gurus. These would have to go. I'd need serious journalistic tomes. *The Pentagon Papers.* Speeches by MLK, something by Chomsky, and that book *We Regret to Inform You That Tomorrow We Will . . . Something, Something.* A guide to digital reporting. That was all the rage. I'd need to get a little cap that made me look smart. Maybe dye my hair and get a cut? A wristwatch. I made a list. It was a short list, and when I got finished, I noticed Jaime watching me. Firehouse.

I pulled out the Firehouse file again and started jotting notes about her "ground-breaking" feminist performances, including her 1981 piece, "Nympho/Pyromaniac," in which Sally masturbated while self-flagellating, and then set fire to her panties. Very soon I had a couple of pages of notes for a story, but it was just about the trickiest bit of cultural translation imaginable, like turning a Friars Club roast of Hugh Hefner into a bedtime story. I couldn't politely conjure a tenth of Sally's act. I tried to describe the protective sheeting and fire-resistant jelly, which she called her "special-formula K-Y," and resorted to the phrase "unsuitable for a family newspaper" five or six times. I drifted back to wondering about Wallace.

Rood arrived an hour later, like Jimmy Cagney back from the joint, smiling and snickering and flashing his gums, while lurching across the newsroom. "Miss Vane," he said, cordially. Then he coughed what sounded like acreage of phlegm.

"Mickey," I said, nodding. "Are you all right?"

"Nothing a few dozen surgeons can't fix," he said. "Or so my doctor tells me."

Mickey had already had one lung removed; I knew that much. I couldn't imagine what they'd be able to do about the other. I was pleased when he opened up his filing cabinet and took out his brown bag. When he started peeling the layers off his lemon sugar wafers, I was reassured. After he'd finished, he opened a folder on the desk, laid out the clippings from the file, and leaned over the papers like an overgrown toadstool. I looked at his wide back for a while before I asked: "Mickey, you worked in the cop shop, right?"

"Fifteen years," he said.

"Ever solve a crime the police couldn't get?"

"Not too often, but a couple of times." Rood leaned back until his chair hit his desk, and he reached for a cigar box he kept next to the picture of his granddaughter. He took out an unfiltered Lucky Strike. "One case was sort of a mistake. A serial rapist attacking prostitutes in the Brooklyn projects. Cops picked up the suspect and I was on the follow. I was collecting string from victims' neighbors, and folks started telling me the cops got it wrong. Then I knocked on one door, and there was a guy there, looking pretty ragged. 'Do you want to talk?' I said. Bingo, confession in my lap. That wasn't anything I did, either. Just knocked on the right door and out comes this cranked-up kid thinking I'm a priest."

"I guess that's a big break."

"Dumb luck."

"And the other?"

"That was all me. That was the big feather in my cap," he snickered like he didn't mean it. "It never ran. Some time I'll tell you all about it, but not now." He tapped the Lucky on the desk's surface and placed it between his lips. He didn't light it. He took it out again and plucked a speck of tobacco from his tongue.

"If you had to do that again—go out on a limb, check something out on your own—where would you start?"

"If I had to, I'd start in the most logical place, with the known facts. I'd follow all the facts back to their source, see if the facts lined up right. Usually they don't. So you find which fact is wrong, you work from there. Then I'd cover my ass. I'd make sure I did everything on the up and up. No side dalliances, nothing that would stop the brass from accepting my word as scripture." He tapped his Lucky on the desk. "You wouldn't want to tell me any more about this thing you're trying to follow, now would you, Vane?"

"Me?" I said. "Oh, nothing. I'm actually just trying to find some of my dad's relatives. Old family history."

"That's good," said Rood, sitting up straight. His chair whacked him in the back, making him cough again. "Because I wouldn't want you checking into something that wasn't within your current realm of expertise. That might lead to a story that was too big for Obits. And that would get certain editors so worked up they'd muss their hair."

Cabeza's call came an hour later. He didn't bother with courtesies. "Did you get news on the Stains?"

"Darla says she sold all of them," I said. "That's all she said."

"Did you get any leads?"

The answer was no. "I can't talk about it here," I said.

"Claro," he said. "I'll be on the Queensboro when you get off work, shooting footage."

"Footage?"

"I'll be there after five. There's a bike ramp on the north side." Before I could ask for directions, I was listening to the dial tone again. I hated that.

I riffled through papers in the Stain morgue file. I picked through the bruised clips. There were lots. I found a *N.Y. Reader* item dated 1985, "Skirmish Disturbs 'Equilibrium.' "

> Everyone knows that the artist Jeff Koons isn't serious. A guy who showcases Hoover Convertible Vacuum Cleaners in Plexiglas cases just can't think he's painting the *Mona Lisa,* right?
>
> At his most recent show, called "Equilibrium," Koons had a basketball suspended in a fish tank. Some patrons didn't get the joke. One visitor to the gallery, an artist

named Stain, pulled Koons's basketball out of the tank, tossed it to one of his cohorts, and pretended to play hoops with his friends against the framed Nike posters—also Koons's "art."

"That was so funny," said one of the teenagers who came with Stain. "But they got upset, as if we ruined something. Come on, man. It's just a basketball."

But the gallery owner, the patrons sipping Pinot Grigio, and Koons weren't so amused.

"This show has nothing to do with basketball," said Koons after the show. "It deals with states of being. I worked with physicists for a year to get that ball to stay suspended."

Apparently, those scientists didn't quite attain their goal. The ball will stay suspended for a while, but eventually it will hit the bottom of the tank. That will turn this piece of art into, well, a basketball in a fish tank.

Stain, the graffitist who won critical acclaim for his first solo show at Darla Deitrick Fine Art four years ago, said he didn't see Koons's work as sacred. "This doesn't do anything but promote Nike," Stain said. "Koons is selling out my people and he doesn't even know it. My response was conceptual. We didn't hurt anybody."

Asked if he thought Stain was a good conceptual artist, Koons said, "No."

No?

"This show isn't about basketball," Koons repeated. "It's about artists using art for social mobility. We're no different from these guys. We're using art to move up to a different social class too."

Maybe that would be true if Koons wasn't himself a successful stock trader until last year. Though I suppose downward mobility could qualify as social mobility, of a sort.

I had to like this reporter's style. It was cranky. It didn't tell the whole story, but it told the good parts. On page two, I saw something else that interested me, a photo of Wallace arm in arm with Darla in front of the SoHo gallery. They looked to be pretty swell pals. She was even putting a few teeth in her smile. In the background was another face I now recognized: Cabeza's. He was twenty years younger, maybe about ten pounds lighter, and his hair had no sign of gray. He was behind Wallace with his arms folded. He had a look of disapproval on his face, but he was leaning sideways, almost as if he wanted to get into the frame. It reminded me of kids who stand behind on-air TV newscasters, mouthing "Hi, Ma!"

Based on what I could find in the clipping file, the incident at the Koons opening hadn't improved Stain's public profile. The next few items I found focused on his public decline: a 1986 story in the *Daily News*, "Staining His Own Reputation? Wallace Undermines His Work with Silly Stunts," followed by a *Village Voice* feature, "Sell-Out Stain Gets Religion," a four-page rant about how Wallace had no right to start "speaking for the people," when he'd already become a parody of himself. A *New York Post* gossip item asked, "What former art star should be voted 'Most Likely to Exceed'? The wall-scribbler named Stain, who can't stop putting his rather large foot in his sizable mouth."

Here it was: the media machine that had built Wallace in his early career was turning on him, taking him apart one pull quote at a time.

The Paper reserves a special place in its heart, and on its fourth floor, for its critics. While most of the reporters who fill the ever-expanding culture sections make their homes in cubes, the critics get offices with walls that smack the ceiling and doors that shut and lock. This alone gives them reason to feel haughty.

Curtis had an office on the floor's west wing, just a few feet behind Tyler Prattle's. He shared it with the second-tier film critic, a British Mensa cardholder named Marvin Everett with the byline M. E. Smarte. I rapped lightly so as not to disturb Smarte, in case he was deconstructing the new Kubrick release. No one answered. I rapped again, this time a little harder. I heard a noise inside, and then the muted rolling of wheels, until the door snapped open.

Curtis was in his chair, his head was tossed back lazily and his eyes were a little misty, as if I'd interrupted him reading Wordsworth. He had a dreamy Sunday kind of look on his face, like he'd just put away a glass of freshly squeezed orange juice and was coming up with excuses to skip the Week in Review.

"Well, I have to say, you missed some serious Bollywood," he told me, and I almost confessed that I'd have preferred to go to the Film Forum than to a funeral. He got up and made ceremonious with the door, then rolled Smarte's chair out from under the other desk and offered it to me. "Can I get you anything? Water? Coffee? Sushi hand roll?" He had a smooth, high voice that kept its pitch.

It had been only a day since I'd last seen Curtis and I should've been able to pick up right where we'd left off, but something had come between us in the last twenty-four hours.

"So, I've got tickets to Celebrate Brooklyn tonight," he said. "Beastie Boys and Kid Creole. Any interest?"

Before I could think of a good excuse, his phone rang. Curtis twisted to answer it. "Just a sec," he said, picking up the receiver. "Culture." He winked at me. "Hey, Clive. Sure, I know—it's in my heart but not in my budget, man. Sure, I'll come down anyway. Sure. Save me a seat up front."

He hung up the phone. "Sorry about that." Before I could answer, the phone rang again. "Oops! Sorry, Val. Just this one."

"Culture," he said. "Berta! Girl! It's been ages! . . . No kidding." He continued on for a while, scribbling something onto his desk calendar and thanking her profusely for the invite I was sure he wouldn't accept. Every box in his desk calendar was already covered with jots: hundreds of invitations to rock concerts, music hall openings, movie premieres, and film festivals. All New York was bumping elbows just to get on Curtis's schedule. Poor culture contenders. The hopes of a slew of aspiring pop stars could be dashed with a single spill of his coffee cup.

"Sorry about that," Curtis said again. "My buddy at Irving Plaza. Screw the Beasties. You want to see Bad Brains tonight? They'll comp me plus one."

"I can't tonight." The moment to offer an excuse came and went, but I didn't know how to tell him I was meeting another man. We rolled around a little on our swivel chairs until the awkwardness went away. "Now, Val, I know you didn't come up to hear me yak on the phone. How can I make myself of use to you today?"

"I was thinking about our conversation yesterday, about the artist you mentioned, the graffiti guy."

"Wallace? The Golden Gadfly. Are you thinking we should've done more on him?" he said. "You know, it wouldn't be bad. The trouble is I really don't have the time. But if you were interested, I'd back you up with Battinger to work on something on spec."

"I guess I'm a little interested, but only because you mentioned it. I mean, if people are complaining . . ."

Curtis thought it over some more. "You know what? This could be a good story to help you get back into The Paper again. If I don't interfere too much, you could get a byline. I'd be really happy to help with that. Maybe even pitch it to Moore and Lessey, or Buzz. Would be nice to get back in Style, huh?" He laughed again, realizing the pun—the same one he'd made the day before. "Sorry."

Curtis's office wall was covered with clips from his two decades as a culture reporter, first at the *Voice,* later at *The New York Observer,* and then ten years at The Paper. He'd been a witness to punk at CBGB's, park jams in the Bronx, and even break-dancers before they were in Gap ads. "Maybe if you could tell me a little bit more about why you think he'd be worthy of a larger treatment, I could start to follow a few angles, you know, just to see where they lead? Do you think Wallace was something?"

Curtis killed the phone again. "I'm actually not a big art buff—you know, music's my thing—and graffiti never did it for me, personally. I was really a young kid when Stain was Stain, so I missed the real fireworks. But Tyler gave him serious props as an artist, I know that."

"It sounded yesterday like you thought he was just sort of a pain in the ass."

"Later, when he was in his prime, he was cool as hell."

"Genuinely?"

Curtis sat up in his chair and lost the dreamy look. "Oh, absolutely. Wallace was a very vivid character. I remember the first time I met him. It must've been about 1985, 1986, somewhere in there. I was still enrolled at NYU and I was trying to break into the *Voice,* and Mike Andatte, this great photographer, was going to shoot some graffiti kids in the East Village and I asked him if I could tag along."

The phone rang again; this time he tapped a button on the receiver to send it to voice mail, which was either out of respect for me or for the memory of Wallace. "It turned out we walked into a great little moment in history. You see, like a week before, Kenny Scharf, Keith Haring, and Jean-Michel Basquiat were supposed to be part of a group photo of East Village artists for the cover of some magazine, but the three of them had all bagged it. They'd just never shown. Major betrayal. So the other East

Village artists thought they had gotten too big for their britches, and now they're part of the SoHo scene. All these writers are pissed off. So, when Andatte and I got to this apartment, we find this whole crew of writers all dressed in zip-up white suits like exterminators—like Devo."

Curtis's phone rang again, and again he sent it to voice mail and kept talking. "Wallace was the leader of this little extermination crew. They were going to SoHo to tar and feather Haring at his opening. They called themselves the Art Crime Posse—I guess Wallace was obsessed with *The Wild Bunch*—and this was, he said, 'guerilla resistance.' It was cool. I wrote it up. My first enterprise story for the *Voice*."

"But that doesn't make sense. Malcolm's dealer was a SoHo dealer."

"No, no, she'd burned him already; told him to get lost," said Curtis. "That's why he was so intense about it. It was personal."

The phone rang again, and this time he lifted the receiver and put it back in the cradle, fast. "Couldn't really blame him. What she did to him was harsh. She'd made him sever his ties to other galleries, to his European dealer, to his folks in the Bronx, and then she'd dumped him, flat on his ass. Told him he wasn't selling anymore. I don't even think that was true. He couldn't go back to any other galleries. He was working as a bike messenger. So it was pretty sad for him."

Curtis could probably read the confusion on my face; I still didn't see the story in all this information. "The thing was, Valerie, Stain made a whole new life for himself after he left SoHo; he did become this kind of powerful force in his own community, in the Bronx. There were a lot of people who didn't like him, and it was hard for him to get the kind of play in the media he had before he severed contact with high culture. But there's a fascinating story somewhere in there, about his second act, if you know what I mean. No one's written that, and if you could nail it I think the editors might go for it. You know at least one thing: no one else is going to beat you to the punch."

I acted as if I were thinking it over, as if I were dubious, but in fact this was the best thing Curtis could've said, under the circumstances.

"You'll need a decent rabbi," Curtis added. "Someone who really knows the graffiti world inside and out. I could give you a few names if you need them."

"I think I might have someone already," I said. I thought of Cabeza, and I had a yen to be near him again.

The phone rang, and then two lines lit up on Curtis's receiver, and then three. "I better . . . ," he said, pointing plaintively to the phone.

I closed the door quietly behind me and waited to hear the click of the latch. When I got back to Obits, I shifted on my swivel chair, listening to the resounding silence of my phone. I went to the printer, stole a few blank sheets of paper, and drew a new map. I put dots on the Queensboro Bridge, in the Bronx, in SoHo, in Chelsea, in the East Village. I couldn't imagine, yet, how they could all possibly connect.

12

Talking Bridge

Summer nights in July, the on-ramp to the Queensboro Bridge is an angry furnace of overworked and overheated nine-to-fivers, fuming as their cars inch toward the bridge. To get to the entrance of the bike path, I had to brave the metallic spew of commuter traffic and the lines of cars its jaws engulfed into the crocodile belly of Long Island.

And the walk up the bike path, entered by way of a tunnel in the bridge's stone pilings, isn't a sunset stroll either. Gray concrete, chicken wire fencing, cracked rusted paint, the sky as yellowish gray as a weathered tombstone, the river that muddy green you get when you go wrong mixing paints. The landmarks: black-windowed corporate towers, the Roosevelt Island tram swaying on its cable, the island they used to call Welfare, where an old castle, once a lunatic asylum, has fallen to rubble. If desolate had a destination, this was it.

I wasn't completely alone as I trekked toward the Queens side. But I didn't know what kind of help I'd get—in an emergency—from the old man walking his yapping Maltese, or the two bikers in orange Lycra speeding past, or the Chinese lady absorbed in silent tai chi. A few workmen high in the cantilevers waved charmlessly. I wondered how Wallace had found himself here at two in the morning when he was supposed to be out buying ice cream. I wondered whether the night air strangled his screams if he was chased, if he was caught, if he was thrown off the bridge. The wind creaked mournfully up through the metal girders and I quickened my pace. I tried to imagine walking up this bridge, climbing up on that high, shaky railing, at night, in the pitch-dark, with just the sounds of cars roaring behind, and that ugly river below, deciding it was time to jump.

In about a quarter of an hour I spotted Cabeza. His look was 1950s Havana chic. Pale yellow short-sleeved guayabera, brown slacks, white boating sneakers, a pair of sunglasses hanging from the V of his shirt. He gave the impression of a man on vacation from his own life. He had a video camera in his right hand, and he seemed to be filming the brown river below.

"What's that for?" I asked, about the camera, when I was a few yards away. He saw me and turned, still filming. He said something but I couldn't make out the words. It was deafening up there. The hum of the steel, the clank and groan of every truck, the wind in the girders, all ate our words. I put up a hand to signal that I didn't want to be in his movie. He let the camera drop to his side. I got closer and screamed, "Why do you have that?"

"The movie version," he shouted back. "Once the story comes out, we make a short doc."

"You really do have big ambitions for this investigation," I said and, realizing he couldn't hear, repeated, simply, "Big ambitions!"

"For you," he said. "For me." Cabeza's full lips curved into a smile. He was cheerful in a place not too many people would've been cheerful. Maybe he felt refreshed and rested; maybe he just liked the feel of all this wind on his face.

There was too much noise to talk, so I leaned with him against the railing and looked out over the river as he filmed the white caps. A pair of speedboats were cutting up the river, each one trailed by a frothy white wake. I watched them until they separated far up ahead.

"What happens if I can't get what you need?" I shouted. "If I can't establish that Wallace was murdered. Do you rat me out?"

"You'll get it," he said. "You will."

Looking down at the water again, I felt the queasy sting of vertigo. I put both hands on the railing and felt the bridge's cold steel rattle. I turned around and put my back to the view. I looked at the latticework of cables above us. I remembered Cabeza's first phone call, the way the wind had howled through the phone and I'd thought it was singing. Maybe he'd been calling from here.

"Were you here when Wallace was discovered?" I shouted.

A convoy of trucks hurtled by and the bridge groaned under us like a body turning in its sleep. He answered but I couldn't hear him; he moved closer and repeated, "Mrs. Wallace and Amenia called me that night. I live over there," he said, his mouth close to my ear, pointing toward Queens. "Not too far. They needed someone to identify the body." He shifted so that he could look into my eyes and gauge my reaction.

"That must've been rough," I said.

"Never had anything harder to do in my life," he said softly, close to my ear.

"Did you see something?" I asked, but he shook his head—couldn't hear. I moved closer. "Did you see something that made you think it wasn't suicide? That he'd been killed?"

A strange smile alighted on Cabeza's lips and creases formed at the edges of his eyes, and then disappeared. Was it a smile of discomfort or something else? "His tongue was black," Cabeza said, and waited to let that sink in, moving back to watch my face. "His teeth were purple. It was like someone had sprayed into his mouth with plum spray paint."

I imagined what Cabeza was suggesting. Somewhere in the Bronx, a man tells his family he's going out for ice cream. He doesn't take much with him—his wallet, maybe, and his keys—

because he's coming right back. Out on the mean streets, someone attracts his attention, maybe puts a hard object to his back, or his neck, maybe hits him over the head, maybe covers his mouth with a chloroformed rag—that's how it was always done onscreen—and prods him, pushes him, drags him, to an unmarked van. Inside the van, he's brought to consciousness, or to awareness, and he sees his captors. Just long enough to know who they are, to understand where he is, to feel the terror of his own imminent demise, maybe even long enough to imagine escape. And then he's given an explanation, if it were the movies, a sermon of some kind about the higher order of criminality or the failures of his own life, or about how he shouldn't have gone stirring up trouble this way or that. And then they make it clear that he will be killed. He hears the familiar rattle—a spray can, this time his death rattle—and next thing he's being held down by someone, some secondary thug, and his mouth is being filled with toxic paint. He tastes it, he swallows. His life's final flavor. Within the hour, his poisoned, slackened body is falling over the railing.

The waning sun was trickling through the cantilevers. I watched the cars drive by on the inner deck of the bridge. A tiny blue Lamborghini zigzagged among a crowd of lumbering SUVs, as if skipping around that way would get him somewhere faster. A blonde in a teal blazer fixed her hair in the rearview mirror of her Toyota as if she could get younger that way. A boy driving a beat-up Mustang convertible leaned forward and changed the radio station; a middle-aged man in wrap-around sunglasses struggled to close the sunroof on his Mercedes while his car idled. I felt sad for them. I felt sad for all of us.

"How was Darla?" Cabeza asked.

"Real down to earth."

Cabeza laughed softly. I didn't hear him, but I could see. "She seem surprised by the news?"

I tried to connect the image of Wallace's death with Darla.

They didn't mesh. "Enough," I said. "You don't really think she was responsible?"

"Someone was. She has friends on the police force."

"Meaning?"

"The police don't take too well to graffiti writers," he shouted. "A graff writer I knew in the early eighties was killed by the police just for doodling on the wall of the L train station. Darla was upset with Wallace because he was snooping around her office for those paintings, getting in her hair. I wouldn't be surprised if she'd asked her cop friends to make sure he stepped off. Maybe they took it a little too seriously." He said it without emotion. "I'm not saying it's what I believe. It's just what people are talking about it in the neighborhood."

I thought of *Sweet Smell of Success*. J. J. Hunsecker has a crooked cop on his payroll, a round Irishman that Sidney Falco calls Hunsecker's "fat friend." The fat friend takes care of things Hunsecker wants taken care of, like his sister's suitor. And at the end of the movie, when Hunsecker turns on Falco, it's Falco who faces the fat friend in a deserted Times Square.

Maybe it wasn't an unmarked van or a hard object against his back. Maybe Wallace was out on Simpson Avenue, on his way to buy ice cream, and he stopped in an alley to paint his tag, like he always did. But this time he hears a voice behind him—it's the cops, saying, *Hold it right there, young man. Put down that can.* So Wallace—no longer a young man—turns slowly and tries to make a joke of it all. But the cops aren't in a joking mood. Maybe they've followed him here; maybe, because of Darla's request, they've been tailing him, waiting for exactly this kind of false move, so they can pick him up. And so they put him in the squad car, and they take him back to the precinct and a few hours later, Diallo-style, they've got him brutalized and they don't want the public to get wind of this new scandal, so they put him back in the squad car, go up to the Queensboro, throw him off the bridge.

"What about graffiti kids?" I said. "Weren't there other writers who hated him, who wanted to get back at him somehow?" If there was another plot in there, maybe it would be simpler. I switched out the cops for a bunch of young graffiti kids who see Wallace at the wall and get pissed. *Hey, motherfucker!* They take the can from him and they try to spray him, instead. Maybe they'd meant to scare him—didn't realize it would be toxic—and he'd just died. So they'd freaked out and tried to cover their tracks. They find some kid with an old beater and they take the body out to the Queensboro and, nervous, terrified, toss it over the side.

"Graffiti beef? Where'd you get that idea?" asked Cabeza.

"Darla alluded to 'long-standing beefs.' And a lot of kids who hung around him, some of them deep into drugs?"

"Darla." Cabeza seemed to think her name was funny. He lifted his camera and aimed it at me.

I flinched. "Hey, let's stop with that, huh?"

"This is good stuff. We're talking through the questions; we're touching on all the possible angles."

He was trying to be playful, I think, but I felt overexposed. "Stop. I'm not kidding."

"Why?"

I pulled away from the railing and started to walk back toward Manhattan. Cabeza grabbed hold of my wrist, tugging. "Come on. I'll stop. I swear."

His hand was on me again. It didn't hurt, and I wasn't scared. He was smiling a rogue's smile and his eyes were playful, bright green dragonflies.

He shouted to me over the traffic's roar, "You're quite beautiful when you aren't trying to look any particular way. I just wanted to capture you exactly as you were just then, with that expression."

He let go of my arm.

I was free to leave now. But I didn't. I needed to know which plot he meant me to follow, which version of the script. "No camera," I said.

"No camera," he said, and put it away. "Look, the truth is, I need you," he said. "This needs a proper investigation and a proper exposé. And frankly, you're the best chance I've got."

I pictured Bogart rolling out of San Quentin in a barrel in *Dark Passage*. What if Lauren Bacall had never driven by in her Packard to save him? I had the strong urge to move closer and put my arms around Cabeza's broad back and tell him everything was going to be fine. Relenting, I took a few steps closer. "Do you know what a rabbi is?" I asked. Before he answered, I added, "For a reporter?"

"Sure I do," he said. "The reporter's guide. Someone who shows you the ropes."

"I'm going to be lost with all this graffiti stuff. These taggers and buffers, or whatever they're called. The high-art stuff I can manage, somewhat, but I need your help in the demimonde."

His eyes flashed gratitude, just like in *Dark Passage* when Bogart realizes Bacall is on his side. "Shalom," he said. "Will I need a yarmulke for this?"

The next few nights, my chair in Obits was spinning empty at exactly six o'clock. I was meeting Cabeza wherever he told me to find him, so I could get schooled in "the art of getting up, getting over," as he called it.

On the first night, he rode with me uptown to a brick schoolyard on East 106th Street and Park Avenue in El Barrio: the Graffiti Hall of Fame. "This is your primer," he said, pointing to the various graffiti murals painted by some of what he called the "old school" writers. "None of these guys are real writers now," he said, with some disdain, "since this is what we call a 'legal wall,' it doesn't take anything to paint here. But I'm showing you the basics of style," he said. He explained who'd invented certain arrows and stars, who'd created three-dimensional techniques, who'd gotten messy and who'd gone figurative or abstract. Some of the "kings of the trains" were there, so he explained old-time train graffiti culture, what it meant to go "all city"—to get your tag on a train that ran in all five boroughs—how writers ranked themselves, and why it wasn't necessarily bad to buff, or write over someone else's tag.

Before we headed back downtown, he showed me where he lived when he first moved to New York. His first tenement on East 103rd Street and Lexington wasn't so different from my first tenement on East Fifth, so I told him a little—just a little—about moving to the city from the farm. What the hell, I thought, this guy had nothing to do with anyone I'd ever know. It was safe to tell him my true history. He didn't laugh about any of it; he didn't think it quaint that I had grassroots roots. "Everybody here comes from somewhere else," he said, and he told me about watching his grandfather kill chickens by hand on his family's farm in PR. I told him that my job on the Eugene farm was to milk the goats in the morning, and not a single titter escaped his lips. So I told him a little more.

On the second night, Cabeza took me on a subway tour of all of Stain's "wild-style pieces"—big mural-style paintings with interlocking letters and symbols, Cabeza explained—on the backs of billboards high above the elevated lines in the outer boroughs. He showed me others that were painted inside the subway tunnels and they flickered past us in the darkness as we rode the trains. Some—the hard to reach ones—might've been around for more than twenty years, but others looked like they'd been finished that month. "Wallace believed in 'keeping it real' as the kids say," explained Cabeza. "He was writing up to the day he died."

Afterward, we had dinner at Nha Trang, a Vietnamese hole in the wall in Chinatown, where the dishes were on our table almost before we ordered. He asked me about my family, and I told him a little about the yippies and Merry Pranksters and the squat, and he said his mother had been a singer in her youth too, and he'd lived a childhood backstage. As we downed rice noodles and cheap Chinese beer, he asked me more—all the questions about my past that no one in New York had ever asked, or at least that I'd never answered truthfully.

As the hours wore on, he walked me through SoHo toward Chelsea and then up to Midtown—pointing out graffiti marks, tags, stickers on the way, explaining styles, histories, techniques—and we passed each green subway lantern that would've put me on a train uptown, we talked and talked and I didn't tuck into my Broadway flat till past two.

The third night, Cabeza gave me the address of his studio in Queens. He said it was time he showed me the documentary he'd made about Wallace long ago, so I could get a picture of "the artist as a young man." "You would've liked him," Cabeza said over the phone. "Maybe you will." I took a cab right over from The Paper.

Cabeza's studio was in a defunct factory, which hadn't been the Eagle Electric plant for thirty years, on a cracked cobblestone street in an industrial district in Queens. It wasn't one of those light-filled lofts of SoHo or a converted Williamsburg warehouse. Even though it was on the second floor, it had low ceilings and the dank feel of a cave. It also happened to be his living room and bedroom, his kitchen and his closet, the couch and the bed pushed into corners behind screens. In the center of the room was a high narrow table that had once lived in a high school chemistry lab, which Cabeza used for editing. There was a sink in one end, a Steenbeck editing table at the other. In the center was an old film-reel projector.

"I was trying to make a series," Cabeza explained, as the projector began to whirr. "Every time there was a new innovation in the style, I wanted to get a 'master' to demonstrate on film. It turned out there was a new evolution in the style just about every six months. From the throw-up it went to the burner, from the burner to the wild-style piece and then the blockbusters. These days it's roller letters and scratchiti. I couldn't keep up with it all."

He went to the kitchen and brought back a bottle of pinot noir. He held it up and raised his brows. I nodded. "Nowadays, style is all anyone cares about. You'd be surprised how petty the beefs can get. Everyone wants to claim his or her rightful place in the graffiti pantheon. In the early days, when they were writing on the trains, it was all about rebellion and subversion. Now it's all about style, who invented what and which arrow came first." Cabeza shook his head while he uncorked the wine. He went back to the kitchen, and quickly brought back two jam jars and poured them both full. He lifted me onto the editing counter and handed me one of the jars. "*Salud,*" he said, touching his glass to mine. "Shall we get started?"

Cabeza cut the lights. The old projector chugged and ticked and a sputter of blue light hit the home movie screen. The room smelled of burning dust. The film was 16 millimeter, black and white. There were no credits or titles, just a flash of light on a young man in a subway tunnel.

It was young Malcolm Wallace, no older than Kamal, but a whole lot slimmer. He was crouched on his haunches, aiming a spray can at a wall. His hair was wild, and his cheeks were soft and hairless. There was the hint of stubble above his lip, but the hair on his cheeks grew in unevenly, like it wasn't fully committed. He was wearing a pair of dark pants and a white turtleneck unrolled up to his chin. On top of that was a white Adidas jacket with stripes down the sides. Around his neck over the turtleneck, he wore a couple of strands of what I thought might be Buddhist prayer beads.

"Guy always looked sharp," said Cabeza. "That was a big part of the Stain mythos. Even when we were just kids, he came up with these interesting combos. A good street look, with a little something from the hippies. He wore those Guatemalan bracelets, or maybe an Indian shirt. He always had the urban ghetto cool, with a tinge of Euro. Something to put you off guard."

On the film I could hear Cabeza's voice from behind the camera. The same voice, minus the smoke: "So, tell us how you got into all this."

"This? Well, you know, man. I mean, I've been tagging for, well, as long as I could walk almost. As long as I could run, definitely." Wallace laughed and pointed at the camera, then shook up his can again. "Well, nah, I mean, I been doing this since the beginning. I was out there with Tonka and Stitch, and Cay, A-1, all those b-boy writers. We started putting our name up, just to get up."

His can started hissing and he started marking the wall with a black curve.

"Hey, let's wait on that, okay?" came the voice from behind the camera. "I want you to talk us through it, show us what you're doing as you're doing it, all right?"

Stain pulled the spray can back from the wall. "Sure, man. Hey, whatever you want. It's your picture, right? I'm just the actor. Or maybe you could say 'the talent,' right?" He laughed. "Am I right, man?"

The voice from behind the camera was impatient, nerdy: "Sure. Talent. Just a minute. Hold on."

The older Cabeza, in the room with me, added his own commentary: "I was just trying to get him to do it in order, but that was hard for him. He was free flowing. Aquarius."

The camera jostled and unfocused and then focused again. Throughout the pause, Wallace looked calm and cheerful. "Okay, so why don't you start painting now," said young Cabeza.

"Ya ready?"

"Ready."

Wallace stood up. "Homeboy, check it out. Today I am going

to teach you how to do a throw-up. This here is going to be like a cooking class, like Julia Child in the rail yards." Stain smiled wide at the camera, showing off the gap where he was missing a canine. He didn't bother to stop and ask Cabeza if he was doing okay. He was perfectly confident. He was a genuine charmer, effortless. "A throw-up is a step up from a tag. Here's my tag, Stain 149," he said, and then demonstrated his basic style, spraying his name in simple script. His signature looped around, the letters overlapping so that the word was barely legible. "And now, here's the throw-up of my name." He sat up on his haunches a little higher, took another spray can off the ground, and began to paint bubble letters in white. These were thick lines and he went over them a few times with his can, until they popped from the wall. He was serious and silent while he painted.

"I bet the girls loved him."

Cabeza nodded. He refilled my jam jar. "*Claro que si*. He had a girlfriend, though, Mae Rose Sims, from Georgia. He was crazy about her. But after he got dropped from the gallery, she left him."

"That wasn't very kind of her."

"It was his own fault, maybe. He was so angry. I know she cared for him deeply, but she didn't want to watch him destroy himself. After she left, though, he started to spiral."

On-screen, Stain was saying, "Now, once you've done the throw-up you can add a fill-in, or you can leave it like you want it." Wallace twisted the cap off the spray can and put on another, thicker cap. "Now, if you get one of these spray starch can caps, you can cover a larger area in a shorter time. That's good, because speed is king." He sprayed, using darker, wider, strokes to cover the area inside the bubble lettering.

The camera moved vertically to take in his whole tall, narrow frame. "Key is, time is your enemy. Along with the Five-0. You have to move like lightning. Get it up; fill it in. Style comes second, once you've mastered the basics. You get fancy and get caught, you be illin'. So keep it simple."

He was a jaunty-looking kid, with energy to spare. Even standing in one place, he couldn't keep still. As he talked, he shifted his weight from one foot to the other, switched his hands from one pocket to the next, took his pick out of his pocket and played with the spokes.

"So, that's it. You think you've got it? I hope so. Because I'll see you on the lay-ups, homeboy. And if you don't know what's a throw-up, you won't be welcome on the Bench. That's the Hundred Forty-ninth Street, my street, my Bench. I'm Stain 149. Word up."

The light flickered and the film unfurled. We sat in the glow of the projector, the celluloid flapping through the reel. Cabeza approached me with the wine bottle, his eyes gleaming. All at once, I wanted to know everything about him.

"Was it Stain who named you Cabeza? Where did that come from?"

He poured my glass full. "*El grande cabeza,*" he chuckled. "'The great head.' Another way of calling me brainy. Where I grew up, it wasn't good to be too smart. I tried to pretend I was an athlete like the other kids, but I wasn't much good at it. Then someone found a hardcover copy of *Don Quixote* in my schoolbag, and he and a few other kids beat me with it. After that, they taunted me: *El grande cabeza, el grande cabeza,* until it just became *cabeza,* and then that stuck."

"Cruel."

"I hated the nickname as a kid, but when I got older, it got to be so I liked it. All the boys who used to tease me for being a smarty were stuck in Aguas Buenas working for their fathers selling kitchen supplies to homemakers. I got out. Good thing I'd been reading all those books. I did think I was pretty smart."

"So, what is it?" I was still on the countertop and he was

standing in front of me as the light danced on the screen behind his head.

"What?"

"Your real name."

Cabeza shifted so that the features of his face were no longer visible against the screen's light, and his head was just a silhouette. "I'll tell you mine if you tell me yours," he said.

I thought it over. I'd told Cabeza things over the last few days I hadn't told anyone else. I leaned forward and whispered the three words into his ear. He didn't snicker; he didn't even suppress a laugh. He kissed me. It was the kind of kiss I'd been hoping for, though I hadn't really known I was hoping for him to kiss me until then. But it felt natural and inevitable, like the kiss to end a scene in any good black-and-white. It was full of a few days' longing.

He put his hands through my hair, "You're beautiful," he said.

"It's not kosher to kiss your rabbi," I said.

"Then I'm done being your rabbi." He put his hands beneath my thighs, and lifted me off the editing table. He carried me to the couch by the wall, and held me in his lap. I pulled away to touch his face, the soft stubble on his square chin. I knew I was getting into something it wouldn't be easy to back out of again. He stroked my hair for a moment, pushing it away from my eyes, and seemed to watch me think.

"No one gets to see this girl," he said. "The one behind the façade. She's pretty nice. Actually, she's terrific. How come you keep her all locked up?"

Now I kissed him.

"Wait one minute." He reached out and found the cord to the projector and yanked it from the wall. The whirring stopped and the light went out. The rest took place in darkness.

13

Crash Site

It was 3:30 a.m. and I was standing next to a grown man sucking on a pacifier. I'd freshened up at Cabeza's and arrived at Twilo right on time, but Blondie was already a half hour late.

I tapped my martini glass and lifted my chin at the bartender. He pointed at the sign above him that read POWER BAR. "Only energy drinks and protein shakes," he yelled above the din. I'd gotten my first drink upstairs. This was no kind of bar at all.

The pacifier-sucker had a long mop of green and yellow hair, a Mickey Mouse nose stud, and eyes glazed thicker than Krispy Kremes. His lips curled at a dancing girl in a glow necklace and a T-shirt that read CLUBBING IS NOT A CRIME.

Not for most people. I hadn't seen the inside of a nightclub since The Incident, and now it was like visiting the site of a hit and run where I'd been both the casualty and the driver. I was back there all over again, slumped over the steering wheel and every tendon ached. The strobe lights were paparazzi flashbulbs; the techno was the soundtrack of my shame. If Blondie didn't show soon and if I didn't get another martini, I'd find the door and use it the way I should've used it that fateful January night.

I'd looked for Blondie everywhere. I'd checked among the zonked-out carcasses on the stadium seating near the fire exits. He wasn't in the throbbing slo-mo dancing mass. A topless beefcake mounted the Power Bar and cleaned up with his washboard abs. That wasn't Blondie either.

"You see, *there* she is, I *knew* she'd come!" came a voice from behind me. I turned around to see Blondie swatting away the pacifier-sucker with the iridescent blue-green eye of a peacock feather. He was walking toward me from the dance floor, followed by a short brawny man with a shaved head and wire-frame glasses.

"Charles," Blondie gestured toward me with the peacock feather, coming so close he almost tapped me on the head. "*This* is Valerie Vane."

Charles came right at me for a quick study. "You're right, Gid, she is *so* much prettier in person," he declared, as if I weren't there. "Those tab shots make her look . . . well, I'll say it—pug-nosed. But, well, she's not at *all*. Her nose is lovely. And the hair. Outstanding. Very forties starlet, very throwback." Then he took my hand. "It's really a shame you didn't get better photos into the hands of the press agents. We have a friend who is an *outstanding* photographer. He's done everyone. Ivana, Monica, Imelda. You'd do well with him. Don't you think, Gid?"

"Oh, I agree. A better picture would've been better, soooo much better," Blondie said. "But I think David LaChapelle. He's done Amanda Lapore."

"You always disagree with me."

"I was agreeing!"

If these guys thought I'd arranged the Club Zero catfight as a photo-op, they were too dim even for the disco. I needed more than a refill. I needed to slosh knee-deep in gin. Blondie was pushing through the crowd in front of the Power Bar and waving some bills. Charles asked me if I needed anything and I told him two martinis. "One for the road."

"One for the road?" said Charles. "Oh, that's funny. One for the *road*. She's got a sense of humor." He was still talking about me in the third person, though we were alone. "She's not leaving already, is she?"

"She might be soon if she doesn't get a martini," I said.

Charles left me to convey the request to Blondie, who shouted back from his place at the bar, "Only virgin over here. Of course that doesn't apply!" He smiled at me and when I didn't smile back, he put a fistful of bills into Charles's hand and instructed him to go find a *bar* bar.

Blondie returned with a Red Bull and I hoped we'd get down to business now, and not clock any more of my snooze time. But I wasn't done with show-and-tell yet. "It *is,*" said a six-foot transvestite in six-inch heels to a midget on a leash. She was in a purple silk number that looked eerily similar to a Vera Wang I owned. He was wearing fur chaps and a mustache. "You know, we were just standing over there looking at you thinking, she is soooo familiar. And Tim said Valerie *Vane,* and I said *no,* and he said, *yes,* and I said, well, I haven't seen *her* face in the papers in *months*. I thought she'd *died* or maybe just *faded.* And which is worse? I'm Sharon Needles," she said, presenting her hand so I could kiss it. "And this is Tim."

I shook hers and then bent down for his, but he bared fake fangs.

"What a pleasure to have you at our club. Of course, it isn't *ours* but we've spent enough money here we might as well own shares," said Sharon with a lilting voice and a bobbing Adam's apple. She tittered at her own joke, putting two big fingers to her lips. "I'm glad to see that your days as a house-frau are over."

"They're not over," I said. "I'll be back in my muumuu soon. Just one night out to see Gideon here. He has something he needs to share with me." I turned toward him to make my point. "Then it's the La-Z-Boy for me."

"Well, then, this *is* special." Sharon looked at Blondie, who was grinning ear to ear like he'd just been crowned Ms.

Chelsea. "You're responsible for Valerie Vane's return? I'm impressed, Giddy." She grabbed Blondie and pulled him closer, looping her arm through his, giving a tug on Tim's chain. He barked. "What was your spot again? Club Zero? We don't like it there. Too many debutantes. The genuine article, not us tranny wannabe's."

I could already see where this was headed. Sharon wanted to get me reminiscing. The spotlights spun around our little klatch and the music boomed faster. "I'm here for work," I said as flatly as possible.

Sharon let her big blue eyelashes lie for a moment on her cheeks, like two butterflies resting on a mound. "Not very much fun anymore, are we?" she said. It was as if she'd put a quarter in a gumball machine and gotten the eraser. "Well, I hope you're at least doing a story on this party. It hasn't really started yet; it gets going around five. I'll take you up to the deejay booth to meet Jr. Vasquez. I can even get you Gatien. But, he's a little press-shy just now. You know, because of those kids who died. But you won't harp on that, I hope!"

Tim was licking Sharon's calf. Blondie stepped in. "Val's not doing a story on the party. I promised her a tidbit on the gallery. You know—" He gestured, a kind of pantomime in which an imaginary box exploded.

Sharon looked at him like he'd stolen the eraser. "The gallery, the gallery. It's all he ever wants to talk about." She sighed. "If I hear another Darla Deitrick story, I may just turn into a piece of art myself. Put a wire through my back and hang me on a wall!" She looked down at Tim and shook him off her leg. "Down, boy." I imagined a pretty domestic scene with the two of them. Sharon in the tub rubbing lavender soap into her size thirteen feet, and Tim in his doggy bed, mewling. Sharon looked back at me, this time right into my eyes. "Say it once?" she said.

"Say what?"

"Don't you know who I am?" Sharon said. "A command performance?"

Tim barked and panted. Here it was all over again, every gut-wrenching headline. I hated Blondie for it. "Enough," I told him. "I don't parrot myself in exchange for tidbits. If you have something to say, you say it, or I'm gone." I started to back way.

"Please, no, Valerie. What I have to say is important. Just one minute." He made nice with Sharon using some words I didn't hear, and she harrumphed. She tugged Tim's leash and off they went, like a six-foot girl and his dog.

"Sorry," Blondie said. "I had no idea they were going to put you on the spot like that. It's just, well, they're fans. We're all fans."

I took a deep breath. Maybe I'd been too hard on Blondie. He probably didn't know how far he'd already pushed by asking to meet at a nightclub.

Charles returned with my martinis. Blondie dispatched him after the dynamic duo. Then Blondie said, "This way." I double-fisted my martinis and followed him down a black corridor flashing with lights and into a lounge. The room was small but Blondie and I found a corner that was darker than the dance floor and even less comfy.

"First off, I'm not working for Style anymore," I said.

Blondie glanced up from his Red Bull. "I figured that when I called your office and they put me through to the obituary desk. That doesn't sound very cheerful," he said. Blondie's freckles looked like perforations in his skin under the black light. His face reminded me of a strainer.

"Then why did you still want to meet me?" I started in on my second martini.

Blondie dropped his eyes. "Before I say anything, I really need to make something clear." He looked at me plaintively. "I went to work for Darla because I really respected her. The way she got her start? A lot of people think all art dealers are just rich kids who dabble. Not Darla. She was from outside Cleveland. Her father is a plumber—don't tell anyone I told you, she'd kill me! Her mother is the 'Muffin Maiden of Smith Street.' No joke. She makes six hundred types of muffins. And we're not talking blueberry, here. Mushroom muffin, celery muffin. Bubble gum muffin! I kid you not."

"Muffins. Got it."

"Okay, she went to prep school, but Darla is basically a midwestern girl. She comes to New York after paying her own way through two years at RISD. She has no money. She has no backers. She has a recipe for Parmesan muffins and her charisma. That's it. She opens her SoHo gallery dealing in unknown artists and—wham!—she's a superstar, a wonder girl. I studied her in *college*. My art history prof had a *crush* on Darla Deitrick."

Blondie was about to give me something. He just had to pay penance first. I drained my martini glass. Sharon and her Chihuahua were already becoming a memory.

"You see, I really admired her. But I've seen certain things—things you wouldn't believe. And I don't think it's right. I mean, even in this business, which is full of sharks, I mean obviously. I just think it isn't right."

We were interrupted by the sensation of someone hovering over us. Dear old Charles. "I have a little something!"

Blondie looked up, right into the black light, and his eyes glowed demonic. "Honeeeeey," he said, as if he were spreading it on toast. "You've had your Valerie time. Can't we just have a *minute*?"

Charles bowed his head and held out his palm. In it were two tabs of Ecstasy. Blondie perked up. He grabbed one, popped it, and then offered me the other. I shook my head. Charles shrugged and took it himself. He held up two fingers—a peace sign—and said, "Number Two! Anything else I can get for you girls?"

I held up my two martini glasses. "How about some refills?" I didn't necessarily want more now, I just wanted to get him gone. Now that Blondie had popped the pill, we were on a clock. I knew that in a half hour or less, he'd be rolling. Then he'd be as useful to me as a headless mop. "You've said your Hail Marys," I said. "Let's hear it."

Blondie moved closer. "Those paintings by that graffiti guy? The ones you asked Darla about? She had them. I saw them in her storage facility, at least until a couple of weeks ago." Now here was something. I looked into Blondie's strainer and I wondered how well it would leak. "There were a lot by that Stain, but that wasn't all. There were all kinds of graffiti paintings back there. Anyway, she was trying to empty out the space so she could close it down."

I asked Blondie why Darla was unloading. He moved closer still.

"She's brilliant in so many ways, like I said, but arithmetic is not her strong suit." He shook his head sadly. "Not her strong suit. It's gotten a little tight at the gallery. And Darla needs cash. There's a Pollock on the market that David Geffen would kill for, and she's been dying to sell him something . . . but I don't need to get into that."

I would've wanted to hear all about it, but I saw sands spilling through an Ecstasy-shaped hourglass. "How many pieces are in the storage space?"

"A couple hundred. Very old work. Some of it she'd taken to sell on consignment maybe thirty years ago. Most of it not worth anything. She asked me to do the inventory. It was just internal—I wasn't supposed to show anybody except Darla. There were probably about ten or fifteen by your friend. I know he was very famous once, but he dropped out of the art world, you know, without croaking, and his market took a dive."

I was fuzzy on math myself, and to begin with, I didn't know how all this worked. "Back up," I said. "Work artists had given her to sell on consignment?"

"Yes, 'consignment.' That means she had promised to sell them, but she didn't own them outright. Like I said, they'd been in storage for maybe twenty, thirty years. I guess she just hadn't sold them and no one had ever come to claim them. They all had different stories. They were mostly unknown artists of no account, except the Stains."

I was starting to settle into my seat. The martinis were helping, but I was also glad about Blondie. He hadn't asked me here just to parade me around like a well-groomed hen at a 4-H fair. "So, does she still have them?"

Blondie thought about it a second.

"I saw a few of them in the viewing room. Darla was shopping them around. She was very aggravated because they were a hard sell. Nobody on the street wanted them. She kept walking around the gallery yelling, 'Crap, crappity, crap, crap, crap.' And of course, once she finally found a buyer and finalized the transaction, Stain comes around asking about them, wanting them back for some reason."

"Do you know who bought them?"

"No," he said. "Could've been more than one person. But probably not too many. The transactions didn't happen during regular business hours. I know that much."

"But you know they were sold?"

Charles was upon us again. He'd returned with my martinis, holding the glasses out to me like twin trophies. "Thank you sooooo much," Blondie whined. "*Kissy, kissy*. Big hug! We just need another teeny weenie minute. Okay, honey?"

Charles pouted for a second, then blew an air kiss like Jackie O and backed away. I picked up one of the martinis and decided against it. This was too good. I needed all my faculties. "What did Darla say to Wallace when he asked about them?"

"I didn't hear that part, either. All I know is after that I went into the inventory log and found she'd erased my notes and penciled in new ones. She had put in the word *sold* next to a few paintings. But in at least a couple of spots I could see that a longer word—*consignment*—had been sort of half-erased."

Definitely something. Even if I didn't quite understand what kind of something it might be.

"The next day, she asks me to take a bunch of stretchers over to the warehouse," he continued. "A truckload, actually. I didn't think much of it at the time. We sometimes stock up on canvases for our artists. But it was odd, considering that Darla was so keen on getting rid of that space."

"Blank canvases? You sure they weren't just white?"

He showed me the whites of his eyes again. "Anyway, there was a fire at the warehouse on Sunday night. The storage space was destroyed and so was everything in it. It could've been a fluke. A bunch of other art dealers had stuff down there too. I don't know if was an accident or—"

This was getting better every minute. "Arson?" I said. "Did she file a claim?"

"I believe so. She told me she thought Wallace might've been responsible. He or some of his goons—that's what she called them. But I don't know. I didn't think that sounded right. That guy wasn't like that. And I mean, I love Darla, but I've seen the way she manages things, and I wouldn't put it past her to, well— Do you see what I'm saying?"

"Sure, I do." I could see the scenario he was suggesting. Darla secretly sells the art, covers her tracks by replacing the works with fakes, and then attempts to cash in on the insurance. It was shaping up to be a pretty exciting club night. Maybe I'd pose for a photo op with his Charles after all.

"A fire. Sunday night."

"Yes."

"The night Malcolm Wallace got dead?"

"I thought he died this week."

"He did."

"No, then. A week ago. A week before Wallace died."

A group of men had formed a daisy chain, rabbit hopping through the lounge. "I'm dancing on the head of a pin," shouted one on tiptoe. "On the head of a pin!"

"Might he have seen something? Might Darla have wanted him out of the way?"

"It's possible." Blondie tented his fingers in his lap and looked down. He might've been praying, but I didn't think so. Maybe he was starting to feel the effects of the Ecstasy. If so, my time was expiring.

"You say that Darla kept these inventory books? Why would she do that if she was up to something criminal?"

"Two sets of books," he said. "There was another set of books for official purposes. You know, auditors and so forth. We get audited about once every four years. I think that's a bad idea—highly suspicious, to begin with—and I've told her so. And simple math, not her forte."

This was the kind of detail I could've easily turned into a transparent blind item at *Gotham's Gate*: *"Why does a certain red-haired gallerist keep one business ledger by her door and another in her closet? Only her former clients can guess."* At The Paper, I couldn't do anything with it. It had way too many holes, like Blondie's face.

"Where does she keep the second set of books?"

"In the safe, of course."

"Do you know the combination?"

Blondie hesitated. "No. Darla likes me, but not that much."

I thought that over. Was there a way for me to get to those books? Could I ask Blondie to try to find out the combination? That would be putting him at risk, but then, he had already put himself at risk by meeting with me. What was his angle, if not to show me off to his pals? Without my asking, he answered.

"Are you still in touch with Jeremiah?" The name jolted me out of the calm I was starting to feel there in the dark. What he wants is his tabloid fix. Only I didn't have anything to offer him, because I'd been detoxing for six months. "No," I said. "The last time we talked was when I gave him the keys to my loft and he moved in with that woman."

"I know all about that," said Blondie, showing me his glowing teeth. "She's still living there, of course, but he's not."

"No?"

Blondie's eyes lit up. "You don't know? You haven't read about it?"

"I don't read anymore."

He turned this over in his mind. "You've missed some juicy news, Valerie. Your buddies have split. Jeremiah had to replace Angelica in the role of Angelica in *Terror in the City*. You heard about that?"

I shook my head.

"Cast and crew agreed: VJ is no Meryl Streep. She floated right to the top of the tank, like a dead goldfish. Jeremiah replaced her with this lovely young ingenue, Claire something, and about a week into shooting Angelica finds the two of them going at it on some medical gurney. She sued him for breach of contract—both ways, movie and marriage."

This was juicy news. I was glad for it. But I didn't ask for more, lest I start to drool. Luckily, Blondie didn't need any encouragement.

"She really got her claws in. She went after him with about sixteen lawyers. She exposed him as a blow fiend and a philanderer—great stuff! She even turned in his stash and gave the NYPD the name of his dealer, Ken something or other. Now he's going to be broke too. His town house is already on the market;

he even came in to Darla's to try to sell his paintings. You have to be pretty bad off to try to sell art to pay legal fees."

I remembered the canvases up in his attic. All those paintings he'd acquired over the years from trendy artists. "Did he sell Darla his Warhol?"

"No, that already went. Gagosian bought it and a few other little items. Jeremiah collected a lot, but a lot of junk, actually. He didn't have a very good eye. Not from what I saw, anyway."

I liked that too. I wanted to ask Blondie a few more questions about Jeremiah, but his face had started to change in subtle ways. His eyes got a little watery. I could see he was swallowing a lot and grinding his teeth.

"I'm just thinking about that guy, Malcolm Wallace," Blondie said. "Your friend who died. He was bothering Darla, but I thought he was cute. You know? To think that he's dead, that maybe he died because of . . ."

"We don't know anything," I said. "Could be totally unconnected. Everything's just speculation at this point." The words made me feel authoritative.

"It's just so incredibly sad," he said, reaching out to take my hand. "I can't believe how sad that is. Wow, your hands are *really* soft. It feels so nice to touch you. Do you mind if I touch your elbow? I love elbows. That sack of saggy skin?"

Blondie was already rolling. I patted him on the shoulder and told him I'd go find him his Charles. I took my elbow with me.

I slipped out of Twilo across a row of slick naked pecs. It was after five and a new round of club kids formed a line up the block. Yellow cabs hovered like hornets. A girl fell headfirst from a cab. She seemed to want to share a secret with the asphalt. Horns blared. Fists raised. She kept right on blathering.

I love this dirty town, I thought, channeling J. J. Hunsecker.

I checked the lineup and didn't notice any of the usual suspects. No Sidney Falcos, no Night Rewrite boys, no socialite shutterbugs likely to call in a scoop. It was a clear night. I breathed in the fresh air. The martinis were starting to wear off. I went west.

On Eleventh Avenue hookers were fishing fares at the one-hour hotels. Hairy lugs in leather chaps trolled the cowboy bars. A cluster of teenyboppers squealed as they dodged traffic across the West Side Highway. I turned north, thinking I'd hail a cab once I escaped club land.

It was another muggy night, but a breeze was blowing off the water. I could feel it cooling my neck, drying the sweat off my back. At this hour, most of Twelfth Avenue was shut up tight, heavy metal grates over storefronts.

As I walked, I read the words painted onto the dingy metal, quick scrawls in cursive, letters packed tight: IKE, MIX, Marty & Shawn 4-Ever, PEEK. Three-d letters, EZ, ROT, SNUFF. Names so jazzed with motion they couldn't be read. On one grate, I could see the edges of lettering, but I couldn't make out the word. I backed up to the curb but still couldn't read it, so I backed up some more. Using what Kamal and Cabeza had taught me, I finally saw it. "Seen," I read aloud. Seen, I thought, as I walked on, picking up speed. That's right, you are.

I crossed the West Side highway to get a better view of the building. I looked up to the rooftops, the white roller letters COST/REVS, a giant name all full of stars and arrows, DOZE. A big name, NATO, sprawled across a wall. Further up, a huge name painted in black and white across roll-down riot gates: ESPO.

The more I looked, the more I saw. Names were everywhere, all over like roaches in a New York kitchen when suddenly there's light. As I walked up Twelfth Avenue, I looked down and saw stencils on the sidewalk, a flower missing petals, a laughing face.

There were stickers on the phone posts: HELLO, MY NAME IS . . . ROY and HELLO MY NAME IS . . . BINGO."

Names scrawled TYRE, tiny illegible scribbles, ergem, ttuffu, big bubble letters, SPY, outlines, jottings, Guru, Anow, doodles, TIE, paint on trucks, JIZ, NST, mailboxes, HC, SIC, stickers plastered on doors, HELLO, MY NAME IS . . . Bigga, scratchiti EXEXEX, a face with crossed out eyes, KAWS, a face in superhero mask, ROACH, loose petals, SIN, AOA, green horse, WOE, a man from Mars, TAR, Aerub Ketsu, Heller, RAE, a white screw, TWIST, letters in circles W, G, letters swinging, letters dancing, KIZA, JRC, a sneaker, VEG, HELLO, MY NAME IS . . . METAPHOR."

Graffiti was dead now that it wasn't on trains? That's what they'd said, and that's what I'd thought. I'd lived in Manhattan for almost five years, and I'd never seen what was everywhere—the writing on the walls. There were anonymous strangers tagging, jotting, scrawling their names for all the city to read. Hieroglyphics, everywhere, signals, signs. In Times Square they turned neon, they turned massive, they were blocks of names in the sky. "Don't you know who I am?" they cried out. "Don't you know who I am?"

My feet chewed up the pavement for a long time and I kept looking until my eyes got weary. I thought about Wallace and I knew that he'd been killed. I didn't know by who or how. But I knew I'd gotten the suicide thing wrong and I regretted it. I thought about what Blondie had given me and where I could take it. I thought about Cabeza and what he wanted from me and Darla and what she wanted from Wallace. I thought about it all while noting the markings, glyphs, jots everywhere, as if the walls were griots telling stories, inchoate texts I had to decipher and reorder from beginning to end. And soon enough, I'd walked myself all the way back to the Upper West Side.

On West Eightieth Street, I looked down Broadway back the way I'd come. It had been a long walk, but I'd hoofed it. And now a band of pale pink light was pushing up the black curtain of night. I wasn't in a hurry to go in. I lingered there for a moment. It was nice, at last, to see a sober dawn.

14

Memorial Wall

I slept the next day until noon. It was an old habit with new charms. I didn't have a headache. I didn't have to harvest cotton from my teeth. Outside my window, some chirping birds sounded like Mozart.

In the bathroom mirror, I looked at my face. It wasn't red and beaten. There were no rings under my eyes. I went to the kitchen and turned on the coffee maker. I cracked some eggs. I toasted toast and drank a little coffee. I didn't need coffee, but I liked the way it went down with my toast.

I looked out the window over the top of the roaring A/C. Across Broadway my good neighbors, the people of New York, were walking with bags of bagels from H&H, picking up their gravlax and Gouda at Zabar's, stopping at the corner kiosk to browse half-price books. There was something comforting about the diurnal life of the Upper West Side, like one of those old-time ten-cent dioramas; slip a coin into the slot and a whole miniature circus lights up and winds into action.

I got dressed in a breezy blouse and jeans and put in a call to Cabeza, telling him I wanted to see the Bigs Cru about Wallace. He said he'd facilitate, and about five minutes later he phoned back. "You're set," he said, telling me where to find them. "They'll be expecting you."

Downstairs, I bought myself another cup of coffee at Zabar's takeout. I didn't need that one either. It just tasted good. I stopped in at H&H to smell the hot bagels, dropping a quarter in the palm of the panhandler outside the door. Maybe I wasn't any richer than yesterday, but I felt like I could spare a few coins for my fellow man. I walked downtown to Seventy-ninth Street to catch the 1/9 subway. The train came in a few minutes, and I hopped on, singing a little tune, *"Con los pobres soy, noble soy."*

The first thing I saw as I descended the stairway from the elevated stop at 207th Street was Stain. Not the man, but the mug. He loomed large in black and white on the sidewall at Diaz Pizzeria, chin to brow, ear to ear. It was the face I'd seen now in so many photos, outlined in Magic Marker, blown up five hundred–fold. He was smiling just the same way as he had in Cabeza's flick, that huge grin like a kindling fire burning up through his face. But this was an older Stain than the one with the peach fuzz; this was a man in his early forties, with age in his eyes, wrinkles fanning out to his temples. It hit me then, powerful and sad, that this would be the closest I'd get to a present-day likeness. The background was already painted blue, and around his head was a giant gold halo, just like in a portrait of a medieval saint.

Bigs Cru was there, too: Clu standing on a scaffold, painting, Wicked Rick, below him on the pavement, and Rx sitting on the sidewalk, his back against the wall. Clu was in the center of Wallace's eye. He was holding Stain's portrait in a frame and painting the outlines of the pupil in black. Then he traded cans, switching to brown to make the lighter circles of the iris; the pavement underneath him was littered with used cans and a couple of milk crates were already full of empties.

Wicked Rick was near the curb, his back to me, looking at something on a piece of white paper. At the curb, a couple of teenagers sat on a tarp, hunkered over an artist's black book. "He's got *mad* skills," one of them was saying. "Look at that arrow, yo." The other one answered, "It's too purrrrty. I like it loose."

"Reporter lady," said Rx, from the pavement, where he was rolling a cigarette, or possibly a blunt, his long thin legs sprawled out across the macadam. He was glaring up at me, like a cat that never got petted as a kitten and now should never be petted at all.

Clu turned around and gave me the once-over. "You're the one who came up for the memorial, right?"

"I am," I said, hoping they'd have forgotten my disappearing act.

Clu nodded ever so slightly, then turned back to the wall as Wicked Rick walked over and took my hand. "We heard you might be on your way," he said, giving me a big, honest shake. "Welcome." He was wearing a FUBU Athletics tank top, showing off two shoulder tattoos—a Raphael-style cherub on one and a Tasmanian devil wielding a spray can on the other.

Rx made an audible noise of disapproval, like a *tsk*, and it was drowned out by the louder and longer hiss of Clu's spray can. Wicked Rick flinched his shoulders ever so slightly as if to shrug off Rx's *tsk*. The dust of Clu's spray paint drifted near us like a cloud; it smelled like rubbing alcohol and burned plastic.

"I hope I'm not coming at a bad time," I said. "I wanted to ask you a few questions about some graffiti writers you might know."

Rx perked up again, straightening against the wall. He threw some of the empties into the milk crates, making a loud clank. "You going to print their names and addresses in the paper? How about mug shots? You want those too?" Rx said.

"Yo, chill," Wicked Rick said to Rx. They obviously weren't in agreement about whether they should talk to me, and I knew exactly who was making which case.

I tried to speak to both of them, in an even tone, at the same time. "I've just discovered some information about Wallace's paintings that you might all find interesting."

It was as if Rx didn't hear. "You ran out of that memorial pretty fast. You could've just told us you were from that paper and why you were really there."

Rick shook his head in annoyance and turned to face Rx. "Let it be, now. We already went over this."

"You did," Rx said back. "Nobody made up my mind."

Wicked Rick crossed his arms. "We have to keep trying," he said to Rx, gently. "We can't just say no, when someone wants to help. Cabeza might be right. You don't know. The police haven't done nothing. They came up here asking us about the Young Lords. They think it was some kind of gang beef."

"Listen," I said, trying to clear my throat. "I made a mistake there, at the memorial. I may have made a mistake on the story—"

"*May* have?" said Rx.

Clu's spray can hiss-hissssssssed.

"I did," I said, with the most assured voice I could find. "Definitely, I did. And this is my opportunity to try to make it right. I should've been honest at the memorial too. But I was scared. You see, I have to convince my editors to do another story, and I need to get enough information together to justify—"

"To *justify*? Are you shitting me?" Rx stood up. I took a step back, unsure of where this was going. "Oh, I'm not going to hurt you, reporter lady, you've got plenty more trouble in store for you—believe it. But if these dumb asses are willing to trust you with anything other than Wite-Out, they making a big mistake, far as I can see." He looked from Rick to Clu, hoping to convince them yet. Clu shrugged ever so slightly and Rick looked blankly at Rx. "Ah-ight. I want no part." Rx picked up his jacket off the ground and threw it over his shoulder. He shook his head slowly as he walked past me. He sized me up one more time and still didn't like what he saw. Then he was off. The two teenagers with the black book got up and followed him.

Clu picked up a new can of Rust-Oleum and turned back to the wall, rattling it up without saying anything. Clink, clink, clink clink—the marble inside the bottle sounded like ringing for alms. He pressed the paint cap and his spray can hiss-hissed.

"Some people are very angry about what happened with your paper," Rick said after a while. "I know how he feels, and he's my blood, so I've got his back, but we just disagree. Your friend, Cabeza, makes a good point. Some more press on this, I think, could help set the record straight."

Clu just hissed on above us, creating small clouds of aerosol dust that drifted past us one after another. He placed a white asterisk at the center of Stain's pupil, and a white cloud drifted. He put a line of pink at the edge of Stain's lips, and a pink cloud drifted. I sensed I was getting covered in it; the smell was dense, acidic. I raised my hand to cover my nose and realized it was shaking, so I tried to put it into my pocket, which didn't exist.

"Here's the outline, in case you're interested," said Rick, handing me what he was holding: a computer printout of the image for the wall as it would look when all the colors were added. Next to Stain's face was the outline of a spray can, which looked as if it had been stepped on and crushed. It spewed letters from its tiny white cap: *R.I.P.* On the other side of the wall were gray tombstones that elongated into three subway trains spreading out into the distance, over a hill and into a city skyline. Wicked Rick said, "We'll try and give you what you need."

"I appreciate it. I do." I took out my notepad, mostly to have something to do with my hands. "You know his old dealer, Darla Deitrick?" I started. Rick nodded. "It turns out she had a lot of graffiti in her warehouse, by some writers who were Stain's contemporaries. Writers I think you'd know. There was a fire at this warehouse and the paintings were lost. It's possible she sold them and maybe the fire happened afterward. I'd like to follow up with these writers. I'd also like to understand what kinds of beefs or gang wars or anything else might have been a contributing factor to Stain's death."

Clu's hissing stopped and he dropped his can onto the pavement with a heavy clunk. He and Rick looked at each other. Rick went to retrieve the can, which was rolling to the curb. "You sure you know what you're getting into?" Clu said. Since he was a man of few words, I didn't take these words lightly. "You sure you're not in over your head? I don't mean any disrespect, but it won't be tea and crumpets."

Rick returned with the empty can and dropped it in one of the milk crates, saying, "Listen, I know you're trying to do your best, but there are some basic things you need to understand. It's not like the old days on the trains when the most graff writers would get was a fine or community service. These days, writers who get caught get jail time. Writing is now a felony offense. Most writers working today, out on the street, don't want anyone to know their names, even if they could get something out of it."

Clu rattled up another can, this one hard and fast, clink clink clink clink. Rick took my arm and led me to the curb. "You need to understand," he said again, "graffiti writers aren't gang members or violent criminals or anything most people think. Maybe a handful, okay? But for most of us, being a writer means being recognized as a solo. An independent somebody with no Crips or Bloods on your back. You see? You write so you don't get mixed up in all that. Number two: my crew, the three of us, we all go way back to the beginning of this thing—twenty-five years in the game and I never heard of no graffiti artist getting killed over a beef. Not ever. I'm not saying there hasn't been friction or there haven't been baseball bats thrown one way or another . . . but killed? Knocked off a bridge after midnight? Floating in the East River? That's some sad shit right there. Ain't none of us ever been so petty to go that far over a buff."

"There's something I need to tell you and it might be a little shocking," I said. "And it seems to me like it might indicate that what you're saying isn't always true. When they found Wallace's body, there was purple spray paint in his mouth."

Rick reeled a little. "No shit?" He thought it over. "How'd you hear that?"

I didn't want to tell him I'd gotten it from Cabeza. I wanted him to think I had sources all over. "I can't say. Doesn't that sound to you like it might be linked to graffiti? Is there anyone who would want to see Stain dead?"

He didn't seem impressed. "No. What it sounds like to me? Somebody's trying to set somebody up. Cover up somehow. I don't know. Now you got me all mixed up. You say Darla Deitrick still owned work by other graffiti artists? Malcolm was looking for those. He told me they were missing too."

"Yes, that's what I heard."

Rick walked down the curb away from me and covered his forehead with his hand. Clu was still hissing paint onto the wall behind us. Stain's face was starting to have more definition, more contoured edges, deeper shadows in his cheeks. I looked at the computer printout Rick had given me. All the cars were covered in graffiti scrawls. One gravestone read, "Malcolm Wallace, 1957–1999," and two others read, "Writing is a crime; the crime is insubordination." Dead center of the wall, underneath Wallace's mug, was his name, big letters, written in the signature style I'd seen in Cabeza's movie.

"You want to know who would want to see Stain dead?" Rick came back. "Maybe half the cops in the Bronx precincts. Maybe about a third of the force in other boroughs, and a whole lot of moms and pops too, because Malcolm liked to agitate. He liked the fact that graffiti would trip up the cops, would make them get angry—dumb angry. He believed in counterculture in the original sense. His art schools weren't about painting pretty landscapes. He wasn't training kids to do what we do—to paint on legal walls, with the permission of the storeowner, out here in broad daylight. He was trying to create an army of bad asses who would get out there and terrorize the powers that be, in the old style. Not with violence, but by putting their marks on the city in a way the city couldn't handle. Remind folks that everything isn't all so perfect. He said, 'Wherever people are neglected and ignored, that's a place where writing lives. That's what graff is about.' That was Malcolm."

I could see he was agitated. He chose a can of red Rust-Oleum from the duffle bag and, shaking it, clink clink clink clink, went to the wall. Then he started spraying the *S* of Stain's name onto the wall, a giant bold letter, letting the emotion out through his arm. He shook the can out again, faster, clink clink, and then hissed new paint, the red hitting the wall, one layer over another as the wet paint dripped and the dust of the aerosol filled the air like a million microscopic gnats. My nose filled with its acrid perfume until I sneezed.

"A lot of people didn't like Stain's philosophy," Rick continued. "But I respected the man. I think what he said was right and the more I think about it now that he's gone the more I think he was dead on. Our communities have been ignored too long. This so-called boom that's happening, we don't see it. How come our subways don't get renovated? How come our parks are still full of dealers? That's not true in Manhattan; down there, it's all squeaky," he made the sound of a window cleaner. "Is that right? Do you think that's the way it should be?"

Wicked Rick's can hissed and hissed, joining the sound of Clu's hissing above, like two instruments in duet. He continued on with the *T,* making long strokes up and down, then side to side. The red paint dripped where it went on thickest, as if the wall were sweating blood.

"You want to try it?" he said.

"What?"

"You want to write a letter of Stain's name?"

I took a step back. "Oh, no, I can't draw a line. I'd . . . I'd mess it up."

He handed me the can. "You can do it," he said. "It's not tough. You just need to keep your hand steady. You can do that, right?"

"Sure, I can, but I . . ."

Clu looked down from the scaffolding to watch, slightly bemused.

"Shake it," said Rick. I did, just as fast as he had before. Clink clink clink clink. The can was cold and heavier than I'd anticipated. I felt the marble somewhere in the bottle knocking back and forth. "Aim the mouth at the wall and stay within the lines. Ever paint your bicycle? Just keep a steady hand."

I positioned the can over the outlined A and pressed down on the paint cap. I heard the satisfying hiss and the tip of my index finger went cold and wet and even a little numb. I did as Rick said and kept within the lines. I finished the letter and stepped back from the wall. I hadn't made a perfect letter A, but it wasn't a disaster. I gave the paint can back to Rick and he cleaned up the edges.

"You ever seen someone paint a memorial wall before?" Rick asked.

"No," I said. "I don't think so."

"We've done them all over the city. We get all kinds of commissions for them, mostly when a body dies young, someone gets shot, gets AIDS. We make a wall and it stays there so people can come by and pay their respects. It's like an epitaph of this person's life. It's for the community."

I was reminded of what Cabeza had said about all the graffiti writers he'd known, how few of them were still alive, how many were in jail or dead. Clu and Wicked Rick were in their forties and still alive, and working, maybe some of the last survivors of the early years of subway art. They'd done it by painting legal murals on sanctioned walls with commissions from corporations. I glanced around, wondering if there were snipers on the elevated subway platform, if any of the passing low-riders could be drive-bys. Did these guys have targets on their backs?

Rick continued painting the *I* and the *N*, using up a can of paint and tossing it to the base of the wall with the other empties. Then he picked up a can of pink paint, accenting the edges of the letters. And after that, he used a can of white, miraculously making the letters pop out into three-dimensional space. I saw now that the *T* was painted as a crucifix.

"This right here," he said, pointing to the words *Graffiti is a crime; the crime is insubordination*. "It was one of Stain's slogans. He didn't want his students to be co-opted by galleries like he'd been. He wanted them to keep graff on the streets, to use it as a tool. 'A tactic to overthrow the ruling class,' he said. He wanted that to be his legacy, but he saw what was coming down those tracks at him. He knew about that fire, the one you're talking about. He told me he thought someone would try to pin it on him."

Rick stopped and looked up at Clu for confirmation of something. Clu was like his silent conscience. "At the time, when he was talking about it, I didn't take it serious. Malcolm talked a lot of shit sometimes and some of it was just jaw flapping. I'll tell you what; now I wish I'd taken it more serious."

Rick picked up Krylon Slate Gray and started painting the width of the tombstone subway train. It sounded like a lot of people didn't listen when Wallace talked. How come? Boy who cried wolf? Or maybe he saw too many wolves. "He thought he was in danger?"

Rick backed away from the wall, assessing the work he'd done on the tombstones. "You know what's messed up?" he said. "He asked us to do his wall. We'd been out of touch for a while because he was pissed we'd taken a commission from Glenfiddich; he always gave us grief about liquor ads. But last week, we were down on 138th Street working on the wall and he came by to watch. I thought he was joking around, maybe to show all was forgiven, and he was like 'Yo, when I die, I want you to do my wall.' "

"Hand me that Tuscan Sunset, will you, man?" Clu called down from the scaffolding.

Wicked Rick rummaged through a duffel bag. "Don't see it. How about Saddle Tan?"

"No, man. The Tuscan Sunset. I know we brought it. I put it in there myself."

He searched around some more. "Oh, here it is. Here you go," Wicked Rick said, passing the brown-topped can up to Clu. "You remember that?" he said, looking up to Clu. "A couple of weeks ago? We're all hanging out joking around, 'blah, blah, blah,' and he was talking something about the new space, how he hoped some of the kids would take it over, now that the mortgage was done. I said, 'Don't get all morose, now, man.' But he kept asking me about his wall; he wanted me to say it out loud, that we'd promise. I kidded him on it for a while then finally I said, 'Right, yo. Who else would do your wall? Nobody else around here can even *stand* you.' "

Rick laughed a few notes before his chin dropped to his chest. He seemed to be watching something invisible snake its way through the pavement. He scratched his neck and the Tasmanian devil squirmed.

He and Clu made eye contact. "Two weeks," Clu said.

"He was expecting something to happen to him?" I asked.

"Maybe not. Maybe it's just a coincidence. I don't know what people know," Wicked Rick said. "We once knew a guy named Tommy Buffo from the neighborhood. You remember him, Clu? He went and shut down his whole T-shirt factory one day and asked us if we'd do his wall. Then a week later, heart attack.

Boom. Gone. Couldn't have known it was coming, could he? Not possible, right? But then, he's dead. Just like that. Got everything squared away. How do you make sense of that?"

"It's no good to try," said Clu, softly. "Some people just know shit."

"Maybe Stain knew something," Rick said to me. "Maybe he thought he was being set up. Maybe it had nothing to do with that Chelsea gallery or anything. I had a dream once that Ruff came after me—another graffiti kid, thought I was buffing him, but I wasn't. After that dream, I was pretty sure for a week there was going to be a memorial wall for me."

We stood around in silence for a while. It was hard to look at Wallace's face, up so close, so large, without feeling sad that I'd never gotten to meet the man in person. I asked Clu if I could look at the portrait he was using to paint the face. He handed it down, wordlessly.

"What did Wallace have against what you do?" I asked Rick, looking at the color photo of Wallace in a gold frame.

Rick laughed. "Ha. Everything. He used to say, 'You're complicit with our oppressors, man.' But we go way back. We had real love."

Though I'd looked at a lot of pictures of Stain, I still wanted to keep looking. There was something behind those heavy-lidded eyes that seemed to have the answer to something. In the new picture, I saw a mature man, one who had lived through disappointments, and who now knew how to take them. He had the eyes of a father with sons that are getting into the same kind of trouble he used to get into. This Wallace, just before he died, looked to me like a responsible man, a trustworthy type. Not at all the rabble-rouser Rick described.

"So, what are you going to be able to do for us?" Rick said. "You going to be able to get this into your paper? You have enough to go on?"

I told Rick the outlines of my plan: I didn't have answers yet. But I had enough good questions to warrant investigation and usually that was good enough for an editor to give the go-ahead. Then I could really start sniffing around, even on company time. I could ask some cop-shop reporters for backup. My working title: "The Bronx Burns All Over Again"; the story would be about the fire at the Darla Deitrick warehouse wiping out eighties art by Bronx artists, how that incensed Stain, and how maybe he'd been pestering Darla about the pictures, just before he got dead. "If I'm right about my hunches," I told Rick, "I could probably report it out all the way to the murder. I'm not saying I know who was responsible, but this at least gives me a chance to try and find out."

There it was, the word *murder.* It was the first time I'd said it with the conviction that I could make it stick. Rick didn't flinch. It seemed to confirm to him that I could be trusted. "Here," he said, dumping the spray cans out of two milk crates and dragging the crates to the curb. "Let's sit a minute and talk this through. You want me to get you a Coke from Diaz or something? How about a slice?"

15

Vanitas

I was looking at Buzz Phipps's BMW face. It was parked next to a gleaming SUV known as Molly Blossom, the chatelaine of Style, or what she still called the Ladies' Desk. She managed the house, kept the books, did the matchmaking, and saw to it that the wedding page included at least one Smith College graduate each month. Women all over Manhattan would've handed over their firstborn to get into her nuptials column.

I'd followed Buzz up the central staircase, through a narrow hallway just past the fourth-floor elevator bank. I wanted to get him alone to have a chance to lay out the whole pitch, just as I'd worked it up with Wicked Rick, something with a big sweep, a long timeline. Buzz had always liked stories that reached.

Molly departed and I figured I'd pounce. I took a deep breath and went over my pitch once again: If graffiti is passé, why is one of New York's hottest dealers moving so many pieces of it around behind the scenes? Someone's buying. It would be a who's who of the Bronx's artistic culture past and present. That's right. I'd just about screwed up my courage when I got to Buzz's desk and saw that he was occupied with Tracy Newton.

"Now, right here, you'll want to get a quote from Chef Le Touffé," he was telling her. "And I want you to put in his real name too. What is it again? Leonard Schwartz? Got to love it! And see if you can get him to say which investment bankers were drinking the Bordeaux. Was this one of those twenty-eight-thousand-dollar wine tabs? Get the figures. Someone's got receipts."

"Well, look who it is. Valerie Vane!" said Tracy, in a tinny screech that the entire Style room couldn't fail to hear. "What a surprise!" She was reclined in Buzz's swivel chair at his desk, a nail file balanced between her two index fingers. Buzz didn't give me a double-cheeked kiss. He didn't usher Tracy out of his seat and offer it to me. Instead, he looked nervous as the room erupted in twittering. A line of stilettoed legs uncrossed and then crossed again all at once, like Rockettes.

The fashionistas in Style weren't on par with the girls at *Vogue, Glamour,* and *Vanity Fair,* our doppelgangers at the Condé Nast magazine empire just across the street. The Conde Nasties. The Paper's Style reporters made half as much, worked twice as hard, and weren't quite as pretty—hips a little too hippy, forearms a little too hairy, noses a little too nosey. As a result, they were all a little grim and a little mean.

"Hi, Tracy," I said. "Nice to see you again."

"I've been meaning to come downstairs and say hello," she said, cheerfully, in the manner of an overscheduled homemaker. "You're one of the *serious* reporters now," she said without a hint of irony. "I think that's really so wonderful."

It was her amiability that I found offensive.

"It's a great challenge," I said, and looked back at Buzz. He'd once told me confidentially that Tracy was a "decent writer without any oomph!" and she was "too eager to make the scene, and not eager enough to dig for news." Now he was beaming at her. She was seated in his chair, eating his natural cheese curls, working, no doubt, on the next Sunday cover piece. And, damn her, she wasn't even lording it over me.

"What are you working on?" I asked Tracy.

"Oh, nothing important," she bleated. "A sidebar to my 'Expense Account, New York' story, about all the hanky-panky that goes on the corporate tab. It's fun, actually."

The fashionista kick line uncrossed and crossed its legs again, with twittering enough for Buzz to get especially antsy. He stood up straight and moved a step away from Tracy.

"So, Valerie," he said. "What brings you up here?"

"I came up to pitch you a story," I said.

"Oh," he said. "Of course. Any time! What is it?" Buzz was glad to get to the business at hand. He folded his arms and placed his right pointer on his cheek, as if he'd been summoned to hear someone declaim a poem. "Go ahead," he said. "I'm listening."

"Okay, well, lately I've been spending some time uptown and in the Bronx," I started. I hadn't prepared myself for a standing presentation. I thought I'd be able to warm up a little with some catch-up chitchat, ease into the pitch, maybe even with a little L'Occitane.

"The Bronx?" Buzz's brow did a little dance before he settled on an expression. "Okay. That's interesting."

"There's a group of artists." I was still hesitant. "Graffiti artists . . ."

The word *graffiti* didn't reverberate well in Style, as if Rx had suddenly settled himself in Molly Blossom's lap. Maybe I should've used the words *public art* or *conceptual art,* even just plain old *art.* But now that I'd begun the pitch, it would've been fatal to cut out. A lot of faces were peeking up over the walls of cubicles, like cats on a backyard fence where there's raw herring.

"These artists may not have gotten a lot of attention in the past, but they've come together around the death of this one graffiti artist. Actually, they called Curtis Wright about it too, and he was saying it might be a good story for me, a little, I don't know . . . something worth pursuing. His name is . . .

was . . . Stain and they're working on memorials for him all over the city." Every word that came out of my mouth felt like a spade full of fresh dirt. I was shoveling myself a little hole.

"Curtis liked this?" said Buzz, waiting for the punch line. "So they're making graffiti murals? We've done some pieces on muralists before."

"The thing is, a number of them are connected to a single gallery in Chelsea, the Darla Deitrick gallery, or they were at one time. And it looks like she might have gotten rid of some of their work under false pretenses."

"So the graffiti artists say?"

"Yes. But I've got sources who would go on the record with it."

"Graffiti artists?" Clearly not the kind of sources Buzz would trust.

"No, well, some of them. These graffiti artists made works about twenty years ago and gave them to Deitrick to sell on consignment. She never sold them—not then, anyway—and these guys think she's really taken them for a ride. Well, see, it's important because this fellow who died, this Stain, he used to run a crew of, well, guerrilla art activists. This was back in the eighties. And I suppose in a way . . ."

The more the words came out of my mouth, the more I wanted to lie down in that hole and bury myself. At least the dirt would be warm, unlike my Style room reception.

Buzz was thinking it over. "Darla has been big news lately. I'm intrigued, but we can't exactly go after her because a few graffiti vandals are upset about something. What kind of substantiation do you have?"

As soon as he asked, I considered taking my shovel and running. My primary source for the story so far was Blondie, the club kid on Ecstasy, who surely wouldn't go on the record against Darla. My backup sources were graffiti writers, some of whom I'd never met and who probably didn't much like the light of day.

With no way to answer his question, I shifted my pitch from the specific to the general.

"Okay, so maybe we don't focus directly on Darla. But I've got a lot on these graffiti writers. Just think, Buzz. Style *does* the outer boroughs." I used both my hands to outline the panoramic lens of it all. "We get graffiti done right, big colorful characters, big splashy shots of art. Half the page is old school, and half is new school. We get a timeline of graffiti art highlights from the seventies to the present, starting with Tonka 184. We could print a map of the city's graffiti landmarks. And we could print a glossary of graffiti terms, like *throw-up* and *burner*. We could show people exactly how to read the complicated lettering. It would be graffiti soup to nuts."

It was a horrendous pitch, ethnic tourism at its most banal—Rudyard Kipling on *Beat Street*. I felt exactly the way he did when he finally said, "Graffiti now?" His BMW face looked crumpled after a crash. He squinted so tight his wrinkles miraculously reappeared. "Valerie, you came all the way upstairs for the first time in months to pitch me *this* story?"

It did sound utterly absurd, even to me. "Well, I—"

"*Style,* sweetheart. That means *fashionable*. I really wish we had more space for the underclass, but our mandate here is strictly *high* culture, *high* society. You get the gist. Gosh, it sure has been a long time since we've worked together. I know it's easy to forget all this stuff when you're in the hard news sections of the paper. Your idea has some merit and the glossary sounds cute—really cute—but it's a bit too, er, down-market for us, don't you think?" The beautiful polish and finesse of his voice took off some of the edge, but it was clear that he thought I'd lost my mind.

The room was a cold bathtub of silence.

Then, suddenly, he laughed. "Oh, Val, I forgot how funny you are! Oh! That *is* funny! I mean, next you're going to suggest I do a story about *bell-bottoms*, right? Ha!"

I hesitated. "Yeah," I said. "Got ya!"

Buzz threw his head back and laughed heartily, as if he'd just been relieved of some terrible burden. He sang, "Gotcha, gotcha," as he tried to poke me in the stomach. "What a relief," he sighed. "For a minute, I really thought you *meant* that!" Heavy sigh. "So, what really brings you up?"

"Oh, you know," I said. "Just missed you! Wanted to see your face!" I'd tried to play along with him, but I wasn't convincing. An awkward silence passed between us like a freight train as he realized anew that I'd been earnest all along.

"Aw." Buzz pursed his face. "You know how much I detest sincerity. Of course, the door here is always open to you, when you've got the okay from Jaime and Battinger. We *love* your ideas!"

Then I swallowed hard and walked out of Style, back down the corridor to the elevators. Ever solicitous, Buzz was behind me. "Val, listen." He waited with me at the elevator. "You know how it is, though. We really need something *fresh*."

I paused in front of the open elevator door and gazed at him. The old Valerie would have said that she didn't really care about graffiti. That all she wanted in life was to write about trophy wives and toy poodles, multimillion-dollar second homes and celebrity divorces, to anoint the next It girl and condemn the city's worst cad. She didn't care about outer boroughs or disenfranchised teenagers or *black* people, for God's sake. *Please* don't make me walk out of Style again, she would have shouted. *I'll do anything!*

But I looked at Buzz's face, shaped and buffed with all the care a mortician gives a cadaver, and I thought, Did he just say *fresh*? What does Buzz know from *fresh*? Fresh like a flower? Pluck it and put it in a vase and it's only a matter of days before it's withered. Before its leaves drop all over the table and its stem smells rank.

"Fresh, huh?" I stepped onto the elevator and pushed the button for Obits. "Buzz, fresh is just rotten waiting to happen."

The door slid shut on Buzz's wide eyes and gaping mouth, and on my ride down that single floor in the elevator it became clear as a sunny-day vista from the Statue of Liberty's crown that I wasn't going to write for Style ever again.

Cabeza called around noon and said he was in the neighborhood. I was so happy to hear from him I almost jumped through the phone. He gave me the address of Manganaro, an Italian deli on Ninth Avenue near Thirty-seventh Street. "I'm taking you to lunch."

The sign outside said GROSSERIA ITALIANA and there was a skip in time over the threshold to the turn of the last century. Salamis hung from the ceiling; the display cases were packed with Italian cookies, cheeses, homemade foccaccia, giardiniera salads, and hunks of proscuitto de Parma. It would've made Michael Corleone feel right at home.

The deli was in the way back, and that's where I found Cabeza, tucked under a café table, playing with his camera. Before he looked up, I kissed him so hard I almost knocked him over.

"I bought us a foot-long sub, *especialidad de la casa,* with soprasetta, mozzarella, and peppers," he said, smiling. "I'll bet a hardy girl like you could handle one on your own, but it was too much for me, so I had them cut it in half."

"Good," I said. "I'm famished." I sat down and took my half, ripping off an edge of the sandwich with my teeth. I felt like a laborer, just finished with a day cutting stones. I gulped down some of the fancy Italian lemon soda he'd also bought me, and wiped my mouth with the back of my hand. "Well, I did it. I ruined my chances of getting a story in Style."

Cabeza looked at me quizzically. "Oh?"

"Yep," I said. "It feels great. I wish I'd done it earlier."

I took another bite of the sandwich and put it down. It was so large—even half of it—that I could be eating it for weeks. Maybe I'd do just that. Sit here in the quiet hole-in-the-wall genuine Italian deli and eat a sandwich for a few weeks. Forget about everything else. "But you know what? I don't care. I never saw it before so clearly. That room! Those women! They're horrifying. The way that everything has to be served up to them with ribbons on a Tiffany silver platter before they'll even take a whiff—and even so, it's got to be as bland as Tibetan food before they'll be willing to taste it. Buzz Phipps has no idea what New York is all about. He cabs it down from his Upper West Side apartment every morning, without even looking out the window, then he cabs from hotspot to hotspot in the evenings so he doesn't get his spats dirty. And he thinks he's writing about style. Well, I have news for him: style is not just what the Montauk set is wearing this year. What about skateboard punks? Are you going to tell me that's not style? Even Bowery junkies have style. How come that's not in our section?"

I picked up my sandwich and started chewing again. The savory blend hit the spot. I chugged a little more Italian soda and looked up at Cabeza, who had his hands folded, watching me.

"They're so incredibly superficial and self-important! As if it's so difficult to write about a scene when people are waiting on you hand and foot—and tooth. As if it's so tough to get sources when everyone in the entire milieu is circling you in a game of Ring Around the Rosie. And you're the Rosie! Ugh. Did you ever notice how every headline for every story needs to be either alliterative or some spin on a popular movie title? And Buzz goes around pretending he's so creative."

Cabeza was chuckling at me. "Now you're seeing your old self through the eyes of Sunburst Rhapsody."

"No one said you could say those two words aloud," I said,

pointing my straw at him. "Not until you tell me your real name, anyway."

He glanced over at the deli man. "You think he's going to tell Rush and Malloy?"

I bit into my sandwich happily. What did it matter anymore? All my secrets were liberated; Cabeza could be trusted not to tell anyone. He wasn't someone who cared about such things; he cared only about the truth.

"So, they didn't take the story?"

"Nope. Too 'down-market,' he said."

Cabeza poured me more soda. "Don't worry about it," he said gently. "When we get this story, we're going higher. Straight to the top."

"Not with our little problem," I said. I filled Cabeza in on everything I'd learned from Blondie at Twilo and from Wicked Rick at the memorial wall. He picked up the camera and filmed me while I talked. "I realized as I was pitching Buzz that I don't have anything yet that could be substantiated and put into print. And my time peg—Wallace's death—is moving further and further away as we speak. So the urgency to write about something that had to do with his art is fast diminishing. I need something to happen, some way to get to Darla."

"That's where your Valerie Vane persona comes in so handy," he says. "This Blondie character likes you, likes to be associated with you. You could work that angle a little bit more, and maybe he'll even take you over there after hours."

I picked up the sandwich and took a smaller bite. "You know, I'm really starting to hate pretending. I don't know, but something about spending time with you, about being able to just be who I am without working any angle with anyone—it feels more and more appealing."

"Just a sec," said Cabeza, getting up to ask the deli counter man if he'd shoot some frames of us together at the café table.

The old man offered a few obliging words in Italian. Cabeza put his arm around my waist and kissed me. "This is nice," he said. "I'll have one of the last known pictures of the girl called Valerie Vane, before she disappears into Sunburst Rhapsody."

Maybe I'd quit The Paper and move somewhere serene, someplace without gossip, without fashion, and without art. Maybe Cabeza would go with me. We could get a little house in Woodstock and grow zucchini and tomatoes in our garden. We'd have kids and name them ordinary names like Joe and Sue. Maybe even Po. I'd known someone on the Eugene farm named Po, and he was happy being Po. Cabeza could edit his films, and I could write a book about my life in the big bad city. We could go on television and talk about nothing in particular. We'd be the Nick and Nora for Woodstock public-access television, not even PBS.

Meanwhile, Cabeza was jotting down some notes on what I'd told him about Darla and the art. "We've got a great story here." He put the cap back on his pen. "We've just got to be strategic and figure out a good way to get it to the right people. We'll just have to figure out a good time peg. Something newsy." He pulled his seat closer to mine and cupped his hands around my hand. "We'll be a great team."

I kept thinking about that little house upstate. Forget the zucchinis. We'd plant hyacinths in the yard. I didn't really know what they look like, but the word itself sounded lovely. Hyacinth.

16

Getting Color

I was in the shower watching water pool at my feet and dreaming about gardening in Woodstock when the phone wailed. I steadied myself against the bathroom wall and kicked open the door. The machine got it, and I could hear Mickey Rood's gravely voice: "Hi, Valerie, nice to hear from you." Pause. "Sure, I'll tell him." Pause. "Yes, definitely. Good you called to let us know." Pause. Rood was having a conversation with me. I figured it was best not to interrupt.

I stepped out of the bathroom and made puddles on the hardwood floor, but I didn't pick up the phone. "Oh, not much, just looking at the call sheet." The morning news roundup from the wires. "There's this breaking item about some dealer in Chelsea named Deitrick. Seems something happened at her gallery last night. I tried to interest Battinger but she won't send a stringer out on it. I don't know, seems like a good story to me. And thanks for calling in to let me know about your dentist appointment. I'll convey the information to Jaime. I'll get a clerk on those faxes. See you this afternoon."

I toweled off, went to my closet, and started dressing. Dentist, I thought. He never forgot a single thing. I had no idea how much Rood knew about my snooping around Darla's. All I knew was he was a pal.

• • •

Yellow police tape decorated a stretch of West Twenty-fourth Street in front of Darla Deitrick Fine Art. It spruced up the place. Gave it a dab of color. TV news crews were posted on the sidewalk like it was red carpet at the Oscars. I wondered whether the Wallace situation was leaving a string of bodies in its wake. I imagined Darla or Blondie sprawled on the floor, outlined in white tape. Another white-on-white.

I pushed my way through the camera crews, trying to get closer. The line of photographers and reporters wouldn't budge. A police sergeant pushed to the front and said, "Let's move this back, folks. We'll let you in to see everything in just a few minutes. But you have to move this line back." I moved left and got yelled at by a photographer, "Heads down up front!"

I still couldn't get anywhere near the gallery. I heard Andrew Siff from NY1 News saying: "Thanks, Frank. I'm standing here in front of Darla Deitrick Fine Art in Chelsea where early this morning a group of vandals broke in and spray-painted an exhibition of white paintings valued in the millions of dollars. Police say the works damaged included Jasper Johns's *White Flag*, on loan from the Metropolitan Museum of Art. The piece is estimated to be worth more than twenty million dollars. The culprits, the police said, could be graffiti artists who, ironically enough, were once represented by the gallery owner. Back to you, Frank."

So, no one was dead. But the exhibition wasn't so pure anymore. A solid news peg. Finally, I pushed through the bank of reporters.

"Excuse me, officer," I said to the closest man in blue over the yellow police tape. "I know the gallery owner and her assistant. Can you tell me if anyone was hurt?"

"No injuries," he said. "The incident occurred during off-hours. Early this morning, probably around two a.m. No witnesses. The chief will be holding a press conference shortly."

Even though I didn't have all the details, I was starting to paint a picture of my own. Did they make a giant *X* across the white flag? Spray the Agnes Martin with red question marks? Maybe they'd mimicked Darla and wrote her famous words, *Paint Makes Art*, over the Robert Ryman. For Darla, it would've been like Piss Christ.

"What's the extent of the damage?" I asked.

The cop squinted at me. I could count the years he'd been working the beat in the rings under his eyes. "The chief will be holding a news conference shortly."

"All right, all right," I said. "I don't need to be told twice."

"Apparently you do." He didn't crack a smile.

I backed away. The more I thought about it, the more unlikely it seemed that there should be so many spray cans loose in New York. Was I following the Krylon, or was the Krylon following me? I'd blabbered on to Bigs Cru about Darla. They seemed a little too sedentary for a break-and-enter job. On the other hand, Rx was excitable, and maybe I'd excited him. Nah, I was taking too much credit. The world didn't revolve around my little head of cherry-blond hair. There were plenty of artists who'd mourned Wallace with an aerosol moan. But one thing I knew: this had some connection to Wallace.

I dove into the press pool and swam to the back. I buried my press card in my shirt and put on my sunglasses, tied my hair into a ponytail, and then I walked down the block to a group of gallery assistants who were watching from a safe smoking distance.

God forgive me, I lisped a little like Bogey in the bookshop in *The Big Sleep* when I said, "Did anyone see Gideon go in there? I'm so worried about Gideon." A young woman with uneven hair and an uneven dress gave me an uneven look. A Brit with floppy black hair said, "He was the one who discovered it. He called the police straight away. As I understand it, Deitrick showed up a bit later and they're both still inside, answering questions."

"Did you see the walls?"

"No," said the Brit. "But I understand it's brilliant."

I assumed he meant brilliant in that British way, not necessarily meaning full of genius. Blondie had been the first on the scene. If I could get him, I'd be set with one or two official comments from Darla. I suspected she wouldn't give me a one-on-one, since I'd failed to accompany Tyler Prattle to her opening. I nodded at my Brit, put on a confident smile and strode toward the gallery door. A copper stopped me just as I was pulling the handle. He was of the Irish model, the ones they mass-produce at the factory in Staten Island with the barrel chest and the broad shoulders and the smattering of freckles and the blue eyes that bore right through you.

"Can't go in there," he said. He put his thick pale arm across the door frame. I reached inside my shirt collar to pull out my press pass, hoping the name of The Paper might grease his elbow. Sometimes flashing the badge worked. Mostly it didn't. If you had to fall back on credentials, chances are you weren't getting close anyway. On blue eyes, I'd gambled and lost. He shook his head. "There will be a press conference in a few minutes. You're just going to have to wait like all the others." He pointed to the press bank. The reporters were like a lineup of restive horses behind the starting gates.

I took off my sunglasses and tried to keep his eyes, figuring calm and authoritative was my best bet. "Oh, excuse me, officer. I should've explained. I'm here at the request of Ms. Deitrick's gallery assistant. He called me this morning just after he got in and asked me to come down. He's worked out an exclusive with my editors."

The copper's blue eyes were so sharp they could've cut glass. "Name?"

"Name? Oh, name of the gallery assistant. Of course, Mr. Gideon . . ." I hadn't played this far ahead in the game. "Mr. Gideon . . . Blondie."

Ah, if only blue eyes would've brightened. I'd have whistled up something right then and we could've had a nice song. Instead, I cringed, awaiting his response.

"Gideon Blondie? I'm sorry, Miss, but nobody goes in until we get the captain's say so. This is a crime scene. You'll just have to wait for the press conference, just like everyone else." He pointed to the steeds again. I watched a few of them whinny into the cameras and scrape their hoofs. It would be a race to the finish.

"Listen," I said in a confidential tone to the copper. "Ms. Deitrick's gallery assistant called me because I have been researching a story related to graffiti. If you could let me in, maybe I could help figure out who did this."

Blue Eyes raised a single eyebrow, making an impressively high arc. "Oh, yeah? I'm sure the captain would love to hand you over to talk to the Vandal Squad. But unfortunately, the New York City Police Department doesn't barter with reporters so they can get in the door before their competitors, and not even reporters with big names on their badges who've attended swanky Ivy League colleges. Now, maybe Steve Dunleavy . . ."

Someone inside yelled loud enough to pierce a steel drum. From what I could assume based on the sound of clacking Cobras, Darla Deitrick had emerged from the back office and was taking a look—presumably not her first—at her gallery. From the timbre of her screech, it sounded like it might be more colorful than a few *X*'s against the white. I tried to crane my neck around Blue Eyes's arm, but he flexed his muscle against my nose. Darla got close enough so I could see her but not the art. A crew of coppers and gallery types trailed her like an Interpol art theft tag team.

"Okay, let's do this," she said, as if she were about to get a tetanus shot. "Bring in the cameras."

A sergeant passed my copper and walked out into the street.

He announced the imminence of the press conference to the assembled pool. The camera crews and their mike-wielding producers picked up stakes as quickly as a traveling circus and made their way to the door. My copper looked down at me to reassert his worldview, that Ivy Leaguers were lowlifes. I almost blurted out, "I only went to Reed!"

As I watched the reporters file past me through the door, I tried to strategize. All I needed was to see the walls and talk to Blondie. Once the presser was over, I could hop on a train uptown and get to Bigs Cru at the memorial wall on 207th Street. I could mine eight hundred words out of that, easy. I'd be back at the office by noon with a daily to put every other hack in the room to shame. I'd get a byline, no contest.

I edged toward the copper and my chin met his arm. "Hold on there, now, little Miss," he said, and lowered the bar of his arm to the level of my chest. Now I'd riled him. He would let even the Brit and the smoker with the uneven dress inside before he'd let me pass. I scanned the crowd filing past me for a familiar face from The Paper. Battinger would probably wise up at some point about the call sheet and send a Metro stringer down. This was too big a story for The Paper to miss. If it were Tracy, I'd kick her in the Achilles' tendon. A little Tonya Harding action.

Now everyone and their cameraman and their stenographer and their pet Chihuahua had been let in the door, and I was still looking at a pale Irish arm. "Excuse me, officer," I said. "I really am on assignment."

He looked down at me as if he'd forgotten all about me. "Well, all right," he said, moving out of the way. I lunged forward, though the entryway, and skittered to a stop in the middle of the gallery, where the press pool stood huddled in stunned silence. It was the quietest moment I'd ever spent among my colleagues from the fourth estate.

That red *X* through a white flag? Nope. A couple of question marks or squiggles scrawled across the walls? No such simplicity. The phrase *Paint Makes Art* scripted with water-soluble spray? Darla should be so lucky.

There were no white paintings anymore. A color bomb had exploded on every canvas, and where there had been nothing, now there was everything—pop-out lettering, squiggles, comic book superheroes, skulls, loops, cubes, rainbows, popping eyeballs, triangles within squares, horses, dogs, waves, apples, pears, and letters, letters, letters everywhere. The gallery walls were still white. But that was it. Everything else was a free-for-all.

Someone—some more than one—had spent a lot of time in here, painting. It was no splotch and run. No break and burn. They'd gotten in and they'd stayed a while. They'd found a way past the locks and the gates and the security guard—the one who came with Johns's *White Flag*. Maybe all night.

There began some murmuring among the reporters, clucks of disapproval, sighs of shock and disbelief. A few TV reporters got down on their knees to start redrafting their scripts. Some of the cameramen who wanted better positions for close-ups were arguing with the coppers who were trying to keep them corralled.

Cy Twombly's white-on-white was now a pink-on-green, a checkerboard design only a preppie could love. Someone had scribbled tiny childish purple letters on Agnes Martin's pale gray lines, like a first-grade homework assignment on a wide-ruled pad. And the little red square on Malevich's Suprematist abstraction had been turned into a square hamburger on a black and tan smoking outdoor grill.

Instead of "essence essentialized," or whatever paradigm of purity Darla had plugged a few days earlier, this was aggression-aggravated, power and glory of color, love of color, messy and unabated. Casper the Friendly Ghost had gotten a makeover by Pucci.

I turned around to face the alcove just off the front door, where I knew I'd find Jasper Johns's *White Flag*. It didn't make use of the stars and stripes faintly etched into the thick paint. There was just one big green word covering the entire painting: *YOU*. I couldn't figure out what it was supposed to mean, until I stepped back and turned to look at the whole gallery. Now I saw it: every other canvas had its own word, and reading it clockwise it formed a sentence: "YOU DO NOT OWN THIS ART."

Then the TV cameras started rolling and the shutterbugs started clicking and the lights were flashing and the questions were flying. "Ms. Deitrick, do you know who is responsible for this vandalism?" . . . "Darla, can you tell us who had access to the gallery other than yourself?" . . . "Were there signs of a break-in?" . . . "Can you tell us the value of the work on display?" . . . "Does any of the work look familiar to you?" . . . "When did you discover this?" . . . "How did you feel when you arrived this morning?" . . . "Have you been in touch with the Met?" . . . "Are you insured?" . . . "Is it going to be possible to save the works?" . . . "What kind of experts will be needed?" And on and on.

Darla closed her eyes while the flashbulbs flashed. No matter how much she loved publicity, this was still a nightmare. The show had been open for only a few days, and she'd soon be wallowing in a mudslide of legal papers, when what she'd hoped for was a deluge of raves.

"Please, please," she said, weakly. She was flanked by two flacks from Rubinstein Associates, the city's top damage-control gurus. I recognized the brunette on Darla's right because she'd taken me out to lunch after Club Zero for a consultation. Now, she leaned toward the bouquet of microphones arrayed in front of Darla.

"Please, ladies and gentlemen of the press," she said, and I remembered her name was Jill. "Ms. Deitrick will make a brief statement and then she will answer one or two questions. Please understand that Ms. Deitrick is very busy, but she would like to make sure you all get what you need."

The press pool hushed, waiting for Darla to take her turn. Jill put a small pedestal on the floor in front of Darla; she stepped up onto it and then steadied herself. She quietly unfolded a piece of paper. Her hands trembled slightly.

"Early this morning at approximately two fifteen a.m., some of the greatest art institutions in the world, along with my humble gallery, Darla Deitrick Fine Art, were the victims of a horrifying and senseless crime," she said, her voice quavering. "Works by some of the leading contemporary artists in the world, such as Jasper Johns, Agnes Martin, and Cy Twombly, on loan from the Metropolitan Museum of Art, the Los Angeles Museum of Contemporary Art, and the Centre Pompidou of Paris, have been vilely desecrated. You see all around you the evidence of that desecration. I consider this violation akin to an art world rape."

Murmuring from the crowd. Notes scribbled. Shushing from Jill.

"The police suspect that there may have been more than one culprit," Darla continued, shakily. "I have no idea who would've committed such a heinous act, and I will not make any guesses to that effect until all the evidence has been accumulated. I am adequately insured to cover the works on loan, and I have already been in contact with the owners of these invaluable works of art. There was no sign of forced entry, and nothing appears to have been stolen." She gritted her teeth. "The violators clearly hoped to destroy masterpieces and to humiliate me personally. I intend to pursue them and punish them to the full extent of the law." Her little nose was flared and her eyes were so narrowed she was almost a Cyclops.

When she stopped talking, she started breathing again. Her breaths were long and shallow in the microphone. She took a step back while the brunette flack named Jill chose her favorite TV talent from the front of the press pool and let them toss some softballs: "Ms. Deitrick, it must've been just awful to walk in here and see this," said Phyllis Chestnut, the entertainment reporter for *Wake Up Call,* the morning report on Channel Five. "Tell us, what did it *feel* like?"

"You can't even imagine, Phyllis. Why, I looked around the gallery when I arrived and . . ." Darla started to get choked up. The second flack, the blonde, put a reassuring hand on Darla's shoulder and softly said, "It's okay, dear. Ms. Deitrick has to get back to work." Flashes went off.

"Okay, only two more," said my old buddy, Jill, sternly, as if she were protecting a toddler from a pack of rottweilers. "Ms. Deitrick is getting worn out." She pointed to TV talent Jinny James up front.

"Darla, you've been such an important supporter of graffiti artists in the past. Do you ever think you'll represent one of them now that they've betrayed you like this?"

Darla looked up appreciatively. "Oh, Jinny, to give of your heart and soul to these people and then to have them turn around and do this." Again, she was awash in emotion, and the cameras were clicking, flashing, exploding.

"A last question please?" said Jill. "Right here, up front."

A man's voice started, "Can you tell us if you've found any meaning in these senseless scrawls?"

But I couldn't take it any longer. I broke in, from the back of the pack: "Ms. Deitrick, is there any connection between this vandalism and the fire at your warehouse that used to contain hundreds of works by graffiti artists?"

Darla's eyebrow began to twitch spasmodically as she peered through the assembled shutterbugs and news hawks to find the face that went with that question. Her flacks began to search for me too, and Jill whispered something into Darla's ear, speeding her twitching. Finally, her eyes landed on me and her face went red as the hamburger in the Malevich.

She lifted her hand and pointed. "Arrest that woman!" she shouted, loud enough for the NY1 News reporter to drop his script. "She is connected to the vandals who did this! She's responsible!"

There was sudden pandemonium as the entire bank of reporters shifted and a few of the cameras swiveled to turn their lights on my face. A couple of coppers edged closer, as if they might do something. But no one made an abrupt move.

"Arrest her!" Darla screamed again. "She knows who did this. She's an accomplice!"

I figured something unpleasant was about to happen—maybe a copper would tackle me or maybe Jill would start pulling my hair. I would've made for the door, but I was stunned into immobility. I just stood there taking in the sight of Darla, standing like Art Gallery Barbie atop her pedestal.

Flashguns started going off in my face and reporters hurled question at me: "Name, please?" . . . "Aren't you . . . ?" . . . "Do you know who did this?" . . . "Did you have a hand in this?" . . . "What was the purpose of this vandalism?" . . . "Aren't you Valerie . . . ?"

Maybe Blondie had gone soft after he'd returned from the Twilo Ecstasy romp and blubbered on Darla's shoulder. Or maybe she'd had him followed that night and she'd tortured him to find out what he'd spilled. Maybe he was getting the hot light and rubber hose treatment in the back room even now. Or worse—Darla had hired Tan Rafifi to splatter his white linen suit with cow's blood.

All I could do was blink into the cameras and promise myself to stand quite still and not do any further damage. I had no interest in fifteen more minutes in the spotlight. So I sighed and said, "Ms. Deitrick is unfortunately mistaken. I'm a journalist.

Check my press credentials. I came here to cover a story." I waved my press badge. A few cameramen snapped it. It gave the coppers pause, but not much. They looked back at Darla, who was still shrieking accusations, even under the muffling hands of her damage-control experts.

"I'll press charges!" Darla shouted, and that did the trick.

My buddy Blue Eyes from the door had his plastic cuffs off his belt and he held them out to me as if presenting a gift. "I knew you were trouble," he said.

I remembered what Cabeza had said about Darla's pull with the cops. Ah, Giuliani New York. It sure was good for some people. "Little Miss, we're going to have to take you down to the station house and sort this all out," Blue Eyes said.

I didn't want Darla Deitrick to become the new Angelica Pomeroy—star of *Terror in the City II*. I had to hand it to her, though, for her skills of misdirection. Her storage facility burns down, her art goes missing, graffiti kids vandalize her gallery, and somehow it's the washed-up journo hack who's to blame. Not bad for the daughter of a muffin maven.

They were on me now. As the coppers tugged me by my plastic cuffs toward the door, I glanced back into the depths of the gallery, to the office in front of the sliding glass door where I'd first met Darla. I saw something white skitter across the space. I figured it for Blondie.

17

The Cooler

Jaime looked different in the pale green light of the Tenth Precinct lockup. Not like the boss who'd forced me to write unbylined death squibs. More like a guy who'd bailed me out twice.

I'd spent three hours in the cooler looking at a dank stone wall while reporters all over the city were filing stories on Darla's break-in. The cell was one of those temporary tanks at the back of the precinct, just big enough for maybe a couple of tricks fresh from the local one-hour motels. It had a cold concrete floor and hard bench suspended on two chains. I didn't have any company or anything to read. That gave me a lot of time to think about how all the pieces might fall into place. It also gave me time to daydream about Cabeza and the nice little tomato salad with balsamic vinaigrette we'd eat one afternoon in our Woodstock cabin once we'd left this dirty town in our rearview.

After the first hour, a sergeant named Suarez pulled me out of the lockup and put me in a windowless room upstairs. The décor wasn't any prettier, but at least I had Suarez to look at. He was bald as a baseball and what he lacked in height he made up in girth. He carried his extra weight like a kid carries an inner tube. Suarez told me Darla said I was personally acquainted with the vandals; I told him I wasn't so well connected. Suarez asked me who I knew who disliked Darla. I said I disliked her.

After a few rounds of twenty questions, I told Suarez that based on what Darla had given him I knew he couldn't get me past the precinct, and I wasn't dumb enough to give him any excuses. I said if he had enough to run me down to Central Booking, he should go right ahead, otherwise I was going to call my boss and he'd call our lawyer. I wish I could say he looked embarrassed when he handed me the phone.

An hour later, another copper clinked keys to unlock my cell and Jaime put his wallet back in his pocket. The expression on his face made me think of a man who's just learned his daughter is a porn star. "Jaime," I started to say.

"Let's not," he said, holding up his hand, "until we get outside."

I followed him out to the street with my head bent and waited dutifully on the curb. It was a clear day, the sky luminous blue. I loved the sound of the traffic and the smell of the exhaust, the people zigzagging through the streets and the scowls on the faces of the fruit sellers. Ah, it was good to be a free woman! I gulped in the fresh air, trying to forget the taste of the dank cell.

Jaime opened the cab door for me. "Come on, Bonnie Parker."

I slid onto the seat and waited. Jaime slid in next to me and unrolled his window, as if he couldn't bear the stench of me. I felt guilty, but I wasn't sure why. I hadn't done anything wrong. I'd been wrongly accused! But I knew Jaime must've had to make up some strange excuses to get out of the news office and pick me up.

"What makes you stick up for me, Jaime?"

"Don't be too sure I will." His eyes were fixed on the driver's royal blue turban. He announced the address of The Paper and the taxi bolted forward, went a few yards, and then skidded to a sudden stop behind another yellow cab. It was going to be one of those lurching rides all the way north—a bad driver and nothing to be done.

"Is it too late for me to file something for tomorrow's paper?" I asked. "I didn't get everything at the press conference but I . . ."

Jaime rolled down his window further, pumping the handle hard, as if he had something against it. "Forget the story," he said. "Tracy got it. It's been filed."

That smarted. I leaned back in my seat. "Jaime, listen, I'm sorry I didn't tell you I was going down to Chelsea this morning. I thought if I could—"

"Save it. When we get back to the office, there is going to be a conference room full of people who will want to know what you were doing at the Deitrick gallery. You can explain it to them."

The cab jolted forward. I caught myself against the divider. I'd never seen Jaime so angry. Actually, I'd never seen him even a little irked. "I let you down," I said. "I'm sorry. I know you must think I'm a total screw-up. I shouldn't have gone creeping around behind your back. I should've . . ."

Jaime unstuck his gaze from the turban. His eyes were bloodshot. His hair sprang out wildly from under his yarmulke. A day without Brylcreem.

"This is very hard for me, Valerie," he said, softly, his low southern twang more guttural. "My cousin had this kind of problem. We lived with it all our lives. After a while, I realized, we couldn't help him. We had to give up trying."

I didn't know what Jaime meant by "this kind of problem." Did Cuban Orthodox Jews get locked up for attacking VJs or for asking unfriendly questions at pressers? It didn't seem like the right time to interrupt. I looped my hand through the window strap and held on, jerking along with the bumpy cab.

"You had such great promise," Jaime said. "Even when you started out on Style, I could see you had a real gift for writing about people. You were tough when you needed to be, and always unflinching."

You *had*. You *were*. Why was he using the past tense? "Thank you, Jaime. I think the world of you too. I think you're a great editor. I—"

"No, Valerie," he said. "I'm not trying to flatter you here. I'm trying to tell you something. When I read your early work, I thought a person with your observational gifts would make a great obituary writer. I had the idea of stealing you from Buzz even before you sabotaged your own career. Then, when Battinger wanted you out of the building, I made my pitch. I told her that I knew you had some personal problems, but I was willing to take you under my wing and see if I could make something of you. I thought you'd been hired too young, that a little fame had gone to your head. People grow out of that sort of thing with the right guidance. Heck, I flattered myself that I could make you into one of the best obituary writers The Paper has ever seen."

This was a new one. "You actually wanted me on your staff?" I felt like a kid who'd discovered a kaleidoscope on a gray day; everything suddenly turned prettier, more magical.

"What did you think? That you were a charity case? The Paper is no place for charity."

We were moving up Eleventh Avenue fast now, the hot wind rushing through Jaime's open window.

"It can still be that way, Jaime. I've almost got this story worked out, and if someone would give me a shot to run it in Metro—"

"You're not listening, Valerie," Jaime said. "Editors are assembling in the Page One conference room at this very moment to determine whether to fire you. And this time, I'm not going to step in."

The cab braked suddenly and we were both hurled forward. Jaime rapped on the glass, "Goddamn it! Take it easy up there!" he shouted. I'd never even heard him raise his voice. The cabbie shouted, "Pothole!" and turned his Gurbani music to blasting. Jaime slammed the divider shut. "I know you think writing obituaries is no fun," he said. "But Obits is a very esteemed section of The Paper. It can be a very prestigious posting for the right reporter. Too bad you blew it."

I took out a pack of gum and toyed with the plastic wrapping and then the foil. "I blew it? That's it?"

"I've got to disengage, Valerie. If you can't help yourself, if this drug thing has got you, I can't do anything about it. I learned that with my cousin. He struggled with addiction for thirty years. It doesn't matter how much you care about someone, they have to do it themselves. They have to go to rock bottom before they turn around. Maybe you're almost there. I sure hope so."

It hit me like a pie-in-the-face joke. Everything was full of creamy good sense. "Oh, Jaime! You think I'm on drugs? This is wonderful!" I reached over and gave him that hug I'd held out on. "Oh, Jaime! Is that why you're disowning me?"

Jaime jerked away, like a man whose porn-star daughter has just attempted a French kiss. I started to laugh. "Oh, Jaime! Who gave you that idea? Was it the sergeant? Was it one of the officers? Darla? Did Darla tell you that?"

Now I remembered: while I'd been in the cooler, Jaime had been chatting with my dear friend Blue Eyes in the hall. They'd yucked it up a little, and then they'd gone hush-hush.

"It's a smear. An old-fashioned Vaseline-on-index-finger smear," I shouted. "Oh, it's terrific! What did that cop tell you?"

Jaime wasn't amused. "He said that Darla's assistant had been doing drugs with you at a club and that you were mixed up with some graffiti artists who might be dealers. They said the dealers had done the vandalism. Is that not the case?"

"All of that is a lie," I said firmly. I leaned back in my seat. Thank God I hadn't accepted Charles's mother's little helper. I was practically a Girl Scout. The cab jolted and my head grazed the gray ceiling. "Drug test me! Go ahead! I've got nothing to hide. I'm as clean as Doris Day."

Jaime was still skeptical.

"The truth is simple, much simpler: I've been moonlighting, Jaime. That's all. I've been working on a story without your permission. I've kept my nose clean, as they say. No—literally. I was trying to get a scoop. I was trying to make you proud."

The part about making him proud hadn't occurred to me until just then, but no matter. I wanted it to be true. Jaime had believed in me when I was at my lowest. He could believe in me again. I would make sure of it.

Jaime squinted and smoothed back his hair. "No drugs?"

"If they had anything on me like that, why wouldn't they book me? Why wouldn't they at least print me?" I held up my ink-free hands. "It doesn't make sense."

Jaime took my hands and turned them over; he put his hands under mine to see if they were shaky, I suppose. Then he leaned close and looked at my eyes. He still seemed to be willing to be convinced the copper was wrong. "If what you're telling me is true, then maybe I've been too hard on you. If you're working on an enterprise story, that's okay, but I wish you'd told me. I'm not sure how I'm supposed to defend you if I don't know what you're up to. I don't know if the other editors will be receptive to that sort of thing."

"That's okay, Jaime. You don't have to defend me this time. I'm a big girl. I've got my dukes up." I raised my fists.

The cab was turning from Eleventh Avenue onto Forty-first Street and I knew I had to collect my thoughts to get ready for the inquest. I went over the whole day, starting with Rood's call, my arrival at the presser, my flashbulb redux, the sergeant moping when he couldn't make me soil myself, and this final news that I'd been painted as a Chelsea-trolling raver. Then I got to thinking about it more and I laughed from my gut. Then I kept laughing until my laugh didn't sound quite right, like a handsaw in a two-by-four, going back and forth but not quite slicing.

Jaime became concerned. "Are you sure you can handle going back into that office?" he said, as the cab jolted to a final stop on Forty-third Street. "You're going to have to face Battinger and Sneed and Richard Antigoni in a couple of minutes."

I stopped laughing and took a few deep breaths. "Whatever happens," I said. "I'll be fine."

Jaime paid the driver and led me into the fortress. We climbed the stairs to the Page One conference room, so named because that's where the editors elected The Paper's most prized stories for A-1. I'd never gotten there yet, and so it seemed like a funny location for a beheading. I would've laughed then, but beheadings aren't all that funny.

I was impressed by my own stature when I saw the witnesses assembled for my execution. It looked like the cast *of It's a Wonderful Life,* without the wonderful part.

Metro editor Jane Battinger and her deputy, Aaron Sneed, flanked Buzz Phipps like a couple of crows on fresh stalk of corn. The Arts and Leisure editors, Liz Moore and Orland Lessey, dressed in black and red shirts, could've been a pair of mating cardinals. Metro columnist Clint Westwood warbled a few notes to them across the table and Tyler Prattle, also present, warbled back. Tracy Newton was balanced on the arm of a chair, chirping away at Curtis Wright. Richard Antigoni, the managing editor, was at the far end of the table, gazing up at the ceiling, using all ten fingers to massage his bald pate. With his long beak and his elbows bent out from his head, he gave the impression of a turkey buzzard.

It was more like Hitchcock's *The Birds*. I hadn't counted on a fatal pecking.

Jaime slid behind me into a seat against the wall. I stayed at the door of the aviary. I felt thirsty, but I didn't dare reach for the pitcher of water, which sat in front of Mr. Antigoni, the most menacing of the flock.

My tongue roamed my mouth for stray gum, and came up with nothing. I thought about that pack in my purse and wondered if they'd let me have a final chew.

"Hello, Valerie," Battinger said, when the door thumped closed behind me. The whole room rustled to a stop, and every beady eye landed on me. "We're glad you could make it. I trust there was no trouble at the station house?" She looked from me to Jaime, who nodded. "Good," said Battinger, pulling out a seat at the table. "Why don't you sit right here next to me, Valerie?"

"Why don't we all take a seat?" said Sneed.

I took my place at the table, suddenly conscious of the stench of the lockup on my clothes. My fingers and palms were grimy and my nails had been chewed to bloody. It must've been me who'd done that.

"You know my deputy, Aaron, and, of course, Buzz, and Clive, Tracy, and Curtis," Battinger was squawking. "I don't know if you've ever met Orland and Liz." They each cheeped a little hello, and Curtis winked. "Mr. Antigoni also asked to join us," she added, as the man at the end of the table nodded gravely. "He's taken an interest in your tenure here."

I did my best to smile. Lethal injection would've been so much more relaxing. I'd even prefer an old-fashioned hanging or perhaps the guillotine. At least that was French.

"I bet you're wondering why we're all here," Battinger said. "I have asked everyone to join us because time is short and I wanted to make sure we were all on the same page."

"Page one," I said. That was about as close as I was going to get to a joke with this crowd, but it didn't go over. All I heard was the sound of ruffled feathers. Tracy twittered. Lessey and Moore offered each other coffee and tea. Curtis shot me a look that said, *Be careful, Val. Watch it.*

Battinger croaked out a few words: "I blame myself for this."

"We blame ourselves," Sneed repeated, nodding.

I wasn't sure if they were talking about my lousy sense of humor.

"You were afraid to come to me and so you went to Burton," Battinger continued, nodding at Buzz, who nodded back. "You pitched him an idea about graffiti artists and something about stolen paintings and he said it wasn't right for Style. Is that right?"

Buzz looked like a crow caught on a corn stalk. He met my gaze and then addressed Mr. Antigoni. "Miss Vane came upstairs yesterday to pitch me a story about graffiti artists connected to Darla Deitrick's gallery. I didn't understand that this piece might have these kinds of implications. The pitch wasn't exactly clear to me, and I was in the midst of putting the section to bed, so I didn't give her an adequate hearing."

Antigoni's beak was bobbing. Curtis was watching Antigoni, but he turned to me and gave me a warm smile that said, *You've got a shot here. Hang in, Val, hang in.*

"It wasn't an appropriate pitch for Style," I jumped in. "I didn't know it would come to this; I just had a hunch. I should've gone to Jane instead."

"That's the point," said Battinger.

"That's exactly the point," said Sneed.

Antigoni nodded. Clint looked up from his pad and down again.

"The point is, Valerie," Battinger went on, "you went about this all wrong. If you had a story of this type, with this kind of angle, you should've come to me. But you know that now, so I won't belabor the point."

"I apologize," I said. "Next time I'll certainly come to you, Jane."

Battinger shook her head. "That's not all."

"Not all," said Sneed, softly.

"The problem here, Valerie, is that you have obligations to Jaime, and you should only be working on an enterprise story once you've completed all your work for Obits. If you get a tip on something big, there's a protocol. You need to go to Jaime and then Jaime comes to me. And then Aaron and I figure out what to do with it. We can't have you sneaking around trying to write stories on your own, without the desk's say-so."

"Say-so," muttered Sneed.

"Is that clear?" Battinger said.

I nodded. That made sense. Help out someone like Rusty Markowitz, who already had two Pulitzers. I could've really used a little water. "Yes," I said. "Very clear."

Behind me, I heard Jaime shift in his seat.

"If we'd gotten the ball rolling right away, we'd have been ahead on this story. Tyler Prattle could've called down and asked a few questions and then when this happened, Ms. Deitrick would probably have called him first to give him an exclusive. We'd have something running even before the press conference, and we wouldn't be playing catch-up, like we are now."

I nodded and picked up a plastic cup; at least those were nearby. Curtis reached for the silver pitcher and passed it to me. I poured, slowly, but it wobbled, and I spilled a little on the table. Curtis handed me a napkin, and I mopped it up as I brought the cup to my lips. Tracy leaned over to Curtis and chirped into his ear. He kept an eye on me, faintly smiling.

"That's the way we like to work around here," Battinger said.

Antigoni nodded a few times from the other end of the table, his pate reflecting one of the track lights.

"But that's why I say it's my fault. I should've made it clear to you when you joined Obits that you were part of the Metro team. I hope you understand that now."

"I appreciate your saying so," I answered, my mouth less parched. "If I'd known I could pitch to you, Jane, I'd have brought it to your attention earlier."

"You just let me talk here for a minute, Valerie," Battinger crowed. "One: you don't go behind our backs and rush out to cover a story you can bring home." She enumerated my crimes on her fingers. "Two: you don't go making trouble and get yourself arrested. Three: You don't fail to communicate with the desk. Is that understood?"

"Absolutely," I said. The beaks were piercing skin, but I could take it so far. Maybe they wouldn't unleash the whole Hitchcockian horror. I placed my palms together to suggest that I'd go in for an eleventh-hour conversion. There was more rustling. Lessey and Moore leaned in to confer with each other, two cardinals on a bough. Buzz extended his neck, ticked his head from side to side, and then dropped his chin.

"I don't like what you did today," Battinger continued. "But at the moment, we need this story, and you're our best option for a lead reporter, so we're going to use you. So, here's what needs to happen," she said, tapping her pen onto a notepad to call all the fowl to attention. "I want blanketed coverage. Moore and Lessey are going to coordinate the arts side." She pointed her pen in their direction. "I want a good think piece from Tyler for Sunday," she pointed her pen at him. "Clint will work up a Metro column." She pointed at him.

I nodded.

"I need you, Valerie, to take the lead on the main piece. I need it to be a feature, and I need it to be comprehensive: everything we know and everything we find out. But you have to work with Curtis and Tracy. You and Curtis put out a nice LaShanniah story together last week. So let's make it happen again. Tracy will be at your disposal if you need any backup. And you should read the piece she did today, of course. It's very solid."

Tracy fluttered her lashes. "Happy to help. I'll bring you my notes."

"I will coordinate," concluded Battinger. "We're aiming for page one."

I couldn't believe my luck. It was like a gubernatorial reprieve. Not only was I going to walk free, I would get another shot at A-1. It was practically a resurrection. "Thank you so much," I said to Battinger. "Thank you so much."

"I want to be perfectly clear, this is not a reward for your behavior," Battinger added. "We're doing this because you're in the best position right now to get this story."

"Not a reward at all," said Sneed, looking stern.

"This is your last chance, Valerie Vane. And if you end up anywhere near a jail, there's no bailing you out this time. And if you don't get the story, it's not going to be Obits, it's going to be the exit. Am I clear?"

"Crystal," I said. "Waterford," I added.

"Very well then," said Battinger. "Let's get to work."

"To work," said Sneed.

Within seconds, Battinger and Sneed, Lessey and Moore, and Buzz and Tracy had all flown the coop. Curtis stood grinning at me from the glass doors of the aviary, his thumb and pinkie to his ear, mouthing, "Call me."

I felt a hand on my shoulder. It was Jaime's. I turned to see his face for the first time since we'd entered the room. It looked much better, like his daughter only got caught making out under the bleachers.

"You knew they were going to do that?" I asked.

"Had no idea," he said. He led me to the door and opened it for me. On the staircase down to three, Clint Westwood flew up beside me. "Listen, I was thinking I'd do a piece on these memorial walls. What do you think of that?"

"A nice idea," I said. "I'd be happy to help with contacts."

As we took the final steps down the stairwell, I felt like one of the newly exonerated, *Dead Man Walking* free. I didn't get the ax. I didn't even get a halfway house. I got off with a warning. My chest broadened. My shoulders felt lighter, and my back started to tingle. Maybe little wings were already budding.

I almost knocked over Mickey Rood with my hug when I got back to our Obits cube. Without his Darla tip, I'd still be on death faxes.

"Not content at the starter gate, I see," said Mickey.

He could still be facing heat for filling me in on the morning's call sheet. "Thanks Mickey, without you," I started to say.

Rood shook his head. "If it weren't for my wobbly knee, I'd have gone down and stolen your scoop myself. Battinger made a bad call there."

"But how did you know I was already—" I started again.

Mickey tapped his temple. "I pay pretty good attention." As if to add, *and speaking of which,* he pushed a file over to my side of the desk. "Some mail came for you," he said. "From Oregon."

I hadn't heard from my mother in a few years. We'd never been very close and after my father died, she sort of disappeared. The other women on the commune did their best to take on the mothering responsibilities, and her mantra was, *it takes a village,* but the village was mostly taking care of itself. I was surprised to see her handwriting, but not surprised by the brevity of her note. It was on a yellow Post-it, in fact, attached to a short list typed on a piece of coarse card-stock. "The past is important," it read. "I know you always wanted to know your father's family. Now that you seem to be staying there, perhaps you can find them." The list had only five names, none of them familiar, and none of them ended with Miller. Was it possible my father had used an alias too?

There was no way to act on the note. I already had a whale of a fish to fry. And whales aren't even fish. I handed the list to Mickey. "Know any of these people?"

"Would I?"

"I don't know. They might've been passed through the desk. Probably famous enough to get obits; moneyed enough, anyway, and they're probably all gone by now."

"Nothing slaps me in the face," he said. "But if you want me to do a search, I will. People are my specialty."

18

Deep Throat

My one shot: my last shot. It's either page one or the exit.

M. E. Smarte clears out for his annual Majorca holiday and Curtis invites me upstairs. Jaime agrees to let me go with a lift of his shoulders, as if to say, *What the hell do I know*?

I kiss Mickey Rood on the forehead and, whistling a phrase or two of *"Con los pobres estoy, noble soy,"* I hoist my cardboard box off my desk. Backing into the elevator for the one-floor ride to Culture, my blood races like the jockeys at Belmont. For the first time in months, I'm sanctioned to ride this pony up.

Curtis clicks shut the office door once I'm in. "Time to come clean. I need to know everything," he says. "How deep are you into this thing?"

I unload my cardboard box of knickknacks and the truth as far as I know it. Recap montage. All the way back to the start: *section geriatric*, *fresh blood*, Pinsky, OB/DNP, *too soon to tell*, Randy Antillo, backspace through Word, fancy stationary, "V. Vane" invite, snake eyes wake, plum face, Blondie's *I love you*! Darla's brand of purity, Rx the cat, Stain's huge face, Wicked Rick's pitch, my failed return to Style, Rood's call sheet call, and my visit back to pure—not so pure anymore. I talk for a good twenty minutes and then it's all on the table, along with my notepads, my antique letter opener, my pens and nightlife guides. I show him the map I made of Wallace's allies and enemies, and he tacks it to his wall.

I've given him all I have. Everything except Cabeza. I keep him out of the story. Just for now, I tell myself. Because that part's a little sticky.

"Okay," Curtis says. "So what do you figure? You think Darla was involved?"

I tell him what I think I've got. It takes a while, and when I get to the end I'm less convinced than ever that I've got anything. "I bet there's some way to paint by these numbers. Darla seems to think I know something about it, otherwise she wouldn't have been so eager to get me locked up. So it's possible I do know something."

"Okay, it sounds like we've got a lot of leads here, and you've done great work already, Valerie," says Curtis. "We need to start with Bigs Cru. They could easily be our perps. There are other people who could've known about it too, though, right? If she had all those paintings, there were other graffiti artists involved. Anyone could've been pissed that she sold those paintings if they belonged to someone else."

"Yep," I say. "Wallace was the Golden Gadfly. You said it yourself. He could've told any graffiti writer in New York. Maybe one or two in Philly. Maybe he told you about it and you let it buzz in your ear. In that case, you're a suspect too."

Curtis pulls his chair up next to mine. "Okay, let's start at the beginning again and jot down every possible angle. We may not be able to solve your murder. The best we can do, if we can do it, is figure out who tagged up Darla's. All we need is motive and opportunity. You lead the way. And we haven't got much time, because Battinger wants it pronto. So get ready for a good long whiff of the grindstone."

We go over it again. And again. We drill it. What we know. What we don't know. What we need to know to make it fly. We make lists. Concise, pointed, nothing wasted. We've got to get well oiled. We've got three days and so far we've got nothing. But we're going to nail it. We're ready. We're set.

I grab a cap off Curtis's hat rack and stick a business card in the brim. It doesn't say "Press," like in the old days, but anyone can read "The Paper" if they get close. I slip off my heels. No more stilettos for this gumshoe. It's time to get serious in my flats.

This time around, I'm a unicycle rider: all legwork.

My first stop is Diaz Pizzeria on 207th Street and the mural of Stain's mile-wide grin. They're done. The wall is complete. Gravestones echo to eternity. The words read: "Malcolm. In Memoriam. You were our inspiration." Votive candles burn on the sidewalk. Bottles of unopened rum. A young girl is there, silently leaving a bouquet of blue carnations. No sign of the Cru. I go inside the pizzeria, where Frankie Diaz is behind the counter throwing dough. He tells me Clu and Wicked Rick are at the shop. Rx left for Jamaica this morning. He suggests I give the office a ring.

"I heard about that gallery job. But no way it's any of my boys. They've got a serious rep to maintain. Otherwise they don't get commissions," Diaz says. "Boys did a job for Glenfiddich up near the mall in the spring. First thing Rx did when he got paid was buy a ticket to Montego Bay."

I ask Diaz for Rx's address anyway. He hands it over along with a number for Bigs Cru. "I'm telling you, it's not these boys. But go ahead and check for yourself." I do. I bang on Rx's door on Fordham Road for a while. I don't get anyone home. I knock on nearby doors, cold calling.

"Have you ever heard of a man named Malcolm Wallace? . . . How about someone who goes by Stain? . . . Do you know your neighbor, a guy who goes by Rx? Ever see him do vandalism? Ever see him break in anywhere? . . . Who was close enough to

Wallace to avenge his death? . . . Did you ever hear about a fire at an art warehouse downtown, in Manhattan? . . . What's your number for follow-up, if you don't mind my . . . "

Just when my wrist cramps up my phone rings. It's Wicked Rick. He tells me to meet him on the boulevard at a swanky joint called Jimmy's Bronx Café. He's there when I get there. He's ordered me an iced tea. He lays it all out: Rx has flown but his alibi is airtight. Clu's wife gave birth on the night of the break-in and they all met up at the hospital to smoke cigars. Rx finished off the Ron del Barrilito at Clu's place before passing out on the sofa. He stayed there until Rick drove him directly to JFK at 6:00 a.m. It's an alibi, sure, but I need to check it. He says, "This is the work of young kids who don't have a lot of experience. We call them toys. We're in our forties, Ms. Vane, we don't have the energy for those kinds of stunts. Not that we ever really did."

I thank him and leave him with the iced tea. I head back out onto the streets, to put more calluses on my knuckles. I get mostly shaking heads. Nope . . . never heard of him. . . . Don't know about that. . . . What's that name again? . . . Sorry . . . not familiar. . . . Wouldn't know . . . ninguna . . . Did you try the guy across the street? . . . Did you try Diaz Pizzeria? . . . Have you tried his house? . . . His mother? . . . The school? . . . His aunt? . . . Why would you ask me? . . . Sorry, no English. . . . Those kids? They're no good. . . . I wish they didn't live around here. . . . Always making trouble. . . . You're from where? . . . Did you say you were a reporter? . . . I'm sorry, you're knocking on the wrong door. . . . No solicitors, please. . . . Following the wrong path . . . This isn't where you should be looking. . . . . Have you tried Manhattan?

By midday, I'm picking up the Bronx's two-three rhythm in my flats. Finally, I get confirms on the Rx alibi. American Airlines says that Rx redeemed his ticket from JFK to Montego Bay. Harlem Hospital says he was indeed in the waiting room that night drinking rum. And the kicker: a vandal squad dick who's been at the gallery says none of the marks at Darla's match the Bigs Cru handprint. Finally, Rx calls me himself, and a Jamaican area code shows on the caller ID. "Rickety told me to get in touch with you," he says over the scratchy line. "You want something from me?" I ask a few questions, but I've already given up on that particular prescription.

Next: I take the A express downtown to meet Curtis at Bomb the System, a West Broadway shop that sells all the paraphernalia anyone would need to fill a paint-stained backpack—fat and thin spray paint caps, grease pencils, stencils, black books, graff-inspired silk-screen tees, fanzines, and graffiti snapshots, or flix, along with concert tickets, fancy cigarettes, and bongs, just in case. We make nice with the owner, who calls himself Skid, though he's so round and pale I doubt he'd leave marks.

Once he's convinced we aren't coppers, he says, "I'll help you as much as I can, especially if you put the shop's name in your paper. We could use a plug. But just so you know: this isn't some kind of taxi stand where I hire out vandals to the blocks I like worst. The customers here are mostly wannabe's, but don't let them hear me say that. The real writers are leery. They won't believe you're not the police. I won't get in your way if you want to ask anyone questions. But I doubt you'll get much."

For a couple hours, we query skateboard punks in line for concert tickets Skid is selling, European graffiti tourists in town to tag our hallowed walls, and a handful of Staten Island teens in search of a fancy stencil.

"Have you heard about the recent gallery graffiti in Chelsea? ("There's a graffiti gallery in Chelsea?") It was on the news. . . . Someone broke into a place and sprayed up the paintings. ("Didn't hear about that." . . . "Just got into town." . . . "Oh, yeah. I heard about that. Who did it?") That's what we're trying to figure out. . . . Know any kids who ever broke into a place to spray paint? ("Why would they do that?" . . . "Plenty left to bomb out here.") Seen any work that looks like this? . . . Or this? ("Wow, those are killer." . . . "They did that?") Look familiar? ("Nah." . . . "If I knew that guy I'd know him, you know?" . . . "That's a dope style.") How so? ("Dunno." . . . "Can't really explain it." . . . "Just different, you know? Look at the curve.") Know anyone who could be hired to vandalize something? . . . Know anyone who knew Stain? ("Oh, yeah." . . . "Sure, I know him." . . . "He's the Bronx guy." . . . "He's old school. Real famous.") Any idea who did this?

Nada. Nyet. Nein. Nu-uh. Ninguna. Dunno. Not a single word closer to the facts in any language. We wash down our defeat with bourbon at the SoHo Grand, flipping through graffiti fanzines and flix at the bar, searching for piecers that place. Curtis tells me about his morning at the courthouse and the cop shop. Seems Wallace had filed a complaint in State Supreme Court against Darla Deitrick Fine Art for ten paintings, valued at $50,000 per. He says he either wanted the paintings back or he wanted the money. If she sold them, she owed him half.

I do quick math. "A quarter of a million dollars is not nothing," I say. "Maybe it was enough to want to knock him off?"

"I don't know about that, Valerie. These dealers trade in more than that at least once a week." Curtis slugs back bourbon. "And why wouldn't she just give him back the paintings if she had them?"

I'm thinking it over. "She didn't have them. She's already sold them. She doesn't tell him that, though. She tells him she'll give them back, but she doesn't have them to give back. So she burns down the warehouse and plans to give him the insurance money instead."

"Could be insurance fraud. If she planned to pay him why would she kill him?"

I keep chewing on the ice from my glass. The barman comes

over and asks me if I want another. I nod. "He found out about the arson?" I say. "Threatened to expose her? He's like that. A big mouth, right?"

"Was." Curtis orders another bourbon. "I don't think it's enough. It would have to be something bigger. Otherwise she wouldn't risk it."

"Maybe some kind of insurance fraud. You get real time for that, right?"

We're all over the ballpark, but at least we're tossing it around. I don't have a lot of practice in this game. I swig my new bourbon. It doesn't make me any brighter. "She sold the paintings to an unknown collector out of state, but didn't collect tax," I try. "Or she had him pay her through a Swiss bank account. I've read about this kind of thing. She promises to get Wallace his paintings, then plants fakes and destroys them. She kills Wallace because he knows about the arson, insurance fraud, and tax fraud."

Curtis laughs out his nose. "Our Darla's turning out to be quite a femme fatale." He shakes his head back so his dreads dance. "I don't know. The plot's too thick. It's got to be simpler. Anyone from August Dupin to Miss Marple will tell you: the solution to a mystery of this sort is always hidden in plain sight. The truth is right in front of your nose the whole time."

"Those are detective classics," I say. "In the hardboiled school, nothing ends up simple. The solution is always 'Nothing is as it seems.' "

Back at the office, Bob Torrens, the red-bow-tied photo chief, is rapping at our door. He wants pix for a layout pronto and we haven't even jotted word one. Now we feel the crunch: a day of reporting and still we have zilch.

That night, I walk a few blocks east of The Paper and hail a cab, telling the driver to drop me near the Steinway factory, just over the Queensboro. It's a short walk to Cabeza's studio from there and nobody trolls the lonely cobblestone streets. No one but me.

Cabeza uncorks a pinot noir and I ask him to list for me names of writers who were close enough to Wallace to factor. He starts with A-1, as the wine glugs into my glass, and he works his way up the alphabet from Ader to Zephyr, ticking off every graff writer Darla might've sniffed or snubbed since 1979. We talk old school and new school, toys and masters, legendaries, kings, all-city, buffers and battles, crews and lone gunmen on every train line from City Island to Howard Beach. We talk scratchiti, stencils, paint rollers, and stickers. We've got lists of names and lists of lists. We're covering ground without getting distance. It's after midnight and all I've made all day is lists.

We stop. We turn down the lights. I stand up to get the bottle and pour myself some more wine, tripping over the leg of a tripod. The camcorder's little red light is flickering. "Did you know this thing is on?" I say.

"Oh, turn it off, will you?" he says, leaning back in his chair and taking off his sandals. "I was filming myself earlier doing monologues. I'm thinking about auditioning again for the screen."

"Again? You've done that before?"

"You're not the only one with secret movie-star ambitions." He turns to show me his best celluloid profile. I get behind the camera and look through the lens. I pluck it off the tripod and zoom in. A few wrinkles here and there by his eyes, sure, but they give him dignity, they make him look tough, worldly-wise.

"Let's do a little screen test."

He stands up and I follow him with the camera.

"Ah, but you underestimate me," he says. "I'm quite a good actor." He raises his wineglass and clears his throat, takes a step back. He's going to get thespian on me.

"Tomorrow and tomorrow and tomorrow creeps in *this pretty face* from day to day." He reaches out his free hand and cups my chin. "To the last syllable of *The Paper of Record*, and all our yesterdays were *fit to print* our way to a dusty death." He puts down his glass and twirls me into the crook of his arm. His nose touches mine. "Out, out, brief candle."

Day two: "Interesting factoid," Curtis says by way of greeting at 7:00 a.m. "I asked Tracy to put together a list of Wallace's biggest collectors. And who should appear at the top of it, but your old fiancé, Jeremiah Sinclair Golden Jr."

"He wasn't my fiancé," I say, putting down my purse.

"Oh, I'm sorry. Your booooyfriend." The sides of his lips suppress a smile.

"That's low," I say.

"Still a little bruised, huh?"

"A little." I move to Smarte's chair and sit, hoping to punctuate the conversation with a full stop.

"Aw. Tell me where it hurts." He pokes me with his pencil eraser. "Here?" He pokes me again. "Here?"

"Okay," I say. "I graduated preschool twenty years ago."

Curtis mock-pouts. "It's a potential issue, though, don't you think?"

"What?"

"Jeremiah's collection of Stains."

"He was always pretty tainted. It was a little bit of a game for him, trying to find the jewel in the rough. It seems he wasted a lot of money on nobodies. He had one Warhol that was worth something and I understand he sold it to Gagosian to pay his legal bills."

Curtis tosses a back issue of *Art News* onto my lap. There's Jeremiah, in all his preppy splendor, hair greased back, cheekbones airbrushed, standing in front of a twelve-foot Schnabel.

"He had good luck early on," says Curtis. "Seems he started collecting before he was even legal to drink. Bought Schnabel and Kenny Scharf, a few small Basquiat drawings. This story says he probably owns a dozen Stains," Curtis says. "He sure knew how to pick them in the eighties."

The art in the attic. "I never saw Schnabel or Scharf, though I didn't get a very good look at his collection. Maybe he'd already sold them by that time."

"He still owns some, at least. They're going to be exhibited in a hip-hop retrospective in Germany. A place called the Ludwig Museum. I'm telling you, it's only beginning. The eighties retro wave is going to hit us like a tsunami. This doesn't present a conflict, does it, Valerie?"

"What conflict? I don't talk to the guy. He doesn't talk to me."

"Do you know if they ever met each other—your fiancé and Wallace?"

"I can't imagine it."

Curtis stands up. "Well, as far as I'm concerned, that qualifies Mr. Golden for your map." He picks up a Sharpie. His hand hovers over the Upper East Side of Manhattan on the wall map. He writes "JSG2" at the intersection of Sixty-third Street and Lexington, then he pauses. "That puts you on here too, Valerie. And where did you say you were from, again? Park Avenue?"

I pull myself in under Smarte's desk, fastening on my phone headset. I punch numbers for the DA's office, largely for effect. The call goes through to Betty Schlachter, the flack, and I make my official request one more time: "Anything new on the gallery vandalism case? Anything on Wallace?"

"We're well aware of your interest in both cases, Miss Vane," Schlachter says. "Both are still under investigation. We'll call you when there's any news."

"I'll call you first."

Tyler Prattle sticks his head through the door. "Anyone got

a moment to let this old codger vent on an idea for Week in Review?"

Prattle is seven feet tall, mostly freckles—a giant pointillist masterpiece. If he moves too fast, he might scatter. I look at Curtis. Moore and Lessey have obviously asked him to check in with us. No way Prattle cares what a newbie like me thinks about his op-eds. Curtis nods, to say, "You go." He's making up for harassing me about Jeremiah.

I follow Prattle into his office next door. Before I've taken a seat, he launches in: "Minimalist art and graffiti are at opposite poles of an aesthetic spectrum, right? Right? One is the ultimate expression of the art world's elitism and the other its most populist, right? Am I right?"

I nod.

"No, I am not right," says Prattle, gleefully clapping his hands. "That's too simplistic. One doesn't have to look very hard to see that these two movements have a tremendous amount in common, a tremendous amount. For one, each genre has an act of aggression at its core. It forces the viewer to overcome an initial resistance, even, perhaps, hatred, toward the artist, toward the piece. Neither provides the viewer with something that's easy to look at. Both require the viewer to be uneasy, or to overcome that unease, to overcome the hatred of the act of painting. But that's not all, is it, not all, right?"

"I'm going to guess it's not."

"No, not all," he says, clapping again soundlessly. His hands are dot clusters, held together by sheer serendipity—sort of like his argument. "There's also the corresponding meta-function. Graffiti asks: Who owns art if art is everywhere, if art is public? Minimalism asks: Who owns art if art is light? If art is the way shadows play against a flat surface? Both say—you own art, you, the viewer. *What you see is what you see,* as Frank Stella said. Brilliant, yes?"

"Brilliant," I agree. It is my place to agree, but I'm also thinking it over. If I'm understanding him correctly, he's breaking down the high-low duality, and saying there's no difference between what Wallace produced on the streets and what Johns produced for the Met. It's heady stuff, but I can't imagine too many grannies who read the Sunday paper would swallow it. He's maybe fishing for letters to the editor. In any case, Stain would've been pleased. I tell Prattle that much.

He giggles and claps his hands. "This is a good one. One for the anthology!"

Back out into the streets for more interviews. This time, Curtis and I tag-team. I query kids in Life Drawing class at the Wallace painting school. He questions art dealers in Chelsea and SoHo; I chat with pencil-tapping art profs who want to plug their books. He rounds up Bronx activists promoting local causes. I interview East Village eighties nostalgics who wish they were back in the good old days when no one but hard-core art lovers and drug dealers went downtown. He tracks down tony art-market reporters who regale him with stories about the exhilarating sales during the last art market boom. Back at the office, feet up on chairs, transcribing our notes, Curtis says, "At least if we don't get the story, we can always compile an Encyclopedia of New York Poseurs."

What we don't get—what it's obvious we need—is legit graff writers, the ones still scrawling, the ones on the street. How do we get to them? They're not at Bomb the System, obviously. They're not at galleries. They don't have union spokesmen or high-paid flacks. They don't attend Life Drawing, and they don't do legal walls. They keep odd hours. They fly by night. They climb scaffolding and rusted fire escapes. They hide. Finding them is like finding prowlers. Like finding Batman in his cave.

Curtis goes in search of his old sources from his days at the

Voice. I track down our subway reporter, Lou Gaines, and ask him to tell me the best-painted tunnels. He tells me a handful of stations. He suggests I wait at the edge of a subway platform, near the NO TRESPASSING signs. He says the kids jump onto the rails once the trains pull out. He suggests I watch and wait.

I do as he says. I start at 6:00 p.m. at the Jay Street–Borough Hall stop in Brooklyn and I wait. And I keep waiting. I see nothing for a long, long while. I hear Gaines in my head: "It's sort of like waiting for rats in an alley. They're there. But they might not be smiling at you. Just keep an eye out." At 10:00 p.m., I finally spot one: the train pulls out, and I look right, and a kid is slipping past the signs. I follow, like a mugger, a thief. I see him sidestep down the narrow edge of the platform, then get to the end and jump onto the empty tracks. I think, "Third rail." I'm afraid. "I'm about to get fried."

But then I hear Battinger's final caveat: *This is your last shot*. Page one or the exit. I don't have a choice. It's onto the rails or out the door.

I jump. I find the kid a few yards up, his spray can hoisted and hissing, the black wall of the tunnel sprayed wetly with the letters *TNL*. He hears my step and he bolts. I chase. I shout, "Reporter! Not cops! Not MTA! I need help! A reporter!" Maybe because my voice is female, maybe because he's just a little kid, he stops. I give him my name. I tell him what I'm doing. I say all I want is an idea how to find another writer.

"Could you take a look at these flix?" I say, holding out the snaps from Darla's vandalism job. He blinks at me through his facemask. Maybe he's amused that I've got the lingo. He looks back at the flix, lit by a safety light in the tunnel.

Finally, in a squeaky voice, he says, "I can't recognize these others. But I'd know those curlicues anywhere. That's RIF's hand for sure."

My notebook is out of my pocket fast. At long last, a genuine lead. "Where do I find him?" I ask my kid. He tells me. I nearly kiss him. "How do we get out of here?" I ask. He leads me through the tunnel down the line. We cross onto an idle track until we're deep under the grid. There's a doorway there that leads to a staircase. We climb up a ladder on the wall to get to the door. We hear something move behind us.

"Come quick," he whispers and he grabs my arm. My heart jolts, I race behind him up a narrow stairwell, circling, heading up. Next thing I know he's pushing a metal grate above him, and we're up and out, a fresh night breeze on my face. He pulls me out and slams down the grate. We're back on the city streets, in the middle of nowhere.

I follow him until he finds me a new subway entrance. My heart slows. "That was pretty awesome," I say. "You're just great."

He chuckles through his facemask. "You're a funny lady. Just don't tell RIF it was me."

I don't need to look at a map now to know how to get to the South Bronx. I find the door for RIF's apartment in the James Monroe Houses, the one I got from TNL. I do the walk-up and knock. An Italian grandma gives me the one up, one down, saying, "Oh, you're looking for our little Picasso." Then she turns and yells, *"Carrrlo,"* as she leads me through the railroad flat. "*Carlo!* You're finally famous just like you wanted. Come explain yourself to your adoring press."

It turns out Carlo and I have a friend in common—a young man named Kamal Prince Tatum. It's been a long trip just to get back to where I started. Before I leave the Bronx, I make one more stop.

No one is home at Amenia's. So I slide my business card under the door with a note: "If I figured it out, the cops won't be too far behind. With me, you have a chance to tell your side."

• • •

Back in Queens after midnight, I prop myself up on Cabeza's pillow and I loop my index finger through one of his curls. "Given the circumstances, this could be perceived as a conflict of interest," I say.

"This? You mean the fact that you're in bed with a source?" he says, dragging his pinky finger slowly up my thigh. "But you tracked Kamal all by your lonesome."

His pinky continues up, making a circle around my navel. "I'm feeling less conflicted every minute."

His pinky takes a tour of my breasts. "That's good, because I haven't lost any interest."

We don't talk for a while. Not with our voices. We drift out, and the faces and names and details and concerns of the day dissipate with a cool fan-blown breeze. I feel the sweat lift off my back. I roll with him like a stone at water's edge, *From Here to Eternity*. I roll again, the water washing over me, back and forth, until all I'm aware of is Cabeza's warm weight and his low, dry moan.

Afterward, I find myself another loose curl and twirl it. "Where would Wallace would be now if he were still alive?"

Cabeza is smoking; his head drops to the side. "Why, here, in bed with us, of course."

I push another pillow under my head and turn onto my back. "I'd love to know what Wallace was like as a teacher. I bet the students adored him. I bet he had some compelling riff about the spirituality of the burner or the transcendence of the fill-in. What it means to 'get up.' "

Cabeza strokes my belly. "You're a quick study, baby."

"When I was in that tunnel with that kid today, I got a taste of what it's like. The adrenaline rush. The feeling of being chased, wanted. It was thrilling. It was the kind of feeling you'd want to have again and again. I can see why people do it. It's not just about getting your name up. It's not just about the fame or the props. You're getting off the grid, all the way off."

"You make it all sound very romantic."

"It was romantic," I say. "I hadn't expected that. I wish I'd had half the chutzpah Stain did, to just keep going for it, even when nobody's watching." I turn to face Cabeza. "I got Wallace all wrong. When I wrote that Obit on him, I thought he was nobody. I didn't even realize how big he was in the eighties. No wonder all these kids thought he was a hero."

Cabeza reaches for a strand of my hair and presses it behind my ear. "Methinks my *linda* is in love with a ghost."

He could be right. "Wallace was like us," I say. "He tried to get inside the machine, and he realized he didn't fit there. But he didn't stick around and just sink into the abyss. He found another way to make his mark. I admire that."

"Maybe that makes sense."

"What do you think, Cabeza? Would you go with me? If I left it all behind? I'm thinking Woodstock. I'm thinking of planting a garden."

"You see? What did I say? Sunburst is shining back through."

"So?"

"I say finish your story," says Cabeza. "I say, once it's done, we can talk about the next step."

The next morning, Amenia Wallace Tatum is waiting in The Paper's marble foyer with Kamal Prince. He's just as I left him: a six-foot mound of uncooked dough. Maybe a little worse for the wear: his mother seems to have dragged him by his ear two hundred blocks south. He jabs the toe of his Puma into the floor. Amenia says, "We got your note late last night. My son has something to say to you."

We go upstairs, find Curtis, and shut the office door. Kamal confesses everything, from the plan for "the action" conceived at the Wallace memorial to the names of his accomplices: RIF, BANG, TRK and N/R. "Stain had the Art Crime Posse, so we called ourselves the Rebel Art Posse," he tells us. "I don't like that lady dealer. My uncle told me she took his paintings without paying, and that's not right. I wanted to get her back." He looks from us to his mother, who is very slowly shaking her head and clutching her purse like a string of rosaries.

"I thought you weren't into graffiti," I say. "I thought you wanted to be another kind of writer."

"Yeah," he says. "But journalists are liars."

I take that a little personally. But I can't exactly blame him. "You didn't have to destroy priceless paintings," I say.

Kamal waves his hands in the air. "No, no. That's just the thing. We had no idea those paintings were important like that." His bottom lip starts to quiver. "I was pretty surprised when my moms said they were from a museum. I mean, they were all just white. I thought they were planning on putting something else up there."

I've got to smile. "But what about the guard?"

"No guard. It was like the place was wide open, anyway. I swear, we didn't mean to ruin anyone's art," Kamal says quickly. He's been waiting to say it for days. "It was just, you know, to make a point that the lady dealer didn't own my uncle's art work. I'm really sorry. I'm really, really sorry."

Amenia's eyes track from her son to Curtis and back. "Prince would never have done anything like this before Malcolm passed," she says. "That man used to look out for him, make sure he didn't get into trouble. Without Malcolm, I think he's all mixed up. I want him to take responsibility for his actions, but I'm worried about going to the police. You can understand. They aren't always sympathetic to poor black children. And Prince is a child, but he looks much older." She glances at me. "We also wanted to make sure the story got out right. We want to make sure Kamal doesn't look like some thug."

Curtis thinks it over for a while, turning from right to left in his swivel chair. He glances at the map on the wall, then at me, then up at the ceiling. Amenia watches his face and Kamal looks up at me from under those angelic eyelashes.

"Okay," Curtis says, finally. "I'm going to give you the best deal I can clear. If you give us everything you've got, and if you let us use some quotes from Kamal and if we can secure some comments from the other writers, we can help you. First, we run the story. Then tomorrow, when the paper hits the newsstands, before the cops send out a goon squad, I'll personally walk you and Kamal Prince into One Police Plaza to submit his written confession. I'll stay with you through the processing, and keep an eye on you in case anything goes awry."

Amenia looks like a few thousand skyscrapers have been lifted off her back. We walk the two of them to the elevator and outside the fortress. I doubt anyone we pass in the hall would finger this kid as a vandal.

"So, any chance I could help redeem your faith in journalism?" I ask Kamal out on the street. The air has cooled a little, but it's a bright sunny day.

"Maybe documentaries," he says. "I've been using the camera for man-on-the-streets."

I look at Amenia and at Curtis. "That's good. Maybe it's a better future for you than all this graffiti stuff, huh?"

"I'm done with that," says Kamal.

Amenia's eyes cloud. "You said it. Now I just hope you remember it." She shakes both our hands, Curtis's especially. "Thanks for being so understanding. Thanks for setting the record straight. We'll see you early tomorrow."

Curtis and I press the final keystroke on the Darla story at 5:00 p.m. While the backfield editors are taking a look at our three-thousand-word opus, we head to Jimmy's Corner and order a couple rounds. "You're a real hardboiled news hawk now," says Curtis. "You've earned the right to drink your bourbon neat."

I drink my bourbon and think of all the rough-and-tumble newsmen who have rolled through this spot in the last thirty years. Did they nurse their beers to the same Billie Holiday on the juke? On the walls and mirrors are tacked thirty years' worth of boxing memorabilia. I wonder, too, through the dusty light in the smoked-out mirrors did they, same as me, love being surrounded by the ghosts of prizefighters?

We head back to the office for round after round of editing. The backfield hands it off to Battinger, and she runs it by Moore and Lessey for vetting, and then Battinger goes over it once again with a fine-tooth comb. From there, the copy editors coax and prod it into standard style, fact-checking every inch, then a page one editors meeting takes a whack. Finally, around 11:30, just before the section goes to bed, Battinger has her mitts on the final version.

She has only one question: "So, Valerie Vane, are you sure you want to continue your career with this ridiculous Style-girl byline?"

19

Headline News

There on A-1, below the fold, 2,624 words, with a two-page jump and four pix:

> ## For Bronx Teen, "Tagging" Priceless Art Soothed Unspeakable Grief
>
> ### Chelsea Gallery Vandals Riled by Death of Eighties Artist
>
> by Curtis Wright and S. R. Miller
>
> All he saw was white. To him, it was emptiness, the void. The white canvases on the walls may have been worth upward of $50 million, but he couldn't possibly calculate values like that. He saw only a blank slate, and the chance, at last, to express some portion of his grief.
>
> For a week, Kamal Prince Tatum, 16, a South Bronx High School sophomore from Hunts Point, had been mourning the death of his uncle, Malcolm Wallace. Mr. Wallace, who used the graffiti name Stain 149, was a blockbuster artist in the early 1980s, showing at prominent galleries in New York, Paris, and Düsseldorf. His work is owned by several

major museums, including the Museum of Modern Art, the Tate Modern in London, and the Los Angeles County Museum of Art. Next month he will be the subject of a retrospective at the Ludwig Museum in Germany.

To his nephew, however, he was more than that. He was a man who rebelled against the art establishment and sought to give a voice to underserved communities. He was a man who stayed true to his heritage, and he returned to the Bronx ghettoes he'd come from to establish a painting school for low-income youth.

Kamal wanted to express his grief in a way he thought would make his uncle proud—by making a statement within the art establishment that had rejected Mr. Wallace.

But the police didn't see it that way. And neither did Darla Deitrick, the owner of the 24th Street Chelsea gallery that was tagged by graffiti artists on July 30, just before dawn.

After all, these weren't blank canvases. The list of price estimates could've put an average Christie's auction to shame: The Metropolitan Museum of Art's White Flag, by Jasper Johns is estimated at $20 million. The Museum of Modern Art's Suprematist Composition: *White on White* by Kasimir Malevich is estimated at $18 million. Cy Twombly's 1955 Untitled, from a private owner, is estimated at $4 million.

The story of Mr. Wallace's life as a painter and the interaction he had with Ms. Deitrick is an art world parable, setting one artist's desire for immortality against the unpredictable forces of the marketplace and the powerful dealers who operate it. Although the reason for his death is still unclear, it seems that his own efforts to control his legacy may have contributed to his untimely demise. . . .

Curtis and I still hadn't nailed down the cause of his death. Instead of writing a reason, this time, we'd done a classic vague-out: "mysterious death," "circumstances unclear," "early suggestion of suicide," "still puzzling police." No one seemed worried about it. All they wanted was more Wallace. The fact that he was both recently deceased and newly famous made him a hot ticket. By midafternoon, representatives from Sotheby's and Christie's and a handful of private art dealers had called the office to find out who was handling his estate. Curtis was down at the district attorney's office with Amenia and Kamal, so I told these callers to try back later.

Meanwhile, I sat in my cube in Obits and received my kudos. Clint Westwood came around and shook my hand. Randy Antillo stopped by to say, "That's pretty cool, Val. Really cool. You know, when I was fifteen, that guy was like, my idol. I remember a few months ago when he was downtown at that rally . . ." Rusty Markowitz gave me a thumbs-up from across the room. Jaime signed me up for a few new advancers.

By noon, I was pretty puffed up with praise, just enough to feel like I could float out the door. Jaime told me I might as well take the rest of the afternoon off—"and hell, take tomorrow off too. It's summer, and I'm feeling generous," he said. "We'll get started on new work on Monday." I was packing up my death faxes when Buzz Phipps's BMW face parked in front of my cube. "Can we still call it the Valerie Treatment?" he asked. "Even with your new byline?"

"Sure," I said. "Nobody's ever calling me Sunburst out loud."

"Whatever we call her, this girl I'm looking at is on to bigger and better things," he said. "I'm proud of you. If you've ever got Style ideas, just run them by me so I can shoot them down."

"Sure." I smiled. "Definitely."

Buzz flashed his expensive teeth and left. I was standing up to make my exit when the phone rang. I took my purse instead.

But when I was almost past Rewrite, the ringleted clerk cried, "Valerie Vane, call on line four." I backed up to Randy Antillo's empty desk and, still standing, picked up the receiver. "Obits," I said. "Vane."

"Vane? I thought it was S. R. Miller now. Or can I just call you Sunburst Rhapsody?" His voice made my legs go weak. I sat down in Randy's chair.

"Jeremiah."

"Congratulations, sweetheart. I always knew you'd end up back on top." His voice was hoarse.

"What do you want, Jeremiah?"

"Nothing, Val. I just wanted to say hello and to congratulate you. To see how things are going. Maybe you've read in the tabloids, things are over between Angelica and me."

"Heard about that. I'm sorry for you."

"Don't be. She didn't mean anything to me. I made a big mistake. I should've stayed with you."

"That's a lovely sentiment, Jeremiah. But I've really got to go now. I'm meeting someone—"

"We're both starting over now," he said. "You with your new byline, me with my one-bedroom in Brooklyn Heights. I'll be moving in a couple of weeks. You ever walk on the Brooklyn Promenade? My real estate agent says it's beautiful in the mornings."

"I'm sure it is."

"What do you say? Could we take a stroll sometime, talk? Just like in the old days?"

I didn't remember a single stroll we'd ever taken. I didn't really remember seeing much of Jeremiah in daylight, and I definitely didn't remember much talking. "I'm sorry about what happened with Angelica, Jeremiah. I guess it was partially my fault. I really regret everything I did that night. But I don't think—"

He chuckled for no apparent reason. Maybe just to put me on edge. "Oh, I see. Everything's swell for you now; you don't need me, huh? Well, just don't get too comfy with your good fortune. It's amazing how quickly the floor can slip out from under you."

I assumed he meant Angelica, or maybe just the bathroom floor. I was about to say something biting, something about how he didn't have any right to talk to me about mistakes. But I didn't have the heart.

"I wish you the best of everything," I told him. "I've got to go now." I hung up and headed quickly down the escape hatch to Queens. Cabeza was there at his studio waiting for me, two martini glasses in his hands.

Some mornings start slow. So slow you think there might be nothing to the day but morning. Nothing but the soft curve of a lover's foot, the sleek hull of a sailing ship. No sound but the whir of the fan forming white caps on the sheets. No smell but the salty morning brine on his lips.

I lay thinking of the ceiling and nothing else. It had cracks. It was a pale, forgiving gray. Its mildew stains were cumulus clouds, puffy and shape shifting. At some point, I knew I'd have to get up. But for the moment, I drifted, and listened to Cabeza's snore, a hush like waves crashing.

Later, when he was stirring, I woke and watched him move around the room. He was naked. Even though we'd been together, I felt strange watching. He had been a muscular man, a tough man, perhaps all his adult life. But there were signs of age in his body now. His torso, a classic V, was sunken slightly under his breastbone; the muscles in his calves and thighs were strong, but the skin under his hips had softened. He reminded me of a leading man just past his prime, trying to suck it in, hold his face at angles that wouldn't reveal the emerging jowl. Robert Mitchum in later life as an aging Marlowe in *Farewell, My Lovely* and the remake of *The Big Sleep*. For a moment, I felt sorry for him, and then I felt a rush of something I might call love. And then I didn't want to be a spectator anymore. "Comeeer, baby," I purred.

Some time later, the morning was still morning. And I was adrift again. The ceiling was forming new cracks, new clouds. His eyes opened and he turned over onto me, again finding my lips. "I can still taste the vermouth," he said.

I got up, lazily, without wanting to. I still wasn't thinking about anything. I was just sensing the room around me, feeling out the day. I looked for my clothes. I found my dress draped over the projector reel, one shoe inside a kitchen cabinet and another in the freezer. I closed the refrigerator and leaned against it, dreamily. There was something on my mind, swinging its legs like a kid on a fence. But I couldn't figure out what it was. Then my cell phone was ringing.

It took a while to find my purse. It was in the bathroom sink. I recognized the incoming number as Curtis's. "Hello there, partner," I said. "I hope you're enjoying all the praise."

"No such luck," he said, his voice all business.

"What's the matter?"

"Sotheby's announced a sale last night. A single owner sale. One of those celebrity auctions that attract big money. And who should be the seller but Jeremiah Sinclair Golden Jr., your ex-fiancé. The fax came in at six p.m., after we'd both left. Battinger checked back late, as she does sometimes, and picked it up from Rewrite. It turns out he's putting a collection of fifty art works on the block, mostly Stain works, and a few other eighties artists. Good timing, it seems, since it will come on the heels of that retrospective in Germany. Battinger is having a fit. She wants to know how come we didn't know about this. Or did we? It has to have been in the works for weeks, because they don't just announce a sale like this without first appraising the works, some preparation. She wants to talk to you, and not Monday."

This was bad. Jeremiah's art? Could this be why he'd phoned last night? Was there some message in his call I hadn't deciphered? Is this what he'd meant about how the floor could shift?

"I honestly don't know anything about that," I said to Curtis. "I knew he was a collector." We'd talked about it. It was out in the open. Curtis had thumb-tacked Jeremiah to the wall map, and then he'd put me on there too, with a line from one to the other. It had been a joke at the time, but now it wasn't as funny.

"We thought he had maybe a dozen Stains. This is a whole lot more. I didn't even know anyone owned that many. Where did he get them?"

"I have no idea." I didn't have any idea. But then my mind started ticking like a taxi meter. Could Jeremiah have been Darla's buyer? The one who'd cleared out the warehouse stash? If so, how did he get the money? As far as I knew he was broke. Could Blondie have been wrong about Jeremiah's reason for visiting the gallery? Could he have been there to buy, not sell? But how could he be buying all those pictures when Angelica was bleeding him? Unless, of course, he'd had a plan to turn them around fast.

"This is the first I've heard of it," I said.

"Battinger will want to hear that from you. She doesn't like the way it fits."

"I don't either."

It was possible Jeremiah had bought those Stains from Darla with the intention of selling once something upped their value. But he would've had to be banking on a story. It didn't tie together. How could I have been helping him if I hadn't been in contact with him all this time?

Curtis's voice softened. "Okay, just get in here soon."

"I'm already there." I rang off and held the phone in my hand, looking at it. Something moved behind me. I flinched, but it was only Cabeza. He was standing in the door frame in his boxer shorts, holding a knife.

"Do you want onions in your eggs?" he said, casually.

I didn't answer him right away. "I'm sorry. I don't think I can stay for eggs."

He looked at the phone in my hand. "The office?"

"Yeah."

"Claro." He smiled. "I guess that means you're in demand now that you're a big star."

"You could say that."

"I thought they'd given you the day off to bask in your success."

"Something came up."

"Too bad. I don't mean to be selfish, but I was looking forward to lazing around for a while and having some brunch, maybe even going out to some galleries, talk about a little town called Woodstock."

The mention of Woodstock suddenly made me queasy. "It is too bad. I'm sorry." I went into the other room. I sat down on the bed, but got up just as quickly. There was something wrong with the way the sheets were straightened. There was something untrue about the pillows the way they were piled on one another. Looking around the studio, it seemed to me the furniture wasn't set up right. As if it had been transported to this place and arranged, a little like a movie set. The cameras, the film reels on the table were just props.

I took a deep breath and told myself it was just the anxiety. Just the office. I was panicking because I was being accused, but I hadn't done anything wrong. But once I made things clear, anyone would be able to see that I had nothing to do with Jeremiah's sale. Why would I do anything that would benefit him, anyway? I hated the man. All I needed to do was put on my shoes, pick up my purse, go into work, and say so. I tried to clear my head, to tell myself nothing was wrong, to not think about anything.

"Everything all right?" said Cabeza, leaning into the room.

"Sure," I said, and he started to back into the kitchen again. Then I ran out of things to not think about. "I mean, well. No. I mean, I meant to ask you." He stepped into the room with me, and I had to swallow air fast.

"What?"

"About the martini you gave me last night when I arrived. It was a Vanitini," I paused, thinking of it. "How did you know the recipe?"

He took a few steps deeper into the room. "The recipe? Oh," he said, looking back into the kitchen as if the answer was there. Then he said, "That's easy. I read it on the Internet."

"On the Internet."

"Of course. You were once a little famous. Or didn't you know?"

Everything in the room started to look wrong. The walls seemed too thin, like hastily tacked-up plywood. Temporary. The windows seemed surprisingly small. There wasn't enough light filtering into the space. It would fool a camera, but cameras had ways of obscuring things, of leaving things out.

"You read it on the Internet," I said. The little lie always reveals the big lie. "And you never met Jeremiah Golden."

Cabeza clucked at me. "You'd be surprised. The Internet is a very powerful tool."

"You didn't answer my question," I said.

Cabeza took a few strides toward me. He was still holding the knife at his side.

"Don't come any closer," I said.

"Valerie, what is it? Has something happened? You're so on edge."

I wanted to take a step back, but my calves were already hard against the edge of the bed. There was nowhere to go on my side of the room. "Could you please back up a few steps? I don't feel comfortable having you any closer right now."

He took another step forward. "Sweetheart, what is it? What's wrong?"

My body went rigid, my chest tensed. "Please!" I very nearly shouted, then steadied my voice. "I need you to take a few steps back."

"*Claro,* okay, okay." He backed up and I moved around the side of the bed. I looked around me for something heavy, like a bat or a frying pan.

"What do you want to know? I'm happy to talk about anything," he said.

"Sotheby's announced a sale of Stain paintings, all owned by Jeremiah Golden. The press release went out last night; that's what they want me to come in to talk about this morning."

"Ah." Cabeza didn't seem surprised. "How could it have anything to do with you that Jeremiah wants to sell paintings?"

"It's weirdly coincidental."

"Purely coincidental. They won't be able to link you to him." The phrasing was wrong.

"You knew about this sale?"

He didn't answer. He seemed to consider it, but then his face formed an expression that said, *You're smart. You figure it out.*

"Then you know about the Jeremiah sale."

"I do," he said, matter-of-factly. "That doesn't mean you do."

He was already reasoning out my defense. But I didn't even know I had a defense I needed to make. I took a deep breath. "Cabeza, when did you meet Jeremiah?"

Cabeza pursed his lips. "A while ago, at a gallery opening at Deitrick's. Just once."

I held my breath, wishing he hadn't said that. I moved to the editing table and grabbed a film reel.

"Is that really necessary?" said Cabeza.

I held tighter to the metal; it felt useful in my hands. Maybe Cabeza had nothing to do with this. Maybe I was behaving foolishly, but I didn't have time to reason it out.

"How much of a cut are you getting from the sale?"

Cabeza laughed. "Okay, well, he is giving me a cut of the sale, but that also doesn't mean *you've* done anything wrong. And maybe it's best if you don't know any of this, if you need to go in and talk to your editor right now. You're not me. I'm not you. As far as your editor knows, we don't even know each other. But anyway, for me, the money isn't the main thing. It's the exhibition that matters."

I gasped. I hadn't expected to be right. But now something solidified in the pit of my gut. My grip tightened around the film reel like it was a ship's steering wheel in a nasty storm. "What exhibition?"

"The one at the Ludwig." Now his body went slack, as if he'd been balancing a plate on the top of his head for weeks, and he'd finally let it drop. He was still shirtless and as he moved across the room I noticed how his skin sagged. He took a seat on the couch and his gut bulged over the top of his pants, like the folds of a curtain. He looked cheap, not like a leading man anymore. More like an impersonator. Everything in the room started to look shoddy. "You really have to trust me, sweetheart. I've protected you entirely. But you might as well know. I'm the curator of the Ludwig exhibition—it's not official yet, but it will be soon, since I was technically working with Micah Stone. The Stain shorts will be of particular interest now." He made it all seem as if we'd been collaborating, and these were the fruits of our labor.

I shook my head. "I'm not getting all this. I don't see how what I did . . ." But even as I said it I was starting to put the pieces in place.

Cabeza studied my face and began to speak again, patiently this time, as if he were working with a very sweet but quite illiterate child. "I didn't get into it earlier because I was protecting you, and probably it's better if you wait until after your meeting to hear the rest of it, but since you seem to be so upset, I'll share it with you now. You see, Wallace was truly a great artist—perhaps one of the best in the eighties—but he'd done himself a disservice. He'd made himself out to be a kind of political clown and then he'd dropped out of sight. This wasn't good for his work. The best thing for him would've been to die in 1987 or so, just after his peak. Then we would've all made money."

I was listening. I didn't want to miss a single syllable. "You mean for his market. For his collectors, that's what would've been best."

"Precisely."

"You own his work too?"

"Stain gave me about twenty pieces over the years, mostly small tokens of affection. They were worthless until a few days ago. But thanks to your beautiful page-one story, they're seeing a remarkable market explosion. Just as we'd hoped. I've technically sold my paintings to Jeremiah to make the whole thing easier, and also, actually, to protect you in case the graffiti artists you've talked to, like from Bigs Cru or wherever, get upset because they know about us. With Jeremiah's celebrity status and Stain all the rage in the press, I'd say we stand to make a killing."

I swallowed. "Poor choice of words." My knuckles were getting white clutching the reel. I was standing in front of a man I didn't know at all.

Cabeza chuckled. "Ha. Sorry. Bad pun. Forgive me."

"I should forgive the pun?" Incredible. "How? How is it possible? Malcolm was your friend; you thought of him as a brother. Didn't you?"

Cabeza stood up, moving the knife from one hand to the other, mulling my question. "That would be harder to explain. Malcolm and I had a very, very long and complicated relationship."

"I'd rather if you sit." I backed up but kept my eyes on him. "I'll take the time."

Cabeza looked up at me with raised eyebrows. Then he looked down at his hand and the knife in it. He held it up and said, "Is this what you're scared of? It was just for the onions, sweetheart. I didn't even know it was still in my hand." He slid the knife under the mattress and then showed me his empty hands. "See?"

I nodded. "I want to know why."

"It would be hard for you to understand, Valerie," he said. "Malcolm got under my skin, I guess you could say. His easy charm, his reckless good looks, the way he didn't have to work for attention like everyone else did; they flocked to him and women, well, he never had a problem there. And he never even rubbed my face in it."

"That's it? That's why you saw fit to—"

"He never used it, Valerie. He let it all go to waste. The guy had everything I never had, everything most people never have, all the tools to get out of the ghetto and to make it big. He didn't deploy it in the right direction. He always had to make some kind of statement. I was tired of always seeing him squander his potential, on some principle. He thought he was better than all that."

"What if he was better?"

Cabeza's look was that of a college professor toward a campus activist, whose ideals he's too busy to humor. "You have a tendency to get swept away with big romantic notions, Valerie. You should be careful."

"Why does everything you say sound like a threat?"

"Relax, darling. You're getting all worked up today." Cabeza stood up again. "May I move around? Is that allowed? Believe me, you're fine. Your editor won't be able to connect you to anything. I swear, you'd think you were completely in the dark about all this."

"I *am* completely in the dark."

He walked toward the foot of his bed and looked out the high window. "It's sweet that you've taken to Malcolm's memory the way you have. He was a rare person. But he was one of these false messiahs, *linda*. He started out for himself and he stayed out for himself. Just like all of us. I know you're feeling more like a crusader today than you did yesterday, but isn't it true that you're basically the same girl who wants to be a big famous reporter? We got you that."

"So you think this corrects it? The fact that you and Jeremiah get rich off this sale? Who else? Is Darla in on this with you? Who else gets rich?"

"Oh, no, no. Darla really had nothing to do with it. She was trying to get rid of those paintings because she didn't want them anymore. Malcolm wanted them back because he had a sentimental attachment to them. Jeremiah wanted to buy them. He knew he could pull a few strings and get the market moving—it's not that hard to make a market move if you know the right people. It takes only a few high-profile bidders out in front of the auctions."

Cabeza seemed to watch something moving outside the windows, a bird or a butterfly. "It's a lovely day out there," he said. "It's too bad we can't go for a stroll." He turned back to face me. "Malcolm kept getting in the way, because he wanted to make a stink about the pictures. Darla told Jeremiah, as a joke really, 'The only way that work is going to be worth anything now is if Stain dies a fast and well-publicized death.' It was an offhand comment, but it was actually also a way to solve it all at once. We were a little bit off, though. We figured Stain would get a big spread when he died, but that didn't happen. I guess times are different now. Only pop stars get really big obituaries. So a few people tried to convince your friend over there, Curtis Wright, but he was busy. Then, of course, our stroke of good fortune: you wrote the obit and made that mistake. We had a second chance."

The queasiness was now turning to bile and it was coming up the back of my throat. "What did Jeremiah tell you about me that made me so easy to manipulate?"

"Oh, sweetheart, if I told you it would make you blush."

There was a rumble in the back of my head and a rush of anger so powerful I closed my eyes. I didn't know I was screaming until my lungs were empty. I had thrown the film reel at Cabeza and I'd missed him. He was laughing softly. It was then that I realized how far I'd removed myself from civilization. At Cabeza's warehouse, no one would hear my screams. No matter how many film reels I threw at him, no one would hear them clatter to the floor. I could kill him and no one would know. But, more likely, he would kill me. He'd committed murder—maybe with his own hands and if not with his own hands then somehow—and I didn't doubt he'd do it again. I picked up another film reel off the editing table and held it tight to my chest like a life jacket. I took a few more steps back and my spine hit the editing table. I looked behind me for scissors, a razor, something that could cut.

Cabeza dropped his voice. "Valerie, you don't have to be afraid of me. I know right now it seems like I've been double dealing, but the truth is, I've been protecting you all along. No one can connect anything to you. Also, honey, the relationship, what's happened between us, that's all genuine. I didn't need any encouragement from Jeremiah to want to get close to you. But I did. That happened all on its own. Once this is over, we're going to have the kinds of lives we've both always wanted. You and me, we're in this together, don't you see?"

I didn't know what Cabeza was capable of, or what he

thought he'd done on my behalf. Did he really believe I wouldn't care what had happened to Malcolm—that a man had been killed, a good man—and that we'd somehow go riding that carousel? If he could believe that, he could just as easily reach out and wring my neck. Then make tea until the cop cars were swarming.

Cabeza leaned forward and put his hands on my face, pulling me toward him. I jumped a little but I didn't pull away.

"Sweetheart, I know this is a bit of a shock, but I know you'll get over it once you see how it all works out," he said. "I know that you won't do anything to jeopardize this, because I know how much it means to you to finally have someone with whom you can be yourself, your true self. Not some ridiculous construction. I know it because I know you. I know you, and I love you, Valerie. And you love me too. We're perfect for each other. It couldn't be any other way."

He kissed me, and the taste of his lips was metallic. I kept the film reel in my hands, but I didn't pull away from his kiss because I was afraid of what he might do.

"But what made you think all this time I wouldn't simply turn you in once you told me the whole truth?"

Cabeza didn't even pause. "Because, *linda,* you'd ruin everything. Everything we've built here together. I mean, I've done most of the work, but I've done it for both of us. I know you wouldn't hurt me. I know it. Just like I wouldn't hurt you. And it's always best to know the truth, no matter how unpleasant it is, right?"

There was that word again. The word he'd used to lure me from the start.

"And just in case that doesn't cinch it," he said, chuckling a little and pulling away from me and picking up his camcorder from the editing table, "I've always got this." He opened the camera and removed the film. "There's some good shots on here that I'm sure would interest both your editors and the tabloids. You and me together—which they could easily link to the Ludwig show—and you and me in bed, et cetera. I'm a little camera shy, but I'm sure we have enough here to suffice."

My eyes burned. I imagined the headlines and captions that would accompany those shots: "Former Gossip Gal Exposed After Exposé!" "New Vane Shocker!" If I'd never had Club Zero, no one would've cared. But since I'd been a media piñata once, there would still be people who wanted to get their licks in.

"You've got me but good," I said.

"That was just a little insurance," he said. "I hope you won't hold it against me."

I was starting to see. He wasn't going to do me bodily harm. His threat was much more grave. He was going to keep me close to him for the rest of my life so that the truth would always be a threat, always be my undoing. I put down the reel. I had to be smart. I had to play it just right. I tried to think of him as the same man I'd watched from bed that morning, so many eons ago, when I'd believed I knew something about love.

"The kinds of things you're saying now," I said softly. "I've been thinking about that too. A life together, a future for the two of us. That house in Woodstock. So, you have this exhibition in Germany and then, a month later, Jeremiah sells these works for a windfall. Okay. Do you really think we can get out? Do you really think the police will stop investigating the murder? And we can live quietly, with no fear that they'll come for us later?"

He kissed me again, the kind of kiss that said, *Thanks for being in it with me*. "We've fixed that, I think," he said, casually. He took the film from his camera and went to his closet and found a pair of pants. He put them on. "All evidence points to Darla. As you know, Wallace was harassing her about some paintings—easy, because true—and she wanted him out of her hair. This gives her motive to get rid of Wallace. Then there's the warehouse fire, which looks ridiculously suspicious, as you know. The police are already investigating the link between those two."

"Very smart. But she wasn't responsible?"

"She's actually a pretty respectable dealer. She cuts corners here and there but she wouldn't do anything of this scale. She just gets kind of trashed in the press because she's one of those people that the media loves to hate."

"Then it was you who saw him that night on the Queensboro," I said.

"All I did was tell Jeremiah when Stain would be going out bombing." He was checking the size of his pants in the mirror, pulling at the waist. Apparently, he was pleased that he'd taken off a few pounds. "I knew he'd be going, because he'd been talking about it for weeks. I told Jeremiah and he took care of the rest. Jeremiah wouldn't have done it himself, of course, but he'd know who to hire." Cabeza looked at himself in the mirror on the inside door of his closet and sucked in his gut. "All rich boys are criminals at heart, you should know that, Valerie. Who was it who said, 'Behind every great fortune is a crime'?"

Balzac, I thought. Or was it Raymond Chandler? Either way, I didn't say anything. Instead, I watched him watch himself in the mirror. He moved closer to look at a blemish on his face, and he poked at it.

"And the paint in his mouth? The black tongue, the purple teeth?"

He turned to me, smiling. "Classic red herring. I liked that one myself."

"Nice touch. You do have a flair for details, don't you?"

Cabeza moved his hand away from the blemish and smoothed it over his chin, checking for stubble.

"And Wallace didn't fall from the Queensboro Bridge. He was dumped from somewhere else. Or he fell from somewhere else," I said after a while.

"You're catching on."

"It wouldn't make sense. Why would Wallace go there at all? He had no reason. It wasn't where he painted. There's no graffiti on that bridge."

"Smart girl. You're doing very well. How did you know he was writing that night?"

"You said it yourself. He liked to keep in practice, 'keeping it real.' Even at forty-two, he liked to have that rush. He wouldn't have been able to live without it."

Cabeza combed a hand through his hair, turned his face to the side, and looked at himself in profile. "It's true. Malcolm was that way. He had to make his mark. Without that, he didn't see himself as an artist." He took a belt off a hook in his closet and threaded it through his belt loops.

"So you figured that he'd do it sometime this month. You found out from him when he was going—going out for ice cream?—and you told Jeremiah and had him tailed. But he didn't go to the Queensboro. It had to be somewhere upstream. His body drifted and ended up practically on your doorstep. How weird."

He thumbed through his closet until he found a shirt he liked, a pale blue short-sleeved button-down. "It was pretty strange," he said. "I have to admit. You're right, again, Val. It was Hell Gate Bridge. Gustav Lindenthal's beaux arts masterpiece." He put on the shirt but didn't button it. "When it was completed in 1916 it had the longest arch of any bridge in the world."

I swallowed. "You love your bridges."

"Oh, sure. That's where my real passion lies. Connections. Look, let's try to find a way for you to get yourself relaxed," he added, slipping back into his sandals. "You're going to need to be calm when you go in to talk to your boss. Maybe we can have breakfast after all? I'll make you a Bloody Mary to take the edge off." He began walking across the room to the kitchen.

"How did you know Kamal was going . . . ?" I stopped myself.

Cabeza retrieved the knife from under the mattress and went to find his onion. He was smiling. He knew I'd figured it out on my own: he'd suggested the vandalism job to Kamal. He'd somehow made Kamal think it was his own idea. Of course that would generate publicity, and Kamal would take the heat. And he and Jeremiah had somehow arranged it so that the guard would be off duty and the doors would be left open so the teens had easy access. It would've been as simple as paying him off.

Cabeza put on an apron and wiped his hands. He smiled at me from the cutting board. "So, would you like onions, then?" He held it up. "I'm going to have some."

"Don't bother," I stood up. "But you go ahead. I better get into the office. Battinger's waiting. I'm just going to tell her I had no idea about the sale. I had no idea that Jeremiah owned Stain's art. I'm just a dumb cherry-blonde, and I only know what I know, nothing more. The best I can hope is that I'll confirm her earlier suspicions that I'm a lousy reporter."

"But it's the truth, sweetheart. You didn't know about any of that. That's the important thing. How could you? It's not like you talk to Jeremiah. It's not like Sotheby's would announce a sale to someone like you—you're only an Obit writer, after all."

I picked up my handbag again. "Thank you for protecting me," I said. "I think I should be fine. I didn't know a thing." I was moving mechanically now, reminding myself with each step and each breath how it was done. I was like a performer on opening night, playing a femme fatale for the first time, even though it was the role that had been written for me. Cabeza had directed me all this time; he'd rehearsed me through the blocking.

"You didn't know a thing."

"Right, exactly," I said. "That's the truth. I just have to stick to the truth."

"The point is, as long as you don't let on you know me, you're in the clear, and everything goes along as planned."

I was about to say, *Just as planned,* but there was a chance it would come out ironic. Instead, I was listening to the *tap tap tap* of the knife on the cutting board, and for the first time in my life, I identified with onions.

"So, what's my cut?" I asked.

Cabeza smiled wide. "I told Jeremiah you'd ask. It's funny, I know you better now. He said I should offer you a third if you'd been a good sport."

"I don't like that math. I'll take half," I said, impressed with my own improvisational skills.

"I'll talk it over with him," he answered.

I picked up my shoes. I walked toward him as coolly as Ava Gardner and pecked him on the cheek.

"Now, what kind of good-bye kiss is that?" he said.

"You're right," I said. I knew he'd want to seal the pact. My heart was pounding, but I kissed him full on the mouth. The air around us smelled of onions. He put down the knife and cupped my face in his hands. It was a horrible feeling, but I endured it. I nearly passed out with relief when he let go, then I made my way to the door.

"I should be gone for only about an hour," I said. "Promise me, we'll talk about Woodstock when I get back?"

"I promise," he said. "I've already printed out a map."

As soon as the door was shut behind me, I ran down the stairs in my bare feet, and didn't stop until I was halfway across the Queensboro Bridge.

20

Memento Mori

In front of the fortress, I caught my breath, leaning over, hands on knees. I'd run all the way west, weaving through a street fair on Third Avenue, dodging window-shoppers on Fifth, swiping tourists at Rock Center. Back in Times Square, my feet were raw with blisters, my clothes soaked through with sweat.

I looked up at The Paper, its dark gray brick looming. Carved into the stone arch above the doors were the words "To Give the News Impartially Without Fear or Favor, Regardless of Any Party, Sect, or Interest Involved." Sweat from my forehead fell into my eyes and stung.

Pressing through The Paper's revolving door, I swallowed hard. My legs could barely carry me, my heart burned in my chest. I took the stairs to the third floor and went straight to Battinger's desk, expecting to find her and Curtis at her computer, fuming. But they weren't anywhere. The Metro desk was like a union hall after the governor's come and gone. A few copy editors clicked a key or two. A clerk answered a call. I ran up the stairs to search for Curtis. The phone was ringing off the hook. It sounded like it might scream itself to death.

Back downstairs, I dropped into my seat and turned around a few times. I took out a pack of gum and shoved a stick in my mouth. Then I took out another piece and chewed that too. But it still wasn't enough. I opened up another and worked my jaws on all three.

On Mickey Rood's computer, the cursor was flickering. *Ms. Steinerman is survived by her Labrador retriever, Chunky Bobo.* Someone was in the office after all. I was unwrapping a fourth and a fifth stick when I heard Rood's three footsteps—two for each foot and one for his cane. He looked a little wobblier than usual, his tie was askew and his shoulders were covered with more than the usual dusting of flakes.

"That's a lot of chew for a little girl." He smiled, showing me his teeth, which had something white lodged by one canine. I opened up a sixth stick. "Jaime gave you the day off, Miss Vane. Shouldn't you be sunbathing in Sheeps Meadow?"

"I'm supposed to talk to Battinger," I said, garbling the words so it came out "gub suppa bat are ure."

"She went out for a sandwich. Said she'd be back in a few."

I nodded, rather than talk through my gum.

Rood eyed me with concern. "There's been some trouble, I take it?"

I nodded again.

"Personal or professional?"

I nodded twice. Both.

"Why don't you go to the cafeteria and get yourself some coffee-colored-water? I'll meet you there once I file this Obit and we can figure it out."

I went to the stairwell and began the eight-story climb. I took the steps two by two, lunging upward, pushing against gravity, swallowing my sugary spit. At the eleventh floor, I went down the hallway and pushed through a turnstile into the cafeteria. Hot plates at one counter, fries at the grill, salad bar, Jell-O cups under cellophane. I felt ravenously hungry for a moment, but then I smelled onions and felt sick all over again.

The cafeteria usually hummed with office intrigue, a senior editor dillydallying with a new blond clerk, investigative reporters hammering out a Pulitzer bid over BLTs. Today it was pretty quiet. A few bleary-eyed overnighters spooned cereal by the far wall; near the windows, a weekend janitor was beating an editorial writer at chess.

I found a plastic seat at one of the scores of empty tables and looked out the picture windows. We were right above the Great White Way, but the view offered no neon lights or glimpses of the tourist throngs. All I could see was water towers, the blinkered windows of adjacent office buildings, and, if I strained my neck all the way to the right, a few threatening clouds. *Way up high, Sam, where it's always balmy,* I thought bitterly, remembering Falco. *Where no one snaps his fingers and says, 'Hey Schmitt, rack the balls.'* The wad of gum swelled in my gob. I chewed slowly, breathing through my nose, trying to make sense of it all. What had I done? How did it happen? Was I doomed to repeat the same mistakes over and over until the end of time? Jeremiah had banked on my ambition, the singularity of my drive. Had he been right twice? Was my fatal flaw repetition compulsion?

Rood arrived carrying a Styrofoam cup, spilling with every step. He put it down with a trembling hand, spilling some more. He smoothed a napkin on the table in front of me. "Go ahead," he said, eyeing my bulging cheek. "It's time to uncork."

I placed the wad of gum on the napkin.

"That bad, huh?" he said.

I nodded, taking a few deep breaths through my mouth and swallowing what was left of the sugar.

"How bad?" he asked.

Then I spilled. It came out fast, because it had to. Because I knew everything. I knew who had killed Wallace and I knew why they'd done it. I'd seen evidence all over the place, and I'd logged it somewhere in the recesses of my mind. I'd even felt it, somewhere in my gut. I remembered the canvases in Jeremiah's attic that night he'd seduced me against his grandmother's rocking chair, Kamal's bitter expression when I asked him about Cabeza at the memorial, Cabeza's photo in the Sunday Magazine, the aristocratic flutter of his hands at our M&G late-night lunch, Jeremiah's parting shot at me the previous day. And that camera of Cabeza's, always rolling. Sure, I'd seen it all, even if I'd tried to ignore it. It had been right there on the walls all the while.

I told it to Rood straight, from the first Cabeza call to the last chop of the onion. I didn't hold back anything, not the embarrassing parts, not the incriminating parts. I told him about Cabeza's offer, my request for half the take, and his eyes glistened.

"Not tempted to take the money?" he said. "That could solve a few problems too, you know."

"Tempted? Sure. I thought about it for about half my run from Queens. But when I stopped running, that felt better. Now I have to decide, because I'm sure Battinger's back from lunch and she's waiting on me. And probably Curtis has gotten back to his desk by now and the two of them are going to want answers."

Rood blinked at me a few times. He leaned both hands on his cane and rested his chin on his knuckles. "Miss Vane, I'm no model of virtue. I've made mistakes ten times in my life that people should never make twice. Everything good I ever had I traded in for vice: one of my lungs, most of my money, both of my wives. I'm not going to sit here and tell you you're a bad girl, if that's what you want."

"I should just march right over to Battinger's desk and tell her to fire me, have me arrested, something."

Rood pushed his coffee cup toward me. "Self-pity is very unbecoming, Miss Vane." The coffee looked about as appetizing as swamp water, but I took a sip anyway. "Did you know everything you just told me when you wrote the piece with Curtis?"

"It all came to light this morning."

"So when you wrote your last piece, you were using your best resources to formulate a story based on what you had in front of you at the time." He didn't say it as a question. "That's what newspapermen do. You have to go with the best information you have on deadline, and then you update when you know better. If you ever know better."

"I was a pawn," I said. "A sap. I should've been able to read the signs here, connect the dots, somehow. I should've seen the whole picture, because it was there all along."

Rood scowled. He pressed his rough mitts against the edge of the table and pushed himself back. His chair legs screeched against the floor. "Did I ever tell you how I ended up on Obits, Miss Vane?" he said.

"No, Mickey. I don't think so."

Rood had a way of making time slow down. Even if the world was a big rush of chaos, when Mickey talked, time gave way. He propped his cane against the table and crossed his arms in front of his chest, signaling that this story would take a while.

"I was a young man then, a beat reporter, like you, except I was working the neighborhoods, the city streets. Back then, nobody cared how hard you hit the bottle, and so I hit it pretty hard, and whenever I was too enthusiastic about it, they moved me to a slower borough to let me dry out. Staten Island was the cruise ship, slower than slow. Incidentally, I was also having an off and on at that time with Jane—that's right, battle-ax Battinger. Don't look so surprised—she was young once, too, and she was a hotshot on Metro, the deputy weekend editor and not yet thirty. I was always impressed with that, I thought I might even ask her to marry me some day, but she wasn't looking for a second stringer; and anyway, it was her career she really loved."

I tried to imagine Battinger as a young woman, and it wasn't so easy to do. Maybe she'd been an Elizabeth Taylor type, curvy in all directions, but with a kind of acid running through her veins, maybe *Cat on a Hot Tin Roof*. No, later: *Who's Afraid of Virginia Woolf?*

"So, a notice came across my desk one day about a pharmacist killed in a Staten Island drugstore; I went over there and got a look around. I thought maybe there was a good story in it—maybe racially motivated, since the victim was black and there didn't seem to be any explanation. But the PD convinced me otherwise. They labeled it black on black, some neighborhood grudge. In those days, that meant we didn't follow up."

Rood didn't need a corollary from one of my old black-and-whites. He was the genuine article. He'd walked the mean streets, he'd worn his press card in his fedora. He'd spat whiskey breath more than once into an editor's face.

"In walks this dame to our bureau one sunny afternoon, a real sweetheart with some prize-winning gams. She's the sister of the deceased and she tells me the cops got it wrong. She says it goes much deeper. She says her brother had refused to pay off some round hats on the take. He could afford it, all right. He just had a conscience, thought it wasn't right for the police to skim the cream off an honest man's wage. I had to agree with him."

Rood traced a figure eight on the cafeteria tabletop. "Sure, I fell for her. But mainly I was interested in the case. I wanted to play good cop. They had a real racket going in the 122, and I had the goods to bust it wide open. But I couldn't get it in the paper no way, no how. For months, I badgered the Metro chief, but he kept telling me I had my facts mixed up. It was a few years before I found out why he killed it. Turns out Jane had found out somehow about the sister and me, and she made sure the story wouldn't run anywhere near the page. I don't know how she did it, because she was still a small fry, but she had a way of convincing people of things when she wanted to. As far as I know, it was the only time she pulled a stunt like that. But it wasn't right of her to do it. I had that story legit. There was nothing wrong with my facts."

Rood's face looked pained. His sadness deepened the wrinkles cutting across his brow. Maybe he'd been over this story a hundred thousand times in his head, maybe he'd told it aloud once or twice. From the look on his face, I could see it still hurt.

"You asked to be transferred off the Metro desk when you found out?"

"That's right. I was pretty easily scandalized for a guy who was supposed to be tough. I didn't mind knowing about corruption out there, in the big bad city. What upset me most was this place. I thought it was better than that. I'd believed in it. The institution. The stronghold." He leaned forward. "Okay, you slept with a source. *Tsk, tsk*. Bad girl." Mickey waved his finger at me and then laughed a little. His laugh turned into a cough. He pounded the table until it subsided. "The more important issue is whether you have the guts to report it out. To see that justice is done."

Rood cleared his throat roughly and wiped his mouth with his hankie. Then he balled it up and tossed it in the nearest trashcan.

"The answer isn't to go to Jane," he said. "She's no father confessor. What you need to do is get the story written. Leave Battinger to me. I'll handle her until you get your ducks in a row. She owes me a little something after all these years. Let's you and I figure out how to make her good for it. That sound right to you?"

"Just right."

"That's my girl," Rood said. "And when we're done with this little expedition, remind me, I've got something for you on those names you gave me last week."

Rood called down to Battinger and Curtis and told them that I was in the building and that I needed a few more minutes to get my act in gear. Then he and I mapped it out, the whole plan, down to the last nickel. We had less than ten hours to move a story, and I had to watch my back. Cabeza would be in contact with Jeremiah by now, waiting to see what I'd do. They'd killed Stain for money and for a little bit of fame; despite Cabeza's claims of love, I didn't think either he or Jeremiah liked me so much they'd spare me if I crossed them.

I found Curtis at the fourth-floor soda machine clunking quarters through the slot. He said he'd already been down to Sotheby's and had talked to the specialists for the sale and it all looked pretty legit. He'd said as much to Battinger, so I needn't worry. She was planning to run a short follow, and they'd be happy to have my assist.

While he stood sipping his A&W, I told him why I did need to worry—why he did too. I reprised all I'd told Rood, but I did it faster now that I'd rehearsed it once already. His eyes were wide when he put down the can. "Battinger's not going to like this. I've already convinced her the sale is on the level."

"That's why we need to get everything lined up just right."

Curtis and I took the back stairs out of the fortress. The first stop was Hell Gate Bridge, the site of Stain's last graffiti stand, the bridge that connected North Queens to the South Bronx. It all seemed so obvious to me now. If Cabeza wanted to get to Wallace, Hell Gate was the shortest distance between two points. We hailed a cab to Astoria, and asked the cabbie to drive under the Amtrak Bridge until we could find a place where it was easy to get onto the rails. As we climbed onto the span, Curtis said, "Abandon all hope, ye who enter." I felt a tingle run up my spine from my hips to my shoulders. Someone could be watching. Cabeza or Jeremiah could be anywhere. They could make sure I slipped.

I tried to focus on the graffiti: Hager, Sane, Tyre, KiK, Tnx, Son, a new name every foot or two. But we were looking for only one name, and a few steps past the landline, we found it. A throw-up, the same signature he'd painted when he was sixteen, just like the one he'd demonstrated in Cabeza's flick, outlined in purple, filled with baby blue: STAIN. It looked fresh. The paint was still sticky and it hadn't been buffed. I saw another, just about a yard ahead, and went to that, then another, another yard ahead. It was like following breadcrumbs out of the woods.

"When I was growing up, this bridge was supposed to be the scariest place on earth," Curtis said, following close behind. "You always heard ghost stories. Kids said they saw lights for trains that never came or else trains full of ghosts. A homeless guy who lived under the bridge who'd snatch kids. Mafiosos dumping bodies. I knew guys who tagged up here in the seventies. Let me tell you, they had *cojones*."

We continued along the span, finding another STAIN and then another, all purple outline filled in baby blue. There were just as many on the inside of the bridge as on its outer face. Wallace seemed to have hopped out onto the ledge to burn his throwie where drivers on the Triborough Bridge would see. About a hundred yards out over the center of the river, we found an unfinished signature: an outline "STA" but the fill-in wasn't done. The *I* started but stopped short, got haphazard, and disappeared off the wall.

The sight was chilling. He'd painted here; that was clear. But he didn't finish.

"He could've decided to stop," Curtis said, reading the thoughts on my face. "Or he could've lost his footing. This doesn't mean murder."

I reached out over to the ledge, asking Curtis to hold tight to my wrist. I felt around blind on the base of the ledge, and when my hand came back, it was covered in something shiny and black. "Tar?" said Curtis.

I recognized the scent from my father's motorcycle shop. It

was a smell you never forgot. I held my hand out to him. "Axle grease," I said.

Stepping back over the ledge, I dialed Betty Schlachter's emergency weekend number on my cell. I told her The Paper had some new news on the Wallace case. Since we'd helped find and deliver Kamal, she was nicer to me this time, but not by a whole lot. I told her we had physical evidence that Wallace had been murdered and it wasn't a gang beef or anything to do with Darla. There was no dial tone this time.

A half hour later, a handsome young assistant district attorney named Mark Detain was eating burgers with Curtis and me at the Neptune Diner near the base of Hell Gate. I asked for mine without onions. I told Detain that I wouldn't give him anything until he promised to get an officer out to a certain warehouse near the Steinway factory pronto. I also said that we needed a guarantee of on-the-record confirms from the DA's office if he found our findings to be correct. No less. No anonymous quotes; no "department spokesperson says . . ." No compromise.

He agreed and I started talking again. After I talked, I took him to see Stain's last tags and the axle grease. He called the Queens precinct to send out a squad. Then he joined us on a trip downtown to Chelsea, to visit Ms. Deitrick.

The defaced white paintings had been taken off the walls at Darla Deitrick Fine Art and all that was left was the outline of the frames where the spray painting had gone outside the lines. There were long ribbons of yellow police tape on the floor. I left Detain and Curtis to admire the new minimalism, while I went to find Darla. She was in the back room, behind the sliding glass door, sitting in front of a mound of papers I figured for insurance documents. Blondie was behind her, standing stiffly in a blue Prada mod-cut suit, holding the "Pure" catalog.

Blondie gasped. "Oh. My. Valerie. Vane," he said.

Darla's eyebrow twitched fiercely when she looked up at me.

"Interesting story you came up with. Too bad it didn't answer any of the important questions, like who murdered Wallace. Made that culprit of yours look like a little saint. Thanks to you, my gallery has been swarming with federal investigators for days. They seem to think I burned down my own storage facility. I wonder why that is?"

I took a long breath in. "I think we can get those investigators off your back rather quickly, Ms. Deitrick, if you'll answer a few questions."

Darla picked up a handful of papers and shook them at me. "You going to take care of all of these too? That the power of the press?"

"Ms. Deitrick, you and I both know I wasn't responsible for what happened here, so let's dispense with accusations. I promise not to get you arrested if you keep your copper friends off my back. How about that?"

"I'm not in a bartering mood today," she said. I had to like her for that.

"You will be," I said. "Once I fill you in."

"Talk, then," she said.

I spilled for the fourth time that day. When I was finished, I said, "I'm afraid we'll need to see the records of the transactions between you and Jeremiah Golden."

She didn't look terribly surprised, but she still resisted. "This will surely come as a surprise to you, Ms. Vane, since you seem to have a very low opinion of art dealers, but our business does follow a code of ethics and unfortunately Mr. Golden is still a private client of mine. My records are—"

"Ms. Deitrick, Jeremiah was responsible for the fire at your warehouse. He was trying to frame you for murder. Does that change things?"

"Jeremiah Golden? He had something to do with these graffiti kids?"

"There was another man too, someone named Cabeza. He was the one who got the kids involved. The link should be all there in your own records. You're lucky that Gideon here told me what he told me, about your second set of books. Those will be able to help clear you."

Darla stood up, knocking into Blondie, who reeled back and dropped the catalog. "Second set of books? Why I have no idea—"

"Let's save the theatrics for the courtroom, Ms. Deitrick. We'll need you to testify against Mr. Golden. And don't be mad at Blondie, here. Those books are going to clear you, and get these federal investigators out of your hair."

I called Curtis and Detain in from the gallery and made introductions. Detain told her everything all over again and made the same request for the books I had a few minutes earlier. If Darla could provide any support for a case against Jeremiah and Cabeza, he told her, he'd see to it that the feds would be waved off. That made her open up in a way she hadn't since prep-school prom.

"She's lucky she has you," I told Blondie as he followed us to the door. "Everyone should have such a loyal tattletale."

Blondie was still trying to piece together the puzzle. "Wait a minute, Valerie, your ex? Jeremiah bought Stain's . . . ? Did you know? Oh. My. Wait. It makes sense. He was so strapped—he was here all the— and he *bought*. I see. But, Valerie, doesn't that make you—"

I turned back to him and smiled. "Yep, it does make me. You're not bad, Gideon. You were reading the signs all the wrong way, but at least you were reading the signs. We'll need you to testify too."

Blondie beamed. "You mean I'll be on the stand? In the trial of Jeremiah Golden?"

"Should be plenty of press. Make sure you get a good head-shot out."

On the way uptown to Jeremiah's town house, I put in a call to Amenia. She told me Kamal was out on bail already. That was good news.

"There's something else that might make the judge go easier," I said. "How well do you know a man named Cabeza?"

Amenia paused. "Cabeza?" She thought about it for a while. "I dated him a long time ago. It was a big mistake. He had some kind of crazy thing about my brother. Like some kind of obsessed groupie. Does that man have something to do with this?"

"We think he's the key to it," I said. "Can you put Kamal on the line?"

Kamal's voice was weak when he said hello. "Remember at the memorial you asked me if I liked that guy, Cabeza?" I said. "Did he put you up to this stunt?"

Kamal was silent for a moment. "He told me when the guards would be off-duty."

I smiled into the phone. "Listen, Kamal, can you meet us down at the office today? We're going to want a little more information from you."

I ordered a cup of coffee at Eat Here Now, a diner on Lexington Avenue across the street from Jeremiah's town house, while Curtis went inside with Detain. Before I was done pouring my half-and-half, Curtis returned with the beginnings of a shiner as big as a grapefruit and a grin as wide as a barn. "He sends you his love," Curtis said.

"That's the prettiest confession I ever saw," said Rood, back at the office, when he saw Curtis's face. Rood filled us in on what he'd told Battinger. We filled him in on our day's expedition. There were two hours left before deadline. Curtis sat down to wait for Kamal and to type. I had something else to do.

Rood walked me down to Battinger's private office just off the hallway from the Metro bullpen, and opened the door. "You'll be fine, Miss Vane. You're a toughie," he said, winking. "Call me when you're done."

The office was tiny and devoid of adornments—not a single picture of a kid or a husband, not a knickknack from travels abroad, and whoever designed it had a special affinity for beige. Battinger was sitting behind a beige desk and Jaime was in a cheap-looking beige seat.

I dropped my letter onto Jane's desk. She picked it up and read it over. It wasn't very long. It expressed my appreciation for the opportunities I'd been given at The Paper. It said I thought it was more than I deserved. She didn't seem surprised, since Rood must've told her pretty much everything, but she still looked angry. She handed the letter to Jaime.

"So, what's this supposed to be?" said Battinger. "Falling on your sword?"

"It's better for everyone concerned if I distance myself."

"Will you be giving us corrections for the story you wrote with Curtis?"

"All the facts were correct in that story. They just didn't go far enough to explain the truth."

"Did you put anything into that piece to help either Jeremiah Golden or this person, this Cabeza figure that was feeding you facts?"

"No, I didn't. I was looking at the picture. I didn't see the frame."

Jaime let my resignation letter fall into his lap. "These are problems, Valerie. But it doesn't sound like you intentionally damaged the integrity of the reporting. The story stands."

"That's right. But the piece serves the wrong ends."

Jane stood up and so did Jaime. She shook my hand, and Jaime gave me a hug so tight I got a nose of Brylcreem. "You've been through a lot this week. Leave your stuff for now," he said.

"Come back once you've had a chance to sleep on it. Maybe there's another way."

"Okay," I said. "But I don't think I'll change my mind."

I went back to my desk. Just as I was about to push in my chair, the phone rang. "Obits," I said. "Vane."

"This is un-fucking-believable material, Valerie," Curtis said. "I wish you were writing it with me. We're a good team, you and I."

"You'll do great," I said. "I don't have any worries."

21

Postscript

Mickey Rood's obituary in The Paper was 250 words, a squib at the bottom of the page. It ran with the headline "Lifelong Newspaperman Mourned by Colleagues," and the subhead "Veteran of Almost Sixty Years Started as Teenage Copy Boy."

He'd died the previous night, in his comfy chair at home in his welfare hotel in Gramercy, reading the late edition of the Sunday paper, the one with a story, "Golden Heir Arrested in Death of Graffitist," by Curtis Wright. A blues singer who'd once sung with his band discovered Rood slumped over just before nine o'clock. A little frazzled and unsure of what to do, she'd called Obits first and had reached Jaime, just when he'd arrived in the office after his Sabbath break. The desk had scrambled, using a clerk and one of the advance writers and squeaking out an Obit at the eleventh hour for the morning edition.

I'd watched Jeremiah do the perp walk on TV the night before with Amenia up at her apartment in Hunt's Point, while Detain was in the other room, prepping Kamal for his court testimony. Jeremiah looked as wrecked as I'd ever seen him, even in the bleary-eyed dawns of our bathroom floor binges. Amenia said, "He's just like all these white boys with too much money and time on their hands." I can't say it felt good because too much of my own frailty was linked to his fate. I wished I could feel superior and righteous, but there was part of the monster in me too. I'd fallen for him, after all. And I'd fallen for another one, just like him, just the same.

The cops had questioned me about Cabeza, but as I was telling them what facts I thought I knew—about his childhood in Aguas Buenas and life on the farm with his grandfather, his stint in Los Angeles as a young wannabe filmmaker, his move to 103rd Street in El Barrio, his early graffiti docs—I realized it was all probably lies anyway. Meaningful, well-constructed lies that seemed to hang together as some sort of truth. I'd have felt superior and righteous about him too, if I hadn't been so good at creating those kinds of narratives myself. In the end, all I could really offer the cops were descriptions of his distinguishing marks.

They did better on their own. My darling Cabeza, it turned out, went by a few names other than "the brain." The one he used to pretend he was a filmmaker was Jose Rodriguez; the one he used when he wanted to act like a curator was Roberto Hernandez-Gonzago, and he'd managed to acquire quite a reputation in Europe, it seemed, for his ability to acquire and exhibit singularly American works of art. But the one on his rap sheet—the one that was now being circulated around New York and across the nation, along with his mug shot—was Raoul Jimenez, from Huntington, Long Island. Turned out he was a middle-class kid from the 'burbs, whose mom was a math teacher and whose dad was a furrier who owned a little store.

He'd always be Cabeza to me, but I didn't get a chance to tell him so. He'd skipped town before Detain could get to his Queens studio and he'd have been halfway to Managua or Reykjavik by the time the cops released his mug shot. Jeremiah might've found some way to tip him off, but it was also possible he'd just had a hunch I wasn't coming back Friday morning while he was eating his onion omelet. It's possible he did know me at least that well.

I was still waiting for the other shoe to drop: Cabeza's little home movie. I was certain he'd release it to all the right people at just the right time; I just didn't know when. Maybe when he felt clear of the cops, maybe once he was settled into a hot tub in Sweden. But I preferred to imagine him south of the border, in Acapulco at a cantina called Pablo's, sipping bourbon with the ghosts of Robert Mitchum and Jane Greer. Maybe someday, if the urge got strong, I'd go down and join him.

Even without Cabeza's flick, I knew I'd be facing new notoriety. The Paper was already preparing a long mea culpa spread, explaining the background to the reporting on the Wallace story and noting the fact that I'd already resigned. Even if the facts in my original reporting hadn't been totally off the mark, the article planned to say, the reporter had no business getting involved with a source, behind the scenes, and using facts obtained through that relationship to drive her investigation.

The German museum's retrospective of early graffiti, featuring Stain, was still under way, except Roberto Hernandez-Gonzago was no longer the curator. Amenia had filed an injunction to prevent the Sotheby's sale, and was also contesting ownership of the paintings Jeremiah had lent the museum. Darla Deitrick was helping. She said her own archival research indicated—as Malcolm had argued when he'd searched for the works the first time—that Wallace had only loaned her the paintings, so she'd had no right to sell them in the first place. The argument would cost her, but considering everything, she was willing to pay. Amenia had another plan: she wanted to get all of Stain's paintings back and establish a Bronx-based nonprofit graffiti museum called Free People.

Of all the men I'd thought I loved that year, the only one left in my heart was Rood. I put down the paper and rolled my swivel chair over to his desk. It was dusted with those tiny white flakes. The tin where he kept the pictures of his grandkids was still on his desk, and the pencil holder with its white plastic fork. I reached for the other tin—the one with his smokes—and took out an unfiltered Lucky, putting it between my teeth.

I opened the filing cabinet and found his brown paper bag, reached inside, and felt the sardine cans, four or five of them, enough to make it through another week before he'd have to stock up at the bodega again. There was a brand-new pack of lemon sugar wafers too.

At the back of the drawer was a yellow manila file, marked "For Miss Vane." I took it out and found inside the list of names my mother had sent, now with a few check marks. Attached to it, by paper clip, were a few other pages of handwritten text, all in Rood's looping script. There were nine pages in all. Relatives of S. R. Miller. Actual people, connected to me. Maybe I did have a history out there, somewhere, after all. I put everything back and closed the drawer, except for the folder with my list. Then I went back to my former desk and began to fill up my cardboard box for the last time.

The phone rang. "Obits," I said. "Vane."

"*Out of the Past* is playing at Film Forum at eight fifteen," said Curtis. "Want to come with?"

"Can't," I said. "Need to leave town for a while. I'd rather not explain, right now, if that's okay with you. You'll understand soon enough."

"Such a mystery lady," he said. "Okay, but you don't get off that easy. I'm going to try you again soon."

I told him that would be okay, and I hung up the phone. In my filing cabinet, I searched for anything salvageable, dumping old death faxes in the recycle bin and saving the odd folder that contained some stitch of worthwhile research. I found yellow pads with lists of old Style ideas: *designer shrugs?? French chefs on private-jets?? What makes Ricki love PETA so bad?* Jottings from a gentler era.

It was a lazy early morning in the dead heat of August. Randy Antillo was snoozing in his swivel chair in Rewrite, his head jerking into consciousness every few minutes when his chair fell too far back. Clint Westwood arrived sleepy-eyed, wearing seersucker, grumbling about the 4/5/6 train. Rusty Markowitz rushed to his desk, put down his briefcase, and swapped his penny loafers for a pair of black velvet slippers. Life here would go on without me, just as it always had, and maybe the world was better off with one less Valerie Vane.

Jane Battinger came by when my box was almost full. I still had the Lucky in my teeth. "You helped Curtis with a nice spread there, Valerie," Battinger said. "It's too bad the way everything turned out."

"Thanks for saying so," I said. "And I'm sorry about Mickey."

She nodded. "Me too."

I watched her walk away. Her gait was slower than usual; her hips swayed with the tune of melancholy. I wondered how she and Rood had spent the day on Friday. Maybe he'd taken her to the park to sort things out. Maybe they'd mended fences. I hoped so. Jane wasn't all bad. It was possible that she'd been a looker in the old days, too, like Rood had said. And I bet Mickey had always kept a spiffy shine on his shoes. I imagined the two of them, young again like Cary Grant and Rosalind Russell in *His Girl Friday*. Maybe for a while they'd been a rat-a-tat duo in a newsroom full of copy boys and newsmen who wore cigarettes behind their ears and pencils in their caps. Rood would've been a go-getter willing to put sources in closets and climb out windows—anything for a scoop. Jane would've been gutsy and straight shooting, calling every card a spade.

Yes, it was true. I'd missed the best parts of Rood's life, the glamorous past. He'd been there for me, all along, though, and the file he'd created that was in my hands was going to lead me to my own past. Whether it was glamorous or not, I didn't yet know. I wouldn't be able to thank him, and I was sorry about that.

But isn't it funny how well you can know someone after they're gone? Better, it turns out sometimes, than when they lived.

graph. My residency at the MacDowell Colony in New Hampshire gave me time to polish the final draft.

For help with the graffiti sections of the novel, I'm indebted to Nicer, Bio, and rrBG183 of Tats Cru; writers Mosco, Kez, and Nato; and Hugo Martinez of the Martinez Gallery, who provided inspiration and helped me with details along the way.

I want to acknowledge all my professors at Iowa: James McPherson, Adam Haslett, Ethan Canin, and Lan Samantha Chang, but especially Margot Livesey and James Hynes, who both went well beyond the call of duty. I really can't thank either of them enough.

I owe my greatest debt to my agent, Nina Collins, for her early and undying support for this book and to my editor, Peggy Hageman, who immediately made me feel as if we'd found the right home at HarperCollins.

Finally, I want to acknowledge my brother and sister-in-law, David and Rebecca, and my parents, Marta and Frederick, who have supported this project and my writing in too many ways to count.

Acknowledgments

The following nonfiction books were useful sources for this novel: *Fame at Last: Who Was Who According to the New York Times Obituaries* by John Ball and Jill Jonnes, *True Colors: The Real Life of the Art World* by Anthony Haden-Guest, *Dark City: The Lost World of Film Noir* by Eddie Muller, *Celluloid Skyline: New York and the Movies* by James Sanders, and *The Perfect Murder: A Study in Detection* by David Lehman. So was the graffiti movie, *Style Wars*, directed by Henry Chalfant and Tony Silver.

This novel would never have gotten past chapter 1 without the early encouragement of Steven Wright, Leigh Newman, John Cassidy, and Lucinda Rosenfeld. My thanks to my aunt and uncle, Marian and Jack Krauskopf, who lent me their house in Chatham in 2001, where I wrote the first pages. I was fortunate, too, for the enthusiastic feedback of my Brooklyn writing group: Leigh, Lilly Kuwashima, Tim Brien, Amy Brill, Joseph Holmes, and Kim Sevcik.

At Iowa, Dina Hardy, Nam Lee, Matthew Vollmer, Nic Brown, Josh Rolnick, Austin Bunn, Amy Belk, and Leslie Jamison were my best critics. I would also like to thank Bliss Broyard for reading early chapters; Rob Sussman, for fact-checking the final draft with me in L.A.; and Jeremy Hobbs for shooting my author photo-